The Lonely H

Charlie Lyndhurst is an award-shortlisted novelist who lives with his boyfriend and cats. He bakes to indulge his dangerously sweet tooth, admires unaffordable classic cars, and drinks pink wine with friends. His favourite sport – of which he's a gold medal winner – is reading a romantic novel in a long hot bath.

CHARLIE
LYNDHURST

THE
LONELY
HEARTS
LIDO CLUB

hera

First published in the United Kingdom in 2022 by

Hera Books
Unit 9 (Canelo), 5th Floor
Cargo Works, 1–2 Hatfields
London, SE1 9PG
United Kingdom

A CIP catalogue record for this book is available from the British Library.

Print ISBN 978 1 80436 026 2
Ebook ISBN 978 1 80436 912 8

Look for more great books at www.herabooks.com

Printed and bound in Great Britain by Clays Ltd, Elcograf S.p.A.

I

To Ford Martyn who does words very well. We started our friendship by exchanging 2,000-word letters as teenagers. Your journalistic skills are way beyond anything I've ever managed. Your knowledge of language and grammar is far superior to mine. Thank you for your love of words, the joy in all things camp, your sense of humour, and for your friendship.

Chapter 1

May

Gabriella pushed a stray blonde hair from her eye. Jack was standing on a step, leaning over the sink and about to put his head underneath the tap.

'What are you doing, Jack?' She lifted him onto the floor.

He looked adorable in his blue sweatshirt, grey shorts and black shoes. He looked up at her with those dark brown eyes, long eyelashes and the smile she knew would let him get away with murder as he grew up. 'What, Mummy?'

Arnie.

She swallowed the ball of grief that formed in her throat. No time to wallow, she had two boys to get ready.

Blinking away the tears she was determined not to let fall, she held Thomas's hand, removing it gently from her sleeve. 'We have to go now.'

'I don't wanna go.' Thomas slowly crumpled onto the floor, sitting with his legs crossed and tucking his hands underneath his armpits. He too looked adorably cute in his blue shorts and red T-shirt. He was old enough for preschool but she couldn't bear the thought of an empty house so had decided to push it back a few months.

Maybe she should take a photo because they looked so cute. They were growing up so fast. Another milestone Arnie would never see.

'Are you sad, Mummy?' Jack asked.

Quickly wiping the tears from her cheeks, she shook her head. 'Mummy is fine. Nothing for you to worry about.' She'd read something about not letting the children see her falling apart, about how they'd mirror her grief if they saw it. So as much as possible she tried to keep her crying to the middle of the night when both boys were asleep.

'Are you sad, like before?' Thomas sat next to her on the floor.

Before, organising the funeral, taking the call, sitting the boys down to tell them.

Before.

Gabriella swallowed the lump in her throat. Someone to talk to about anything other than nappies and school runs. 'No, Mummy isn't sad like before.' She glanced at the wall clock.

Seven forty-frigging-five and neither boy showed any signs of being ready to leave. Somehow they'd removed their shoes and jumpers, their hair messed up again, after she'd taken so long combing it earlier.

She lifted Thomas to his feet, kneeling down to his eye level. 'You said you wanted to go to school like a big boy, didn't you?'

He stuck his bottom lip out and nodded, looking away.

'So, you're going to be a good boy and Mummy is going to take your brother to school. And if you're very good, one day, you can go too, when you're a little bit bigger.'

He nodded, taking his brother's hand, whose face formed a smile and he copied.

'Can you be big boys and put your shoes on again for Mummy?'

They set about finding their shoes in the kitchen and Gabriella cursed herself for having not one, but two children who were under five. Her plan had been to wait for number two until number one could dress himself. But Arnie had other ideas, he persuaded Gabriella that another baby wouldn't be any more difficult than one, since he was such a great dad. And Gabriella had agreed because of the prospect of having another boy who looked just like Arnie, or even a daughter, someone she could dress in pink, braid her hair, do all the girly stuff Gabriella had missed as one of six, brought up in a council flat in the East End.

She rushed to collect her handbag and car keys. Just the looks from the other mothers at turning up in a car when they could easily walk it had Gabriella bracing herself.

'Come on you two!' She raised her voice hoping they would rush into the hallway, dressed and obedient.

Instead she found them spreading peanut butter on each other's sweatshirts and faces.

Bloody brilliant! 'Come on you two.'

In the car, Jack was talking about his friend's birthday party. 'Can I go, Mummy?'

'Of course, love.'

Golden sun shone through the windscreen, Gabriella pushed the sun visor down so she could see better. The boys had the windows open and warm spring air, filled with flowers and mown grass scents of late spring, filled the car.

'Robert is having a bouncy castle and a clown and someone who paints everyone's faces,' Jack went on. 'There's gonna be jelly and ice cream and cream and everyone can play on the slide and climbing frame…'

The traffic was worse than usual, of course, and Gabriella tried to remain calm, while talking to Jack about his friend's party. She lowered her window and enjoyed the sun's heat on her arm.

'Robert is having party bags for everyone and there's sweets and cakes and a toy in every bag. The boys have blue bags and the girls have pink bags. Robert is having four flavours of fizzy and you can go back and have as much as you want. Robert's mummy wanted to put a book in the bags and Robert said he didn't want a book, he wanted a toy. So now he's having a toy. And you have to do them for me too. For my party. I said there won't be books in my party bags, mine are going to have sweets and toys and all the good stuff. Will you, Mummy?'

'Of course I will…'

Jack continued chatting to himself, a stream of words about everything from the flavour jelly his friend was having to the name of the clown who was doing face painting.

Gabriella nodded and agreed when she thought she should, all the while trying not to scream and tell the traffic to fuck the fuck off out of the fucking way.

They arrived at school a good ten minutes late, only able to nod to a few of the mums she was on waving terms with. One thought it was really funny to tap her watch.

'Thanks,' she said through gritted teeth. *As if I don't know I'm late.*

4

'We must connect and organise the playdate for the boys – Elisabetta and Christopher are super keen to spend time with your two.'

So you can check out my interior décor more like. Gabriella stared at her.

'I'm Jessica. Elisabetta and Christopher's mother. It's so brave of you, honestly, I don't know how you manage it,' she said.

Gabriella held both boys' hands to prevent the children running off. 'Brave?' *If she says something about losing Arnie, I'm going to fucking well punch her smug lights out.*

'Moving so far from your family and putting your boys in this school, when quite obviously you've not had the… You know… Of such a salubrious educational history.'

'Didn't need A levels to stand about modelling clothes, did I? But I done okay, I reckon.'

With pursed lips, Jessica looked her up and down. 'It must be such an eye-opener when they return from school telling you all the wonderful things they've learned. In some ways it must feel like an education for yourself too.'

Patronising bloody cow! Despite being physically livid, she gritted her teeth, she reckoned least said soonest mended, as her old mum used to say. She would always be the East End girl, out of place on this side of London, in the rich suburbs, never really able to make friends. 'I've gotta shoot.' She stormed off towards the school.

Somehow she'd bundled both boys out of the car and into the school. Somehow she'd not lost her temper. Somehow she'd not let the sadness overtake her. Well, not since last night anyway. So, somehow, she was determined to smooth this over with the school and convince them she wasn't as much of an unfit mother as most of the mums would have you believe.

She was just going through a difficult patch. Her heart squeezed, as she wished she could call her mum. Turn up to the spacious split-level maisonette in the concrete tower block in Mile End, sit at the kitchen table where she'd been when she'd first met Arnie and told her parents she reckoned she was gonna marry him.

A mum hug was what she needed now.

The secretary turned from her computer and peered through her glasses. 'Mrs Denmead, I see you've missed registration again.'

'You wouldn't believe the morning I've had.'

The woman held her hand aloft. 'If you'll wait, I'll register Jack for arrival – late. And then perhaps we could speak about Thomas, who's already due for our preschool intake?'

'Can we do it another time? I've had a right morning of it, I could just do with…' Anything but this really. Gabriella narrowed her eyes, leaning on the desk, looking down she realised she was wearing two odd shoes.

'If you don't register Thomas, you may not get him in and you'll have to send him elsewhere when he moves to reception.'

Not a private school for poshos, is what she meant, but didn't say so. Gabriella had been against sending the boys to a private school, but Arnie had insisted, said they could afford it, so why not give them the best?

If she took them out now, it would always have the unmentioned phrase – it's what Arnie would have wanted – associated with it.

'Will it take long?' Gabriella asked.

'I'll ask Miss Simms to take Jack to his classroom. Then perhaps we could…' She waved a form she'd retrieved from a filing cabinet.

Jack was taken away without too much whining and crying. All things considered – Gabriella thought as she stared at the admission form for Thomas – she hadn't done too bad recently.

Except for the screaming and crying into the bath. And the sleepless nights. And not dressing all weekend, and not showering most days until she caught a whiff of herself and thought she better had.

All things considered, maybe not so—

'I said,' the receptionist asked. 'You'll receive thirty percent discount on Thomas's fees since you'll have a sibling at Cygnet School.'

Am I definitely going to do this? Do I have enough money? I wish I could work. Gabriella never had much to do with that side of things, not when Arnie was around. She put it all on the credit card and magically it was always paid.

'I've got some money stuff to look at first, all right?' *Understatement. And speak to the in-laws.*

The look of disgust on the secretary's face was hilarious. The designer logo on her glasses and handbag told Gabriella somehow this woman didn't need to worry about money. Another someone, since the school was full of them.

'I see. I was under the impression all of that side of things was taken care of since…'

'Arnie died. Is that what you're trying not to say?' Christ on a bike, what was it with these people never wanting to say the actual words *death*, *dying*, or *dead*. It wasn't as if it made any difference now.

The secretary nodded. 'Insurance or such like.'

'Do you want to know how much I got?'

She shook her head. 'Of course not, that would be most impertinent.'

7

'As I'm sure you know, their grandparents pay Jack's fees, but I don't know about Thomas's.' *Because I've been avoiding them since…*

'I assumed… Especially since you're now in, shall we say, very different circumstances…' She smiled.

'Yeah, and me and my circumstances aren't any of your business, okay?'

The receptionist folded the form in half and stared at Gabriella.

Nothing more to say from this busybody. Gabriella smiled. 'Right, well in that case, I'll leave it at that, if it's all right with you.' Gabriella picked her handbag off the floor, waved a hand in the sign that Thomas knew meant time to go.

Thomas stood from the corner where he'd been playing with wooden blocks. 'Want to stay!' He looked exactly like Arnie had at that age.

Arnie's mum had shown the pictures to her the first time they'd visited, much to Arnie's embarrassment and his mum's pride.

It had all seemed so simple back then. She was going to date him until she got bored of him, then she'd marry a famous actor. Except she'd never become bored of Arnie. He was always there, by her side, powerful, calm and such a gentleman. The photographer who didn't try it on after the swimwear photo shoot.

Arnie was a prince among men, her mum had said, and so giving up modelling to have a family with him had seemed such an easy decision.

'We'll play when we get home.' She picked Thomas up, turning to face the secretary. 'To be honest, never mind the money side of things, but the timing's not great. I

8

know I need to do something, but at the mo, I… I've got plenty else on my plate. All right?'

She removed her glasses and they hung around her neck. 'Mrs Denmead, I can put him down as provisional. So you don't lose his place. We'll come back to the financial matter. Do you want me to ask if you can pay them all monthly?'

She didn't want to assume Arnold's parents would pay for both boys, and didn't want to look a kind gift horse in the mouth, so said, 'Great, ta.'

'For both of them?'

'Both what?' Terms, a year, no, doesn't make sense… Seasons… No that didn't work, people involved in their schooling – her and Arnie's parents… Probably not that either. *Must speak to the doctor about how my memory's screwed, must be the pills I'm on.* She was sleeping some nights now, and the weeping during the day had stopped, so that was something, right?

'Your boys, Mrs Denmead, monthly payments. Do you want a cup of tea? Pause for a moment, maybe?' She spoke slowly as if Gabriella was a half-wit or something. She tilted her head to one side and smiled tightly.

Gabriella shook her head. 'No time to hang about. Whatever you think. The monthly thingummy.' *I've had enough of this.* She left the room.

The secretary shouted something but Gabriella only caught part of it, something about taking time for herself.

That was a joke, she thought as she strapped Thomas into his car seat – all she'd had since Arnie died *was* time for herself. Those were the worst times, watching the home movies they'd made, listening to his voice, noticing how precisely like their dad both boys looked. They were brown haired, dark brown eyed, with rounded heads, just

9

like Arnie, as well as having his smile. Jack had developed Arnie's sense of humour too – Gabriella didn't think a sarky five year-old was possible, but Jack had proved otherwise.

'Where are we going, Mummy?' Thomas asked as he waved his arms and legs excitedly. 'Can we go home? I want play Lego.'

As she slid into the driver's seat and started the car, she looked at his cherubic face in the mirror and a tiny version of Arnie stared back. 'Not home.' Because even that reminded her too much of Arnie. His kindness at indulging her when they'd bought the only house like that for miles around: white walls, orange roof tiles, dark wooden doors and windows, and balconies for every bedroom. Nope, returning to her and Arnie's hacienda wouldn't end well today. Scrolling through the map on the car's sat nav, she tapped 'places of interest' and a list of options appeared.

Restaurants? No, she wasn't hungry.

Petrol station? Could do, something to kill time – *Christ what am I thinking, what's happened to me?*

Oh yeah, that's what's happened.

Shops – could always kill a few hours with some retail therapy. Gabriella, ever since her first job as a Saturday girl in a café off the Roman Road in east London, had enjoyed a purchase. The searching for the perfect item, the trying it, and finally taking it home in one of those bags that told everyone you had money to spend. Of late, she'd not done much retail therapy – who was going to see her all dressed up to the nines? Why bother? Even now, she reckoned there wasn't much that could touch that feeling.

Except maybe a hug from—

Stopping that thought screeching in its tracks, her finger hovered above a point of interest she'd not considered before: Lido.

One of the school mums had mentioned it. According to a quick internet search there was a café, gym and two swimming pools, so more than enough to keep her and Thomas amused all day. At the time Gabriella had dismissed the suggestion, thinking it was just an outdoor pool and knowing after two babies there was no chance she was going anywhere near putting her cossie on again.

With the most determination she'd felt since... Since...

She pressed the sat nav screen and waited for it to calculate a route. Her nails had seen better days too.

Unsurprisingly, the weekly shellac appointments and six-weekly trips to the hairdresser, to touch up her dark roots to keep her as the blonde she'd always wanted, had fallen by the wayside. She had once looked quite glam. She had been a model. Swimwear and some glamour stuff early on. All very tasteful: covering her boobs with her arms, knickers on, that sort of thing. Then catalogues, hand modelling, eyes, lips – it just came and came. Not that anyone would think it now if they saw her. Showing her parents the picture of her as the face of a women's high street face cream in a magazine advert had been the proudest moment of her life.

Her mum had bought all the copies from the local newsagent, sent them to the family and framed one for their lounge.

How could that only be eleven years ago? And how can the fresh face of the best high street night cream now look like this? Glancing in the mirror, she pulled on a baseball cap from the glove compartment to cover her greasy blonde hair with its dark root growth.

I wish I'd kept in touch with my modelling friends… They had all seemed to melt away after Arnie died, probably worried her grief would rub off on them.

'Mummy, I need a poo.'

'Can you hold it?' She made eye contact with him through the rear-view mirror.

Thomas nodded and smiled.

'Good boy.' She slipped into the traffic, following the car's directions the short distance to the lido, determined to make this move, no matter how small, to break the cycle she'd been in since Arnie's death, to do something different, go somewhere new, to take the smallest step forwards to building something approaching a life without Arnie.

Her joy at what seemed like a good plan to avoid going home was soon gone as the unmistakable smell filled the car. She scrunched her nose as they stopped at traffic lights. 'Do you still need a poo?'

'I think I done it, Mummy.' He shrugged.

Chapter 2

Helen Liphook held her coffee mug close to her body as she stared into the garden. It wasn't for warmth, but because she used to savour this time of the day.

The garden was in full bloom, lush green grass in the centre, perfect stripes running up and down, the flower-beds full of reds, purples, yellows and lush green foliage, as the plants put on their best for the summer just around the corner.

Despite never needing to rise for work, her body clock had remained resolute in demanding she rise at 6am every day since becoming a mother. It had, at one point, been her favourite time of the day. A period when there seemed to be so many possibilities, so much that could and indeed would happen. Seeing her son off to school, then uni, then watching him leave with the contents of his bedroom in the car, leaving his bedroom as a sort of half mausoleum to his childhood and half extended walk-in wardrobe for Helen.

It hadn't been the medical director post that had done it; she'd quite enjoyed being Mrs Liphook, married to Mr Liphook the medical director. It hadn't even been the fight he'd had to get the top job when his and a neighbouring hospital had merged – she'd quite enjoyed that, she reflected now with a smile, gazing out at the garden as it stretched far into the distance, down a slope until it met the woods at the bottom where her son and his school friends had played.

A smile crept across her face at that.

Sipping the coffee she then took an illicit toke of the vaping cigarette – better than smoking apparently, although nowhere allowed you to do it nowadays, which somehow made it feel slightly pointless.

No – she saw the final straw, the thing that had really and truly finished things for her, was when he had decided to semi-retire and go down to a three-day week.

While he was busy at that bloody hospital five days a week usually twelve hours a day, occasional weekends for on-call, she'd managed to convince herself things weren't so bad. Things were, as her friend had once said, 'Not too bad, all things considered. Men.'

But since then, she'd had to get used to seeing Bill in the house, getting under her feet, doing something that seemed ever so urgent at his computer every day he wasn't at the hospital. And just like that, Helen's dreams of a happy retirement together had melted away.

The house phone rang.

Bill wouldn't answer it, he would be too absorbed in his endeavour to even notice. Of course, she'd asked what it was he was doing, and had received a grunt and a waved hand, followed by, 'Why do you want to know anyway?'

'Because I'm your wife, in case you've forgotten,' had been on the tip of her tongue, but she'd done what she'd so equably managed for nearly forty years, and bit her tongue and left the room.

The phone continued ringing.

It would be one of the committee friends, they all seemed to insist on using the landline rather than Helen's mobile.

Placing the coffee cup on the work surface, Helen then answered the phone.

It was Rosemary, the secretary at Caring for Children, the charity she found herself on the board of, among other charities. Rosemary had just returned from a fortnight's cruise around Europe with her husband and asked if Helen wanted to see the pictures.

'Very probably,' was all Helen could manage as she longed for someone with whom she could sail around the world, eating and drinking as much as they could manage.

'Are you okay? You seem a little... distant.'

'I'm absolutely fine.' The three most uttered words from Helen's mouth. In particular of late she'd found herself repeating them ad nauseam, so difficult was it to convince even herself of their truth, never mind anyone else.

'Is Bill at home today?' Rosemary asked carefully.

The light in the dining room indicated this to be true. He'd set himself up there despite having a perfectly serviceable study from which to work. He'd bought a new laptop, set about the room with such vigour that Helen had worried for his mental stability, and now he spent the two days when he wasn't saving the sick and in need of Uxbridge at their dining room table.

Helen said, 'Yes.'

'Must be nice, you know, after all these years, having some quality time together. How's he acclimatising to reducing his consultant hours?'

'Very well.' It was, in theory, wonderful for them to be approaching the autumn of their lives together and for Bill to be finally – five years after he'd said he would – semi-retiring. But the reality – this three-day week facade – had brought into sharp relief all the worries and concerns

15

Helen had kept to herself about him, and about which Bill had done nothing for decades. Because, as her late mother-in-law had said, 'Bill is Bill and he will always be Bill, and do precisely what Bill wants.'

Some days those words haunted Helen so frightfully that she had to leave the house, grabbing her keys frantically and rushing from the home they'd shared, without a word, just to get away.

'What do you do when he's off work? Ted and I have been discovering the deep relentless joy of being able to have three fortnight-long holidays back to back.'

Helen closed her eyes tightly, her jaw gritting her teeth so as to be painful.

'We,' Helen began carefully, 'we're sort of pottering about. And I've been swimming quite often. Few times a week, at the lido – they've refurbed it. Beautiful art deco café, curved windows, flat roof, all painted white. They've fixed the crumbling concrete. Repainted it. It's wonderful now the scaffolding's gone.' Seven days a week – was that a few times, she wondered.

'Sounds wonderful.' Rosemary didn't sound convinced. 'What's he doing now? I expect he's getting ready for your next adventure.'

Helen hadn't told anyone about Bill and his office setup in the dining room. She'd barely been able to make sense of it herself, never mind explain it to others. 'He's doing something with computers at the moment. I'm sure he'll soon hurtle into the kitchen, disturbing my morning cup of herbal tea to suggest we book a weekend in Rome for our anniversary.' Never.

'I didn't know it's your anniversary. How many years?'

'Forty.' Helen had been eighteen when they'd married, first relationship, first kiss, first man. First everything really.

He came from money; Helen liked that, and him, at the time, so it had seemed eminently sensible to accept his proposal of marriage.

Bill, five years older, and much wiser she'd thought then, had gone to medical school and they'd lived in a small house his parents had bought them. Helen had been young, full of anticipation of what their life could be together. Every time he'd made a suggestion she'd gone along with it, since every time he had such splendid ideas. She'd done a bit of secretarial work at a magazine when she'd been in her twenties, when stick-thin with lashings of mascara had been the in look. It was easy enough to give it all up since Bill pointed out they hardly needed the scant money she brought in.

A picture from those days rested on the mantelpiece. Helen was still slim, her hair in the same sharp bob she'd always favoured, but now the lines on her face had deepened. Her fingers looked like an old lady's, she reflected holding one out as she held the phone.

'Are the kids doing anything for you?' Rosemary asked.

Helen shook her head. Peter was in his thirties, and had far better things to do than organising a party for his parents' anniversary, especially when at least fifty percent of his parents had no interest whatsoever. 'Don't expect he'll even know. Who remembers their parents' wedding anniversary? I certainly didn't.'

'But Bill will have something in mind, won't he?' It was more of a statement than a question. Rosemary's Ted had taken them to Paris for a long weekend on their fortieth anniversary, they'd climbed to the top of the Eiffel Tower, taken a river trip down the Seine and Rosemary had even tried snails and frogs' legs since it had been an ambition since she was a little girl learning French. Rosemary had shown the whole committee the pictures one evening at her house and Helen had warred within herself between feeling happy for her friend and colleague, while also fighting a deep, dull aching pain at the realisation that Bill would do no such thing when their anniversary came round.

'I expect so,' Helen said. 'Little surprise for me.' She tried to keep her tone light. No sense bothering everyone with it.

Rosemary continued, asking further questions about what she thought Bill would do for their anniversary and Helen couldn't bear it any longer.

'Sorry, did you have some business you needed to discuss?'

'Yes, I mustn't keep you any longer. Is Bill standing at the door, ready to spring an idea onto you?'

'He is,' Helen lied, only the loud tapping of Bill as he two-finger pecked at his keyboard were audible.

'It's just about Saturday's meeting, are you coming?'

Helen checked the calendar and just as she'd thought, two stars over the weekend indicated Bill was on call at the hospital. This meant he'd turn up, just in case, and spend the whole weekend there, probably even sleeping in the doctor's mess on Saturday night. She'd asked why, when he was meant to be taking it easy, and he'd replied that they couldn't manage without him.

The fact that Helen had been managing without him for years wasn't obvious to Bill, then, as now.

'Can I let you know?' Helen wasn't spending the day at home, but equally she had better things to do than the committee she'd been on for nearly a decade. They were well-meaning people, but somehow they seemed to lack the gumption to really get things done. The whole point of not having a career and volunteering instead was to give herself the flexibility to simply not do any of the activities she was given, when the mood took her. Her late mother-in-law had explained the virtues of this with such relief when Helen had given up secretarial work.

Rosemary bade her farewell and they ended the call.

Her coffee had gone cold. She had friends, people with whom she could share a small talk chat at one of the many cafés nearby, or attend one of the endless coffee mornings put on for people of a certain age with a lack of anything else to do. She would attend, alone, of course. But she was lucky enough not to live alone. And yet, the terrible piercing pain of loneliness seemed to stalk her.

The silence was punctuated by the keyboard tapping from the dining room.

She stood by the door, coughing gently.

Bill looked up – he still had that smile she'd fallen in love with all those years ago, and his eyes too: they'd been azure blue, but were now waterier. 'Yes? Who was that on the phone?'

'Rosemary.'

'Who?'

'The secretary at Caring for Children.'

He'd returned to his laptop. Looked up, shook his head. 'Did you have a question you wanted to ask me?'

This was why she didn't usually bother disturbing him. It wasn't worth marching herself up hill of hope, only to come tumbling down when faced with this. *I was going to ask if you'd like a coffee.* 'What are you doing?'

He let out a protracted sigh, shaking his head. 'You wouldn't understand.'

'Try me.' She stepped closer, placing her empty coffee mug on the table.

'Can you not put that there, if it spills over the computer it'll ruin it. This cost a great deal of money. I'd rather you didn't spoil things.'

She picked it up. 'What are you doing?' She shook her head at the laptop screen. There were many internet tabs open and a spreadsheet filled half the screen.

He waved her away dismissively. 'Research.'

'About what?' she persevered.

'Figures.'

'What sort of figures?' She was determined to press more than she'd managed before.

'Reviews.'

'Of what?'

He removed his reading glasses, pinched his nose in obvious irritation. 'Major tourist attractions around the world. Eiffel Tower, Empire State Building, Niagara Falls, Leaning Tower of Pisa.'

Her heart sped up at the possibility of holidaying in all those places with Bill. Perhaps he wasn't so bad after all. 'What are you doing with the reviews?' Working out which is the best one, using some mathematical formula probably, as was his wont.

'Sorting them into themes, ratings and then, well, that's it so far.' He looked at her, frowning. 'It's a work in progress. I wanted something to do totally different from looking after patients.'

Helen nodded slowly as it hit her: he was doing nothing, nothing of any consequence anyway. He was analysing the reviews as simply something to do. 'I'm going out.'

He didn't look at her, peered at a screen of reviews for Stonehenge.

'Do you want to do something together?'

'What? Today? Now?'

She nodded, collecting her mug and holding it to her stomach.

'Why?' he asked, staring at the laptop screen.

'Why? Oh, I don't know, perhaps because I'm not working.' *Nor have I been for decades…*

He stared at the computer screen.

'And you're *clearly* not doing anything that can't wait.' Helen bunched her free hand into a fist, holding it by her sides. 'The world is, as they say, our oyster. We could go for a drive, have lunch out, a wander around the shops perhaps. There's an antique mill near Oxford I've been reading about.'

He continued to stare.

'Anything?'

Nothing from him.

'Don't you want to do something? Together?' *Anything.*

He looked away from the screen, staring at her with his watery blue eyes. 'Antique mill? Shopping? Why on earth would I want to do that? We've a house replete with things, a fridge full of food, there's no need to traipse all the way to the countryside to *eat*.' He spat the last word out with such disdain it was all Helen could do not to slap him across the face.

She banged a fist on the table.

'Darling, what is the matter?' He carefully shuffled the papers into piles.

'For fuck's sake! What's the matter with me? What about you? You…' she struggled for the right word, eventually settling on '…idiot!' She knew this would rile him, he took great pride in his long and illustrious educational history.

Bill shrugged, returning to his computer, staring intently at the screen and carefully pecking the keyboard with two fingers.

'Did you hear me, I called you an idiot!'

He shook his head. 'You're clearly overwrought, why don't you have a lie down?'

'Lie down? Lie bloody well down?' She shook her head, as the heat flushed her cheeks, pure undiluted fury raging through her veins.

He tutted loudly and smiled.

Fucking bloody well smiled. All she wanted was a proper row, to at least show that he gave a shit about her. That he cared enough to fight with her about something. Anything. To prove that he saw her, noticed her more than as someone who prepared his food and kept the house tidy. She wasn't bothered about being appreciated, that had long since gone, but being noticed would have been a start.

She left the room, carefully and deliberately rinsed her mug in the sink, left it upturned on the draining board. She'd stopped using the dishwasher during the day because washing up by hand gave her something to do. Gripping the sink tightly, she stared at the ceiling and screamed.

Bill did not come.

He no longer saw or cared about her. No one really did. Her coffee morning friends were just filler, people to share small talk with; none of them would want her spilling out her feelings with them. They simply sat up straight, talked about the news, house prices, what their children and grandchildren were doing and left with a brief hug until next time.

At that thought, the sadness of that realisation seemed almost too much. She grabbed her bag of swimming paraphernalia and left the house for the only place she felt able to, when her emotions overcame her like this.

Chapter 3

Ian Oakley sat in his car staring at the single storey white building with curved windows and a flat roof. It was flanked by tall conifers with flowerbeds in colourful bloom at their bases. The whites, blues and reds of the bedding plants contrasted against the tall poker-like green trees.

The anxiety about taking his clothes off made his hands sweat and the beginnings of a headache formed behind his eyes.

A quick glance at his grey suit trousers jolted him back to why he was here. *This is who I am now. This is what I do.*

A woman crossed the car park pushing a pram.

A man wearing sportswear jogged to the building, pausing to stretch his legs before entering through the double doors.

Ian reckoned he should have become used to this by now, and if not, why not? He wiped his hands on his trousers. A quick swipe of his phone and the headlines didn't catch his attention – he didn't have much interest in current affairs since—

His thumb hovered over the email icon. He knew he should have unsubscribed from the newsletters he'd signed up to after leaving. He'd told himself it would help keep his hand in, remain up to date with policy developments. Pretty essential for a head of policy. *Ex.*

Something something, new health minister, something something cabinet reshuffle, something something another reorg of the NHS.

It used to be his job to keep abreast of these sorts of developments. Now, he'd have been better spending his time signing up for job alerts.

I'll switch the phone off – just a quick swipe through social media. His friends were all posting about their amazing lives: perfect holidays, unbelievable partners, adorable kids, interesting jobs.

The really unbelievable part was that he'd been doing this for three months. Twelve weeks. Next week would be his thirteenth week – unlucky for some, maybe it would be his lucky week, maybe a recruitment consultant would call and offer him one of those perfect jobs everyone seemed to have.

Everyone, except him.

Losing his job wasn't just that, for Ian it was the most important part of who he was, who he had been since leaving university. Ian was the earner, the provider, the main breadwinner in his relationship and he'd enjoyed that. It was part of – no, the key element of – who he was in their relationship.

He was an expert in the health policy professional field he'd chosen and that had afforded him respect and validation of his life up to that point. When they met, three years ago, Drew had said he'd never met someone who knew so much about such a wide range of subjects as Ian.

And now, they'd taken all that away from him.

The work bag sat on the passenger seat. Normally it would be full of Health Service Journal, The Economist,

The Times – plenty to keep him occupied on the journey into London from the far reaches of the Piccadilly Line.

Reaching into the bag, he pulled out the towel and found the bright blue swimming shorts. Drew had bought them for him, he'd worn them during their last holiday to a sunny Greek island filled with white buildings and azure blue roofs. Not too dissimilar to the gym and café he was staring at. The gym was called a wellness centre apparently, although the name above the door didn't really fit with the art deco building.

I can do it! I've done it every day this week, this month, why am I sitting here now?

With a sigh he switched the radio on and the nauseatingly upbeat breakfast DJ was waffling on about the weather and asking people to call in with their favourite morning songs.

At least this place opened early. Six o'clock meant he didn't have to wait after his journey from the small Oxfordshire village. The first fortnight had been the worst, driving around aimlessly, unclear what to do, where to go. Sitting in the supermarket car park until it opened and then browsing clothes he didn't need, books he couldn't afford and food they already had, was probably the low point of this whole thing.

One day, having parked at Uxbridge tube station, ready for the commute into London he wasn't doing for the job he didn't have, he'd meandered around the town centre, not spending money and had happened upon the lido. He'd worked out the longest he could spend in a café was a couple of hours, and the library had proved too depressing with people studying and reminding him of his optimism as a graduate at getting a decent job. And now, here he had been, sitting next to pensioners, reading the news in an actual physical newspaper, watching the clock until he could return home. Besides, the library shut too early and he'd arrived home at an impossible hour and Drew had asked why.

The lido stayed open late and had a variety of activities that he could fill his day with, alternating between them, so a day would pass much quicker than sitting in a café or library. All different people moved through the lido's facilities, meaning he didn't feel awkward at spending the day there, Monday to Friday. Besides, the car park was free, so that was a saving too.

BD (Before Drew), he had once completely run out of money. A new car, larger flat in a nicer area, new clothes for his swanky new job, eating out every night as he was dating furiously in his early twenties, determined to find a boyfriend, had all combined. Nine months after graduating he sat on the floor of his empty flat, having let bailiffs empty it, and watched his car being lifted onto a lorry and driven away, knowing he'd made a big mistake.

Feeling powerless at his own stupidity for getting in that situation was one thing, but the mess afterwards had been enough to teach him he was never going to run out of money again.

Except this time, *they* and their bloody departmental restructure had taken the ability to earn money away from him.

At least here – the West London Lido – there was no waiting around, he could arrive and go straight in for a swim. Clear his head, butterfly stroke away what had happened. Front crawl his way into a solution. Backstroke himself into a new career maybe.

Oddly, no one seemed to be interested in a just-shy-of-forty ex-head of policy for a health think-tank. They'd all had their fill of people like Ian. And nowhere else wanted his skills.

The lido had a café, in which he'd spent a third of his days – the rest of his time was spent in the lido and the gym and wellness centre. Ian liked a plan, enjoyed the neatness of spreading his daytime hours between these three places. He knew Drew would never come there; he used the Soho gym near the fire station where he worked or went for long runs through the Cotswold countryside near their home.

The white towel and blue swimming trunks jolted Ian back to laying on the soft sandy beach next to Drew, sipping their third cocktail before lunch.

'We're on holiday!' Drew had said as he'd requested the first. 'Besides, it's all inclusive.'

Reluctant to start drinking so early at first, Ian had soon become accustomed to it. They'd have a swim in the sea, boozy lunch, sunbathing, and then back to the hotel room for kisses and cuddles and oh so much more…

Ian hadn't wanted to book a gay holiday, in a gay resort, too… Much. But Drew insisted on holding hands on the hotel's private beach and the odd kiss while eating or laying by the pool.

It had been such a perfect holiday. Away from the drudge and worries of real life.

Now, guilt filled his chest at the lie. The repeated, ongoing, continuous lie.

What Ian wouldn't give now for a bit of the regular daily drudge he'd enjoyed. Daily drives to Uxbridge station at the far end of the Piccadilly Line, the tube train clattering all the way to Piccadilly Circus, reading the latest HSJ scoop, getting his head around new legislation from the Department of Health and Social Care, arriving bursting with ideas at the office.

The comforting routine of employment. Less drudge now he remembered it fondly, more providing him purpose and income.

His phone beeped, signalling a text message. His bank confirming his balance was over a certain amount. Money had been deposited in his bank account in an imitation of his salary. His modest redundancy payment rested in an account and each month he sent his old salary into his current account, meaning most of it could join Drew's in their joint account, as before.

Drew wouldn't check Ian's account, he wasn't like that, but Ian wanted to make everything appear as normal as possible. Hence the suit, the drive every morning, returning at the end of the day, as before.

By his calculation Ian had another two months before the money ran out. Before he had to tell Drew the truth. What had really happened.

But first, before he could do that, he'd need to make sense of it himself, and then hope Drew wouldn't leave. Ian knew he was punching way above his weight being with Drew. Firefighters don't go out with men like Ian. Boys who grew up into men like Drew used to bully boys who grew up into men like Ian. It was the natural order of things.

A *ten* doesn't really fall in love with a *six*. Except in some books maybe.

Ian allowed himself a smirk, looking up from his towel and swimming shorts.

Perhaps if I stop wearing the shorts Drew bought me, maybe that'll reduce some of the guilt. No matter what he wore, it would still remind him of Drew.

'I've started swimming at lunchtime,' Ian had said the first time Drew commented on the chlorine smell.

Ian had never done anything at lunchtime except work so that had come as a surprise to Drew who'd raised an eyebrow and continued without further thought.

Because he trusted Ian. And this is what Ian did with that trust. Screwed it up like a used towel, discarded it like one of the plasters he saw floating in the pre-swim foot pool.

Gross. Ian shuddered.

No, he told himself, what's gross is you, in the tiny swimming shorts your boyfriend bought you, just to be kind, because you don't deserve him. Because you're useless and when he finds out precisely how useless, he's going to leave you. And if not for that reason, because you've been lying to him.

Maybe I'll sit here a little longer before going in.

Ian thought he'd got used to this new routine, but the part he hadn't quite appreciated was the hopelessness and guilt from saying goodbye to Drew every morning as if nothing had changed since before their Greek holiday.

Ian changed the radio station – news. Instinctively he waited for the headlines, then listened intently for the health reporter – why?

With a sigh, he banged it off with a finger. Shaking his head he knew something had to change, but except for getting a job, he didn't know what else to do. He couldn't now tell Drew what he'd been doing all this time, could he? He was committed to the lie now, he needed to see it through until he'd landed a new job. Casually drop it in that his office had moved, Drew wouldn't pay enough attention to know he'd moved from one think-thank to another, it wasn't something Drew followed in much detail, and a world about which he knew nothing – only what Ian had told him.

More guilt at the deceit stabbed in his gut. It was like a nervous stomach ache.

Blinking furiously as the enormity of his situation threatened to swallow him whole, Ian wiped his cheeks of tears and turned to his phone – social media, news, email...

Chapter 4

Gabriella stopped her car outside the wellness centre. There was a single-storey white building with a flat roof and rounded windows – it looked old. Next to it stood a taller glass and metal building; there were people running and cycling on equipment on the other side of those windows. Behind a wall to the side of the older building lay an outside pool: the lido itself. Although the whole complex centred around the old lido building, apparently it was so much more, with a gym, indoor swimming pools and a café – hopefully, it would be her little slice of normality.

Unbuckling Thomas from his car seat she said, 'Are you hungry?'

He nodded, sticking his thumb in his mouth and looking up at her with huge dark brown eyes, framed with long eyelashes.

Arnie hadn't liked Thomas sucking his thumb, said it made him babyish, but Gabriella loved it. She preferred the babyish stage, when they would cuddle up to her and Arnie in bed, sucking their thumbs, laying their heads on her lap.

Everything about that stage was full of joy... Except the nappies part. Still carrying a bag of clean-up essentials and spare nappies at all times had made quick work of Thomas's earlier accident.

Gently she removed Thomas's thumb from his mouth. 'Plenty to eat inside.' She lifted him from the chair, placing him down, his tiny shoes tapped the ground.

Taking his hand, they walked towards the lido as the warmth of the sun heated her bare arms.

A man was sitting in his car with red eyes, wiping them with his shirt sleeve. He looked very unwell.

She caught his eye, raising her eyebrow and smiling briefly, hoping he'd return with a grin.

He quickly looked away, staring at the steering wheel.

Shall I check he's okay? They were next to the car.

What would Arnie do? He'd definitely check. Except I'm not Arnie, and he's not here, so I'm walking past.

Gabriella strode past with purpose, catching the man out of the corner of her eye.

The horn blasted and he seemed to be banging his hands on the steering wheel.

He was definitely not okay.

Shaking her head, she strode towards the lido. *None of my business, leave him to it.*

They were at the entrance now. A man held the heavy door open for Gabriella to go in.

The car horn beeped and the man made a noise of something in a lot of pain.

Now, Gabriella had to see if he was okay. Her bar for speaking to strangers was much higher than Arnie's. She briefly imagined him standing shaking his head if she'd continued inside the building.

'Sorry,' she said to the man holding the door, turning around and marching back to the man's car. She rested her large sunglasses on her head and smartly knocked on his window.

He looked up, red-rimmed eyes open wide, wet cheeks, hair ruffled and messy. It seemed really out of place with a grey suit jacket hanging in the back and he wore a smart white shirt and tie.

'Are you all right?' she asked.

He nodded furiously.

'You don't look it.'

'I'm fine.'

She crouched lower so she could see him better, still hanging on to Thomas's hand. He was clean shaven, looked as if he'd made an effort that morning, and now something must have happened to upset him. 'Do you want me to get you a coffee?'

He stared at her blankly.

Emboldened by a big dollop of her mum's courage, she tapped the window, motioning for him to lower it.

He did not.

He leaned closer to the glass. 'I'm fine. Honestly. Absolutely okay.' He smiled weakly.

She recognised that smile, she'd done it a lot since Arnie had died. The '*I can't be bothered to tell you how I really feel, and to be honest you're not interested, so I'm just going to tell you I'm okay*' smile.

Knowing when she was beaten or outstaying her welcome, she nodded and left him to it.

The main doors opened into the reception desk, with turnstiles leading to the, she presumed, paid-for facilities. The café was to one side, with a slight scent of chlorine mixed with coffee and frothy milk in the air. To the left lay the outdoor pool, and the right to the indoor one and beyond it the wellness centre, which just looked like a plain old gym to Gabriella.

The man at reception explained she needed to pay to access the facilities behind the turnstile.

'Can I look at the outdoor pool?' she asked.

He opened the gate and showed her through. It was enormous, full of people swimming and playing. Each end had a fountain squirting water high into the air.

'Where do you get changed?' she asked.

The man pointed to one side of the lido. 'Those booths. Or if you're swimming inside, there are changing rooms.' He smiled. 'Want to see the gym?'

She shook her head. 'Not for me, ta.'

From the other side of the gates he said, 'Would you like to swim?'

It all felt a bit much, so she said, 'Not today. I'm just gonna sit and have a coffee, if that's all right.'

He nodded towards the café. 'Of course it is.'

At the thought of the café and a coffee, she remembered the man in the car. She told the barista. 'Does he normally come here?' She described him.

'Wearing a suit?' the barista asked.

Gabriella nodded. 'Dirty blond hair. But it's not dirty, it just looks not blond blond, you know?' She'd run out of words and it wasn't even nine o'clock.

'Comes here every day in the week, spends most of the day here.'

'In the café?'

'And the lido, both the indoor pool and the outdoor one, and the wellness centre.'

'What's he drink?'

'Decaffeinated espresso.'

She scrunched up her nose. 'What's the point of that, eh?'

The barista shrugged.

'One of them, please, and a large latte.'

As they made her drinks, she pondered on what sort of man would arrive at a lido in a suit, spend the whole day there, and drink caffeine-free espressos.

With a shrug at not working out any of those questions, she paid the barista and left the building and Gabriella knocked on the man's window. 'Got you this.'

'What?'

'Your usual.' She tapped the glass with a nail that had chipped nail polish. 'Wind it down, will you?'

He did and accepted the drink gratefully. 'You didn't have to. I'm perfectly okay, thanks.'

She smiled. All done with trying to convince strangers otherwise, she nodded. 'Have a nice day!' She deliberately tried to Americanise her accent in some sort of vain hope it would cheer up this man.

'Thanks.' He was searching through his wallet, handed some coins out of the window.

She shook her head. 'Not necessary.' Taking a deep breath, she said, 'See you, then.' And off she walked, with a frown, trying to decide what, if anything, that all meant.

They had placed her order on a table in the corner, as she'd asked. She nodded with thanks as she walked past, soon settling into the seat. It gave her an uninterrupted view of everyone in the café, all the comings and goings of the gym, and, if she turned to one side, the outside pool. At either end sat fountains, with brightly coloured wooden changing booths along one wall. Wooden sun loungers were scattered in the sunny patches around the Olympic-sized, heated, outdoor pool – so all the signs said. It did look attractive.

Thomas banged on the table and had managed to cover his face with Gabriella's avocado and poached egg on toast. It looked like the least weird thing on the menu. No chance of a full English breakfast here. Part of her wanted to scoop it off with a spoon so she could eat it – her stomach rumbled – and the other part wanted to rest her head on the table and just cry.

She wanted to call her mum just to hear her reaction to this strange breakfast concoction: 'Nothing's better with avocado.'

Scooping the mess off Thomas's face with a napkin, she then gave him a drink from his sippy cup and ate what was left of her breakfast.

Why did you have to go and bloody well die? she wanted to ask Mum. She tensed her fingers around the knife. Sometimes she found herself feeling… Stabby, like this. Sort of physically livid at everything and everyone. But in particular Arnie.

Not just him though, seeing men Arnie's age – early thirties – who weren't dead, annoyed her. As well as their wives and girlfriends. Smug cows. And kids who had two parents too.

A man slipped into the deep end of the outdoor pool. He wore a swimming cap.

A woman, who looked about her mum's age, had been doing lengths in the lane to the left side for the whole time Gabriella had been sitting there. She did the one where your head is under the water, except when you turn to one side and breath, presumably. This woman was like a human submarine, slicing through the water, without a worry to hold her back.

Lucky cow.

'Want juice!' Thomas shouted.

It brought her back to the task in hand. Parenting her youngest child. Alone. She could weep just thinking about how tired she felt. Her body ached, her eyes felt heavy, her skin seemed to sag everywhere.

How she longed for some additional adult company. Additional adults were something she'd grown up with – a parade of aunties and uncles who'd taken her when her parents were working.

There was no one who she could hand the children over to – unless you counted Arnie's parents. And Gabriella didn't. Not if she could avoid it. Their parenting methods for Arnie went out with the Ark, and Gabriella wanted to avoid them rubbing off on her kids.

'Stay there.' She ordered another juice from the counter, by miming drink, then pointing to Thomas.

It was practically like she lived here already. Never did she think she'd feel at home somewhere like this. In a pub, of course. God, she loved a pub. Clearing glasses as soon as she could, then serving behind the bar when she turned eighteen. Her dad used to play an upright piano and her mum used to sing. Stepping into their local in Mile End had felt like another world. She didn't realise they were the odd ones out until she met Arnie. And his parents.

'We'll take Thomas, if you can't cope,' Pru had said.

It wasn't that Gabriella couldn't cope, as such, it was that the slightest thought of Pru thinking that to be true was enough for her to do the complete opposite. She had said to Gabriella, 'You don't really think you'll marry him, do you, dear?'

And since Arnie had asked her to be his wife, Gabriella had nodded. 'Yeah, I do, as it goes.'

Pru had shaken her head, tutted loudly and said, 'I shan't hear of it. Arnie is destined for big things, grand in fact. Not some budget Marilyn whose only talent is taking off her clothes.'

It wasn't Gabriella's fault that people kept comparing her to Marilyn, in her looks mainly. Arnie had remarked on the fact when they'd first met. She'd bitten her lip. 'I love him.'

Pru had laughed. 'What do you think that has to do with anything?'

Gabriella knew she'd never understand them, so had stuck to her mum's advice – least said soonest mended. Unfortunately if she'd really fallen out with her mother-in-law she wouldn't have had the added pressure of their wanting to see their grandsons at every bloody opportunity.

Now, the lane woman climbed out of the pool. She had thin legs and arms, hardly any hips – she couldn't have had any kids – her breasts were small also. Yet she moved slowly and deliberately, laying on a sun lounger in the first of the morning sun. Reaching into her bag she pulled out a cigarette. It didn't need lighting, so it must be one of them fake, vape ones.

Taking a long drag, she lay back, then exhaled.

The lifeguard blew his whistle in her direction from the chair high on a platform at one end of the pool, next to a fountain.

The woman continued regardless until the lifeguard walked over, pointing his finger, gesturing to a sign on the wall.

There was one on the wall in the café – it clearly said no vaping was allowed.

The old woman nodded, put the fake ciggie in her bag, shaking her head, adjusted her sunglasses, then lay back.

'Fair play to the old bird.' She turned to Thomas as if he'd know what she was on about. 'Do you want to see Granny and Grandpa?'

He nodded, banging his cup on the table enthusiast-ically. He'd only known one set of grandparents, since her parents were gone when he was born. At the time, it made sense to move nearer to family, since hers were still in Mile End but six feet under and not much use as nan and pop-pop, as her boys may have called them. And so they'd found a big house in the outer west side of London, an area Gabriella knew nothing about – it might as well have been outer Mongolia for how much she'd had to do with that side of London as a girl.

Her phone rang with a withheld number – at least it wasn't anyone who'd want to speak to her about the life insurance, or his will. She'd had those calls up to her eyes. What was the point of paying a bloody solicitor if you still didn't understand what to do?

Best answer it. She pressed it to her ear. Her heart sank as the voice greeted her.

'My dear,' Pru said, 'you really are very difficult to track down. I've left you a number of messages asking when we can see our dear grandchildren.'

'Speak of the devil! I've just been thinking about you,' Gabriella said with a smile.

'My grandchildren, when can I see them?' There was an imperious silence – she'd done this to Arnie and it'd worked on him – he always gave in to her demands.

Gabriella bit her bottom lip very hard.

'Are you still there?' Pru asked. 'It sounds as if you're in some sort of market. You've not gone back to that dreadful pub where your father used to work, have you?'

She gritted her teeth. *When is this bloody woman going to give it a frigging rest?* The only reason Pru spoke to her was because she wanted access to her grandsons once Arnie had married her – they'd eloped and had a register office do in east London where Gabriella's parents had wed. Since then, Pru had realised the Gabriella-not-marrying-her-son ship had well and truly sailed so instead focused her efforts on belittling Gabriella at every opportunity.

Very carefully, Gabriella said, 'I'm grieving.'

After a long sigh, Pru replied, 'We're all doing that. I lost a son. We, I mean.'

'And I lost a husband. A lifetime together, retirement, getting grey, seeing grandkids—'

'Can I ask where you are? We can be there in a jiffy and take Thomas off your hands.'

Tempting as it sounded, she knew the day all alone would be worse than with Thomas. Without the constant need to look after and mother him, her thoughts would spiral into a negative black hole. and she would soon find herself standing on a bridge, kneeling in front of the oven, or staring at a bottle of sleeping tablets. Until she imagined her sons' faces when they found out what she'd done.

'You gotta keep on keeping on,' Mum used to say. It had seen her right when she'd started out in the modelling game, endless grubby photo shoots with photographers who'd tried it on, no money and no prospects. Until after winning a magazine competition she met Arnie at the photo shoot and he'd told her, 'You've got a bright future ahead of you.'

And for some reason, probably because he'd seemed so much older and wiser than her, twenty-four to her twenty had felt so different, she'd believed him and then he'd shown her.

There was silence on the phone line until Pru said, 'Are you at home?'

Gabriella laughed. It was hilarious that she'd even consider spending any time *there* when she had any choice.

Except sleeping, she aimed to be out of that house as much as possible.

'What's so funny?'

She shook her head. Pru had no idea.

'Where are you?'

The lane woman at the far end of the swimming pool was reading a book and nipping behind the fountain and putting her head in her handbag, followed by a mist. She was having a crafty puff on her fake ciggie, then returned into the water.

And with that, at the pure undiluted impressiveness of the lane woman, Gabriella said, 'I've got to go,' ended the call and switched off her phone. Taking Thomas's hand, she said, 'Come on, love.'

'Where are we going?'

'It's gonna be like a holiday, all right?'

He nodded vigorously and smiled.

It made her heart leap with the tiniest bit of joy she'd experienced since...

They left the café and made their way to the outdoor pool where the lane woman was swimming.

Chapter 5

Helen was in the middle of completing her forty lengths, in complete silence, without interruption, alone with her thoughts, as usual.

If she was going to escape Bill and her empty house, she'd long ago decided squandering the days drinking in cafés, browsing the shops for things she neither needed nor wanted, or even volunteering somewhere, would just be pushing her problem to one side, rather than facing it head on, like she should have done years ago.

The lengths gave her an almost beautifully mindful time at the start of each day, to consider her situation and what she could do about it. Over the months, she'd dreamed up elaborately complicated plans to deal with Bill's not seeing her, and had, without exception, failed to implement a single one. She didn't mind because she knew the next morning, she'd come up with another... And another...

The warm sun heated her face and she no longer squinted since she'd started swimming in tinted goggles. She counted to herself in time with the swimming strokes: one, one, one, two, two, two, three, three, three... It was the best way to completely empty her mind.

Every five lengths she'd swim underwater for as long as her lungs permitted.

Those submerged lengths were often her favourite part of swimming here. Beneath the water she could be anyone, forget what Bill was or wasn't doing at home, that her son was now an adult and didn't need her, that she didn't have grandchildren for perfectly valid reasons but how it didn't fail to jab her like a stomach cramp when, inevitably with friends and meeting new people her age, the subject of grandchildren came up.

'None. At this stage,' had become her stock response to that question.

After a thoroughly exhausting swim, with the germ of an idea about how to face up to her problems, she towelled herself down, enjoying the warmth of the sun's rays on her arms and neck. She was basking in the sun and reading. It was an unusually warm day for May and she was determined to make the best of it, notwithstanding Bill.

She slid a hand over her calves – she could do with shaving her legs, but then again why bother? Bill wouldn't notice. Bill wouldn't notice if she walked into the kitchen in a space suit, singing Liberace.

She put the book to one side. Maybe that's something to consider. It would at least start a conversation with Bill.

A petite, blond woman in a long dress, holding the hand of a small child, was walking closer.

Her heart squeezed at the memory of being in her late twenties, and having young children. The stage at which they *really* loved you. Couldn't do without you, hadn't yet learned to be stroppy or want to be independent. The being completely relied upon element had felt strangely comforting in comparison to when her son had become a surly teenager, needing Helen's help less and less until they'd left home.

I wonder what Peter's doing now.

The woman crossed her legs and sat on a sun lounger a short distance away. She was giving the little boy something from her handbag.

Helen's heart ached at the lost happiness for that stage of her life. She'd never felt more useful, more purposeful, than devoting all her time to raising their baby as he had turned into a toddler, then a small person.

Sometimes she would dig out the home movies Bill had put on DVD and spend a whole afternoon watching Peter when he was that small and perfect. More than the longing for the younger, line-free, brown-haired version of herself, she missed, more than almost expressible in words, the vitality she had in their lives. In everyone's lives, then, as the mother to their child. The primary caregiver, isn't that what they said now?

Helen saw the woman seemed to be looking at her – was she slipping out of the dress into her swimming costume? A quick glance and she confirmed she was not. The woman with the toddler would look splendid in a bikini, just like Helen had used to wear.

Helen pretended not to be bothered about the other woman and her child and picked up the book to read, occasionally glancing over the top to confirm the woman and her child were still there.

After a few more pages about the woman in New York City getting to know the birth mother she'd never known existed, Helen noticed a shadow cast over her.

The blond woman stood next to Helen's sun lounger. She was short with a petite build, the fact she'd given birth to a child seemed impossible. 'It's a bit of an odd request, but I wondered if you wanted some company. I'll go if not. I've got Thomas, but I think it's always nice to have some additional adult company.' She smiled. Bright white, probably-capped teeth shone back.

Helen lowered the book, turning to the woman. The way she'd said the last phrase hit something inside Helen. 'This is empty.' She gestured to the next sun lounger.

The woman sat, indicating for her son to join her. 'Good, is it?'

Helen frowned. *Is this woman on something perhaps?*

'Book,' she added, pointing as if it were necessary.

'It's okay.' Helen put it to one side, sitting up slightly, pulling her sarong over her lap in a moment of self-consciousness about her tired fifty-eight-year-old body next to this woman's shapely curves.

'I never have time. Never used to read much before kids, but now…' She shook her head tutting loudly.

'How many do you have? Children.'

'Two.'

Helen looked around for the other one.

'He's at school. Five and three. Jack and Thomas.'

Helen was enjoying this. 'What are they like? What does their father do?'

The woman swallowed, blinking furiously.

Without thinking, Helen put her hand on the woman's shoulder. 'Did I say something wrong? I'm sorry.'

The woman shook her head, took a breath and said, 'Gabriella. By the way.' She held out her hand.

Helen shook it. 'Helen. By the way.' She chuckled. 'Bill used to call me Hell.' Not for a long time though. He'd not cared enough to call her anything much.

'Your hubby?'

Helen involuntarily shuddered at that word. It was one of her pet hates. Best not mention that at this stage.

Gabriella seemed a touch fragile for some reason. 'Yes,' Helen said, then swallowed carefully.

'Don't he swim with you?' Gabriella looked about.

There was quite a lot to unpack with that question, and because she wasn't quite ready, Helen asked, 'You never said what he's like, the other boy. Two boys, that must be quite a handful. I had a boy.'

'Had?'

'Have. I mean of course he's older than you now.'

'I thought maybe you'd...' Gabriella looked at the ground, tucking a hair behind her ear.

Helen shook her head. 'No. I was lucky. Textbook pregnancy and birth.'

'Had a friend, in the local mum's group. First baby and it had taken her ages to fall. I just used to look at Arnie and I'd fall.'

Helen nodded, it had been the same for her. Bill and her started to try for a family in the February and she fell pregnant that month. She told Gabriella.

'Lucky us,' Gabriella said. 'This woman, she lost it. Her. Stillbirth. Imagine that, all the pain and suffering and—' Gabriella looked away, wiping a tear from her cheek.

Helen sensed there was a lot more going on behind that than she was letting on. Another squeeze of her arm, then she rubbed Gabriella's back. 'I wanted a girl too. Well, another child. Whatever it was, I'd have been happy. Another boy, a girl...'

'What happened?' Gabriella asked.

Helen swallowed, carefully considering how to describe what had happened. 'Bill said one was enough, and of course I didn't want to go through all that again, did I? Interfered with his work. He found it all very much of a strain.'

'You?'

'I loved it. I'd have had four.' Helen blinked at the realisation, she could have had three adult children now, had she put her foot down to Bill's refusal.

There was silence.

Helen shook her head, as if to rid herself of that thought. 'Are you having a swim?'

Gabriella indicated no. 'He's still in nappies. I've not tried him swimming yet. Besides, I come here for a rest.'

'Have you seen the film, *The Water Babies*?'

'Disney?'

'No. But it's a cartoon. Part of it anyway. I used to sing the songs when I was giving my son a bath.' Helen smiled at the memory. This was the first discussion with someone she found interesting in too long and she didn't want it to end. 'Do you want something to eat?'

'No, ta. I must let you go. I've disturbed you enough.' Gabriella took the little boy's hand and stood.

'You're not disturbing me. This is the first proper conversation I've had in months.' Years possibly.

'What about Hubby?' she asked brightly.

Another shudder at that bloody word. Helen resolved to mention it if she did it again. Or maybe she shouldn't. Helen stood, raising her eyebrows at Gabriella.

She smiled. 'Go on then.'

'My treat.'

'I can pay.' Gabriella seemed to puff herself up at that.

'I don't doubt it, but I'd like to. All three of us. We'll eat here, save getting in cars and all that palaver.'

Gabriella bobbed her head from side to side and giggled lightly.

'What?' Helen asked.

'Mum used to say that. Must be something from your generation.'

'Maybe you *should* pay. Since I now feel about a hundred and five.'

Gabriella patted Helen's back. 'Soz. Never thought. Mouth Almighty, that's what Arnie used to call me.'

As they walked inside and found seats in the café, Helen reflected on the two times Gabriella had said 'used to' – indicating her mum and husband were both no longer with her.

They settled in the corner, Gabriella had found a high chair for the little boy.

'What do you want?' Helen asked.

Gabriella stared long and hard at the menu as if it were a complicated legal document. Looking up with a worried expression, she said, 'I've not long eaten. You go ahead and order yours, I'll get mine once I've chosen.'

Helen sat. 'No rush.' This was a woman who'd made a lot of very difficult decisions in a short space of time – no doubt linked to the "used to" of her husband. 'Take as long as you need.'

Chapter 6

Ian had been sitting in the car for nearly forty-five minutes.

He'd been watching people enter and leave the lido, some going straight for a swim, others hanging around the café, others heading for the gym and its rowing machine, weights or treadmill. The glass building to the side of the original white one housed the gym, giving him a clear view of everyone doing their gym activities in what they believed was isolation, but in fact on show for everyone to see.

His phone rang, withheld number. *Probably a recruitment consultant. Must be. Hope it is.*

'Hello?' Ian asked with uncertainty.

'It's me,' Drew replied.

Why's he calling from a withheld number? 'How are you?'

'All right, you?' Drew asked.

Ian swallowed, he wasn't expecting to hear from Drew at this time. 'Fine.' He sounded unsure. 'Everything okay with you?' One of the risks of having a boyfriend who was a firefighter was him being called in for extra shifts at short notice and the impending threat of you-know-what, which most other jobs didn't include in their job description.

'How come you're not underground by now? Was expecting to get your voicemail.'

Ian blushed, shook his head furiously. Stupid mistake. He should have switched his phone off by now, rather than endlessly scrolling.

Ian coughed. 'Stopped for a coffee.' It was the best lie he could come up with at this much notice. Once you started telling lies, they kept coming and coming.

'Nearly ten, shouldn't you be in your daily stand up meeting, now?'

Shit. He really should. How long had he been sitting in the car?

'Are you still there?' Drew asked.

Ian did his best to compose himself, his reflection in the rear-view mirror told him otherwise – he looked like a kid who'd been caught with his hands in the sweetie jar. In fact, he had been that kid, before losing all the weight. 'Fine. Yeah. Sorry. It's been a lot this morning. A lot.'

'Right?'

'Flat tyre on the car – that's what made me late, then I missed the train so had to sit waiting for the next one for ages. Then I forgot I had an early meeting, so missed that. Should have done it in the car park, but…' *The dog ate my homework*. He might as well add that for good measure, since the lies were tripping of his tongue without a second thought today. 'I sent apologies for the ten o'clock since…' *It's a lie…*

'Babe, it sounds like you got out of bed the wrong side this morning. Wish I could give you a hug.'

Christ, that made it even worse. Eliciting sympathy from Drew for stuff that hadn't happened. The guilt was the hardest part of all this. Ian swallowed the lump in his throat. *So that's what guilt tastes like. Right.*

'I was only ringing to remind you we're seeing that show tonight.'

More money they didn't have. Great. It was a show Drew had wanted to see since his birthday and they'd booked it then and waited almost six months for seats. So in some ways it had already been paid for, when Ian was earning.

'Of course,' Ian said. 'How could I forget? Really looking forward to it.' He gritted his teeth and tried to inject more happiness to his tone.

'Are you okay?'

Ian huffed.

'Only, you sound funny.'

Ian debated coming out with it all, the whole big ugly lie he'd been living, telling, or not telling for all these months. But then he'd have to face the worst part – Drew's disappointment. And then his inevitable upping and leaving. They relied more on Ian's money. Although Drew's firefighter money wasn't bad, he'd refused to go for a management promotion so was stuck on the normal firefighter wage, about half what Ian used to earn. Not nearly enough money considering what he did.

'You still there?' Drew asked.

Ian blinked away tears, fought back the gasping wail he'd let go of so well before while in the car alone. He couldn't just let it all out, he had to man up, deal with this on his own, because he was strong, and shield Drew from the mess. A mess of Ian's own making. He stuck his fist in his mouth, biting the knuckles as tears squeezed from his eyes.

Swallowing, it took all his strength to say, 'Tired.' Deep breath. 'Today's been a lot, you know?'

'I know,' Drew said. 'See you tonight. We're meeting the others for drinks in Soho, you remember, right?'

'Yep.' Ian nodded.

'I'll let you go.' Drew ended the call. Clearly he suspected nothing. Clearly Ian was a good liar. Even at the sort of elaborate, long-term lie he was tangled up in at the moment.

A lot. Ian shook his head. What a bad lie. And yet Drew had believed it, because he trusted him.

Shit.

The guilt shot through him again.

If anyone knew about a day being a lot, it was Drew. The things he'd tell about his work were enough to make Ian's hair curl. It really wasn't all rescuing cats from trees. He'd had days of cutting people out of crashed cars, rescuing children from burning bedrooms and much more.

When Ian thought of it, today, even today's fake morning, hadn't been a lot, by any measure. Neither was the little blip he found himself in at the moment. All the more reason not to bother Drew with it.

Ian switched his phone off – because now he was meant to be in back to back meetings until at least lunchtime. Rather than walking into the lido for a swim.

Chapter 7

From the corner of the café, Gabriella saw the car man walk through the door.

His eyes were red, he'd definitely been crying. He looked so weird in a grey suit, white shirt and blue tie, surrounded by people in sportswear or casual clothes.

He carried a leather satchel, placing it on the desk as he spoke to the receptionist. He looked to one side at Gabriella.

She smiled, hoping he'd recognise her from earlier.

He looked away, head down, clicking through the turnstile with the token the receptionist had given him, scurrying through to the outdoor pool.

'Someone you know?' Helen stirred her fennel tea.

'He was crying in his car this morning. I asked if he was all right and bought him a coffee.'

'That's nice of you.'

Gabriella shrugged. 'Be kind, isn't that what everyone says now?' She sipped her decaf latte, the bitterness hitting the exact spot she needed.

'It is. My son is always telling me. The part I don't understand is whose definition of kind are we using? And at what point is it okay to stop being kind and walk away so you can be kind to yourself?'

Gabriella sat back, checking Thomas was okay.

He was contentedly munching through a bowl of macaroni cheese.

'Don't know about that. But I only spoke to him, mainly for my own reasons.'

'How does that work?'

Could she tell Helen why she came here? How she felt as if she was carrying a huge backpack of grief that weighed her down and some days it was all she could do to get dressed and get the two boys dressed, and drop Jack at school, and how she used to sit in the lounge staring at the TV while Thomas kept quietly amused gazing at the screen. All Gabriella could think was she didn't know what she'd do without the one-eyed babysitter, as her mum used to call the telly. How she'd briefly considered ending it all and then hadn't even been able to go through with that.

Swallowing, she carefully said, 'I can go all day without speaking to an adult. I never use self-checkout at the supermarket because then I can talk to the cashiers.' She shook her head. 'God I'm such a sad sack.'

Helen stroked Gabriella's forearm. 'You're not. Really, you're not.'

'I wanted to check he was okay, but I also just wanted to talk to him.' A pause, and then: 'Like we're doing now.' She swallowed. 'I think that overpowered wanting to see if he was okay. See? Selfish.'

'What did he say?'

'He was quite rude actually. Well, not rude, but a bit... Off with me. You know? I can see why people don't bother helping strangers. Not worth all the aggro, you know?'

'Be kind without an expectation of thanks.'

'Right. Who said that?'

'Me. Just now.' Helen smirked.

'Right. I like that.'

'My son told me. It's Maya Angelou, or Elizabeth Gilbert, I think.'

Gabriella shrugged. Helen might as well be speaking Swahili.

'Authors.'

'Like I said, I don't read much. Not with two kids there's not the time, see.'

'Do you want another?' Marie gestured to the mugs.

'My round.' Gabriella stood, leaning on the table. 'You all right to keep an eye on Thomas?'

'I'd love to.' Helen stroked his cheek.

Gabriella knew it wasn't clever to leave your kids with strangers, but she didn't class Helen as a stranger, not now they'd spent the last few hours together. Okay, so she could, in theory, be a child-snatcher, but it was pretty unlikely. Besides, Gabriella didn't let Thomas leave her sight while ordering their drinks, before returning to Helen and Thomas talking about nothing and smiling at one another.

As she sat, she said, 'I came here because sitting in an empty house, all I can think about is that Arnie isn't alive. Surrounding me with other people, watching them, talking to them if they'll let me, overhearing them – not in a creepy way, just little bits of their conversations – all keep me busy and help me forget that he's gone.'

Helen closed her eyes and nodded. 'How did you meet Arnie?'

Usually, people asked what he used to do for a living, or how he'd died. Both really shitty questions. But this was a good one. Just remembering the first time they met had Gabriella smiling.

'You have a beautiful smile.' Helen shook her head. 'Sorry, didn't mean to be creepy. I mean, it's pretty.'

The smile continued to spread and Gabriella said, 'When I'm here I can imagine he's in his studio working. We met at a photo shoot. I'd won a magazine comp and he was the photographer booked to do the shoot. Swim-wear. He talked and joked with me, making me feel really relaxed and they're still some of my best photos. Course, I was only twenty and everyone looks pretty then.' She shrugged.

'I'd love to see them, if you're happy to show me.'

Gabriella reckoned she could do that. 'At the end of the shoot he asked if I wanted to go for a drink.'

'And you said yes?'

'No. What do you think I am?' She laughed.

'Sorry, didn't mean to—'

'JK.'

Helen frowned.

'Just kidding.'

'Right. What did he do to convince you to go out with him?'

She thought back, a decade ago, before kids, before marriage, before everything that had made them the couple they were, before Gabriella had truly known what love could be. 'I'd been dicked about by men before. Sounds more fun than it is. Trust me.'

Helen smiled. 'I can imagine.'

'After the swimwear shoot was over, he gave me his card, said if I needed any other pictures, I should call him. I thought he was giving me a load of old flannel, but later, he introduced me to someone from a magazine and I got a *proper* modelling job. Nothing mucky. Proper class. You know?'

Helen raised her eyebrows. 'I can imagine.'

'That afternoon he said he had another photo shoot to do, but he'd like to take me out for a drink. I said I didn't drink – lies, but I'd spent enough evenings with men, buying me drinks with only one thing on their minds, to know better. So I suggested a coffee and a bagel off the Roman Road.'

'Where's that?'

'Mile End. Where I grew up. Dad ran a market stall. Mum did whatever. I reckoned if he really wanted to see me again I'd make him work for it.'

'A woman after my own heart.'

'Right?! He met me at my favourite café and we drank tea and coffee, ate bagels and he paid. He kissed me on the cheek and said he'd love to see me again. Asked if he could have my number, so I gave it to him. Well, he had come all the way to see me.'

'And then you got married?'

'No fear. I made him wait. We used to hang out together, I took him to the pub Mum and Dad liked and he showed me his manor. West London, Ruislip, Hillingdon, all that lot far out west on this side of London. It's like another world. Well, you know, cos you live here now. Nothing like where I grew up.' She thought wistfully about her parents' home in a tall concrete tower block in Mile End. They thought it was a palace when the council re-homed them from a damp, cramped terraced house nearby.

'What made you fall in love with him?'

It was too much to explain. 'Him. There's no other way to describe it. The way he was with me, the way he made me laugh, the way he looked after me, but never controlled what I did. He never patronised me when we came across stuff I didn't know. He took it as an opportunity to learn, grow. He was always on about growing as a person. Suppose that's why he ended up where he ended up.' Gabriella swallowed the lump in her throat.

'How long were you together?'

She thought for a moment. 'Just under a decade. I'd just turned twenty and I'm twenty-nine now. But he's been gone…' She squeezed her eyes. She was bloody well not going to dissolve into a pile of snot. Not in front of her new friend.

Helen put her arm around Gabriella's shoulder. 'How long ago?'

'Six months.' Gabriella sniffed loudly. 'He was almost thirty-four. And I'm still physically livid about it. It was so stupid. One of those terrible things that can happen. But it happened to him.' She couldn't say any more. Gabriella sat upright, blinking furiously to stop the tears falling.

'Tell you what, do you want to have a swim?'

'Told you, I can't. Not with this little monster.' She nodded towards Thomas. It all felt too much. She was comfortable at the moment, didn't need anything else.

'All right. We'll just sit.'

She liked the sound of that, just sitting with some additional adult company.

'Tell me about your modelling days? Glamorous photo shoots, jet-setting around the globe…' Helen winked.

And so she did, although it had been more Southampton than San Marino and Portsmouth more than Paris. She'd loved it, earned good money and made great friends.

Gabriella hadn't laughed or smiled this much since Arnie's death. Briefly, she hoped Helen would want to see her again. Even if only once, another afternoon like this would keep her going, give her some hope in what had been a bleak, shitty, miserable six months.

Chapter 8

There was something behind her reluctance to swim, but Helen wasn't sure what. Not yet anyway. 'I usually have a swim in the morning, some light exercise in the gym, then food, and return for another swim in the afternoon. It's a good variety. The wellness consultant recommended it to me.' Well, her counsellor actually, but she wasn't about to spill that quite yet.

'Are you sure it's all right for Thomas to swim?' Gabriella asked.

'You can get special waterproof nappy covers. They sell them in the shop. Let me get it, and you can pop home for your swimming costume.'

Gabriella leaned her elbows on the table. 'Can you still do your swimming up and down? I don't want to spoil that for you.'

'Lane swimming is always open, that's why they have a lane to one side. You can use the shallow end. I see mothers and their toddlers doing it all the time.' It was always accompanied by a pang of jealousy, particularly when an older person was helping – clearly the grandparent. She pushed that thought aside very swiftly, neatly filing it away, not for later consideration.

'Look, do you want me to speak to the receptionist and confirm you can take him swimming, even if he can't swim and isn't potty trained?'

'I don't want him to empty the pool cos he, you know... In the pool.' Gabriella looked both slightly lost and determined. She simply needed a gentle push in the right direction.

'Bear with.' Helen shot over to the receptionist, asked the appropriate questions, bought the waterproof pants and returned to their table. 'Sorted. You must not take your eyes off him, if he can't swim. Not that you would.' She handed Gabriella the waterproof costume.

'How much?' Gabriella reached into her leather designer handbag.

'Don't be so ridiculous. Go home, fetch your things, and I'll see you in the original pool outside, the lido.'

'I'll buy a cossie in the shop.' Gabriella left.

A short while later, Gabriella re-joined her at the table, holding a paper shopping bag. 'I'm really nervous. Feel like I'm about to take an exam. Never was any good at them. Maybe I should just watch. Sit by while you swim. I'll sunbathe and...'

'Not read? What's it like, this new costume?'

Gabriella removed a bright red one-piece swimming costume from the bag.

'You'll look beautiful.'

Gabriella shook her head, blushed and clutched her stomach. 'Butterflies.' A pause, and then: 'I meant to ask earlier, why are *you* here? Where's hubby?'

That word again. Ignore it. 'Bill's at home.'

'Doesn't he like swimming?'

'I don't know.'

Gabriella frowned. 'If he likes swimming? Haven't you been married for donkeys?'

'Forty years.' Helen said it as if it were nothing. But it had been anything but that. It had been a lifetime of being together, raising a child, supporting Bill's work, running the house, volunteering on countless charities' boards, leading her to this moment now. The moment when she was going to tell another human being how she felt. A near stranger. In many ways that made it easier than trying to tell someone who knew her. Knew Bill.

Gabriella said, 'How comes you don't know if he likes swimming?'

'I don't know what he likes. Full stop.'

'I don't understand.' Gabriella sat and frowned.

Helen shook her head leaning it forwards, closed her eyes. 'Neither do I. I don't understand how one goes from a perfectly normal marriage to this. It's not like it was one day when he flicked a switch, it's been slow, like watching a pan of water come to the boil.'

'Right.'

'He's stepped away from me, very gradually. We're not like husband and wife any longer. Two people sharing a house. Not even in the same bed.'

Gabriella put her hand on top of Helen's. 'Marriage is hard, whatever happens.'

'I have a very privileged life. A wonderful son and husband, everything I could ever want.' *And yet, I feel so desperately lonely. Painfully, sadly alone, for so many of my waking hours.* She blinked away a tear. 'Thank you.'

'Didn't do nothing.'

'For talking to me.'

'Talk too much, that's me! Never stop rabbiting on. You'll soon be sick and tired of me.'

Helen doubted that very much. Because Gabriella was a stranger, didn't know her or Bill, she had felt, for the first time, able to open up to someone. That showed how long it had been since she'd spoken to someone new, like now.

She must get a grip of herself. 'I used to work on a fashion magazine. You're too young to have seen any of them. But I was, for two whole seasons, the secretary to the editor of *A La Mode* magazine.'

'What happened?'

A long sigh then: 'Bill. That's what happened. And me. I can't lay it all at his door.'

'Shall I get some more drinks? Or do you fancy a walk, maybe? We can go swimming another time.' Gabriella set aside her bag, leaned forwards on the table.

Helen wasn't sure how to proceed now. She was not going to weep. Not in public. And not in front of a near stranger. She'd had enough of that with her counsellor. Terribly emotionally incontinent and she could not bear it. 'The summer of 1990, I turned twenty-six, pretty much the same age as you.'

Gabriella nodded. 'Near enough.'

'Gaunt heroin chic models with pale faces and dark eye makeup were very much in vogue. So I fitted right into the magazine staff. I loved it. That summer I helped at photo shoots for a new car launch, a perfume, a watch, a clothing brand and some shoes.'

'I feel bad but I've never even heard of the mag. Soz.'

'Folded in 2002. It's all in the recycling now anyway. Magazines are such ephemera, really.' Helen didn't quite understand herself how she'd gone from the bright independent career woman of 1990 to the withdrawn, lonely woman now.

'Why did you stop?' Gabriella asked.

'Why do you think?'

'Bill?'

Helen nodded. God, how pathetic. Gabriella must think her terribly old-fashioned. Going along with what her husband had wanted. Fitting neatly into the mould he'd created for her as the dutiful wife, mother.

'I gave it up an' all. Not cos Arnie wanted me to, but cos I wanted to. He said I could do whatever I wanted. And at the time I only wanted to be a mum. Reckoned I'd have plenty of time to get back to it. Didn't realise we'd end up having two and then—' She looked at the floor.

She was so damaged, hurt, broken, still. Only months after losing Arnie, somehow – she'd still not managed to tell Helen how Arnie had died, and here she was the one trying to comfort Helen, when really it should be the other way around. 'Perhaps we should have a swim. Clear the air. Take a break.'

They changed in individual booths at the far end of the swimming pool, behind another fountain. Helen gave herself a stern speaking to in the privacy of her booth: 'She doesn't want to hear all that nonsense. Stop being so bloody embarrassing. Another forty lengths and it'll all be well.'

Triumphant and entirely resigned to not continuing with the conversation from before, Helen emerged into the afternoon sun as it warmed her skin. She squinted and wished she'd remembered sunglasses.

Gabriella, with her bright red one-piece swimming costume, perfect curves and hair tied up neatly above her head, was standing at the shallow end, holding Thomas by the hands and splashing his feet in the water. The little boy smiled and giggled.

A jolt of pure joy shot through her and Helen was jealous that he wasn't *her* grandson.

Silly old woman! She walked carefully around the edge of the pool, meeting them at the shallow end.

'I love your cap,' Gabriella said.

'I think it's designer. Don't know who. Doesn't matter much I suppose.'

'You do your lane thing and we'll be here. He seems to really like it.'

Thomas was sitting in the water up to his belly button, splashing gaily.

Helen knelt in the water. 'I'll go and do my lanes, now. Is that all right?'

Gabriella was sitting in the water, playing with her son. 'Magic.'

'You look stunning by the way. Front page material.' Helen smiled and propelled herself towards the deep end of the pool, counting in time with her breast stroke – one, one, one – until she reached the far end. Forty lengths and she'd have cleared her head, as usual.

Each time she reached the shallow end, she'd nod and smile at Gabriella and Thomas splashing in the water. It had been a while since she'd felt like this, a genuine smile and the lightness that accompanied it, happiness, the slight bubbling of joy that had been so elusive for so long.

Chapter 9

Ian changed in a booth, emerging in his gym wear.

He couldn't stay at the lido all day since he had to go to the West End for real for the theatre tonight. He'd quickly got used to this new routine; the thought of travelling all the way into London filled him with the same dread he'd had at showing off his body to swim the first time, and this morning.

What if he saw an ex-colleague? What if he missed his stop?

He walked past a woman in a cap who was swimming lanes as if her life depended upon it. She didn't look to either side. A woman on a mission who knew what she was doing. Enviable really. He caught her eye, but she didn't return with a sign of acknowledgement – maybe she had smiled but it was obscured by the water.

The woman who'd bought him coffee was in the shallow end with her little boy. They were having a great time splashing together.

They'd talked about having children, but that was all it had been. Talk. At least he didn't have another mouth to feed as well as all this shit. Being a father and out of work felt worse than being a boyfriend and out of work.

The woman in the red swimming costume nodded at him as he walked past. He smiled, continued striding along the edge of the pool, past sun loungers with people bathing, reading, drying off.

He made his way to the running machine because he knew the rhythmic thumping of feet would help him forget everything else for the time he remained there.

Sweating, he refreshed himself with water, panted and leaned against the wall. The rowing machine followed for the same reason as the treadmill, and then he tried some small weights. Drew had said if he wanted to build muscle he needed to lift weights as well as the cardio Ian did, mainly for his heart.

After a shower in – thankfully – individual cubicles rather than communal, he dressed and went to the café. *I deserve a treat now.*

He found a seat in the corner and started the other part of his daily routine: job hunting. Phone calls with a few recruitment consultants garnered what they always said: now wasn't a good time, there weren't many vacancies in his field, but if he wanted to branch out they could help.

Branching out meant taking a massive pay cut. Ian had been on the same horse since graduating from university, so losing all that to start from below graduate level wasn't appealing. Yet.

Another few coffees and he had completed three job applications. Job hunting is really like a job itself. The irony of this wasn't lost on him.

The café was full, every table taken. Why aren't all these people at work?

He searched the main think-tanks for job vacancies. Then decided that wasn't proactive enough, so he wrote an email introducing himself and his impressive credentials with a view to sending this to potential employers. That had to be better than sitting back and waiting for the phone to ring, didn't it?

Or was he better off giving up on this horse and changing direction, taking a pay cut, because a job was better than no job, surely?

If only he could speak to Drew and ask him. He'd know the answer. The irony of that didn't escape him either. He wondered if he could take another job, any job and whether Drew would notice there was less money in the joint account…

When a man who is his job loses his job, what does that leave him?

It would be much easier to share the problem with Drew, rather than having to keep it a secret, but the feeling of failure, the pity he'd no doubt receive, the admission that he'd failed to even secure an interview, all combined to make it easier to keep up the lie and get another job so he'd never have to come clean with Drew.

He knew that gym membership wasn't free and nor were daily swims, but if he stopped buying any tech, clothes and cancelled the other subscriptions it would pay for his Monday to Friday trips to the lido.

If I linger out this coffee for an hour I can buy a nut bar that'll see me through the next hour, cheaper than another hot drink…

Ian felt for his little black spending book in his pocket. Had he entered today's spending in it?

'Excuse me, are these seats taken?' The voice broke him out of his thoughts.

It was the woman from the car park who'd bought him the coffee. What did she want? He bit back his instinct to be brusque and instead smiled. First time in a long while for that.

Chapter 10

'We sat here this morning,' Gabriella said. They'd continued hanging out together after swimming and made their way to the café, back where they had first met that morning.

'I didn't know you'd saved it. Sorry.' The man stood, started packing up his laptop and papers.

'We hadn't. I was just commenting. Stay. Please do.'

'Right.' He sounded uncertain.

'We don't bite.'

'I do,' Helen said, chuckling.

'We wondered if we could sit here.'

'I was just about to leave anyway.' He checked the time.

'Rubbish,' Helen said. 'You were settled in for the afternoon. I've seen you here before. Every day.'

'You're here most days too.'

'No judgement.' Helen held her hands up in surrender. 'It's just after Gabriella saw you in your car this morning, we wondered...'

Surprise covered his face, turning to embarrassment. 'I'll leave you to it.'

Gabriella held his wrist as it rested on the table. 'Please don't.'

'Why shouldn't I?' He removed his hand, narrowed his eyes and thinned his lips.

'Because people don't just sit in their car crying for no reason.' Gabriella nodded at Helen.

'Indeed,' Helen said, folding her arms. 'Stay as long as it takes to drink the coffee I'm going to buy you, and then you can leave.'

His chin stuck out determinedly. 'I'm leaving now.' And he did.

'What's that all about, do you think?' Gabriella asked.

'Men.' Helen shook her head. 'They never want to talk about how they feel and then they wonder why they're sitting in a car crying.'

'Right.' Gabriella nodded. 'He's obviously got a lot on his plate,' Gabriella said, crossing her legs.

'Who hasn't?'

'Exactly.'

'Grief, I reckon. Maybe he's lost someone.'

'That's a maybe, but he needs to seek help if he's crying in his car most days.' Helen raised her eyebrows.

'What about the suit?'

'He's always wearing one. I've seen him a few times, always in a suit.'

Gabriella paused. 'He seemed pretty buttoned up, don't you think?'

'Wound tight.'

'Indeed. I hope he's all right.'

There was a comfortable silence between them. Only the background noise of the café continued.

'Tell me if I'm being silly, but would you mind if we swapped numbers?' Helen asked.

'I was just about to ask the same.' Gabriella smiled, relief washing through her that they'd both been on the same page.

'I have plenty of friends, but…' Helen stared out of the window.

'More than me. I lost touch with all the ones from the old days.'

They swapped numbers and Gabriella felt like she'd just taken a positive step away from being swamped by her grief. 'Thanks.' She smiled.

'No PTA friends?'

Gabriella shook her head. 'Not my scene. Arnie used to call it the PITA.'

Helen frowned.

'Pain in the arse.' Gabriella smiled.

'Truth be told, it wasn't really mine, but I just sort of ended up doing it.'

Gabriella reckoned there was a lot of pain behind that, but she decided to keep that chat for another time – the next time they met, or maybe the time after that.

A few days later, Gabriella was at the lido. She'd done a few lengths and splashed about with Thomas while Helen was doing her lengths. She seemed to like to be left alone while doing them.

Gabriella walked past the gym and saw the man they'd met before running. She still didn't know his name, but she waved and he nodded and waved back, smiling.

Taking Thomas by the hand she walked into the gym, straight over to the man.

'Fancy a coffee?' Gabriella said, determined to find out what had made him cry in his car, while wearing a suit.

He sipped water from a bottle as he slowed his tread-mill, rubbing his forehead with a towel, then wrapped it around his shoulders. 'If anything, I owe you one.'

'I'll be in the corner. Bring it over, will you? I'm Gabriella.' She held her hand out.

He looked at her with confusion. 'Okay?' He said it as a question.

'Cappuccino would be nice. And I should ask your name...'

'Ian.' He shook her hand.

Gabriella smiled 'In the corner, see you soon.' She left.

He moved to another piece of equipment, sitting and pulling his arms up and down, lifting weights attached with wires.

She joined Helen at their seats in the corner of the café. 'Ian, he's called.'

'Right.'

'He's coming over. Owes me a drink. Be nice, he looks like he could do with a friend. Everyone needs some additional adult company, I reckon.'

'You got all that from talking to him in the gym?'

'I did, as it goes.' Gabriella could feel it in her bones this time, Ian would want to stay and talk.

'Drink?' Helen asked, seemingly very confused.

'Water, I'm waiting for Ian's drink. What's so difficult to understand? He's probably mortified at me seeing him like that in his car. I would be. And he's a man, so...'

'And your plan is?' Helen asked.

'Wait and see. He needs us, it's just he doesn't know that yet.' Sometimes people didn't know what was good for them until it was right in front of their eyes. And for some, that was too late. She was determined not to come too late to help Ian.

Helen left to order their drinks.

Ian arrived at the table, holding a coffee cup. 'Cappuccino. For Gabriella.' He smiled weakly, then looked at the floor.

He looked very broken in many ways, but Gabriella was determined to find out how to help him. 'Thanks.' She nearly gabbled off nervously, but sensed he had something to say.

'I'm all right today. In case you're wondering. That day, just a one off. I've been having a great time since. Just a blip. I don't make a habit of that sort of thing.'

'I cry all the time. Most days in fact. Does me good to get it out, I reckon. Nothing to be ashamed of.'

He looked at her, placing his drink on the table. His eyes widened and filled with sorrow. 'Can I sit? Just for a bit. I don't want to go home, not yet anyway.'

Gabriella patted the chair. 'Course.'

He sat, resting his elbows on the table, looking like a crumpled paper bag.

Helen returned with their drinks. 'Hello.'

He stood. 'It's all right, I'll leave you to it.'

Gabriella held his arm, gently pulling him down to sit. 'Do you have to be somewhere else?'

He poked out his bottom lip. 'Nowhere.' He sat, looked from Gabriella to Helen. 'I'm fine. Not like before. Absolutely fine.'

Helen shrugged. 'Well, I'm not.'

'Me neither,' Gabriella said. 'I'm a total mess.' She looked at Helen.

'But that's normal. Everyone's just doing their best every day.'

Ian nodded. 'That's all I ever tried to do.'

Gabriella rubbed his forearm. 'You looked like you know what you're doing in the gym. I wish I had the stamina.'

'Or the inclination,' Helen said with a smirk. 'Swimming doesn't involve all that sweating and deep breathing.'

He leaned backwards, his shoulders relaxed. 'I don't do much. A run or a row here and there. Some weights. Really small ones. Not like Drew, he's a firefighter.'

'Drew?'

'My partner. Husband. I don't like partner. It sounds so formal.'

Gabriella thought for a moment. 'Partner, I agree, is shit. Sounds like you formed a company together. Not very romantic. No love there.'

'Very magnanimous of you. What's your husband called?' Ian asked Gabriella.

'Arnie.' She didn't want to jump straight in with the fact that he *was* called that. One dead husband conversation a day was plenty. 'Well, whatever you say, any weights, or using any machines in the gym, is impressive.' She smiled. He looked like a child that had been caught doing something wrong. He wanted to talk about it, only he didn't know where to start. Same as she'd felt.

'Helen,' she said as she shook his hand. 'Mine's called Bill. Although maybe not for much longer.'

There was a silence and Gabriella decided to just let it hang there. Helen would open up about that when she was good and ready.

Gabriella smiled at Ian. 'Looks like Ian's a bit of a gym bunny. Plenty of stamina.'

He blushed, and shook his head. 'I'm really not. Otherwise why was I crying in the car park a few days ago?'

'I was gonna ask you the same. But I'm nosy like that!'

'Well, I for one have no stamina for weights.' Helen looked about her. 'I couldn't lift much more than a bag full of groceries. Swimming on the other hand...'

Ian sipped his drink, looking over the rim from one woman to the other. 'How do you two know each other?'

'We don't!' Gabriella said. 'Not too well, anyway.'

Ian frowned. 'What do you mean?'

'We met here. Few days ago.'

'I've seen you here before,' Ian said to Helen.

'I've been coming for ages,' Helen said, stirring the sweetener into her fennel tea. 'Christ I wish I could smoke here. It's no fun anymore.'

'Why do you come here then?' Ian asked.

'Why don't you go first?' Helen asked.

Ian swallowed. 'I lost my job and I've been coming here instead of going to work.'

'To job hunt?' Gabriella asked.

'Yes, but I could easily do that at home.'

'So why are you here?'

'I haven't told Drew I've lost my job.'

'Well, that's okay, I mean, giving it a few days to sink in before—'

'How long has it been?' Helen asked.

'Three months…'

'I said you had a lot on your plate, didn't I?' Gabriella looked to Helen.

Helen nodded.

'What's yours, reason for coming here?' Ian asked Helen.

'It's preferable to being at home.'

'In an empty house, because your husband is at work?'

'That would make sense. But no.'

'Oh,' Ian said, as confusion clouded his expression.

'Bill is a doctor. A consultant.'

'That must be…'

Helen shook her head. 'Whatever you think it might be, I can confirm it most definitely is not.' She looked out of the window for a moment.

Gabriella had wanted to ask this earlier, but hadn't dared. 'That's enough for now – if you want, we can move on to me or Ian.'

Helen sat up straight. 'I shall tell you and then I shall go outside for a vape, and then we shall not speak of this for the rest of today. Am I understood?'

They both nodded.

'Bill has always worked. Loved it. Ate it up. All hours, all days. Now he's seventy he's trying to ease into retirement.'

'Nice.'

'No, not nice. Not nice at all. I have remained by his side for the last forty years in anticipation of enjoying retirement together and now he's reached it, he hasn't the first idea what to do with it.'

'I don't understand,' Gabriella said. 'What's he doing that you come here instead?'

'Nothing.'

'Nothing?'

'Nothing.' Helen swallowed. 'He has no interest in doing anything with me. Speaking to me in fact. He's started some new project that involves a laptop and he won't tell me what it is. He barely speaks to me all day. I've tried to talk to him about it and he says there's nothing wrong and I should stop nagging him.' Helen blinked away a tear, covered her mouth with her hand. 'So I come here, because it's less lonely.'

Less lonely than staying at home with her husband. Crikey, Gabriella thought, when you put it like that, it was worse than being widowed. She squeezed Helen's hand on the table.

'Now, I'm going to smoke, I mean vape, and when I return we won't speak of this.' She blinked slowly. 'Have I made myself clear?'

'You have,' Gabriella said.

She left.

They sat in silence for a few long moments.

Finally, Ian said, 'What about you? Or do you want to wait until she's back?'

'Helen knows. We're old friends!' It was said as a joke, but in many ways Gabriella meant it. Helen was the first person she'd properly opened up to about Arnie's death, how seeing the boys was both wonderful and painful, and how she could barely breathe most days when she remembered what had happened, as the grief pressed down on her stomach, as it had this morning.

'What brings you here to the lido?' Ian asked.

'My husband died. I'm bringing up our two boys alone, and they both look like him. As in, completely spitting image of him. Same eyes, same gestures, same accent.' A pause as she took a breath. 'It's kinda lovely because he lives on. But also it's like the most painful thing you can imagine, being shown what you really love, but can't have, every. Single. Day.'

Ian nodded, blinked, wiped a tear from his cheek. 'Sorry. I'm a mess. You saw that morning. Sorry. I didn't mean to cry. It's just…' He swallowed.

'Really shit?'

He nodded. 'Yep.' The words caught in his throat. 'And really fucking sad.'

'I know, right.' She allowed herself a small raised corner of her mouth, at the shared experience of loss, grief and how life really could do the worst thing to you and expect you to carry on living.

Helen returned. 'That's better. I can think straight now. Bloody nicotine, it's addictive isn't it?'

'That's kind of the point,' Ian said.

'Has she said what Arnie died of yet?' Helen sat.

Ian shook his head.

Ordinarily, Gabriella would have been really upset by that, but because it came from Helen and she knew there was no malice behind it, she simply said: 'Not today. Like Helen, I've said enough for today.'

'So when are we next meeting?' Ian asked.

'Tomorrow morning, here?' Gabriella suggested.

Ian and Helen shrugged.

'Is that a yes?'

Helen said, 'I suppose so.'

Ian nodded. 'Haven't got anything better to do.'

'Charming,' Helen said with narrowed eyes.

'Have you?'

'No, but that's hardly the point.'

'I think it's precisely the point.' Ian smirked then laughed.

Helen joined in.

Calling them to order, Gabriella asked, 'Can we have a WhatsApp group please?' She'd muted all the school ones because she always asked questions people laughed at. Or they would correct her spelling and punctuation. But with these two people, she reckoned she had another chance at friendship.

'Whatever,' Helen said.

Gabriella set up the group, naming it 'TheLonely Hearts Lido Club' before posting the first message: *hello peeps!*

Helen shook her head, tutting loudly.

'What?' Gabriella asked with concern.

'I know it's a generation thing, but I struggle with these colloquial versions of certain words.'

'Like what?'

'Hubby for one. I can't bear it.'

'Yeah, you mentioned it.'

Helen was obviously thinking for a moment. 'But when it comes out of your mouth it doesn't make me hallucinate with anger, as with others.'

'Thanks?' She wasn't sure if that was a compliment or what.

'Ignore me. I'm a grumpy old codger.'

'None of that,' Ian said, shaking his head. 'If this is a pity party for three, then I'm out. I've had enough of that in my own head.'

'Agreed.' Gabriella lifted her phone as if they were toasting. She nodded for the others to copy.

They picked up their phones, touching them together.

Helen shrugged. 'If you insist. But if anyone starts posting inspirational memes I shall have no compunction in leaving the group.' She shuddered.

'Isn't it a bit of a sad name?'

'Not if our main aim is to stop each other from feeling like lonely bastards,' Gabriella said.

And with that, the The Lonely Hearts Lido Club was born.

Chapter 11

The next morning, Helen was in bed while Bill got ready for work.

He rushed to the en suite bathroom wearing his baggy pyjamas. She tried to remember the last time she'd seen him even semi-naked. As newly-weds they'd quickly agreed sharing showers and the bathroom was part of being married, but on their honeymoon in a hotel by the coast in Tenerife that had a bathroom within the bedroom, separated by only a curtain and wall, they introduced a rule involving number twos and solitary bathroom time. 'To keep the magic alive,' Bill had said, as a twenty-five-year-old man. And Helen had agreed, kissing him, greedily wanting to gulp more of him, and taking him back to bed.

The shower was loudly running.

Helen climbed out of bed, remembering their honeymoon and smiling. She knocked on the door.

'Yes!' Bill shouted from inside.

'Can I come in, or are you…'

'I'm showering.'

She entered, watching him soaping his body through the glass shower screen. His head was bald, and the hair on his chest had long since gone grey, but like her, he'd managed to keep relatively trim. No abs or washboard stomach like when he'd been twenty-five, they'd both become rounder at the edges.

'I wanted to talk to you about something,' she began, biting her bottom lip. Her palms were sweaty. She wiped them on her cotton nightie, staring down at her slender legs – in need of a shave.

'Can't it wait?' He shut off the water, opened the glass door then climbed out. He stood dripping onto the tiled floor. Unapologetically naked he held out his hand. 'Can't you pass me the towel?' He shook his head. 'Make yourself at least semi-useful, won't you?'

She handed him the towel.

He dried himself. 'I've got a seven-thirty, I need to leave very soon. If you've something to say, can you please just spit it out?'

He always did this. Making her flustered, rushing her, and putting it all into her court so she had to express precisely what was the matter, in as few words as possible.

He left the bathroom and pulled on a shirt from the wardrobe. He should have looked ridiculous, completely naked except for a buttoned-up shirt. Some of her girl-friends said they didn't find all that particularly attractive, but Helen had always thought it rather splendid, the way it sort of sat there wobbling about until it was on and then it became something else entirely. Entirely fascinating and how it fitted perfectly within her and... But he didn't look ridiculous at all. In fact, she reflected, he looked rather splendid. A sort of distinguished Daniel Craig playing James Bond in fact. Echoes of Sean Connery possibly, with the grey beard...

She felt an unfamiliar coil of desire threading its way from her stomach, starting as butterflies, then heating up in lower, and settling at her core, her centre.

She longed to be able to just grab him and pull him on top of her, as they had all those years ago. She'd been the one leading him to the bed from the shower on their honeymoon. Now she was frozen.

He'd pulled on underwear, suit trousers and jacket, and socks. He was rifling through the ties in his wardrobe, trying to find one that matched properly. He picked a beige one – one of the ones he'd had since the nineties and now looked particularly dated.

'What about this one?' She handed him a navy blue tie she'd bought for his birthday. It went perfectly with the single-breasted suit that clung to his frame wonderfully.

He nodded, discarded the beige one and put the blue tie on. 'Surely it wasn't to tell me which tie to wear?'

'What?'

'What you wanted to speak to me about?' He walked to the door, speaking without turning back to her. 'Walk and talk.'

She followed him. Not because she wanted to, but since she didn't know what else to do. It was as if the words she had were stuck in her throat and the more he continued to ready himself for work, within the set time frame he had, the less able she felt to speak to him.

In the kitchen he made a black coffee from the expensive bright red and chrome machine. He'd been given it as a leaving present from the hospital, before returning – while taking his pension – the following Monday. It had been another discussion she'd felt completely unequal to continuing, after many prior attempts and failures.

He poured corn flakes into a bowl, added milk, sitting at the table he turned to The Times he had delivered daily. Briefly, he looked up, staring out of the window. 'Are you going to spit it out, or is the point now moot?' He never seemed to look at her, make eye contact.

When had that started, she wondered. And why hadn't she noticed?

'Do you want to plan something on your next day off?' Goodness, she could be so forthright and decisive if she wanted to. Not.

'Something like what?' He was reading.

'A trip to the coast maybe. There's a lovely National Trust home in Buckinghamshire.'

'I shouldn't think so. I've got a serious amount to do back here.'

'I said I'll get someone in, no need to worry about the little jobs around the house.' They could afford it and Bill had always hated DIY, even if it had been a necessity.

He folded his paper, leaving the spoon to clatter in the bowl. Shaking his head as he stood, he said, 'Not that. I mean the project I'm doing. The reviews.'

'Right.' Helen bunched her fists until the skin went white. Why is he so bloody impenetrable? 'You don't fancy spending time together, nice meal out, we could take the new car for a spin maybe?'

'I'm going in it now. Unless you wanted to join me. I can drop you off in town. Spend the day shopping maybe?' He looked her up and down. 'Only if you want to, you'll need to dress sharpish. I'm going in five minutes.' He strode upstairs.

The tap was running signalling he was brushing his teeth.

No, the point wasn't quite going shopping, but doing something together.

Helen leaned against the wall in the hallway, folding her arms, rubbing them as a shiver of cold ran through her.

He clattered downstairs, taking two at a time – she'd told him about that, one slip and he'd break his neck, but he never listened. He put on his jacket, grabbing the keys from the table by the door. 'I'm leaving now, so unless you're able to dress in superhuman speed, I shall be leaving alone, yes?'

'I meant,' Helen said, with some force, 'spending time together. When you're not working.'

'Maybe when I've finished the other project.' He frowned, clearly confused. 'Besides, why would we do that, we're together all day for the rest of the week.' He smiled, briefly made eye contact – the first time this morning, then he left, slamming the door.

Helen waited until the car had left the drive, crunching gravel on its way, until she let out the breath she hadn't known she was holding. Except, quite unexpectedly this time, it came out as a scream.

How is this my life? What should I do? He has no use of me now Peter's grown up. I should have left him when Peter went to university.

Regret stabbed her gut. As if she'd have had the gumption to do that in her thirties.

Ridiculous.

Later, after she'd taken a long bath, listening to the radio and scoring rather higher than usual at the quiz, she dressed in something that made her look like she did more than sit around in her home all day after a swim at the lido (floral dress with sensible but smart heels). At eleven o'clock, she stood in the hallway, remembering how he'd been that morning. Tentatively, she dialled

Peter's number, removing a shoe and smoothing her foot over her leg – definitely need to shave them soon – and felt overjoyed when Peter answered.

'Dad, is that you?' Peter asked.

'It's Mum. Sorry to disappoint.'

'You're the only people who insist on using the landline to call me. It comes up as Mum & Dad Home.'

'Are you busy, darling?'

'I'm working. But for you, I can make time.' A pause, and then: 'You sound different. What's happened?'

'Can we have lunch? My treat.' That usually worked. She held her breath.

'When? Not today, surely?'

Helen bit her lips. 'I was hoping.'

Peter made a clicking noise down the phone. The same noise he'd used when thinking since he was about five. 'Two o'clock. How's that?'

It was rather late, and all Helen could think about was the yawning chasm of time laying in front of her until she'd leave to meet him. Over three hours of it, in fact; she did a quick calculation, staring at the grandfather clock in the hallway. 'Perfect. I'll book somewhere.'

'I've got a three o'clock. Come to the house.'

'Ah. I'll bake a cake.'

'You don't have to.'

I really do. 'Bye, darling.'

'Nice of you to call,' he said, almost as an afterthought it seemed.

'I never know when you're home, when you're free or busy.'

'Just call and we can work things out like this.'

'Thank you.' She tried very hard not to sound desperately lonely and probably failed.

'Bye.' He ended the call.

Helen stood staring at the phone in the empty hallway, rubbing her other leg with a stockinged foot and wondering if she ought to shave them. Peter wouldn't notice or care either way. Bill... Well, Bill wouldn't comment if she served dinner in a Father Christmas beard, the great white furry thing coming down to her stomach.

She smiled and almost chuckled at that. Perhaps that's one option then.

After baking the cake and cleaning the kitchen, which killed a good couple of hours, she arrived at Peter's detached house in a new housing estate tucked away in the last sliver of green between Uxbridge, Hillingdon and Ruislip. The front garden looked as if it had been designed as a show home and hadn't received any attention since: bedding plants past their best and a few shrubs in need of a good pruning.

She pressed the doorbell. She had a key, but it always felt slightly intrusive, arriving at Peter's house, she was never sure if she'd walk into something she'd rather not witness. She'd had enough of that when he was a teenager.

He opened the door – he towered over her, had obviously been cultivating a beard, made him look older with the grey flecks. He let her in, cradling a mobile phone between his ear and shoulder. He pointed to it, gestured her towards the kitchen. Peter lifted up three fingers, signalling he'd be done in that many minutes, Helen assumed.

In the kitchen she placed the cake box on the table, then helped herself to one of the herbal teas he tried to drink to reduce his caffeine intake, but never seemed to succeed at.

The kitchen had red shiny cupboards, white walls and tiles. The appliances were all hidden. The first time she'd seen the house when he'd just moved in, it had taken her a not inconsiderable amount of time to locate the dishwasher and oven in an attempt to make cheese on toast and tea.

Why do they always make show homes appear as if they're the bridge of a spaceship?

She settled herself at the glass kitchen table, slipping into the curvy metal and clear plastic chair and wondering why on earth someone would think that suited a kitchen.

Placing her handbag on the floor, she retrieved her phone. So many green numbers, telling her no doubt she had multiple messages in many and various places. With a sigh, she unlocked her phone – why on earth young people were glued to these contraptions was beyond her, they were simply a time-suck.

The *Lonely Hearts Lido Club* group had half a dozen messages – it was Ian and Gabriella arranging to meet at the outdoor pool at the lido earlier that morning. Then some guff – kindly guff though – about missing her and wishing her good luck with whatever she was doing today. One of them had included a picture of someone who she didn't know from a programme she also was unaware of, with the text: *you got this!*

'What's that? Didn't think you did WhatsApp, Mum.' Peter stared at her phone.

She set the phone face down on the table. 'Nothing.' Opening the lid of the box, she said, 'I made this. Victoria sandwich. Fresh cream, strawberry jam. Sponges didn't rise as I'd have liked, but…'

He peered into the box. 'I'm sure it'll be delish. Thanks. I've got an hour, well nearly.' He checked his watch. 'I thought cheese and tomato on toast.' He raised his eyebrows. 'All right?'

'That used to be your favourite, when you were a little boy. Whenever we went out to eat, you always asked if they could make that. I remember your father becoming very cross about it when he'd taken us to somewhere very swish in the West End.'

'Bibendum? It was an old car garage just off Park Lane.'

'The Riley.' Bill's father had owned one. She'd been very impressed when she first met Bill's father. Almost as impressed as she'd been about Bill. Funny how all that fades...

'That's it.' He turned to grate cheese and slice bread, then cut tomatoes into thin slices. 'Are you enjoying Dad being retired?'

'Semi-retired. Three days still.' Just saying it had her almost in tears. Christ, she needed to get a grip. She needed to remind herself that she had this, or whatever the phrase had been from Gabriella's message.

'And?' Peter asked, turning to face her. He looked the spitting image of her own father at that age. The same long slender limbs, dark hair and blue eyes.

'Unclear as yet,' she lied, biting her tongue.

He talked for a while about his work, the new team he'd been recruiting until there was a budget cut and how he had to do it all himself now, which was why he needed days at home, so he could concentrate without inter- ruption – he did something for the nearest non-London council about customers and marketing, much more than that she was unable to say – he seemed happy and good at it, which was the most important thing. Finally, he carried two plates with cheese and tomato on toast, placing them on the table.

'Don't you want place mats?' she asked automatically, realising how, without even noticing, she'd somehow turned into her mother.

'Sit, eat, it's fine. The table's very robust. Trust me.' He waggled his eyebrows. Probably something rude.

'Can I have cutlery please?' She stood.

'I'll get them.' In a flash he'd retrieved them, from a concealed draw at the far side of the kitchen – it probably also housed an eject button and emergency escape route.

'Thanks.' She smiled as he handed them over.

'What's funny?'

'Nothing. I just always think this kitchen is a bit…'

'Expensive? Ostentatious?' He chewed.

'Spaceship-like.'

'Show homes have got to really show off the best.' More chewing and then: 'What's Dad doing today?'

'Working.'

Peter nodded. 'Of course. What do you do when he's not? Trips to the countryside in the car with a tartan picnic blanket and wicker basket?'

She wished. Rolling her eyes, she said, 'If only. He's doing some sort of project about reviews. I have no idea what he's doing.'

'Ask him.'

'I have.' She tried to keep the irritation out of her voice, but mostly failed.

'And?'

'He's not interested.' *He doesn't even look me in the eye.* But she couldn't say that. It made her look pathetic and would crush Peter's view of his father. Wasn't her place to do so.

'What does interest him?' Peter sipped some sparkling water he'd poured them both.

Helen shrugged. 'He doesn't say. Except work. And this review thing.'

'What do you do all day? I'd go very swiftly mad.'

'Indeed.' *Me too.* 'I bake, like today. I take long baths with a book. I've become quite proficient at the quiz on the morning breakfast show on one of the channels. I swim too.'

'Where?'

'The lido.'

'Didn't they close that years ago?'

'Since I've been swimming in it every day your father is at home,' *and more besides…* 'I can confidently say no to that question.'

'That's good. Exercise. Better than sitting around watching TV.'

'It is.' Although now, her rule of no TV until six o'clock had somewhat been allowed to slip. It wasn't as if she was actually watching daytime TV like students, the unemployed or stay-at-home mums. She taped things Bill didn't want to watch during the evening and she would prop herself on the sofa, laying down, with a slice of her latest creation and a coffee, and watch. At first she'd felt very ostentatious, slightly naughty, but when she realised no one was going to tell her off, she'd somewhat leaned into it more.

Peter had finished eating. 'Aren't you hungry?'

She had taken a few bites from hers. 'Not terribly.' The cream horn in the bath earlier had probably done for her appetite. That was another thing she'd recently taken to doing – eating in the bath. So much comfort she seemed to elucidate from food now. But only particular types of food.

'Mum, what is wrong with you? You seem like you're not there. What's Dad done this time?'

'Nothing.'

'Well then, what's the problem?' Peter stood. 'Want a slice?' He held her cake aloft, brandishing a knife.

Suddenly her appetite seemed to return. For that, it was raging once again, unlike the decidedly plain and lacklustre meal Peter had lovingly prepared for her. God, she was such an ungrateful old cow. 'He's not interested in anything. Me, doing anything.'

'That's just Dad being Dad.' Peter shrugged.

She accepted the slice of cake and ate it in contemplative silence. 'Is there anyone special in your life? A man, a woman, we wouldn't mind either way.'

Peter sighed. 'I thought you promised not to ask me that any more.'

'I can't help myself. I want to see you happy. Settled. With someone.' It had always been such a worry. He'd never shown the slightest interest in a relationship, with either a man or woman it seemed. Having married so young, it felt so alien to Helen. She'd told him this many times.

Peter stood, tidied away the plates. 'I am happy. The more interesting question is why you think I need someone to be happy. Although you have friends, and Dad, you're patently not happy, are you?'

She shook her head. 'And yet you don't have any suggestions for what I should do.'

Peter looked at the clock on the oven. 'I've got time for a tea before my three o'clock.'

It was lovely spending time with Peter, but it was also somewhat disappointing. She wasn't sure why she'd expected someone who'd never had a relationship – to her knowledge – to have anything useful to say about her relationship with Bill. 'Okay,' she said with some effort, folding her hands in her lap.

He busied himself with the tea then stood behind her chair, placing a kiss lightly on the top of her head.

'What's that for?' she asked.

'I want you to be happy too. And you're obviously not.'

'I can't speak to him about it. I don't know where to start. He's always so dismissive. Says I'm nagging him.'

'What would show you that he cared?'

'I don't know. Seeing me, that would be a start. He doesn't see me, never mind talk to me. It's almost as if I'm not there.'

'Leave him.' Peter said it as if he were suggesting she get a new hairstyle. He handed her some raspberry tea.

'Don't be so ridiculous. I can't do that. What would I do?' She had no idea how to be on her own, never mind where to start if she wanted to leave him.

'Not permanently, just so he notices. So he realises what he's missing.' He sipped his coffee, nodding at a cupboard. 'Biscuits in there. Let yourself out, will you? I've got my call now.' He paused to hug her, then clattered upstairs.

She sat at the table in silence, rubbing her legs as she'd crossed them over one another more than once. It was something she did when worried. Unconsciously she wanted to make herself take up as little space as possible. Be as little bother as she could.

Peter's deep voice boomed from his upstairs study – he'd be giving them what for from a marketing perspective, she expected. A small smile crossed her face; he'd turned out well. He was the sum total of Helen's life's work. Of course, Bill had been there for high days

93

and holidays, paid for everything, but it had been Helen who'd changed the nappies, potty trained him, taken Peter to school, put plasters on his cut knees, nursed him when sick off school, fed, dressed, seen him off to university – Bill had been too busy.

Glancing at the cupboard, she decided she didn't want a biscuit. Better to be hung for a sheep as a lamb. She helped herself to a generous slice of the Victoria sandwich, greedily gobbling it after licking the cream off her finger. Bill would have been looking on disapprovingly had she done this at home.

He was no fun anymore. That's what it boiled down to. She neatly stacked the crockery on the draining board after washing it. Couldn't face tracking down the dishwasher once again.

As she stared out at Peter's back garden, she remembered him playing in theirs as a child, the summer they'd bought the paddling pool. Bill had filled it, then they'd played with a ball for the afternoon. It must have been a weekend because otherwise he'd have been at work. Peter had used to look forward to Daddy returning from work, telling his friends proudly that he made sick people better.

'Bye, love,' she called at the front door, slipping out and closing it behind her. Sitting in her car, she said to herself: 'Leave him? As if that's even possible.'

Chapter 12

Ian met Gabriella and Thomas at the shallow end of the outdoor swimming pool. It was another warm May day, blue sky and the scent of summer just around the corner.

Gabriella was holding Thomas's body as he splashed about happily in armbands. 'You've got a nice *visique*,' she said, looking at Ian's chest.

He folded his arms and turned away. 'Sorry?'

'I mean to say, I don't know why you're self-conscious of swimming. There's all shapes and sizes come here, I can tell you.' She giggled.

'Thanks?' he said with a shrug. She meant *physique*, but had the word wrong. There was something refreshingly unselfconscious about her that he admired. It wasn't as if she had an agenda, knowing he was both gay and attached had seen to that. But Ian knew no one else who'd simply come out with a comment like that, unbidden.

'Don't mention it. Thought I should say. I know you said you was worried. Your Drew, he's a lucky man.' She looked from side to side. 'Have you told him yet? About the job situation?'

'Not yet. I will though.'

'When?'

'You're worse than my mother.'

'Bloody right too.' She winked, returning her attention to Thomas who seemed to almost be managing without her help.

'I'm going to…' He dived underwater, swimming into the lane and there he remained until he'd completed his thirty lengths. He was going to tell Drew. Definitely. Some day. At a point in the future.

After they dried from the pool, the three of them relaxed on sun loungers, Thomas drifting off in Gabriella's lap.

'Tired?' Ian asked.

'Wish I'd known this trick before. I tried all sorts to get him off. Driving around in the car, playing with his toys. This works a right treat.'

'Not bad here, is it? Could almost be on holiday, catching some rays.'

'There are worse places. How was your do last night? Can't remember the last time I went up west.'

'I thought I'd miss it, but I don't. The work bit I miss. Purpose, a reason to get up. But London itself, not so much.'

'What did you see?'

'One of those juke box musicals.' Ian recounted to Gabriella their night in West London.

They had met at a restaurant and Drew hugged Ian, kissing him on the lips. 'How was work?'

'Busy. Only just got here in time.' *Because I was travelling from the West London Lido, and not the West End.* He sat at the table next to Drew.

'You look tired, are you okay?' Drew held his shoulders and looked him up and down. 'Somebody's been to the gym.' He squeezed Ian's biceps.

'Like I said, busy day.'

'Are you sure? You've not been yourself for a while. Do you think you should see the doctor?'

He probably should, but not for being unemployed, but Ian didn't want to think about that. 'It's nothing.'

Drew squeezed his hand. 'If there was something wrong, you'd tell me, wouldn't you?'

Ian couldn't meet his eyes. He nodded, looking at the menu. 'Who else is coming?'

Drew was still staring at him. 'I'm worried about you.'

'No need. I'm fine.' Absolutely fine. *I haven't cried in days. Almost a week in fact. And the other problem – that'll pass, surely, won't it?*

There was silence until the waiter arrived, asking when the other members of their party would be arriving.

Drew checked his phone. 'Five minutes, all right?'

The waiter nodded, then left.

'I think I'm going to have a pizza. What about you?'

Drew put his menu down, folded his arms. 'I know there's something wrong. Why won't you tell me, let me help?'

Ian concentrated very hard on telling the lie. He raised his eyebrows, stared straight into Drew's eyes and lied. 'There's nothing wrong.'

Drew shook his head. 'You're always like this.'

'Like what? There's nothing for me to be like anything about? Can't you just leave me alone?'

'No. Because I love you.'

Ian took a deep breath. 'Isn't love about giving someone space too?'

'When they need it, yeah.'

Before they could get any deeper into that particular discussion their friends arrived. Two male couples, one was a school friend of Drew's and his boyfriend, the

97

other one of Ian's colleagues from a previous job plus his husband. They hugged and kissed cheeks, before the conversation moved on to what they were going to eat and when they needed to leave for the show.

Later that evening, at home, after Ian had fallen asleep on the tube journey home having drunk too much wine at the meal, Drew handed him a pint of water. 'What was that?'

'What was what?' Ian asked, sliding lower.

'Drinking like there's no tomorrow. What happened to no alcohol on school nights because you had work the next day?'

Ian waved away an old maxim of his. 'People change.'

'They do. But there's always a reason why. That's what I'm trying to work out about you. Because this Ian, this isn't the man I married.'

'Why did you marry me?' Ian blurted out in anger and drunken ill-thought.

'Because I love you.'

Ian thought he heard hesitation in Drew's voice. This was precisely what he had always worried about. Drew was finally realising the mistake he'd made in marrying him. 'I wouldn't marry me.'

'You didn't marry you, you married me.'

Ian shook his head, took a sip of water and then turned on the TV. It filled the room with noise and the screen cast a flickering light. Ian lay back on the sofa, making himself comfortable. He didn't want to discuss this with Drew any longer.

Drew stood, shaking his head. 'I don't understand.'

'Nothing to understand.'

'So you say.' Drew sighed, folding his arms across his chest. 'Am I so scary that you can't talk to me, your own husband? We should be able to talk about anything.'

He wasn't wrong, Ian admitted, and yet he couldn't say it. Spit out the words that he'd been holding inside for months. 'Sorry,' he said finally, looking at Drew and feeling it very deeply.

Drew shook his head, then kissed Ian's forehead. 'You don't need to say that.'

'Love is never having to say sorry, isn't that right?' Ian asked. He'd read it somewhere, or heard it... Couldn't remember where.

'No, Ian.' Drew crouched in front of the sofa, staring directly into Ian's eyes. 'That's not my definition of love. Love is never having to hide who you are from someone.'

Ian could no longer make eye contact, continuing with this lie, while staring his husband in the eyes. He stared at the TV as a nurse stood by a patient's bed and spoke to him.

'Night,' Drew said, kissing Ian's cheek, then leaving the room.

Ian remained with his guilt and his thoughts and his sadness, all alone, thinking that now the fact he'd lied for so long was probably worse than the lie itself, and at that thought he fell asleep with the TV still flickering.

Now, Gabriella smiled, folded her arms in her lap as she reclined on the sun lounger. 'I've seen all them. Juke box musicals. Went to the Queen one five times. Arnie said I was addicted.'

Ian smiled. Her late husband sounded really special. He could literally feel the love she'd had for him, every time she mentioned his name. Guilt at abusing the love Drew had for him stabbed in his gut.

'I said to him, it's better than being a drug addict, or an alcohol addict. I bet there's not an AA for people going to musicals.'

'If there is, I've not heard of it. As far as addictions go, it's pretty benign.'

'What's that? Sorry, I'm thick. I didn't go to a good school, not like where my kids are. Well, one of 'em. Other's soonish. Should have started preschool now... They said any time between three and four. But I don't want to leave him so soon after his dad... When they're both at school, most mums'd be relieved, but I'm dreading it. Just me and the empty house. At least now me and Thomas can make noise if I don't come here. Fill it with something. When it's me on me tod, I...'

'Benign means harmless. People talk about finding a lump and it can be malignant or benign.'

'Right. How's it spelled?'

Ian spelled it slowly.

She nodded, closing her eyes as he repeated the spelling. 'I got a letter from the school and there were three words I'd never heard of. Looked 'em up. I had heard of 'em, but didn't know that's how they were spelled. Like I said, I'm dim.'

'Don't say that. Please. Your modelling career is far more interesting than anything I've ever done sitting at a desk behind a computer.' He turned to look at her, noticing her very striking good looks. She definitely had a touch of the smouldering Hispanic film star about her.

'How did you get into modelling? I imagine it's very cliquey.'

Gabriella sat up on the sun lounger, her long limbs shiny with sun cream. 'You wouldn't believe. Mum was really pushy. Entered me in all the competitions. Miss East

London, had me on carnival floats all dressed up. I was a pretty little girl.' She blushed.

'You're very attractive now.'

'Thanks. I did well in a few magazine competitions and Mum took me to an agency. Got me on their books. Kept calling every week asking for work. Whatever it took to get me more work. I've got the clippings at home somewhere. Mum kept them all. Big break was getting a catalogue job. Every year they used me for the clothes and toys. Someone scouted me, noticed I'd been doing all this work. Steady like. Then I won the magazine comp for swimwear. I knew I would, cos the photos I sent in, well, they wasn't just a few snaps Dad done for me. Got 'em done proper, professional like.'

Ian frowned, in confusion.

'It was meant to be an amateur comp. New talent spotting. Send pics in, tell them about any other work you'd done. I didn't lie, but the pics, well, they weren't, technically speaking, amateur.'

'Didn't anyone realise you'd done modelling work before?'

'Could you tell me what a model looks like from a clothes catalogue you've flicked through?'

Ian shook his head and smiled.

Gabriella raised her eyebrows and winked. 'Mum kept saying one day I'd hit the big time.'

'And you did?' Ian asked, fascinated.

Gabriella shook her head. 'No. But I made enough to help Mum and Dad with housekeeping when I left school. After I met Arnie I bought them a car. Only a Fiesta, nothing too flash, but new. Top of the range. I splashed out on 'em. Power steering, chrome around the windows, five gears, alloyed wheels. The whole shebang. Theirs. They'd never had that before. Mum cried when she picked it up at the garage. They wrapped it in a big red bow, just for her.'

'Fascinating. Never think you're less than. You're amazing, in your own way. Right?'

Gabriella shrugged, seemingly unconvinced.

'Besides, you're raising two boys on your own. It's more than I've done, or will ever do.'

'Fancy kids yourself?'

'I don't think so. I like them, but I enjoy being able to give them back at the end of the day. We've looked after friends' kids, and Drew's brother has two. I like being cool guncles too.'

'Guncles?' She frowned.

'Gay uncles.'

'Right. I like that. Guess who won't though.'

At the same time they said: 'Helen.'

Gabriella said, 'Wonder how she's getting on today.'

'Has she said anything in the group?'

Gabriella checked. 'Nope.' She took a picture of Thomas sleeping, leaning his head on her chest. Then one of Ian.

'Why'd you do that?'

'You looked nicely chilled out.'

He shrugged.

'Anyway, change of subject: maybe we should go see a show sometime. Maybe you can meet Drew.'

'You enjoyed it that much? Bit of normality?'

Ian nodded. 'I didn't enjoy having to lie about what I'd done at work during the day. Or the expensive meal we couldn't afford.' He looked at the ground. He was doing his best to eke out the money, and Drew... Well, he wasn't. Why should he? He told her.

She raised an eyebrow. 'You know what I'm going to suggest, don't you?'

He sighed, shaking his head. 'I didn't really think it through. I thought I'd do this—'

'The lie?'

'The lie, while I searched for another job and it would be over before it became a problem. Except now, the deception is worse than what I'm lying about. I think.'

Gabriella nodded. 'That's what I thought.' A pause, and then: 'When are you gonna tell Drew?'

'When I've found a job.' It was the only answer he knew how to give. Anything else was unthinkable.

Chapter 13

Gabriella saw the sadness on his face. Guilt too. And regret in his eyes. She reached her hand out, gesturing for him to hold it. She was always too friendly, over-familiar, or so Arnie's parents often told her. Mum used to laugh about it, right from when, as a bold ten year-old she made friends with a teenager on the beach at Southend, bringing the gangly boy back to them, sitting down and asking if he could have lunch too.

She smiled at the memory, brushing Ian's fingers gently. 'It's gonna be all right, you know?'

He nodded slowly. 'Is it? Wish I had your confidence.'

'I'll come with you when you tell him. How would that be?' It felt like a stroke of genius and she puffed up her chest a little as she said it.

'Who would I say you are?' He sat upright, rubbing his eyes furiously. 'It would be really helpful. Don't get me wrong.'

'We can't be from school, cos...'

'I went to an all-boys school.' He shook his head.

'Right. And cos I'm—'

'I've told you about that. No more putting yourself down. I insist. We could have gone to the same school. If mine had girls in it.'

'Well, if you insist, then I suppose I should.'

He looked at her from the corner of his eye, smiling. His hand rested on the table.

She liked that Ian wasn't a snob. She felt she could ask him questions without worrying he'd think she was thick. It gave her a burst of confidence she'd not felt in months.

Thomas was sitting on the ground, playing with a plastic toy car. It seemed to keep him endlessly amused. Gabriella wasn't about to question that so had started bringing it out with him.

They sat in comfortable silence for a few moments, their hands almost touching while resting on the table.

People were swimming, some going silently up and down in the lanes section that Helen seemed to like. There were children throwing a ball in the shallow end with their parents.

The sun loungers were filling up, about half of them had people sitting reading, looking at their phones, occasionally talking. It seemed most people tended to come here alone. Maybe they were here to get away from a busy life, take a break for an hour. It seemed ironic that she, Ian and Helen were doing the exact opposite.

'I will tell him. If you come with me,' Ian said with a serious frown and nod.

'Sorted.' She lifted her fist towards his.

His hands remained by his sides.

'Don't you know nothing? Fist bump.' She showed him.

He bunched his hand into a fist and tapped hers. 'Right?'

'Sorted.' And for the first time since Arnie had gone, in those long six months, she felt something light within her stomach. It had replaced the heavy darkness she'd been carrying there for so long. A lightness that rose in her stomach, up through her chest and into her throat. Unclear what it was, but it felt good.

Ian smiled.

'I'm ready to tell you,' Gabriella said, with a confidence she'd not thought herself capable of.

'What?'

'How it happened.' She nodded to Thomas. 'He can't hear. I told him Daddy was hurt, like the cat we had after it got hit by a car.' The lightness in her stomach was replaced with the heavy sadness of before. *Maybe this isn't such a good idea…*

'Sure?'

She nodded quickly. Wanted to get it over with. Knew if she didn't tell him now, she probably never would.

'Want to dress and have a coffee?'

She pursed her lips, shaking her head. 'Think I just wanna get it over with. Rip off the plaster, you know?'

'What about Helen?'

'She's not here.'

'I can tell her, if you don't want to go over it again.' He smiled and his eyes crinkled at the edges. This was a good man. She'd known that the first time she saw him. She had a sort of sixth sense for people. Never once had her intuition about whether someone was kind, dangerous or otherwise, been off. Ever since a little kid, she'd just known what sort of person she was standing in front of. Known, with a confidence she'd doubted at first, when she'd told others. But now, she knew, as surely as she knew anything, she was always right. And Ian was a good man. Helen was a lost soul and she reckoned Bill wasn't a bad person, but she'd need to see him to be sure.

'It's all right, I'll tell her. Put it in the group.'

'Sure?' he asked, looking concerned.

It didn't feel right, making Ian tell her most painful memory to Helen. Gabriella bit her bottom lip as she blinked. 'No.'

'Sure?'

She nodded. 'Yep. I want us to be together when I do it. Don't feel right just us two and then me dumping it on you to tell Helen.' She shook her head. 'It'll keep.'

'It will. When you're ready, and not before.' Ian stared at her and smiled. 'Fancy hearing about my really slutty phase at uni?'

Her eyes widened, and she smiled. 'Bloody right! You, slutty? I thought you were a one man… Man.'

'I am now.' He looked away. 'Even if I'm lying to him.'

'Told you, we'll sort that. When *you're* ready.'

Ian pulled his phone from his pocket and showed her a picture of a spotty teenager with a wispy thin moustache, smiling uncomfortably in his too-tight school blazer and shirt.

'Who's this?'

'Me.'

'Fuck off!' She peered closer and recognised Ian's eyes. But everything else was different. His square jaw, muscular build, and clear skin nothing like the boy in the photo.

'Puberty kind of hit me like a sledgehammer.'

'What's with the moustache?'

'I couldn't shave it because my acne was so bad. They asked my parents to do something about it. Facial hair wasn't allowed. Except for religious reasons.' Ian shrugged.

She shook her head. 'What's up with the jacket?'

'That year I went up a few sizes. It fitted me and then… Well, it didn't.'

She leaned her elbows on the table. 'What's this got to do with your slutty phase at uni?'

'Once testosterone had done its thing with me, I discovered the gym and, well, there was less of me than when I was at school.' He coughed. 'At uni, I sort of went a bit mad really.'

'Like how?'

'I went to uni as a virgin and after going to the LGBT soc we ended up at a gay club. I'd never had the guts to go to one before.'

'You were a virgin at eighteen?'

Ian blushed and nodded.

'Hang on a minute, LGBT soc, what's that?'

'A club for lesbian, gay, bisexual and trans students. There were all sorts of clubs at uni, chess, sports, films, drama…'

'And one for being gay? Like you didn't know how to do it?'

Ian laughed. 'Well, I didn't. Honestly, not a clue. I was more… Gay in theory, but not in practice.'

Gabriella laughed, banging her hand on the table. 'Honestly, this gets better and better.'

Ian coughed. 'So I went to this club and this guy offered to buy me a drink. We danced, he kissed me.'

'Had you kissed anyone before that?'

'Not properly.'

Gabriella had been kissing boys at school from eleven and had lost – what her mum called her innocence – at fifteen to a boy in her class at a party, on his parent's bed, on top of her classmates' coats. 'So you kissed this bloke and went home with him?'

Ian nodded. 'He was a third year, on the music course. Lived in a shared house off campus. I was in halls of accommodation next to the uni main buildings. We were kissing on his sofa and his housemate walked in, said we should get a room and...'

'You did?'

'Correct.' Ian blushed. 'Ran upstairs into his room. Afterwards, when I went back to the club, it was like I had this new superpower. If a man talked to me and I fancied him, I'd go home with him. I'm not shaming anyone for any sort of body shape. But I wasn't happy before. I had a terrible time at school when I looked like that. Puberty hits everyone differently.'

'It does.'

'What about you?'

'I started kissing boys at eleven and didn't never stop. God, fifteen is too young to... you know... lose it. I know that now. But at the time, I just sort of wanted to get it over and done with. Like it was a bad spot that needed bursting.'

'That is young.'

'He was the same age. He said he'd be my boyfriend if we... And you can guess how that turned out.'

'Men, eh?' Ian shook his head and smirked.

'Right!'

'Fancy a walk?'

'Don't you usually run in the gym?' Gabriella asked.

'Unless you want to watch me running.'

She thought for a moment. 'Bit creepy.'

'It is.' He stood. 'I know a nice route to the town centre. We could go shopping.'

'That would be nice.' She stood, taking Thomas's hand and they walked the fifteen minutes to Uxbridge town centre where she bought the boys some clothes, some toys – letting Thomas choose for his brother. She bought herself a summer dress, long and floaty with bold geometric patterns. As she looked at herself in the mirror, she could almost fool herself into thinking Arnie would say how much he loved it on her, and she'd promise to wear it the next time they went out, and he'd kiss her and he'd pull her close and she'd feel his hard body next to hers and…

They spent a lovely few hours popping into shops, for stuff Gabriella needed and stuff she didn't need.

'Thanks,' she said to Ian.

'Didn't do anything.'

'I've gotta pick Jack up from school. This afternoon, it's been really nice. Normal.' She smiled.

They were walking back to the lido, where her car was parked. Ian carried most of the bags. He'd been the one persuading her to buy herself something, having filled three bags with clothes and toys for the boys. The money certainly came in handy, but it didn't make up for losing Arnie.

He winked, nodded, turned and walked towards the lido. Probably going to the gym, Gabriella thought. It was mid-afternoon, and Ian couldn't arrive home yet without explanation – until he'd finally told Drew the truth.

As Gabriella arrived at the school, she reminded herself of the promise she'd made to Ian, to be there for him, just like he'd been there for her today.

'All right, shall we see what your brother's been up to?'

Thomas smiled. 'Yeah, Mummy.'

A man was standing outside the school gates. Rare, one of those. It was usually the mums who did this.

Gabriella nodded at him in recognition.

He smiled back, his eyes twinkled slightly. 'How many?' He nodded at the school.

'One, and one just about to start.' She raised her eyebrows.

'Two.' He saw two girls running towards him, knelt and pulled them into a hug. Taking their hands, he led them away, smiling at her briefly.

Chapter 14

It was just light outside and Helen sat in the kitchen sipping fruit tea, watching the sun rise higher in the sky. She really should get the hang of caffeine, didn't people swear it helped them in the morning? She was going to leave before Bill woke. She couldn't have the same conversation again. The same non-discussion with Bill.

Her legs were crossed and tucked underneath her. She wished she had someone to talk to, but everyone knew Bill better than herself. So it would feel like a betrayal of sorts. Emotionally incontinent, spreading her worries among her friends. They'd surely talk and she'd be the subject of gossip within days.

Friends had asked why she rose so early now she was retired.

'I always have,' she'd replied. For the children, getting them ready, taking them to school. And then Bill had become used to her soothing presence as he readied himself for work.

'Why don't you do it any longer?' Bill had asked a while ago.

'I had been labouring under the misapprehension that you would have retired by now. Hence giving me a break from assisting you. But since you seem to show no inclination towards retiring, I'm giving myself the gift of retiring.'

He hadn't known what to say and had simply stared at her, open mouthed. 'So am I to make my own lunch, iron my own shirts and press my own trousers?'

It was perfectly clear to her that he only saw her as a means of delivering those things to him. 'I think retiring and then returning to work shows a not inconsiderable lack of imagination.'

'Pardon?'

'Imagine all the other things you could be doing, rather than continuing to go to that bloody place.' Helen had clenched her fists so tightly her knuckles went pale white. She tensed her jaw and later gave herself a headache.

So he'd started buying lunch at the hospital, and she'd arranged to have his ironing done, all their ironing in fact, she remembered with a smile, by a lady called Joan who collected them on a Friday and returned them on Sunday evening.

'You're up early.' Bill's voice shook her from the memories.

She looked up from the mug into which she'd been staring. 'Yes.'

'I'm off today.'

'Wednesday. You work Wednesdays.'

'I was on-call over the weekend, so I'm not working today. I offered to go in, but they said some guff about working time directives. I told them when I was a junior, we used to do eighty, ninety-hour weeks and not to bother me about that nonsense again.' He chuckled.

That smile reminded her of Bill as a young man and how he'd looked at her when he'd proposed and how she'd had no choice but to agree. Forty years ago and she felt like a different person.

'What are you doing today?' Her voice came out quieter than usual. She was disappearing. Curling into herself, folding inwards, until she would one day be nothing but her strong decisive haircut and her reading glasses.

'I heard you getting up and wondered...'

A small glimmer of hope. 'What?'

'If Peter had called you. It's always you he turns to in times of crisis.'

'Why wouldn't he?'

'Because I'm his father.'

'Are you?'

'What's that supposed to mean? I am his father.'

'Biologically yes. But as to whether you parented him as I did, the verdict is significantly different.'

'What's that supposed to mean?' He looked bemused.

Hearing about Gabriella and Arnie's marriage made Helen realise how fantastically wrong she'd got it all these years. 'Do you want to have lunch out?' She couldn't be bothered to explain to him that they turned to her because it had been her who had raised them. It seemed perfectly obvious to Helen.

'Today?'

'Yes.'

'We have a fridge full of food.'

'Correct.' Helen stood, placed her mug in the dishwasher.

'Why should we eat out if that's the case?' He opened the fridge in emphasis.

'Indeed.' She raised her eyebrows, wishing, hoping very strongly indeed that he'd care enough to have at least a small argument with her.

'What's wrong?' he asked, with an expression of bemusement.

She shook her head. 'If I said no, let's stay here for the day and we'll have luncheon together, would you be interested?'

'Should I be?'

'Interested?'

He nodded, raising his eyebrows, with the same look of confusion. 'Well?'

'I'm going shopping. I may spend a disgusting amount on clothes I neither need, nor have any place to wear them.'

Bill waved it away and shrugged. 'If you wish.'

She left the kitchen, walked upstairs to brush her teeth and collect her swimming kit. Shortly after, she walked downstairs.

Bill was sitting at the dining room table focused intently on his laptop.

Turn around and have a bloody conversation with me! Tell me I'm forbidden from spending money on clothes I don't need. Let's have a fight, if we can't have a discussion. 'I'm going out.'

She grabbed her coat, keys, then opened the door. 'How much is the credit limit? Ten thousand, fifteen?' She waited for a response, something about how she mustn't waste money like that. As he'd done before, when money had been tighter and when Bill had given a shit what she did. When he'd seen her.

Silence.

'I wonder how you'd react if I bought a pair of ridiculously expensive shoes, the designer ones with the red soles, five thousand pounds apparently.'

Slow, two-finger pecking on the keyboard of Bill's laptop. 'Marvellous.'

Helen closed her eyes, took a deep breath and bit her bottom lip with frustration. 'I wonder how you'd get on if left entirely to your own devices.'

Silence.

'I'm considering joining the circus. Or perhaps I'll book a one-way ticket to Greece.'

Bill's voice came from the dining room, a sense of confusion and irritation unmistakably present. 'What are you shouting about? I thought you were going out.'

'Nothing. Nothing of any consequence.' Closing the door, she held onto that thought during the short drive to the lido.

Arriving at six-thirty, the car park was nearly empty. Blue sky, not too hot, as the sun hadn't had a chance to warm the air and ground. She changed quickly in a blue booth, then slid into the deep end. She'd told Ian and Gabriella that she would be there as early as possible for a swim.

She'd done ten lengths, counting in time with her front crawl strokes, when she recognised Ian's face coming towards her in the lane.

'Morning,' he said, continuing to swim breast stroke.

She smiled, continued her determined front crawl, preferring to maintain the silence, to give herself time to process the morning's conversation, and what it probably meant for her life.

How does one even get a divorce at this stage, when there's not another person to blame? Do people cite feeling fed up, or emotional cruelty perhaps. Was Bill's behaviour cruelty? She wasn't sure. If a distinct lack of emotion could be described as cruelty, then Bill had that in gallons.

She held onto the edge at the deep end, treading water, catching her breath.

Ian joined her. 'How's it going?'

'I've been better. I've been worse.'

'Want to talk about it?'

'Is it possible to get a divorce citing emotional barrenness, do you think?'

'I'm sure a solicitor could advise. Shall we swim?'

'Together?' Helen frowned. The main purpose of swimming was to be alone with her thoughts. Particularly at this time. Although at the moment her thoughts weren't very pleasant to spend time with.

'If you want.'

'I don't know what I want.'

'Let's take it slowly. Breast stroke, all right?'

'So we can talk, I suppose?'

'If you want to.' He kicked off from the side and slid into a serene breast stroke.

Helen followed and they soon moved into the slow lane, after receiving angry stares from Mr Fast Front Crawl.

'What happened this morning?' Ian asked.

'Nothing big. No massive row. No throwing plates.' She really wasn't enjoying trying to talk while swimming. 'Do you mind if we don't talk at the moment? I'd rather...'

'Course.'

They continued swimming in silence until Helen had completed her usual thirty lengths. She reclined on a sun lounger while Ian continued swimming

A short while later Ian joined her, standing and dripping onto the concrete floor, with a towel around his shoulders. He sat next to her, shading his eyes with a hand. 'Can't you talk to a friend?'

'That's what I'm doing.' She stared at him.

'That's very kind of you, but what about someone who knows you both, and for a bit longer?'

'They're all Bill's friends' wives from the hospital.'

'You must have some of your own. From when the children were small. Local mums maybe.' He shrugged.

'I don't know where you think I live, but we don't know our neighbours. Well, only to nod to. I didn't have time for friends, not when I was bringing up Peter. And as for local groups, I don't know where I'd start. I have no interests other than my home and children. And they're both mostly redundant now.' An icy chill passed over her as she realised she was somewhat surplus to her own life.

'I don't understand.' Ian looked perplexed.

'Bill encouraged me to befriend his colleagues' wives. We used to host dinner parties. All part of him getting to know the right people, how else do you think he became the youngest medical director at that hospital?'

'He bribed someone?' Ian's eyes widened.

'Goodness no! I don't mean that. A game of golf here, a dinner party there, invitations to one another's children's birthday parties. It all goes towards greasing the wheels of power.' She sighed. 'I would have thought you'd be much more of a man of the world than this.' Helen tutted loudly.

'No wonder you're lonely. I'd be terribly sad in the same situation.'

'He discouraged friends he thought served no purpose.'

'And you went along with it?'

'It's easy for you to say that now, but thirty to forty years ago, times were different. I was the corporate wife, helping my husband get on. I agreed to give up my job as a secretary. I wanted to. I really did. To be the perfect wife, the strong woman standing behind Bill, *nothing* could have made me happier.' She bit her lip at the thought.

Chapter 15

'You don't sound convinced.' Not remotely, but he wasn't going to say it. He was enjoying himself, for the first time since the restructure at work. Working with people, talking to others, that was what he missed most about work. That and being the expert in his field.

'I thought you were meant to be helping me.' Helen sounded snippy.

'I'm trying to understand why you can't speak to him.'

Gabriella arrived with Thomas and sat on a sun lounger. 'That's what I thought.'

'Don't you think I've tried?' Helen looked from Ian to Gabriella. 'I get nothing in return. He doesn't even say goodbye when he leaves in the morning. He looks straight through me. It's as if I'm not there.'

The way she said it showed Ian how hurt she felt. To not be seen, the ultimate expression of being taken for granted, was the worst sort of cruelty. 'I'm lucky, we have a wide friendship group.'

'Tell me about it, will you? I'm in the mood to live vicariously through you and your husband's social life.'

'Just because we're gay doesn't make it any more gripping than any other couple's social life.'

'I'll be the judge of that,' Helen said.

Ian told them.

Earlier that week, Ian had returned home to find Drew there, watching TV in the living room.

He silenced the TV and looked up at Ian. 'You look well. Shaken that dark cloud that was hanging around you before?' Drew asked with concern, pulling Ian in for a hug and a kiss on the lips.

'When?' Ian was doing his best to appear normal, as if nothing had changed from before.

'When we went up west. You were very maudlin that evening.'

Ian's hangover had been epic and he'd dragged his sorry carcass out of bed and into the car, pretending to go to work, but had slept in the car at the lido until Helen's knock on the window had woken him.

'Red wine. It does that to me sometimes.' Ian waved it away as if it were nothing. 'And London.'

That weekend, they went for a drive farther into the Oxfordshire countryside, visiting a small village with a green and houses at the edges in yellow Cotswold stone. The pub had recently received a glowing review in a newspaper Ian trusted, so he'd arranged lunch there with friends.

It was one of those lunches that spread from midday until early afternoon, with more wine and food and laughter and chatter sloshing around for hours. Ian, the designated driver – he was off the wine for now, decided it made him more liable to tell Drew the truth and a much less pleasant husband – had shepherded his drunken friends and husband into the car.

After dropping them off, and over-familiar kisses on cheeks and hugs, Ian returned home.

Drew was keen to get inside and held Ian's hand, masterfully leading them through the kitchen until they fell on the sofa, first Drew, and then Ian on top.

Drew seemed to have a hunger, an almost desperation then, kissing Ian, and grabbing at his clothes, slipping off his T-shirt, and unfastening Ian's buttons until they were wearing only underwear.

Ian wanted this, loved his husband, needed to show him he wasn't a different man to who he'd married, that the drunken night was the alcohol and the maudlin talking, not the real Ian. And Ian willed himself to give into the moment, to just feel, enjoy, experience what they were doing... And yet...

Drew smiled lasciviously and stood, hooking a finger into Ian's waistband and walking towards the bedroom.

The door closed, the lights off – Ian insisted unless he were a little tipsy, much to Drew's protestation – and both on the bed and Ian knew it was useless. He was useless. His body was useless.

Drew lay to one side on the bed and had explored Ian's chest, navel, and began to remove his underwear.

Ian lay frozen still, his body rigid except the part that should be. He turned away from Drew as shame and remorse washed through him.

'What's wrong?' Drew asked carefully.

Ian shook his head. 'Tired.'

Drew lay behind him, like spoons and reached around the front to continue what he'd been doing.

But it was no good, game over before it had begun. Ian shuffled out of bed, stood, grabbed a dressing gown and left the room.

He was sitting on the sofa with his head in his hands, when Drew joined him a short while later, wearing a T-shirt and underwear.

Drew put his hands around Ian's shoulders. 'Do you want to talk about it?'

Ian shook his head.

'Okay. Can I hold you?'

Ian shrugged. Didn't seem any harm unless Drew expected more than a hug.

Drew did so. 'Doesn't matter, you know.'

Ian said nothing, a tear forming in his eye and falling down his nose. It tasted salty. He huffed. As if it didn't matter.

'Is this why you've been acting funny recently?'

Mood swings, feeling withdrawn, repeatedly saying he had a headache if Drew indicated wanting more than a kiss. Ian shrugged.

'I love you. You do know that, don't you? I'm not going to trade you in for a new husband. Forever means forever, right.'

In sickness and in health. Except Ian reckoned this, combined with losing his job, were surely grounds for separation. Who would want a man like him?

The crippling anxiety about whether he'd ever earn again had made him anxious much of the time around Drew, and that was neither sexy nor relaxing.

Drew made them dinner and they cuddled up on the sofa, with Drew stroking Ian's arm, face, stomach, doing his best to show Ian he meant what he said. 'You've had a lot on your plate. Work stress, and maybe the commute's too much for you…

'And what happened to that person in your team, who was going to take some of the work off you?'

'I'll ask.' *Never.* They were the starting point for the restructure and why he'd lost his job.

The lies kept coming though. One meant he had to tell half a dozen more and then constantly having to keep track of them. They were like weeds in a flowerbed, growing and spreading, intermingling and tangling up with his feet, ready to trip him up. He felt moments from falling at any point of every day.

Now, he left silence after telling them about that night with Drew.

'It's hard to feel in the mood when you don't... Feel in the mood,' Gabriella said.

'Indeed,' Helen added with a smile.

Ian turned to Helen and squeezed her shoulder. 'I'm sure he does see you, Bill. It's just he's forgotten how.'

'The practical upshot is the same as not seeing me, regardless of the route he took to get there.' She turned to face him, running her hand over a slender leg. 'How about if I were to tell Drew about your job?'

'You've not met him. Won't he think it's a bit, well, random?'

'I could be there with you. Do it one day when he comes home from work.'

Ian didn't like the sound of that at all. He shook his head. 'Gabriella has offered to be with me when I tell him. I think that's better than someone else telling him.'

'She's right. Sorry, I think I'm trying to mother you. Solve your problems for you, rather than simply being there to support you while you do it yourself.'

Gabriella had a clever way of knowing simply being with someone, there to listen, or standing beside them, was often all it took to feel supported enough to take the leap they hadn't managed before. 'She's sort of like a sister who takes no shit, but lets me get on with it.'

'Far preferable. I'll step away. Sorry to interfere.'

'What if he kicks off?'

'What do you mean?'

'Gets angry, smashes things up. You know. Even if Gabriella's there.'

'Is he likely to?'

'I've never told him I've lost my job before.'

'But you've given him bad news?'

Ian thought for a moment. He stood. 'I'm going for a run.' He scurried to the gym, changed, then after waiting for a woman to vacate it, jumped on the running machine. He set it at medium speed and settled into the rhythmic thuds of his steps.

With disappointment in his gut, he saw Helen walking into the gym.

She smiled, winked at him, and was soon standing next to the treadmill. 'All right?'

If he told her to go away it could only be interpreted as rudeness. He continued running, counting to ten in his mind in time with the steps. It was unsurprisingly good at shutting out all other thoughts.

'I'm not an expert at anything. Never was, until I found work. Now I don't know who I am without it.' Drew wasn't going to want an unemployed husband, particularly one who had Ian's other little problem.

He wiped his face with a towel and switched the machine off, smartly dropping to the ground at the back, sipping his water bottle.

'Why do men so entangle themselves with their work? Bill does this. Probably half the reason for our problems.' She shrugged.

'I used to be an expert. Now I'm not an expert at anything. People used to listen to what I said, requested my opinions, listened to them. Acted upon them even.' He needed to shower and it would give him a convenient exit to this conversation. Taking a shower. Great, another opportunity to be faced with his useless body. Or one particular part of it. A shiver ran through him.

'Is there something else that's stopping you telling him?'

There really was anxiety about Drew thinking he deserved a better husband than Ian, but it wasn't something Ian was about to spill his guts about in a busy gym on a Wednesday morning. 'Can I get changed first?'

'Aha, is that a yes I detect?'

He nodded. 'Not here.' Not ever. He'd need to be much more desperate to tell Helen that.

'You don't think you're an expert, but I'm sure you're an expert on Drew. And you're mis-judging him completely. Honesty is always the best policy.'

Ian smiled stiffly. Ha! He'd tried that about the other little problem and failed. Not being able to love Drew was all mixed up with Ian losing his job. He worried and worried, and so he worried when they were in bed and then he couldn't... 'See you in the café.' He left for the changing rooms, standing in the shower cubicle, unable to look at his body. The shame he felt for lying to Drew seemed to have worsened. Combined with the sure knowledge that he was, without doubt, completely useless as Drew's husband, meant he sat in the changing room staring into space as he decided it was still the best option to keep his job loss a secret from Drew.

Eventually, with each limb feeling as if it weighed a tonne, he dressed and left the changing rooms.

Chapter 16

Towards the end of May, Gabriella was sitting in the café with Thomas. The school had called her to explain Jack had been misbehaving. She held the letter they'd handed her after what she could only describe as a bollocking.

Ian arrived, taking a seat at their table. 'All right?'

She nodded. She didn't want them to feel she was always asking for their help. Couldn't cope on her own. She could. Had been, mostly, up to now.

'What's that?' Ian asked.

She handed it to him.

He read it. 'What's wrong with Jack?'

She shrugged. 'They called me, bollocked me, this arrived in the post and now they want to speak to me in person. It's like a triple bollocking.'

'Helen will know what to do.'

Shortly after, when they had been drinking their beverages for a while, Helen arrived.

'Sorry I'm late.' She looked exhausted and out of sorts.

Gabriella stood, pulled out a chair and offered to get Helen a drink.

'I'm fine.'

She didn't look it and Gabriella wouldn't take no for an answer. 'Look after Thomas.' She made eye contact with Ian, indicating as best she could, that he needed to make sure Helen was okay.

She returned with drinks and Helen looked more together, she sat, staring at the laminated menu. Accepting her drink with thanks, she smiled at Gabriella.

'How are we all today?' Helen said, stirring her drink with a spoon.

Ian leaned his elbows on the table. 'Gabriella has something she wants our help with. Well, yours.'

'What is it?'

Gabriella shook her head. 'We don't have to. I can see you're not right.' She folded the letter, placing it in her handbag. 'We can just chat. Chew the fat.'

'I am perfectly okay. I will not have more people ignoring me. I have enough of that at home. If I say I'm well, then please can you take me at my word?'

That certainly told them. Gabriella handed her the letter. 'I had a phone call. Jack's playing up at school.'

'What's he doing?'

'Hitting other kids, throwing stuff all over the shop. He's being a right little tearaway.'

'Do you know why?'

Gabriella shook her head.

'How long has this been happening?' Helen asked.

'Last few weeks or so. Out of nowhere.'

Ian said, 'I've not got children, but I don't understand why you need our help.'

Gabriella bit her bottom lip. She didn't want to tell them the teachers scared her and made her feel stupid. 'Arnie used to do all the school stuff.'

'You didn't have anything to do with your boys' schooling?' Helen made a face of obvious disapproval.

'Course not. I went along. But only for the ride. Arnie done all the talking. My parents never bothered with parents' evening.'

'Why not?'

'Cos they knew I'd leave as soon as I could. I never did well at anything they taught me. It's not like there's a GCSE in modelling, or hair styling, or beauty and makeup.'

Helen pursed her lips. 'I'm very happy to join you. I've been a school governor, I shan't take any nonsense.'

Gabriella liked the sound of that. 'Yes please. I could do with some of that. If that's okay.'

'Wouldn't have offered otherwise.' Helen handed back the letter. 'Although, I do think it's worth considering what may have led Jack to start misbehaving so suddenly.'

'I've wracked my brain and nothing.'

'Anniversaries, birthdays, anything changed at home recently?'

Nothing, except their dad dying. 'Nothing.'

'Has he been not allowed to do something he used to do?' Ian offered. 'Ignore me. I know nothing about kids.'

'I like that,' Helen said.

And then it hit her, Gabriella remembered Jack telling her he'd been invited to a birthday party of a boy in his class and asking if he could have one. She told them. 'I said yes and...' She shook her head. 'Shit. I am the worst mother. Unfit. They should take 'em off me.'

'What happened?' Helen asked, stroking Gabriella's shoulder.

'That's just it. Nothing.'

'Nothing? I don't follow.'

'He never went to the friend's party. I forgot. That's not so bad. But then he asked what about his party, could he invite his little friends, could he have a bouncy castle, and face painting like his friend had. They must have talked about it at school. He doesn't know what day is what. He can barely tell the time.'

'When's Jack's birthday?'

Gabriella checked the date on her phone. 'A month ago.' She put her head in her hands and closed her eyes. 'What sort of mum forgets her own kid's birthday?'

'Did he tell you?'

'Probably. Definitely. He asked about his friend's birthday and then he said something about his party. I thought it was months away, I'm not great with dates at the best of times, but since… The weeks and days blend into one. Jack's always rabbiting on and normally I listen to it. But so much of it's just nothing, just him talking to himself, I can't listen to all of it.' The horrific realisation about what she'd not done finally dawned on her. He'd been looking forward to both going to his friend's birthday and having his own very similar one.

'It's not the end of the world,' Helen said.

'It's not as bad as losing their dad, but it's not far off, is it?' She remembered him saying something about his friend's party bag and that he wanted the same. He said it needed to have a balloon, some bubble-blowing kit and sweets. 'I thought it was just stuff he wanted, in general.'

'Will he know he's missed his birthday?' Ian asked.

'Don't know. Possibly. Probably. Like I said, he's not good with dates. Neither am I. But they do know everyone's birthday at school, they like to ask them to make something – a story, or a model – about their birthday party.'

'I see,' Ian said.

It got worse. 'I need to go now, tell him we're having a party for him next weekend.' She stood. 'Before he tells his grandparents. As if they don't think I'm a useless mother already.'

'I'm sure they don't.'

Gabriella turned to face him. 'You've not met them. Never thought I was good enough for their son and now I'm an unfit mother. If they were looking after them...' The pain of that seized her heart.

There was silence.

'I need to do everything I can to keep this from them.'

Helen nodded. 'Understood.'

'Ta.'

'Do you think that's why he started hitting his class-mates?'

'Wouldn't you? Teacher has gone and asked him what he did for his birthday and he said nothing. The other kids laugh at him and...'

Helen held Gabriella's arm. 'You can't take him out of school now. Why don't you sit here and calmly think about how to give him the best birthday party a five-year-old's ever had?'

'Six.' She sat. It wasn't the worst idea. She took a deep breath. 'He was a photographer, Arnie, and he wanted to do more serious stuff. Not just fashion shoots, like where he met me. I said he was better than that. So he got some jobs for newspapers, mainly in London, covering big news stories. He was really good. If you Google his name, you'll find the pictures, they were used in all the main papers. I was so proud.' She sniffed. She wasn't gonna cry. Definitely not. 'Still am really.'

Ian squeezed her shoulder. 'You don't have to do this, you know.'

'I know. So, one day he gets a call from one of the journalists he'd worked with on a paper. Did he want to fly to India and report on this story. Course he said yes.' Another sniff. 'He always said yes. I used to call him Mr Yes. Stupid, innit?'

Ian said nothing, smiled carefully at her.

'It was some story about a British boy who'd gone missing. His parents were on holiday in Mumbai and he'd gone missing while they were shopping in the city centre. He let go of his mum's hand, wanted to see something.'

'I remember that, did they ever find him?' Helen asked.

'Yep. Not long after, he turned up at their hotel,' Gabriella said.

'That's right.'

'Arnie was photographing the main shopping street, can't remember what it's called, and they were interviewing people. Spoke to British tourists staying at the same hotel as the boy's parents. Same one as the big white palace everyone has photos taken in front of. Lady Di had a picture there.'

'The Taj Mahal Hotel?' Ian asked.

Gabriella nodded. Carefully she continued, 'So, this one morning Arnie was in a jewellery shop on the main shopping street. Can't remember the street's name.' She swallowed, blinked away a tear. 'Seven twenty-nine it went off. Somewhere on the street. A bag dumped in a litter bin. Everyone in the jewellery shop and the clothes shop and the shoes shops either side, was killed. They don't know why. Who even. It was just something that someone wanted to do. Some people said it was cos the shop was used by the British tourists and they wanted them to go home. No one knows.' She blinked and tears rolled down her cheeks.

Helen and Ian hugged her, making a sort of Gabriella sandwich between them.

She nodded, indicating she was okay.

They released her from the hug.

Helen handed her a tissue.

Sniffing, wiping her eyes, Gabriella went on, 'Mindless. Pointless. Don't make sense, but there you have it.' She stood. 'Sorry, it's a bit heavy all this, for ten o'clock in the morning. Watch him, will you, I'm just gonna wipe my face.' She left for the bathroom, wiped her face, sat down and really let it all out and had a good old cry.

It felt good to have told them. She couldn't explain it, but back then she'd finally felt ready to talk about it and although she didn't want to hog the conversation she worried if she'd waited it might have passed her by.

Having put herself back together, she returned to their table in the corner of the café, feeling much lighter.

'You're doing very well,' Helen said. 'And don't let anyone tell you otherwise.'

'You're a warrior, strong and impressive.' Ian squeezed Gabriella's shoulder.

'Don't feel like one.' She sniffed, wiped her nose on a tissue.

'We say you are, and therefore you are,' Helen said.

Gabriella shrugged. Although she knew she wasn't strong and impressive at anything, Helen and Ian certainly made her believe it was true, and she smiled at that.

The next day, having established that their theory was right, Gabriella went with Helen in the middle of the day for her appointment with the headmaster.

They sat outside in the corridor in uncomfortable plastic chairs that were too small.

'Reminds me of school,' Gabriella said.

'Unsurprising,' Helen said.

'Not the school, but being sat outside the head's office.'

'You didn't have a good time at school, did you?'

Gabriella shook her head.

'The school system does, unfortunately for some, favour traditional measures of attainment. There is no GCSE in the skills you undoubtedly have.'

'It is what it is.'

'I'm very happy to be here, and I'm sure you won't need my help, but I wonder, do you have any family who could help?'

'I do have five siblings. Three brothers, two sisters. We don't keep in touch.' She pursed her lips. Better not to say anything if she couldn't say something nice.

'Families are such complex things.'

She'd thought losing their parents would have brought them closer together. But emptying the maisonette in the tower block and fighting over who got what had finished it for any love between them. 'People always say things are just that, things, and people are more important.' She chuckled to herself. 'Funny how people are always falling out over things, eh?'

'There's not much you can't sort out over a cup of tea.'

Gabriella shook her head. 'You've not met my family. Once they get an idea into their heads, there's nothing you can do to shift it.'

'What idea would that be?'

'They used to call me The Duchess of Dalston when I used to visit them.'

'Ah,' Helen said.

Gabriella had tried to build bridges with her siblings, but the distance wasn't the hardest part. They were convinced she'd married above herself and had forgotten who she was, and where she came from along the way. 'They resented me buying Mum and Dad a car, and our house, well, they visited it once, but not again. Too flash. I should have stayed in the East End and got a terraced house, like they done.' She paused for a moment. 'Who doesn't like nice things? Why shouldn't I send my boys to a good school? Doesn't mean I look down on people who can't.'

Helen rubbed her shoulder. 'Families are complicated beasts at the best of times.'

They sat in silence and Gabriella wondered if, when she'd got herself back on her feet, she should give it one last try with her brothers and sisters. After all, her boys had cousins they'd never met and family was family, right?

The door opened and the headmaster – a fifty-something man in a suit – looked from side to side. 'Mrs Denmead, about Jack.'

The man she'd seen at the school gate left the room looking exhausted, in a smart suit and tie. 'Hello again,' he said.

All good, she wanted to say, but couldn't. 'Hello again. We must stop meeting like this.' An awkward smile, bright white straight teeth.

Reminded her of a movie star from one of those black and white films her mum used to enjoy. Slicked back hair, dazzling smile, sharp suits. Men who swept you off your feet, before you'd even had chance to notice.

Where did that come from?

The man shook the teacher's hand. 'Thank you for all your advice. Plenty of food for thought. I shall discuss it with the girls.' He turned, waved at them, then left, his shiny leather shoes clip-clopping along the hard floor.

Gabriella stood, holding her handbag close to her chest to disguise how much her hands were shaking. She was that misbehaving thirteen-year-old girl again. Chewing gum, not understanding why she needed to bother with all this school bollocks and wanting desperately to be sixteen and away from school and everything the grey stuffy building represented.

Mr Coats gestured for Gabriella to enter.

'My friend is coming with me,' she said quietly, noticing how her voice wavered with nerves. 'If that's all right.'

The teacher wore a too-tight suit, and on a coat stand he hung the black cape that Gabriella had been told they received when they graduated from uni. It had always seemed a bit stuck up to her. But then again, she wasn't used to private schools. It had always been Arnie's decision to send them here.

He frowned. 'It's not actually.' Turning to Helen, he said, 'I hope you understand, Madam.' Back to Gabriella now, he shepherded her into the room.

'Excuse me,' Helen said from the corridor.

They stopped, turned to face her.

'I'm sure you're aware that Mrs Denmead is recently widowed. I presume you'd normally allow her husband to attend?'

'Of course,' Mr Coats replied.

'As I suspected.' Helen stepped forward, through the door into the office.

Mr Coats stood still looking from one woman to the other. 'Usually we reserve this privilege for parents or nominated guardians.'

'I can only apologise. Unfortunately Mrs Denmead has had many other matters to attend to since the sad passing of Mr Denmead. Among those, she's not yet found time to nominate me as someone she'd wish to accompany her for meetings such as this. She will afterwards.' Helen stood in the office, the door closed behind her.

With the facial expression of a man who knew he'd lost, Mr Coats walked to his desk and sat, indicating for the woman to do the same.

They did so.

Mr Coats went into great detail about Jack's poor behaviour. 'It is unacceptable. We can't condone violence and an inability to follow simple rules. Even if he's only...' He cast his eye over a list '...six.'

Helen nodded to Gabriella.

She leaned on the table to steady herself. 'About that really. I think I've worked out why he's doing it.'

'That would be helpful. Do you think he'll start behaving again?'

She nodded.

'It seems such a shame because up until now, he's been a model student. I was most impressed that he came to school the day after Mr Denmead's funeral, which I understand he attended.'

It had been the hardest decision in her life, but Gabriella had thought it the only way to show the boys what she meant when she said Daddy was dead. She'd tried that he'd gone away, or was in Heaven and they'd both immediately asked if they could visit him in Heaven, or when he was coming back from Heaven. So, in the same way that her parents had insisted she go to her great auntie's funeral as a little girl, she'd taken both boys.

'I'm not sure they get that he's never coming back, but so far they seem to understand he's not here anymore.'

'Indeed.' Mr Coats nodded and smiled.

Gabriella explained she had a big birthday party planned in the next fortnight and was inviting all Jack's classmates. She was going to make a big fuss of him, and explain that it was still his big day and he could have whatever he wanted.

'Is there anything we can do to support you, Mrs Denmead?'

Bring Arnie back from the dead. 'What like?'

'We can keep an eye on Jack, ensure he's not withdrawn, or misbehaving. We can give him more one-to-one time with a TA, if that would help.'

'TA?' She knew she should be aware of what this abbreviation meant, because she'd probably been told it before, but today her mind felt like a sieve, all the words and things to remember just flowing through it, lost forever.

'Teaching assistant. We have them to support students with their learning.'

'He's not...' *What was the right word to use?* Of course it had slipped her mind. '...special needs.' That felt inoffensive enough.

'Jack is very bright. He will do exceptionally well in his exams, and I'd be very surprised if he didn't go to university, one of the red brick ones.' He leaned his elbows on the table, looking from Gabriella to Helen and back. 'This significant life event is understandably affecting his behaviour and therefore his ability to learn. A little assistance to steer him back on track would be our pleasure to give.'

Red brick universities, exceptionally well in his exams... Well, she'd been told this before but hadn't actually heard it from a teacher so clearly. Gabriella looked to Helen.

She nodded.

'Yes. We'll take that. As long as Jack's okay with it. Yes. Any help. Thank you sir. And I'm sorry for Jack's behaviour.'

He shook his head. 'No need to apologise. We simply wanted to discuss and agree a plan of action for your son. Is there anything else you think he'd benefit from, Mrs Denmead?'

Except his daddy back, she reflected bitterly. Swallowing the ball of grief she shook her head.

He mentioned some paperwork needing to be completed and asked her to have a conversation with Jack so the TA didn't come out of nowhere.

They shook hands and said goodbye.

In the car, she thanked Helen. 'I don't know what I'd have done without you.'

'I did very little. You were magnificent.'

She'd not been called that before. Not about anything to do with school, definitely. A warmth filled her stomach. She felt as if Helen had come into her life at the point when she most needed a mum. 'I meant to ask you, what did he mean about red brick unis when he was talking about Jack?'

'Older ones, in big cities, difficult to get into and renowned for their research.'

'That's good, is it?'

'Indeed it is.'

Gabriella smiled, imagining Jack going off to uni and coming back in the holidays, telling her about what he'd been learning. 'Don't suppose you know anyone who'd like to help me organise a party for twenty six-year-olds, do you?'

A look of concentration crossed Helen's face. After a moment, she said, 'I'm not really au fait with the paraphernalia for children. I'm still rather glum, so probably not the best person to help organise a party. Ian, however, hasn't got an awful lot on at the moment...'

'I'll ask him.'

'Sorry.'

'No need. Totally get it. You can come if you want.'

'We'll see,' Helen said.

Chapter 17

Helen had tried to have the same conversation with Bill, asking him if he wanted to spend time together and he'd ignored it, batted it off, dismissing it as if it were the most trivial request.

Helen arrived at the lido, enjoying the sun as it warmed her shoulders.

She completed fifty lengths in complete silence, still turning over the idea in her mind, wondering if she could, where to start. She saw Gabriella with Thomas in the shallow end, by one of the fountains. Thomas was splashing and Gabriella paddling in a clearly designer, brightly floral swimming costume.

They waved.

Helen swam towards them, feeling more than usually glum.

Gabriella looked her up and down. 'I was just saying that you look like you've got the worries of the world on your shoulders.'

Helen didn't reply. Best not. She pursed her lips.

'What's wrong?' Gabriella asked.

'I don't want you to feel sorry for me. Couldn't bear that.' It was very important to Helen that she tell her this.

'I don't feel sorry for you.'

'Good.'

'At first, I just wanted to talk to you. Some additional adult company never goes to waste.'

'Indeed.'

'But now, I care for you. You're my friend. I want to see you with a smile, not with a face like a wet weekend in Clacton.'

Perhaps she was telling the truth. Gabriella struck Helen as an uncomplicated woman. A person who wears one's heart on one's sleeve. If only Helen could behave this way.

'If you're sure?' Helen asked carefully.

Gabriella nodded.

Without further thought, Helen knelt in the water, and put her arms around Gabriella, pulling her tightly into a hug. The sobs of relief were barely kept inside as she gasped, determined not to make more of a show than absolutely necessary. 'Thank you. From the bottom of my heart. Thank you.'

From over her shoulder, Gabriella said, 'What for? I've not done nothing.'

Helen stood. 'You really have.' She'd been there, she'd *seen* Helen, she'd been herself. And Helen put her goggles on then pushed off the bottom of the pool, propelling herself into the water, swimming most of the length submerged.

She returned to the shallow end, where Gabriella and Thomas were playing with a ball.

'Seen Ian about?' Gabriella asked cheerily.

Just like that, no histrionics, no embarrassment, Gabriella would take it on face value and move on. Helen wished she'd mastered that skill at Gabriella's age.

'He was on the running machine. Running as if his life depended upon it.' Quietly, Helen said, 'I wonder what he's running away from now… See you at our table. I must get on.' She nodded towards the changing booths.

Shortly, Helen joined Ian and Gabriella at their corner table with their usual drinks awaiting them.

They had been talking, but when Helen sat, there was silence.

Helen wasn't about to fill it with unnecessary chatter, unlike some people who didn't know how to appreciate silence.

Cutlery rattled against crockery. The chatter of people in the distance competed with the music Helen failed to recognise since it wasn't from her era and sounded the same as all modern music.

'I think,' Helen began carefully, 'I'm in need of your assistance.'

'At your service,' Ian replied.

'Poised and ready,' Gabriella said with a smile.

'It's no laughing matter.' A lump formed in her throat at the enormity of what she was about to say. 'I think… What I mean to say is, I believe… I'm leaving him.' She swallowed. 'Bill. Of course.'

'Can we help?' Gabriella asked.

'I'm not sure.'

'Why not?'

'Because I'm at a loss as to where to start. Is it even possible? Can I really do it?' She felt completely unequal to this. Hopelessly lost in a sea of memories of their forty years together, contrasted with the last few years of his unbearable emotional frigidity.

'I've never left someone,' Gabriella said. 'Well, not a husband anyway. But I've left plenty of boyfriends, if that's any good?' She put her hand on Helen's forearm as it rested on the table.

It was such a gesture of kindness and friendship that Helen couldn't hold in the emotions any longer. She blinked slowly and two large tears rolled down her cheeks, landing in big splashes on the table and in her fennel tea.

Ian did the same. 'I've been dumped plenty of times. If that's any use too.' He shrugged.

'I'm not sure if I can. If I can be on my own after living my whole adult life as part of a couple, and not just any couple, with Bill.'

'You can stay at mine,' Ian offered. 'Spare bedroom. Own bathroom.'

'What am I meant to do? Simply pack a suitcase and leave?' It seemed far too simple.

'Yep, that's right,' Gabriella said. 'Not to sound big-headed, but I've got a massive house,' Gabriella said. 'You can have your own wing if you want. In fact you'd be doing me a favour.'

'How so?' Helen had an idea why, but perhaps a little unkindly, wanted Gabriella to spell it out.

'Additional adults. At home. It's been too long. Someone to have a good natter with.' Her eyes shone at the very mention.

'Right,' Helen said with uncertainty.

'You'll stay at mine,' Gabriella said.

'So I just pack a bag and leave?'

'That's what I did when I'd had enough of a crappy boyfriend.' Gabriella shrugged as if it were the simplest thing in the world.

'I wish I could say the same, but...' A wistful look crossed Ian's face.

'How do I decide what to take? Forty years' worth of stuff.'

'Whatever means something to you, or you need. It's surprising what you can do without once you've forgot you ever had it.' Gabriella blinked quickly, looking away for a moment. 'Things, of course.'

Not people. Helen was certainly not going to miss Bill. 'I don't think I know how to exist without being part of a couple.'

Ian gestured at her, from head to toe. 'We've known you, what, a few weeks, and never seen Bill. I've only ever heard you talking about doing stuff on your own.'

Alone is how Helen would describe it, the emphasis being slightly different from on one's own. 'You really think so?'

Gabriella said, 'You were wicked good at Jack's school.'

She scoffed, dismissing it. 'Whatever. It was nothing.'

'You're stronger than you think.'

'I'm really not.' Helen shook her head.

'Do you want me to help you pack?' Gabriella asked.

'That would be really helpful.'

And so, somehow, with nothing more than a plan to do it and someone to help her, Helen seemed to have agreed to leave Bill.

They moved on to other topics of discussion, she drank much more tea than she'd anticipated, and before she knew it, Ian and Gabriella had said goodbye and left her alone at the table. She returned for another swim and reminded herself what she'd just agreed to do.

Bill wouldn't understand, possibly he wouldn't notice.

That was why, Helen decided while vigorously drying herself with a towel, she had to leave him.

Chapter 18

Much to his surprise, Ian enjoyed helping Gabriella organise Jack's party. He bought balloons and party bags, and sweets and toys to put in the bags. He booked a face-painting clown and a magician.

The sun shone, golden and warm, in a blue sky. The flat-roofed Spanish hacienda-style white house was well suited to the heat. Inside it remained cool, without the need for air conditioning.

Ian had filled the pool with buckets to keep within the terms of a hosepipe ban that had been in place for a while since the heatwave had continued.

Tables and chairs were placed under the shade of the house, laid with a colourful paper tablecloth and balloons tied to the chair backs. Helen reclined under the shade of a tree, watching the children playing.

Ian led a game of pass the parcel while Gabriella continued making food inside. 'You'll be fine,' she'd said, before leaving him.

There was a paddling pool and a water slide where the children went slipping and sliding on their stomachs all the way to the end, before running back to the start and repeating it.

Gabriella appeared from the house. 'Can you help me bring the food out please? When's the clown arriving?'

Ian checked his watch. 'Now. I'll call him.'

She smiled, returning to the kitchen with Helen.

The clown arrived in a car with each panel painted a different colour. 'Are you Ian?' he said as he collected his bag from the seat.

Ian nodded. The clown scratched his red frizzy hair, sitting in the car, he changed shoes to long wide blue ones. He stood, put his hands in the pockets of the over-sized blue dungarees. 'Where's the birthday boy?'

'Jack's out the back.'

'Before we go, can I check, does he like clowns? I ask because some kids are terrified. I just wanted to make sure.'

'He loves clowns. Although his friends, I can't vouch for. Now, if you don't mind.' Ian led the clown to the back garden.

The children turned and shouted when they saw him, running closer and jumping up and down.

Jack ran to Ian. 'Is he for me?'

Ian knelt on the ground. 'Unless there's any other birthday boys here.' He looked in an exaggerated way from side to side. 'I can't see any.'

The clown began his act, juggling, balancing a ball on his nose, squirting water at himself, and the children watched in awe.

Helen appeared holding a tray of sandwiches. She placed them on a table along with the other food. 'Where's Thomas?'

A pair of shoes emerged from beneath the buffet table. Lifting the table cloth, he crouched and found Thomas sucking his thumb and looking thoroughly glum.

Helen joined him, holding out her hands. 'Aren't you going to join in the fun?'

He shook his head.

'There's a clown. And ice cream. Mummy's making lots of nice food. Are you hungry?'

He nodded, shuffling out from underneath the table, then stood. 'Where's the food?'

Helen took his hand and led him to the table where she had placed a large birthday cake. 'Food is served!'

The children stood around the table, grabbing paper plates, loading up with crisps, sandwiches, slices of cake.

Helen looked at the ground and shuffled from one foot to the other.

'Are you all right?' Gabriella asked.

'I really am. I hadn't appreciated how much I missed being around children. They really are pure joy, aren't they?'

Gabriella nodded. 'Until they're not!' She winked.

'I used to organise Peter's birthday parties. Loved it. I'd forgotten what it felt like.'

'What felt like?'

Helen held Thomas's hand, wiping off the crisps and sandwich debris. 'Being needed. Being seen.' She looked at the far side of the garden, composing herself.

Gabriella hugged her.

'You get used to unhappiness. And then this.' She gestured at the garden filled with children playing happily. 'I've made up my mind, I shall leave him.'

There was silence as they all appreciated the importance of Helen finally coming to this conclusion herself.

'I was wondering where you'd disappeared to, Gabriella,' came a woman's voice behind them.

'Speaking of unhappiness,' Gabriella whispered to Helen and Ian. She turned to face the other woman. 'Hello! How lovely of you to come.'

They air kissed.

Gabriella introduced them to Amanda who wore a flowing yellow and blue dress, large sunhat, and oversize designer sunglasses.

'You've done such a good job, all things considered.' Amanda looked at Gabriella, tilting her head. 'I think I'd die without my housekeeper. There's only so many hours in the day, aren't there?'

Gabriella smiled and nodded.

Another woman arrived wearing long dangling gold earrings and a white blouse. A small boy was suspended on her hip. She greeted Amanda and Gabriella before turning to Ian. 'And who are you? I'm Emily. I've not seen you at the school gates. A father who parents; you're a dying breed.'

Ian introduced himself. 'I'm just helping out today.'

'No children? Wife?' Emily gave him a pitying look over her sunglasses.

'Nope.'

'Single? Oh dear.'

'Gay,' Ian said, beginning to enjoy this. 'Very.'

'Are you? Well, you don't look gay.'

Ian wasn't about to cause a scene by asking her precisely what a gay man should look like, so he said, 'Is this your little one?'

Emily shifted the boy on her hip. 'Yes, this is Beau. And Dora is currently eating a month's worth of sugar at the end of the table.' She turned to Gabriella. 'Are there more natural options for the children?'

'No... Ice cream and jelly is next,' Gabriella said.

There soon followed a conversation about the weather and Gabriella and Ian extricated themselves from the two women while Helen returned to her chatter with Thomas.

Gabriella emptied a large packet of cheesy crisps into a bowl and placed it on the table. 'Dig in!'

A tall man with dark blond hair, wearing a jacket, shirt and jeans, walked up to her, and they shook hands. Gabriella nodded towards Amanda and Emily.

He laughed, led her gently by the shoulder to a table, where he produced a bottle from a bag, and soon they were drinking wine from plastic glasses.

Must be Simon, Ian thought, so he left them to it.

Later, as they were clearing up the mess once all the children had left, Gabriella confirmed this, said she'd had a wonderful time chatting to him but that she felt guilty for having wine while in charge of a children's party. Ian said he and Helen were more than capable.

'He's very handsome,' Ian said.

'Is he? Can't say I've noticed. Tall, is all I picked up.' Gabriella bit her bottom lip and blushed.

Ian nodded and continued folding up the chairs from the lawn.

Ian couldn't believe that as well as being unemployed and lying to his husband, he had another problem. Although he'd mentioned it to Helen and Gabriella, he found discussing it very difficult. He wasn't sure if it would be easier talking to another man about it. At least they would have some idea what it felt like.

He hoped.

Drew was standing in their kitchen contemplating what to make for dinner. He wore jeans that showed off his muscular behind and a polo shirt that did the same.

By rights it should in some way get Ian going, but he felt nothing.

Ian had spoken at length to Helen and Gabriella about the big lie he'd continued telling to Drew and they'd agreed he needed to come clean.

'Why were you home so early yesterday?' Drew asked.

Ian had left the lido after having his fill of being told by the other two that he should tell his husband he was unemployed.

'I wasn't feeling well,' Ian said.

They had insisted they hadn't ganged up on him, but given it was the sole topic of conversation for most of the morning, with them persuading him it would be for the better to share the problem than keeping it to himself, he felt it was much more than strong-arming.

'What's wrong?' Drew asked.

The problem, Ian reflected, with a lie, was that it begets more of them. 'Nothing. Twenty-four-hour bug, or something.' He bit his bottom lip. He looked at the time on the kitchen clock.

Helen was due shortly, to accompany him while he came clean with Drew.

'Are you late for something?' Drew asked.

'A friend is coming round.'

'Who?'

Normally Drew knew all of Ian's friends, but he definitely didn't know Helen, nor how they'd met. 'Helen,' he said simply.

'Haven't heard of her. Where do you know her from?' Drew busied himself making toast. 'Will she want feeding?'

The doorbell rang.

'I shouldn't think so,' Ian said, walking to answer it. He let her in.

'You look terrible,' she said. 'Have you not slept?'

He hadn't, but that was no change from normal. Well, the new normal. He shook his head.

'I'm going to tell him, as agreed?' she asked.

'I'll do it,' he said tightly, as his brain started frantically back-pedalling.

'If you're sure.'

He nodded. 'Yes. You're just here for...'

'Moral support?'

'That's the one.' He led them into the kitchen.

Drew was sitting at the table eating toast. He stood, extended a large hand for Helen to shake. 'I'm Drew.'

She introduced herself, shook his hand then sat at the table.

Ian couldn't sit, he was fidgeting and felt unsettled and shaky. *I wish I'd cancelled on her.* Bloody woman, interfering. He knew that was uncharitable and Helen was only trying to help and go along with their plan. Without asking, he made Helen a herbal tea.

'Thanks,' she said accepting it.

'How did you know what she liked?' Drew peered at the mug.

Helen laughed. 'Oh, we go way back. Worked together at the... Err, that place...' She laughed nervously. 'He's well aware of my peculiarities of taste.' She sipped it. 'Raspberry, so wonderfully refreshing.'

'What brings you here?' Drew asked.

Helen put the mug on the table, folded her hands in a praying position, placing them on the table carefully. 'I'm afraid I have something to tell you. That Ian should have told you but wasn't able.' She looked at him, made eye contact.

He looked away, staring at the floor as his palms sweated and sickness filled his stomach.

Helen nodded, indicating he should go on.

'There's something I've been keeping from you that I shouldn't,' he said unsteadily.

Horror clouded Drew's face as he looked from Helen to Ian. 'You can tell me anything. You know that, don't you?'

In theory, Ian knew this. But in practice it was another thing entirely.

Helen said, 'It's rather delicate. Ian has—'

'I,' he stared hard at her, widening his eyes to show her she definitely didn't need to go on. 'I—' *Just say it, tell him you've lost your job. That you're looking for a new one. That all will be okay.*

'Go on,' Drew said, holding Ian's hand.

He remembered the day when he was told his skills were no longer required. The pain of being thrown on the scrap heap at his age still burned to his core.

'Is it work?' Drew asked.

'I'm unwell,' Ian said.

'What's wrong? You've seemed not yourself lately. Withdrawn, quiet, less sociable.'

Ian hadn't considered his behaviour had changed that much to warrant that. He wasn't sure what to do with that information.

'It's all linked,' Helen began carefully. 'I read a very interesting biography about it. Happens to the best of people. Takes away part of one's identity it seems. In particular for men.' She looked to Drew, indicating he should continue.

'I should have told you. I know that now. But it's so difficult. Once you've told one lie, they grow and multiply.'

'It can't be that bad,' Drew said with feeling.

'There are plenty of resources to help, something of an online community it seems. Which surprised me. It's the lack of structure to one's day that many people struggle with. Once you...' She folded her hands on her lap.

Oh shit, she's going to tell him. Reveal the big ugly lie I've been telling Drew for months. Nearly four months now. And no sign of a job either.

'I'm impotent,' Ian said, more through desperation than anything else.

Helen looked away in obvious shock.

'Are you?' Drew frowned.

It had been going on for some time, and Ian had made excuses: that he was tired, he'd been drinking, he was too bloated from food. But each time he'd rejected Drew's advances because he knew he couldn't respond. His stupid body wouldn't respond.

A look of horror and confusion crossed Helen's face. She became very interested in the contents of her mug, staring at it intently.

'You're... I don't...' Drew glanced at Helen, then back to Ian. 'Don't you think we should talk about this privately?'

Helen stood, collecting her mug. 'I agree.' She left it next to the sink. 'I'm away now.' She left.

'I don't understand. Why would you tell me that, while she's here?'

Ian didn't know either. Except that it had seemed preferable to coming clean about the real lie. He shrugged.

'I didn't know. I thought it was a one off, that you were stressed. How can I not know this about my husband? It doesn't make sense. How long?'

'Few months.' The truth was, it had come on at the same time he'd lost his job. His opinion about himself had slipped, affecting his self-belief, and anxiety had started to dog him with everything. Who was he even without a job? Would Drew want him? Ian wouldn't want Ian, not like this.

Silently, Drew stood, strode closer, and hugged Ian. Pulling him in for a powerful hug, his strong arms wrapping around Ian, like a seatbelt in a car. Holding Ian together after so long when he'd felt his unstructured days and directionless self-opinion had led him to this now.

Over his head, Drew said, 'We'll sort this. Trust me, it's all going to be fine.'

Ian hadn't thought it possible, but he felt even more guilty than before. Not only had he failed at telling Drew one of the root causes for this problem, but he'd rejected the one person who'd agreed to help him, and told her the most private and intimate problem he had. Because, at the time, it had seemed preferable to coming clean about the big ugly lie of how pointless a person he really was. As a man, as a husband, as a friend too.

Oh god, why did he make things so hard for himself? Ian screwed his eyes tightly closed, hoping the tears he felt forming wouldn't fall. At least not yet anyway.

Chapter 19

'Is it bad to hate the only two grandparents my kids have?' Gabriella asked.

'Hate is a very strong word,' Ian said.

'I need more information,' Helen said. 'What happened to *your* parents?'

Ian nodded.

They were sitting on sun loungers next to the lido's outdoor pool, with the fountain loudly splashing in the background. In the full sun, she enjoyed the heat on her skin, made her trick herself into believing she was abroad.

The lido was surprisingly full for that time of morning on a weekday. TheLonely Hearts Lido Club had claimed their usual pitch in the corner, taking advantage of the morning's sun, while retaining a parasol if Ian's light skin colour meant he had to take shelter.

'Mum and Dad died.' She swallowed the ball of grief in her throat.

'Did they meet Jack and Thomas?' Ian asked.

Gabriella shook her head. 'They saw me carrying Jack. Dad died of a heart attack, that's what forty ciggies a day and all the fried breakfasts you can eat will do to you.'

'I'm so sorry,' Ian said.

'Mum didn't smoke. Well, passive smoking, she did. But anyway, after Dad went, she sort of faded away. Curled up into a ball, like a crumpled bit of paper.'

'What do you mean?' Helen asked.

'Stopped caring about anything. Didn't get up, dress. I'd pop round the tower block and she'd still be in her dressing gown in the middle of the afternoon. I helped her organise Dad's funeral and she sort of went along with it. But after they put him in the ground, the offers of help sort of dried up.' It had been the same for her, when Arnie had died. Maybe this was a known thing, get the funeral over and done with and the grieving person is good to go back to their life.

Gabriella rubbed factor ten sun cream into her arms and legs, called Thomas over by offering him a sip of juice, then holding onto him with one hand, smothered him in factor fifty.

'Let's leave it there for today. It's obviously painful for you to recount,' Helen said.

'It's fine. She's with Dad now, so that's all that matters.' Gabriella sniffed. 'I used to put her hands on my belly, letting her feel Jack kicking. I had him three weeks later, to the day. Called the police, they come round with an ambulance crew, certified her dead. Asked what I was doing in her place, why did I have me own key. All that bollocks. I told 'em. Didn't have nothing to hide. Once they'd done what they needed, I opened the window.'

'Why?' Ian asked.

'To let her soul out.' Helen looked at Gabriella, tears in her eyes, as she blinked. 'That's right, isn't it?'

Gabriella nodded. 'I done the same for Dad, when he was in hospital. Got told off for it, but I didn't care. Mum liked that. She thanked me.'

There was a silence as they all absorbed what Gabriella had just told them.

Quietly, Gabriella said, 'So I miss 'em. They were on my side, always... Whereas Arnie's parents...'

'Aren't?'

Gabriella tried to think how to explain the attitudes of her parents-in-law. 'They told me they wanna see the boys. How they hadn't spent time with 'em for ages. How they were the only thing they had of Arnie left.' Gabriella sighed as the wave of grief crashed over her, winding her.

'That must be very challenging,' Helen said diplomatically.

'I know it's not normal to lose a child. It's meant to be the parents who go first. I get that. But...' She shook her head. She couldn't explain it. 'I've had enough of people making me feel bad with the school mums. I don't mind that cos it's for Jack. But family, is it too much to ask they aren't such bloody hard work? Or critical of me?'

Helen shook her head. 'Family is complicated. You can't choose it and it's laden with all this emotional baggage because people assume it's better to see them than not.'

'Exactly. If it wasn't for the boys, I'd never see Arnie's parents again. No need. If I could, I'd tell them to fuck off. The way they speak to me. Always have.'

'It's admirable that you haven't,' Helen said, 'that you're keeping your mouth shut for the boys' sake.'

She felt a bit better at that. Wasn't sure Pru and Edward appreciated it though. 'I grew up with both sets of grandparents. Mum's were in Mexico and we saw them once a year; Mum and Dad saved up for their plane fares and they'd live with us for months. Dad's were round the corner, and we saw them every day. I loved them both.'

'Sounds idyllic,' Helen said.

Gabriella shrugged.

'When are you summoned to see Arnie's parents?' Ian asked.

'That's the right word. Summoned. It's like I'm only there because I come with the boys. They don't actually want to see me.'

'I'm sure that's not true,' Helen said. 'If Peter had a life partner, I'm sure I'd welcome him or her into my life.'

'When and to what have you been summoned?' Ian asked.

'Friday night. They've suggested we make it a regular thing. Implied it's what Arnie would have wanted.'

'Tell them no. It's impossible.' Helen shook her head.

It wasn't that simple. 'Arnie's parents are their godparents and named in his will as guardians if anything happens to him.'

'But not while you're still alive, surely?'

'No. But they don't half bring it up. It's what Arnie would have wanted, after all he trusted them to bring up his kids if he couldn't. It would have been simpler if it wasn't for the hold they have over me.'

'I thought you were okay for money,' Helen said.

She had said this, very openly explained that Arnie's insurance pay-out had paid off the mortgage and left her with enough to live off. What she hadn't said, because it was happening now, was that Arnie had made no provision for the boys' school fees. She'd assumed the insurance would be so much that she wouldn't have to worry, or think about getting a job.

'I can live off the money. No mortgage. I'm not poor. It was one thing that Arnie sorted. Thank Christ!'

'How can they have a hold over you?'

'The boys. If it was up to me, I'd have put them in a normal school. Before they started. I didn't know anything about private schools. I didn't even think it was an option. But Arnie said he wanted them to go private, like he had. Only child, rich parents, why wouldn't they send him private? Both of ours he wanted to go down that road. I didn't know nothing about private schools, but he seemed to, was always going on about how it had given him confidence and a bloody good education, small class numbers, all the outside school activities. So that's what we done.'

'So what's the problem?' Ian asked.

Gabriella felt embarrassed, talking about money.

'I thought the money was enough. I never used to worry about it. It was a lot, the insurance pay-out. I'm very lucky. Don't get me wrong. I own the house. But I can't work, wouldn't know where to start, and well, it's not enough.'

'What are you spending it on?' Helen asked.

'Who knows? Food, house, cars, life.' Gabriella shrugged.

'Why do you put up with your in-laws treating you like this?'

'They pay nearly fifteen grand a year on school fees for Jack, and Thomas will go soon, making it thirty grand.'

'Ah,' Helen said. 'I see.'

'They set it up monthly, have done since Jack started. Goes straight to the school.'

'So you're stuck with them, and their disapproval?' Ian asked.

Gabriella swallowed. 'Or I take the boys out of school. Put them in a normal one. Jack got top ten percent in the entrance exam and Thomas top twenty. Doubt I'd get fifty percent.' She looked at the ground. It was definitely not what Arnie would have wanted. Nor was it really what Gabriella wanted for their boys. She knew she wasn't academic but both boys took after Arnie in that.

'So what does this have to do with your being summoned for dinner on Friday?' Ian asked.

Helen shook her head, leaning back in her chair. 'I should think it's perfectly obvious.'

Ian shrugged.

'They're happy to pay for the school fees, but only if they see their grandchildren more often. Am I right?' Helen asked.

Gabriella nodded. 'Except they didn't say it like that.'

'How did they put it?' Ian asked.

'It's what Arnie wanted,' Pru had said, 'I know that for a fact. We are happy to continue paying for Jack's school fees. Plus, when Thomas starts, we will happily pay for that too. Although, of course we would very much want to hear how they're getting on at school. Jack at first, and in advance of Thomas starting preschool. Every week should suffice.'

'Doesn't sound too bad,' Ian said.

'You have no idea.' It would be fucking awful. They always were. She knew it was a boring stereotype about the evil mother-in-law, but ever since first meeting her, she'd looked down her nose at Gabriella, right from her background, her career choice, how Arnie had met her and now everything they'd believed about her being an unfit mother had come true.

'What's up?' Ian asked.

Gabriella shook her head. Too much to explain. Too many issues from the past to dredge up. 'It's complicated.'

'Families always are,' Helen said.

'Not this bad.'

'Do you want me to come along this week?' Ian asked.

'Why?'

'Be your human shield. Take some of the pressure off you.'

'They'll love you.'

'Why?'

'Cos you're posh. Don't you think they'll reckon I'm dating you, or something?'

Ian held his left hand, waggling his ring finger. 'Married. To a man. So... Probably not on both counts.'

'Sounds eminently sensible to me,' Helen said.

'Have you agreed, to them paying for Thomas too?' Ian asked.

'I don't think I have much choice, do you?' Gabriella asked.

'One always has choices. It's one of the wonderful things about being human. Even if the choice is to do nothing. Remain as is.' A faraway look crossed her face.

'Nuff about me,' Gabriella said, sensing she'd over-stayed her welcome conversation-wise.

'What will you do?' Helen asked.

'I can't take Jack out of his school. Imagine the upheaval. Thomas has been looking forward to starting there ever since he started dropping off his older brother with me. Haven't they had enough change already this year?'

Helen smiled and raised her eyebrows.

'That means yes, doesn't it?'

'It means,' Helen said, 'You're their mother. You know better than anyone else what's best for them. This has to be a head decision not a heart one.'

That had been what Gabriella feared. 'Six o'clock on Friday.' She looked to Ian. 'All right?'

It still surprised her that Arnie hadn't sorted this in his will. He was always so organised and careful about this sort of thing. Perhaps, Gabriella acknowledged briefly, he always knew his parents would be happy to pay, long after he was gone.

He'd always refused to see how badly they treated Gabriella, brushing it off as a joke, or just wanting the best. The problem with that was it left Gabriella feeling she was far from the best, both for her children and Arnie.

With a sinking feeling, she agreed for Ian to join her at the first dinner. The first of many, she wondered...?

It was a warm evening, a cloudless sky, much more pleasant than during the day which had, at times in the full sun, felt slightly oppressive.

Pru opened the door, looking down at the two boys, pulling them in for a hug, holding them tightly. She stood. 'Welcome, Ian.' A hand was offered for him to shake.

He did so. 'Lovely to meet you, Mrs Denmead.'

She looked him up and down, smiling with approval. 'Enchanté.'

French. She never speaks French to me. I knew she'd love him. Gabriella leaned in for a brief and awkward hug from Pru.

Pulling back to look at her, Pru said, 'Gabriella, my dear, I don't know how you manage to remain so down-to-earth in your look, while coming from such a glamorous career.'

Gabriella shot Ian a look that indicated, *See what I said?*

Ian stood back, letting Gabriella and the boys enter first.

They sat at the large wooden dining table. Pru placed Gabriella at the far end of the table, the two boys were along one side, Ian opposite them with Edward and Pru at the end opposite Gabriella. Gabriella felt as if she was being interviewed for a job, and not doing well at that.

'Perhaps,' Pru began, 'you'd like to tell us how you know Gabriella?' She looked at Ian.

'We met locally. Swimming actually.'

She frowned. 'I didn't know you went swimming?' She looked at Gabriella.

There was a lot she didn't know about Gabriella. But she kept that to herself. 'It's great to keep me in shape. I know I'll never return to my modelling days, but it's important to look after yourself.'

'It is.' Turning back to Ian, Pru said, 'What do you do? Do you live locally?'

Such boringly predictable questions – Gabriella could have bet she'd ask Ian this. Pru was obsessed by stuff like this. She sighed.

'Something you'd like to share?' Pru asked her.

'No. Ian might not want to talk about that.'

Ian removed his elbows from the table. 'I'm head of policy for a think-tank. Was. Currently... Well, exploring other options.'

Why couldn't he just tell his husband that. As he'd described it, Gabriella reckoned it didn't sound too bad.

'I assume Gabriella has filled you in about our agreement?'

Ian mercifully said nothing. He raised his eyes at Gabriella. She said, 'I think it's better to talk about that without small ears listening in, don't you think?'

'I don't see why. Perfectly ordinary for grandparents to wish to see their grandchildren. Especially since they have no other grandparents to speak of.' She seemed to smile, but Gabriella couldn't be sure. Was she really that spiteful?

'It's very generous of you. Too generous in fact.' Gabriella reckoned she'd just grab the nettle by the horns or whatever the phrase was.

'Don't be ridiculous. Impossible. No such thing as too generous. A gift should always be accepted, for fear of offending the giver.'

Gabriella reckoned she'd heard something similar from her parents, mainly about Christmas and birthday presents, and she was pretty bloody sure it didn't apply to ongoing financial gifts, especially not ones that came with strings very firmly attached.

'Perhaps we'll eat and then we can return to this,' Pru said.

She served a complicated salad that the boys were suspicious of, asking Gabriella what most of it was, and ended up picking out the tomatoes and cucumber as the only bits they trusted. Smoked salmon, as she'd expected, didn't go down well either. It was almost as if they wanted to not try because they knew they'd see the boys next week whatever.

'Don't like it, Mummy,' Thomas said, spitting out the salmon onto the table.

The food was cleared away and over a dessert of ice cream, which the boys thankfully ate with enthusiasm, Pru asked, 'How has everyone been?' beaming at the two boys.

An answer didn't come as they busied themselves with spoonfuls of ice cream.

'I think Grandma means school,' Gabriella offered.

Jack shrugged. 'Can I have more?' He grinned in a way that could only be recognised as an Arnie look.

Gabriella's heart simultaneously burst with joy and broke into a thousand pieces with the pain that Arnie would never see this. 'Ask Grandma. And remember to say please.'

'Can I have some more, Grandma, please?'

Pru rose, left and returned shortly with the tub and a silver scoop, doling out more to both boys. 'Easy when you know how.' She sat.

The implication that Gabriella couldn't look after her children was obvious. She debated taking both boys by their hands and leaving. But she knew it wouldn't do any good. She couldn't cut their grandparents out of the boys' lives. It would upset Arnie and she couldn't bear to see their sad faces about not seeing Grandma and Grandpa any more. She wanted, with some care, to show the boys it was far more than giving them ice cream and it actually involved, on pain of death, expecting to see them every Friday night. Which was way too controlling.

She'd told Ian this.

Now, having remained quiet for some time, he said, 'I think what Gabriella is trying to say is the offer to continue paying for the boys' school fees is very generous. She would love for them to have more grandma and grandpa time in their lives. But an expectation of it every week is a tad excessive.'

'Forgive me, Ian, but when I want your advice I'll ask for it.'

He gave Gabriella a look, widened his eyes, biting his lips. 'I think—'

'We were seeing them almost this frequently before.'

Before Arnie died was unsaid. It was true, but Gabriella had gone along with it for Arnie's sake. Now that he was gone, his parents had dropped all pretence of liking her.

'You were,' Gabriella said. 'What happens if we can't see you? Do you stop paying the fees?'

'Don't be so ridiculous. Besides, we'd pay in advance, so we're hardly likely to ask for a refund, pending your behaviour.' Pru narrowed her eyes.

'Right.' It didn't feel as bad as she'd thought. 'Monthly?'

Pru knitted her eyebrows in an expression of disappointment. 'For paying one and shortly two boys' school fees? I don't think so.'

'I'd feel guilty if we said weekly and I couldn't manage it. Every other week, how's that sound?'

'Once a fortnight isn't satisfactory either. At this age they grow and change so quickly. You must understand we don't want to miss that, as Arnie obviously has.' She looked heavenwards, then back to Gabriella.

Way to guilt-trip me.

'Of course, we understand things come up. A busy mother's day is always full. But we should like it very much if you could do all you can to see us, with the boys, weekly. Unless you'd prefer we picked them up and they spent time with us without you.'

That, of all options, was the worst one imaginable. She'd believed them to be almost incapable of any kindness unless it was met with something in return. She'd never told Arnie this, and he dismissed as their own brand of humour the digs and jibes his parents made towards Gabriella. But the thought of them spending time with her children alone made Gabriella's mind up.

Finally she said, 'That's all right. We'll stick to me bringing them here. If I can't, I'll let you know. Plenty of notice.'

'Of course, these things inevitably happen. But with you not able to work, we hope this arrangement will make the most of your time and limited resources to the benefit of all concerned.'

'Yep.'

'We'd be very disappointed if that were to happen. Of course.'

'Course.'

The boys had ice cream around their mouths and were trying to spoon the last remaining mouthfuls of it into themselves.

'There, that wasn't so difficult, now, was it?'

The rest of the evening went in a blur and as she reached the car, and they had left the drive, she turned to Ian who was driving. 'I had no choice.'

'There's always a choice. Besides, I don't see they're so bad.'

'Tonight they were on their best behaviour. Well, she was. He's always along for the ride. It's all led by her. God, no one ever sees what I see.'

'This is what families do. How bad can they be? Why don't you accept their offer to look after the boys some-times?'

Because then it shows I really can't manage without Arnie. Because then I've well and truly given up. Because then I'd have great empty days I wouldn't have a clue what to do with.

'You could go back to your career,' he offered, not very helpfully.

She scoffed. 'Yeah right. Like they'd want me now.'

'You're very beautiful. Your eyes are the darkest brown and largest I've seen on a woman. Your hair would be great for a shampoo or something.'

'Piss off.' Her hair was one of her favourite features, when she allowed herself to admit it. Some women had gone grey by her age, or soon had it cut short. Hers was long and blonde and even though some days it would have been much simpler to cut it all off, she hadn't. It was one of the most striking things Arnie had noticed about her. When the style had been for short cuts, she'd kept hers long, flowing down to her waist, and tied it up instead.

'Piss off yourself,' Ian said with a laugh. 'Imagine what you could do with some time to yourself. Maybe you need to let go sometimes. They are their grandparents. How bad can they be?'

Gabriella wasn't going to tell Ian some of the stuff Arnie had told her about his childhood: being packed off to a boarding school at seven, crying in loneliness while his parents insisted it would toughen him up. The bullying at school was bad enough, but it was the fact that Arnie's parents hadn't done anything about it, told him it was to be expected, it was just boys being boys.

She'd promised never to tell anyone. Besides, they were thirty years older now. She was sure they would say they'd moved on, as had attitudes about parenting, and they weren't those people anymore, but Gabriella believed that some things stuck to you, no matter how far in the past they were. And even if they didn't, she didn't want Pru and Edward parenting her boys, so she decided if they were to see the kids, she'd make sure she was always there too.

Chapter 20

June

Helen was in the kitchen, wiping the work surface furiously. Her suitcases were leaning against the wall. The house felt empty, even though she was still in it.

The doorbell rang. Helen opened the door.

Gabriella stood there and smiled. 'Ready?'

'I ought to be, since I've had years to get ready.' She shrugged. 'Shall we have a drink first?'

Gabriella shrugged. 'If you want. When's he due home from work?'

'Six, which means eight.' Helen turned and made them a coffee on the machine Bill had bought her last Christmas. She placed them on the table, sitting carefully. She told her when she had received the machine as a gift.

'I didn't think you liked caffeine,' Gabriella said, sipping her drink.

'I don't.'

'And so why?' She pointed to the mug.

Helen raised her eyebrows. 'Reminds me why I dislike it so.' She sipped her coffee, then put the mug on the table and pushed it away slowly.

'I think we should go. There's plenty for you to do at my place.' Gabriella had finished her coffee. 'Are you writing a note? I think no. Leaving is the note itself.

Right? A text maybe. But a note, it feels a bit... Old-fashioned.'

'That's Bill and me.'

'Not you.' Gabriella shook her head. 'Ready.' She stood.

'Can we sit for a little while? Please?'

'Of course.' Gabriella put her hands in a praying position, resting on the table, closed her eyes.

It must be some comfort, like Gabriella, to have religion to fall back on, upon which one could rely for succour. Helen had been C of E, but then had lapsed and given what she'd seen more recently, had decided if God did move in mysterious ways, he was behaving inordinately mysteriously of late.

Helen made hot water and a slice of lemon and she slowly sipped it while writing a note to Bill. Finally finished both, she stood back to admire her handiwork.

Helen's phone rang, it was Bill. 'I'm packed.'

'Splendid, going anywhere nice?' he asked.

'Staying with a friend.' Helen bit her bottom lip.

'When will you return? I don't remember this being on the calendar.'

'Spur of the moment. It's not a holiday, it's...'

'Look, I'm just calling to let you know I'll be home late tonight. Didn't want you waiting to eat. I'll grab something in the canteen.'

'Very considerate of you. But you needn't have bothered.'

'Are you okay?' Bill said with uncertainty.

'I'm leaving.'

'You said. Look, I'm terribly busy, I just wanted to tell you to eat on your own. All right?'

'What if it's not?'

'Not what?'

'All right,' Helen said, marshalling her temper, but only just.

'Why are you talking in riddles? Have you been drinking? I said that lunchtime drinking on your own was a slippery slope, did I not?'

Helen's jaw tightened. 'I'm leaving you.'

'What?'

'There's a note. I'm packed, and I'm off. Not a holiday, more a parting of the ways. If I'm to live alone in this life, I might as well do it properly, without having to worry just in case you change, start seeing me.'

Bill chuckled. 'Is this some kind of joke?'

'Not in the slightest. I'm stone cold sober, have never been more serious in my life. I'm leaving you.'

'You can't do this!'

'And yet, here I am, bags packed and ready to go.' She paused, waiting to put the phone down, hoping against all previous experience that he'd beg her to stay, fight for her, tell her how much he'd miss her and that he loved her.

'I can't talk to you when you're like this. I'll call later when you're talking sense.' A pause, and then: 'Bye.' He ended the call.

Helen stared at the phone.

'Is he coming round, begging you to stay, confessing his undying love for you?'

'No, no and for the avoidance of doubt, no.' Helen blinked away a tear. Stupid really, for it had confirmed what she believed to be true. Bill didn't care for her nor see her, and had become so used to her being there, in the background, that he refused to believe she'd do anything about it. Well, she'd show him.

'Ready?' Gabriella asked, standing, stepping towards the door, collecting one of Helen's suitcases.

She nodded, smoothing the paper as it lay on the kitchen table.

'Can I read it, your note?' Gabriella asked.

'Of course, it's hardly *War and Peace*.' She chuckled.

'*I give up, M,*' Gabriella read. Looking up, she went on, 'Short and sweet. Let's go.'

Helen had said it all, over the years and just now, on the phone. She couldn't have the same conversation with Bill again. Bill had defeated her. In the face of her optimism, Bill's inability to change had beaten her.

Helen collected the smaller suitcase as Gabriella had taken the larger. They wheeled them out of the kitchen, into the hallway, where Peter's coats had used to hang by the door. Where his shoes had stood neatly in two rows to one side. Where once, Helen had tried to have a stand-up row with Bill, shouting that she would not be treated like this, that she would not be married to a man who behaved like this. And Bill had looked back at her with his watery light blue eyes and said, 'Well, you very much seem to be,' and left.

Now, Helen shut the door with a satisfying click, stepped onto the drive – that she'd had laid – and into her car.

Gabriella's car was reversing and now faced towards the road.

Helen backed hers out and followed Gabriella to her home.

A short drive later they were at Gabriella's place. Helen stopped by the roadside, switched off the engine. A white building, dark wooden door and window frames, orange tiles, balconies filled with bougainvillaea and bright blue and yellow plants stuck out at all first-floor windows. A Hispanic casa. It looked perfectly incongruent with the other houses, but it was wonderfully Gabriella.

Gabriella opened the car door. 'Come on. Welcome to the first day of the rest of your life.'

It sounded so dramatic and Helen wasn't remotely convinced it would be such a monumental change. She held onto the steering wheel, staring straight ahead.

'Coming?' Gabriella asked brightly.

'In a minute.' And then something occurred to her. 'Where is Thomas?'

'First day at preschool.'

Helen's heart jumped with joy at the sense of opportunity and new beginnings it stirred within her. But it warred with her dull, dead-end memory of her last holiday with Bill, before she'd decided not to bother again.

Helen stepped out of the car, retrieved her bags from the boot and walked into Gabriella's spacious, well-kept home.

Standing in the hallway, next to her bags, Helen admired the spiral staircase, the room was filled with light from windows in the ceiling. The walls had dark panels of wood, and stained glass stood atop the large, heavy front door. It reminded Helen of an old Catholic church. She supposed it was deliberate, given Gabriella's religion.

'Your home is very beautiful,' she said.

'Thank you. I'll show you to your room.' Gabriella took the heaviest case, despite Helen trying to wrestle it off her. She led them up the marble stairs into a bedroom with a double bed, wardrobe along one wall, en suite bathroom and a balcony.

Helen wondered what the balcony overlooked… Well, it wouldn't be much, it would just overlook suburban Ruislip, but a balcony nevertheless.

Gabriella opened the French windows, led her onto the balcony. Half of it was in dappled shade, the other full sun. It contained a small table and two chairs, and below were rows and rows of Victorian terraced houses, stretching as far as Helen could see. In the far distance were green hills and forest, signalling the ribbon of moving traffic between the homes and green that would be the M25.

'Is it okay?' Gabriella asked.

'It's beautiful. I feel as if I'm on holiday. I shan't outstay my welcome.' Helen reached into her handbag and found her purse. Opening it, she found some money and pressed it into Gabriella's hands.

'I won't accept.' She motioned as such.

Helen knew she could do with it, since hearing about the new arrangement she was resisting with her parents in law. 'I insist.'

'I think you'll be gone very soon and we won't need to worry about any of that.' Gabriella put the money into Helen's handbag.

'I wish I had your optimism.' Helen rolled her eyes.

'I'll leave you to make yourself at home. I've gotta do some cleaning and then I wondered what you fancied doing today?'

'When do the boys finish school?'

'Two thirty.' Gabriella left.

Helen checked the time – they had over four hours to kill.

Wonderful.

Helen met Gabriella in the kitchen, making some food. Her back was facing Helen as she rolled something on the work surface.

'I don't know what to do,' Helen said.

'Then you'll help me with this.'

'What are you making?'

'Sausage rolls but Mexican.'

Helen stood next to her – there was a bowl of pink meat and herbs, sheets of pastry rolled thinly on the floured surface.

'Arnie used to like sausage rolls and I thought they was boring. Mum used to make them with Chorizo, guacamole and spicy meat. So I made up my own recipe. The boys loved it. Arnie loved it. So because today is the first day when I'm in the house on my own, I thought I'd whip some up for us.' She stood back, admiring her handiwork.

'Very sensible.'

Helen became Gabriella's sous chef, rolling, cutting, seasoning and baking until they had two dozen perfectly golden Gabriella rolls.

They ate some for lunch and Helen, for the first time in a while, actually tasted them. Rather than eating in silent frustration as Bill read next to her.

'How's your room? Settled in okay?' Gabriella asked after they'd finished.

'I am. I think the balcony is a wonderful touch.'

'So did I. And Arnie after I convinced him. He wanted to remove them all. The house was built in the Mexican style, a hacienda, just like my grandparents'. Some architect designed it himself apparently. I fell in love with it. It was a total fixer-upper when we bought it.'

'Very impressive. You must be very proud.'

Gabriella nodded. 'It's important for me to stay here, for the memories of the house.'

'I understand.' Their house was the same, except of late the memories had become less happy and had somehow sullied the earlier ones of bringing up the children there.

'What are you thinking?' Gabriella tidied up their plates.

'Nothing. You don't want to hear it. Trust me. I barely want to hear it.'

'Fancy going shopping?'

'I don't need anything.'

Gabriella shook her head, tutting loudly. 'That's not the point of this sort of shopping. You have so much to learn.'

'Shall we tell Ian not to expect us at the lido today?' She'd become not only used to, but quite reliant on their daily meetings there. They had become more important than the swimming, which now seemed secondary. The sure knowledge of adult company, conversation, a problem shared being a problem, even if not halved, certainly easier to manage. Gabriella and Ian had become, in the absence of anyone else, if not actually, a very strong substitute for her family.

'He's probably grateful for a break from us, after my family dinner.' Gabriella sighed, shaking her head.

Summer was in full swing, too warm to walk outside in the full sun, and everyone wearing shorts and T-shirts. They went to the welcome, air-conditioned cool of the shopping centre in Uxbridge and bought a variety of items, none of which Helen particularly needed, but it did pass the time and stop her wondering when Bill would call, having seen her note.

They collected the two boys from school, who were pleased to see Helen in the car.

A dashing looking man waved at Gabriella from his car.

'Who's that?' Helen asked.

'Simon. He came to the party, remember?'

'Yes. Friends, are you?'

Gabriella shrugged. 'Waving terms.' She stared at the man as he parked, stepped out of his large car and hugged two little girls, before helping them into the car.

Good father. 'Married?' Helen asked.

'Dunno. If he is, I've never seen her.'

'Right.'

Jack, from the rear seat said, 'Mummy, who is the lady?'

'I told you, this is Mummy's friend, Helen. Remember?'

Jack nodded. 'Do you know Grandma and Grandpa?'

'Because you look similar, I suppose,' Gabriella said by way of explanation as they drove home.

Over dinner – chicken risotto with lots of tomato and garlic that Helen was very impressed both boys ate without complaint – Helen checked her phone obsessively.

'Put it in your bedroom,' Gabriella said firmly. 'Better still, switch it off.'

'What if he thinks I'm dead.' The thought of Bill not knowing her whereabouts was too much to take.

'Let him.' Gabriella took Helen's phone, switched it off and they resumed dinner.

She helped read the boys bedtime stories – the memory of doing so with her children hit her like a warm hug – her ability to do it without thinking impressed her and surprised Gabriella.

'Like riding a bike,' Helen had said, as Thomas cuddled up to her while she perched on his bed and read to him.

Gabriella had mouthed 'thanks' and gone to Jack's bedroom.

Helen had switched her phone on and was disappointed to find no messages.

As they sat not watching TV and drinking wine, Gabriella said, 'Anything?'

'I don't think so. But I'm never one hundred percent sure when I've switched it off. Can you check?' She handed her phone over.

Gabriella inspected it, pressed a few buttons, handing it back. 'Nothing.'

There was no further conversation as the TV's noise filled the room. Helen was unsurprised at their companionable acceptance of quiet in this way. She supposed it was because they were used to this, while sitting in the café, laying by the lido's pool, or even observing Ian in the gym. She had friends of many decades who were pathologically incapable of comfortably sitting in silence with her. Always needing to dive into the quiet and say something, no matter how trivial or pointless.

Helen's shoulders relaxed with tiredness as she carefully turned the wine glass between her fingers.

'Do you think I'll ever find another husband?' Gabriella asked.

'Like Arnie?' Helen enjoyed this, it gave her respite from her own circular thoughts, from worrying if Bill would indeed even notice she'd gone.

'No. Impossible. Just someone who makes me feel loved, safe, cared for, like he used to. And who can fit with my life.'

Helen thought it was quite a lot to ask, but didn't say so as it felt unkind. 'I think love can come along at any age. Well, most ages. Human beings are creatures with an enormous capacity for love of all kinds, if we let ourselves.'

'Do you think that's Bill's main problem?'

'I don't follow.'

'Not letting himself love. Like he's sort of forgotten how to do it.'

'Because we've been together so long?'

'Maybe. Or just because.'

'Because what?' Helen placed the wine glass on the small nested table Gabriella had placed there earlier.

'I don't know. Because he's forgotten. Or he fell out of the habit. I think loving someone is a habit you have to keep. Like daily exercise, or eating healthily.' Gabriella shook her head. 'Ignore me, what do I know?'

Helen liked that theory. She said so. 'It's possible you will find love again. You're young.' The thought of a woman who wasn't yet thirty never having the love of a man filled Helen's heart with sadness. More sadness than when she considered her own situation – being unloved by someone who'd forgotten how, who'd fallen out of the habit of caring and making an effort. Who had, when she boiled it all down, taken her very much for granted.

'I'm going to bed.' Helen stood.

'Want to come with me to take the boys to school tomorrow?'

Although it was mostly pointless, except for the odd part of shepherding the children, it gave her purpose, at least for that time. Would make the long morning pass swiftly she hoped. 'Yes. I'd like that very much.' She turned to walk to the door.

'What about goodnight?'

'What about it?' Helen asked, turning.

Gabriella stood, holding her arms wide, gesturing for a hug. 'In this house, we always say goodnight. Arnie and me used to do it, even if he was working away, he'd video call me and we'd say goodnight.'

'Every night?'

Gabriella nodded.

Helen hugged her. Gabriella's arms tightly around her, patting her back as they said good night to one another.

She said, 'Tomorrow is another day and we will face it together. Right?'

It felt a bit inspirational-meme-like and Helen was not a fan of those. She pulled back from the hug. 'Of course.' Helen walked upstairs to her room and, contrary to all instincts, fell asleep very swiftly, even before she'd had time to check her phone once more.

It wasn't until the following morning, at six o'clock when she woke naturally, that she confirmed Bill had not been in touch.

She would not let this upset her, she told herself. Bill wasn't worth enough for that.

She would, despite feeling to the contrary, continue to live her life in spite of his behaviour, not because of it.

And with that thought firmly lodged in her mind, she made herself a fruit tea and took it back to her room until she heard noises along the corridor, as Gabriella and the boys showered and dressed for another day.

At lunchtime two days later, Helen's phone rang. Gabriella had insisted Helen not get in touch with him. It had been difficult, but necessary, Helen later realised.

'Bill?' Gabriella asked.

Helen nodded, turned away and stared out the kitchen window. 'Yes?' Bright sun flooded the garden.

'Where are you?'

'With a friend.'

'Where have you gone? I was worried. When are you returning home?'

'Don't know,' Helen said, biting her bottom lip.

'I thought this was your attempt at a joke and you'd gone on holiday without telling me. Well, that you'd told me but I'd not processed it fully. Looked on the calendar and nothing.'

'Nothing.' That it had taken him two days before worrying enough to call her was the least of her concerns. She closed her eyes slowly, trying to marshal her temper.

'When are you coming back?' His urgent tone was obviously masking anger.

'Don't know.' Hearing his familiar voice, and the pain so obvious, spiked her heart with longing. Although she'd kept herself busy since leaving, she did, as much as she didn't want to admit it, miss him. Forty years with the same man by her side and now it felt as if she'd lost an arm. A useless, withered, unresponsive, unloving arm, but an arm nevertheless.

A long and awkward silence preceded Bill's next question: 'When are you returning home?'

'Unclear.' She would not let her missing him cloud her judgement. She had decided to take this course of action and was determined to see it through. If she went home now, it would have all been for naught. And they'd swiftly fall back into their old patterns.

'I don't understand.' He was quiet, anger having been replaced with confusion.

'No, you don't, do you?' Helen shook her head in deep disappointment. 'I am safe. That's all you need to know.'

'Come on now, when are you going to end this nonsense? I've got the hospital board coming round for supper at the weekend. I need you.'

'I'm afraid that's where you're wrong.' He didn't need her, he just needed what she could do for him, with no consideration for herself.

He chuckled. 'Is this some sort of practical joke?'

'I am not laughing.'

She ended the call and switched her phone off at Gabriella's insistence.

Clutching the phone in front of her chest, she felt strangely euphoric and empowered – alongside deep grief at the death of their marriage – for the first time in as long as she could remember.

'Well done.' Gabriella held her palm aloft. 'High five.'

'If you insist.' Helen felt it unnecessary and overly dramatic, but did it all the same. Didn't feel like she had much to celebrate.

Chapter 21

Ian wore a suit, as usual, sitting on the Tube line, not as usual. His right leg jiggled up and down as he leafed through his notes, turning to the email with details of the interview.

As the train rattled from the suburbs into central London and underground, the stifling heat that Ian had forgotten returned worse than before, it seemed. The window at the front of the carriage was open, giving a weak stream of air, the vents above his head did the same, only less effectively. Sweat trickled from under his armpits, down the sides of his body. He loosened his tie as his mouth felt dry.

Focus on the positive.

At last, he finally had an interview and he'd spent the last week preparing for it.

He got off at the nearest station, found the building and gave his name to the receptionist. 'I'm here for a job interview,' he said, feeling the wobble in his voice.

Not many months ago, he'd been used to public speaking in front of half the company, doing talks at conferences to hundreds of people.

He took the lift to the thirteenth floor – unlucky for some – and gave his name to the man at their front desk.

'I'll tell them you're here,' he replied, indicating seats where Ian could make himself comfortable. He rang his colleagues, explained the second candidate had arrived. 'They'll buzz me when they're ready for you,' he said to Ian.

He tried to relax, knowing if he didn't know the answer now, he didn't know it. Sure in the knowledge that he'd prepared as much as he could and all he needed now was to share it on cue when asked the questions he'd anticipated.

He held the papers he'd printed and his hands shook. His stomach was heavy with anxiety.

Almost an hour after his interview time, the receptionist man said, 'They're ready for you now,' gave the room where he was to meet the panel, and pointed in the right direction.

Later, he couldn't remember the questions they'd asked, but did recall how he'd felt. Each response he gave had stuck in his throat and copious sips of water hadn't improved the situation. There was a question about why he'd applied for such a role when he was clearly over-qualified.

To this, he said, 'I'm very excited about this role. Being out of work isn't as much fun as I expected. I thought I wasn't fungible and well, turns out I am.' A little chuckle at the silly joke he'd made at his own expense.

The panel – two women and a man – hadn't raised a smile, simply turning back to their list of questions, holding their pens ready to mark his answers out of ten, he supposed.

'How can I not get a job I'm overqualified for?' he asked now, in the lido café, to the other members of their club.

They had all been swimming before deciding they deserved a hot drink.

'Don't ask me,' Helen said, 'I'm very much out of the loop job-wise.'

Gabriella sipped her coffee. 'If you did your best that's all you can ever do.'

They asked how it had gone, what the panel had asked him and Ian recounted as much as he could remember – which wasn't much. 'I was very nervous. Like GCSE exams nervous.' *Like, first date with Drew nervous too.*

'Why?' Helen asked. 'You prepared, did you not?'

'Yes, but they kept me waiting…' He'd been exhausted, nerves run ragged, shaking, by the time they'd called him through.

'Did you tell Drew?' Gabriella asked.

'He'd have wondered why I'd applied for a step down rather than a promotion.'

'Would he have known that much detail about your career trajectory?' Helen asked with a cynical tone.

Ian shrugged. He reckoned Drew would have done. Or perhaps it was because he didn't want to say anything until he knew he'd got the job, and then perhaps he'd only mention it after being at the new place for a while. Smooth over any gaps in his story.

'If you don't get it, just forge on with the next one,' Helen said as if it were nothing.

She continued, 'You know what I'm going to say, don't you?'

'Tell Drew.'

He hadn't spoken about the other truth he'd told Drew when Helen had accompanied him. He'd told Helen she could tell Gabriella, but that he didn't want to discuss it with them. It wasn't personal, it was just a man thing.

Every time Drew touched him, if he didn't instantly become aroused, it portended something much worse. He worried he wouldn't rise to the occasion and, as usual, the underpants department failed to reach the top floor.

Drew had been more than understanding, so soft and gentle that it had irritated Ian beyond all words. Not least because Drew wasn't a soft and gentle man – although he was very caring, Drew was a large, imposing, hulk of a man and that had been one of the things that Ian found sexy. And if there was anything guaranteed to make Ian feel less attracted towards Drew it was him being painfully and awkwardly supportive wrapped up in too much soft and gentleness.

'Arnie had the same thing. After Jack came along – he said he didn't know what to do, how to be a father and we went to bed, cos I knew it would take his mind off the worry and well… It didn't. Only that one time though.' Gabriella bit her bottom lip briefly. 'Yeah, just the once.'

If Arnie had been alive, Ian would have liked, in some way, he wasn't sure how, to have asked Arnie what he'd done to solve the problem. And thinking about that now, imagining communicating with a man he'd never known, was entirely less embarrassing than this conversation now.

He said nothing.

Unbidden, Helen said, 'I wouldn't know about Bill, I'm afraid. It's been so long since we've… He could be as he'd been upon our first meeting. Doubt it though. I'm not, so I don't see why he would be. I find myself less and less considering that side of things nowadays. Used to make me terribly sad, but I suppose one becomes used to it, even if one doesn't want to.' She raised her eyebrows, obviously expecting Ian to respond.

He did not.

After a pause he felt long enough to signal a clear change in subject, his cheeks heating up, Ian said, 'I didn't even really want the job. Only applied because I needed one. Normally I would never have bothered. And I couldn't even get that one. Shows how much use I am.' He felt defeated, exhausted and entirely disinclined to continue the conversation about his sexual failings with the other members of theLonely Hearts Lido Club.

'Don't you think,' Gabriella said, 'if you told him you needed a job, he could help you?'

It was an entirely reasonable line of questioning. 'I'm not inclined to give him any more reasons to think I'm any more useless than he already believes.'

'That's not fair. You don't know he thinks that about you.'

'He's not said it, but the look in his eyes.' When they'd been in bed and Drew had been gently trying to coax desire from Ian, it appeared to be a look of confusion, pity, sadness... Anyway, enough of that. But the look then told Ian that Drew considered him almost entirely without use.

'Windows to the soul,' Helen said, apropos of nothing.

'What's that?' Gabriella asked.

'Eyes. That's what they say.'

Ian stood, hugged them goodbye and left. Although they were well-meaning, he couldn't listen to any more of their talk today. He needed to sort out his problems for himself, without relying on others, and before Drew found out. He just needed to work out how to do so. If only he hadn't ballsed up that interview and therefore scuppered any confidence he'd had.

His car felt like an oven when he opened the door, a blast of hot air greeted him. Should have parked it in the shade. The air con provided blessed relief, cooler than the café certainly and almost as nice as sitting in the shade beside the lido pool. His forehead was covered in sweat and he felt thirsty, wishing he'd grabbed water before leaving the lido.

Arriving home, he then changed out of his suit – fat lot of good that had done – had a cool shower – such blessed relief, he stayed under the water longer than necessary – and, after checking the calendar to confirm Drew was due home late evening, descended upon the biscuit cupboard. Soon, he sat himself on the sofa, with three packets of cookies and a pint of milk, into which he dunked each biscuit half, took a bite, then the other half, before eating the rest. After watching a great deal of very bad television, he realised he had, unbeknownst to himself, finished all three packets of biscuits.

It was late evening when the door clicked and Drew shouted his arrival. 'What have you been doing?' he asked, surveying the crumbs and empty packets around Ian on the sofa. 'Bad day at work?'

If only! 'Something like that.' And Ian made up a story about how his day hadn't gone to plan and he hadn't the energy to make dinner, so he'd commiserated with biscuits because Drew wasn't home until late. With every word of the lie, he felt as if he liked himself progressively less and less.

Chapter 22

Gabriella hadn't been in the mood to... Well, do anything, when she got talking to the charming man she kept bumping into at the school gate. Sheltering from the summer heat in the shade of the buildings opposite the school, she held Thomas's hand and waited for Jack to appear from the school, walking towards the gate. She noticed a tall, wide-shouldered man with brown hair with light flecks.

They exchanged a raised eyebrow, hello. 'I'm Jack's mum. The party?'

Recognition crossed his face. 'Great party. You don't fancy organising one for a very particular six-year-old girl, do you?' He grinned.

A tiny flutter of *he's handsome* scurried across her mind, but nothing more. Only briefly.

'Saw you at the headmaster's office. Looked serious.'

Gabriella nodded. 'I wished I was in your shoes. He was very happy, whatever he'd been saying to you.'

'More issues than solutions, but still, it's a good problem to have.'

Gabriella raised her eyebrows.

'Sorry, I don't normally do this, boasting about one's children is so...'

Boring, obvious, tedious...

'Annoying.' He raised an eyebrow.

'I know, right.'

'The head said if my eldest had extra tuition for her GCSEs, and she did well in her A levels, eventually she stood a good chance of—' He blushed. 'Doesn't matter.'

'What? Go on!'

'Eventually. In many years… Oxbridge was mentioned.' He smiled.

It felt as if Gabriella were starring opposite him in their own romantic movie. She was so wrapped up in his smile, his twinkly eyes, his square jaw and his understated pride in his daughter, that she almost forgot why she was there.

Earlier, she was so focused on checking Jack had been okay, having received a frantic call from his teacher at lunchtime saying he was unwell. Upon arrival at the school she'd been told he'd seemingly made a full recovery and she was no longer needed.

She suspected it was attention-seeking – he'd been doing it more and more lately since Thomas had started preschool and Gabriella had Helen staying with them.

Focus on my son, rather than this man and his brainbox daughter.

Two girls, about the same age as Gabriella's boys, ran up to the man.

He knelt and hugged them both tightly, holding them for longer than usual. It looked as if he had been sniffing them too – later he confirmed this to Gabriella.

'I'll never get used to leaving them all day,' he said to Gabriella, taking both girls' hands.

She wasn't sure he was talking to her, so she'd ignored it until he'd repeated it then asked: 'Which year is yours in?'

'Reception and one's at preschool,' she replied. 'I've already been here twice today for Thomas.' Half days of preschool were, in some ways, more of a pain than full days. She knew it was the right thing for Thomas, but hadn't expected to be at the school twice as often as before.

'Two?'

A really sarcastic *yeah well done, you can count* had been on the tip of her tongue, but her mother's cry, that anyone could be sarky but it took a lady or a gent to be kind, stopped her.

'Yes,' she said, looking to her side at him.

It struck her then, how similar he looked to Arnie. *I must have a type. But I can't remember his name, except he has two adorable daughters.*

'I remember. Simon,' he said holding out a hand.

Simon, that's it. Why had that slipped her mind?

Gabriella introduced herself, then noticed Jack running to the gate shouting Mummy at her. She hugged him. 'Are you okay?' she asked.

Jack shrugged. 'Will you take me away, cos I was naughty?'

Gabriella blushed bright red as heat filled her cheeks. She laughed. 'It's something I say. If they're being,' mouthing the words now, she went on, 'right little tear-aways.'

Simon gave her a knowing look. 'I'll remember that. Not used to all this. My wife used to do it all. Classic man, eh.'

Used to. People only said that when… Gabriella said, 'Any time. If it makes you feel any better, I'm crap at all the stuff my husband used to do.'

'Divorced?' Simon asked. 'Didn't see a man at the party, but that doesn't mean anything.'

'Widowed.' That one word had caused dozens of different reactions since she'd started saying it. 'You?'

'Widower.' He said it like he'd just told her he didn't take sugar in his coffee. He'd obviously been saying it for a while, like she had. He'd not mentioned that at the party, perhaps didn't want to put a downer on the birthday party. *How considerate of him.*

'I'm sorry,' Gabriella said.

He smiled – a sort of fixed forced grin. 'Do you fancy grabbing a coffee sometime?'

It took her by surprise. She smiled, nodded. 'Yeah.'

'Playdate, with the children. I think mine are in the same years as your two.' He smiled. 'Aren't yours in reception and preschool?'

'They are, as it goes. Sounds nice.'

'Better give you my number, or unless you want to give me yours and I'll call and then you have mine...' He looked adorably awkward.

She took his phone and entered her number.

Hers rang.

'You've got mine now. Choose to ignore me if you wish. I won't be offended.' Another awkward smile.

I won't ignore you, I'm really excited to have coffee with you. With or without our kids. You, me, coffee, sounds wicked. She grinned, wondering if this was really happening.

'Best get on.' He left.

Out of the corner of her eye, between snippets of conversation with Jack and wondering whether she needed to walk into school to find out what had been wrong with him, she saw Simon walking away, holding his daughters' hands. He wore light jeans – fitting very snugly around his behind – and a pink shirt that showed off his wide shoulders.

'What did you say?' she asked Thomas.

He shook his head, put his hands very firmly on his hips, stamped his foot and said, 'I said. Why didn't you listen, Mummy?'

'Mummy was distracted. What did you say about Jack?'

'He was with the doctor.'

Gabriella removed her sunglasses, placed them on her head, knelt down to his level, looking very firmly into Jack's eyes. 'Which doctor? Where?'

'The school one. I said.' Jack sighed. 'Can we go home?' With reluctance he added, 'Please?'

She gathered him to her and strode into the school and was greeted by the officious school secretary who informed her that, yes, Jack had been sitting with the school nurse, they had telephoned earlier but she had not answered.

'What was wrong with him?' Ian asked now, sitting by the outdoor swimming pool in the shade.

They had gathered sun loungers and two parasols, plus a low table for their plastic containers of fruit mixed with cream and flavours. No one had fancied coffees in this heat.

'Nothing. Sometimes Jack cries so hard he makes himself sick and it looks like he's really rough, but he's just doing it for attention.'

'At least,' Helen said, with a tone of approval, 'you're not one of these modern parents who coddle their children. It does them no favours in the long run.'

'Why was he crying?' Ian asked.

'He wouldn't say. Sometimes it's anything, sometimes it's nothing. But really he misses his daddy.' With that, Gabriella broke the promise she'd made to herself this morning, that she would not get upset. She'd had a run of bad days, crying all the time, totally unable to stop herself and rationalise it away.

Helen had been some comfort to her, just being there, but Gabriella still felt it showed weakness.

'I don't think I should see him again. It's too soon to date.'

'I think you need to slow down a bit before you get there,' Ian said.

'It feels like I'd be cheating on him. Arnie.'

'We got that, dear,' Helen said.

'Why worry about that, he's not asked you out, has he?' Ian said.

'I don't know,' Gabriella said with care.

'What do you mean?'

'He asked me to have a coffee with him.'

'How, precisely, did he ask you for this coffee?' Ian asked.

'It was the third time that week that we'd been chatting at the school gates, and when my two turned up and I was leaving, he just said it. Did I want to grab a coffee sometime? He said he's always open for a play date for the kids.'

'That sounds a bit sexual, don't you think?' Ian raised an eyebrow in question.

Gabriella shook her head. 'It means letting the kids play around each other's house.'

'But he said you could come round his place for a coffee?'

'With the kids there,' Gabriella said simply.

'A date,' Helen said, 'with the children as chaperones.' Ian nodded.

Gabriella shrugged.

'To accompany you, make sure you don't get up to anything naughty.'

Gabriella hadn't thought of it like that before. She'd taken it at face value. 'There are never dads at the school gates. Well, almost never. If they are, it's like they're doing their wives this massive favour. He wasn't because—' She stopped herself. Because he was a widower, like she was a widow. She shook her head. 'Anyway, the kids will hate each other, they're bound to. So it'll all be off anyway.'

'What are you going to do?' Helen asked. 'If it were me, you'd tell me to grab it by the balls or something equally as crude yet encouraging.'

She would do that. Definitely. 'We'll see,' she said. The thought of kissing, holding, going to bed with anyone other than Arnie felt so wrong, she almost felt sick. She knew it wasn't cheating on him; you can't cheat on a dead person. But imagining the horrified faces of school gates mums as it went around that she was dating Simon, sent a wave of repulsion running through her from head to toe.

'Too soon, definitely,' she said finally. 'I'm not interested.' She wanted the subject closed, but wasn't even convinced of this herself, never mind convincing the other two members of theLonely Hearts Lido Club.

Was it the worst thing if Helen and Ian encouraged her to find some way of being less lonely? Of moving on from her grief and edging towards happiness?

In her mind, after thinking she'd never be with anyone else ever again, she'd softened and had set herself an imaginary three years after Arnie's death, before returning to love. Three years to honour Arnie's memory and then…

Helen said, 'You're thinking about him, aren't you?'

'Arnie?'

Helen nodded.

'Yep,' she said, and yet he had barely featured in her thoughts, except as a time restriction on her moving on. *I am a terrible person for not thinking about my dead husband more.*

Three years, well less now. That's what she needed to remember.

Chapter 23

July

Helen had been living with Gabriella for a few weeks.

The heatwave continued with temperatures reaching the low thirties, no rain since May and the country descending into a mild panic about hosepipe bans and garages unable to keep up with requests to fix cars' air con units. The ice cream van arrived twice a week, playing a song from Helen's childhood. She wished Jack and Thomas were there during the day so she could treat them. Gabriella said she was watching their teeth after a bollocking from their dentist, but it was kind of her to offer.

Helen had returned to her home, hoping to meet Bill, but hadn't.

He had phoned her after four days, asking where she was. 'Are you okay?'

'Depends how you define that.'

'Can you not speak in riddles, please?'

Helen wanted to tell him it was none of his business to dictate to her how she spoke, but didn't have the energy to argue, so she'd ended the call.

He tried calling back again – which filled Helen's heart with not quite hope, but a flutter of optimism – until she turned the phone off and resumed her life in Gabriella's home.

'And?' Gabriella asked now.

Helen shook her head solemnly.

'I was going to take the boys into town for shoes and clothes. They've grown out of everything. Don't suppose you fancy coming with, do you?'

'I do. Very much so.' This, having spoken to friends her age, was a grandparent rite of passage she'd missed out on. *Must call Peter, see what he thinks about my moving out.*

Peter had sent her a text a week after Helen had left, it simply read: *WTF you've left Dad???*

She'd texted back: *Correct. And???*

Peter: *Why???*

Helen: *Because he doesn't love me.*

Peter hadn't replied to that and Helen hadn't felt the need to explain herself any further. Perhaps he thought it best not to become embroiled in his parents' marriage.

'Are you okay?' Gabriella asked. 'You looked miles away.'

'Nothing. Just thinking about Peter. Wonder how he's coping with all this.'

'He's a grown man, he'll be fine. It's hardly like you've split up when he was nine.'

Helen shrugged.

'Sure you want to go shopping?'

'Absolutely so!'

They bundled the boys into Gabriella's large van-like car and went to Uxbridge town centre. She sat them on a bench, explained to the sales assistant they both needed new shoes and went on to explain which type.

It seemed, in a feat that Helen found impressive, they had both grown out of different types of shoes at the same time, meaning Gabriella couldn't hand down the too-small shoes to the younger sibling, instead needing to buy two different varieties of footwear at the same time.

She started to ask if her parents-in-law helped with this sort of thing, but Gabriella had changed the subject. Evidently the regular dinners must be putting some sort of strain on her she wasn't ready to discuss.

Thomas tried on a new pair of plain black school shoes – his old ones far too small for his brother.

Jack kicked his legs back and forth as he sat, and the sales assistant tried to fit a pair of white designer trainers on his feet, while his old ones lay on their sides on the floor.

She marvelled at how Gabriella calmly marshalled each boy in turn, all the while carrying on a conversation with Helen that had nothing to do with her boys.

She was, Helen decided, a very impressive mother. Not really in spite of being a single parent, but because of it. Her ability to put the needs of her children first, remain calm while both boys did their own special brand of disruption, all while carrying on a conversation with Helen, put herself to shame.

They were talking about holidays and how Gabriella hadn't dared have one without Arnie, the thought of looking after two boys in a new place she'd felt unequal to. 'We used to be like a tag team,' she said. 'Taking either one, sticking by their sides no matter what. We took Jack to a theme park, before Thomas was born, and me and Arnie nearly killed each other.'

'I don't believe that for an instant,' Helen said, putting Thomas back onto his seat.

The sales assistant returned with a box of shoes and carefully slid them onto his feet.

'True,' Gabriella said.

'Did you take him again?'

She shook her head. 'Thomas hasn't been.' She made an awkward face. 'Bad, right?'

It didn't strike Helen as particularly bad mothering to not have taken one of her children to a theme park. 'We could go. I'll do the tag team thing, whatever that is.'

Gabriella chuckled. 'That would be nice. Have you been away with young kids before?'

'Of course. Years ago. I have one of my own. How hard can it be?'

Gabriella laughed, looking out of the corner of one eye. 'Right.'

The boys stood and held their boxes of new shoes. Gabriella paid for them while Helen watched the two children.

'Mission accomplished,' she said returning and putting the receipt in her handbag.

They decided not to eat lunch out because Gabriella had a fridge of food at home. At the clothes shop, Helen was given strict instructions for the clothes Thomas required.

It occurred to Helen that he could probably have worn hand-me-downs from his brother, as she'd sometimes wished with her Peter, despite only having one child. She admonished herself and regretted not pushing Bill further on having another child. Still, that ship had most definitely sailed now.

Later, she returned to the changing room, where Gabriella was helping the two boys try their clothes on.

'These all right?' Helen showed her the clothes that Thomas had chosen.

'There's an empty one at the end.' Gabriella pointed. 'Are you all right helping him change?'

Helen nodded. She'd not done it in decades but felt sure it would all come back to her.

Thomas tried on the clothes and settled on a few that matched Gabriella's list of what he needed.

He sat next to Helen and Gabriella, while Jack changed without anyone's help.

'Apparently he's a big boy now and doesn't need Mummy's help.' Gabriella kissed Thomas, pulling him close in for a hug.

'Happens to them all,' Helen said with a smile.

'We used to have some wicked holidays. As a family,' Gabriella said.

'I bet.'

'This reminds me. We used to buy them a new summer wardrobe so they had new stuff to wear when we went away.' A pause: 'Spoilt, I know but…'

'Loved, that's how I'd describe it,' Helen said. 'Where did you used to take them?'

Gabriella thought for a moment until Jack burst from the changing room wearing a new T-shirt back to front. She rectified this. 'Spain, France, Italy, Portugal, but Greece was my fave.' To Jack she said, 'Want it?'

He nodded.

'Try on the shorts. Do you want Mummy to help you put them on?'

He thought for a moment, nodded, and she followed him in.

Shortly they reappeared and Jack wore new blue shorts that came down to his ankles.

'I think they're a bit big. Auntie Helen is going to get them in a smaller size.' Gabriella pointed.

She left, returning with the items, handing them to Gabriella.

'Greece was my fave. We went to the little islands, not just the mainland, you know?' Gabriella asked.

Helen did know and it filled her with sadness as she recalled their last holiday before Bill had pronounced them pointless because they were retired. What was she needing a holiday *from* anyway?

Helen blinked away a tear.

Gabriella sat next to her. 'Okay? Did I say something?'

Helen shook her head. 'This, it's all very emotional.' She felt, for the first time in a long while, as if she were useful. As if she had a place in a family, rather than being an afterthought. Having brought up a child – and now Peter was an adult – she felt somehow surplus to requirements. With this, she felt firmly rooted in having a use.

'Has Bill been in touch?' Gabriella asked, gathering up the boys and their chosen clothes.

'Not in any useful sort of way, no.'

They paid for the clothes and left the shop, each boy holding the bag of his new purchases.

'Home?' Gabriella asked gently.

'I think,' Helen said, choosing her words with care, 'you and I spend enough time at home, don't you?'

'Right…' Gabriella looked unsure.

'I was thinking we could have P-I-Z-Z-A for lunch.'

Jack shouted, 'Pizza! Can we, can we, Mum, can we?'

Gabriella raised her eyebrows. 'Private school can be a right PITA.'

Helen winked. 'My treat.'

They went to a pizza restaurant and drank cooling milkshakes as the boys ate contentedly, sometimes standing on their chair, before Gabriella told them off, other times shouting for more food before finishing what was on their plate, Helen found out why Gabriella had loved her Greek holidays with Arnie and the children most, and Helen remembered what she now recognised as the beginning of the end for her relationship with Bill.

'We used to eat mostly fish,' Gabriella said, 'and the boys loved it. Not at first though.'

'Better than fish fingers.'

'Exactly. And we would swim in the sea, sit on the beach and take them to the water park to knacker them out for the day.' She got a faraway look in her eyes. 'We came home and they were all too tired to eat, so went to bed straight away.' She smiled. 'And so did me and Arnie.' Her dark brown eyes shone with undisguised lust and desire.

Helen felt both sorry for her, at losing someone who was so clearly very special, loving and caring, and also pleased that Gabriella had known that sort of love.

The boys had finished the pizza on their plates and Gabriella said, 'One more slice, eat that and then another, okay?'

They both said: 'Yes Mummy.'

'Did you take your son abroad?'

'Camping in Brittany – France, a hotel in Paris for Euro Disney as it was called then; the Amalfi coast. Yes, yes we did,' Helen said, overwhelmed at the memories.

'Not Greece?'

'Not with a child. When Peter was young, Greece wasn't what it is now.' Helen didn't want to be rude, but forty years ago, Greece had been very different from now. It felt like stepping back in time: small fishing villages, undeveloped beaches and a feeling of optimism and modernity being not far away since joining the EU.

But all very undeveloped and much rougher around the edges than now.

'You said you've been.'

'Recently, without Peter.'

'You liked it?' Gabriella asked.

She had. Very much so. 'Yes. But it's difficult to remember now.'

'Why?' Gabriella checked the boys had finished. 'Who wants ice cream?'

Two hands shot into the air, with shouts in the affirmative.

While they gave their dessert order, they talked about the pizza and the successful day they'd had. Gabriella thanked Helen for helping.

In the silence when the boys were eating strawberry, chocolate and vanilla ice cream globes, Gabriella said, 'Tell me to mind my own business, but why's it so hard to remember that holiday now?'

'Because,' Helen said, 'it was the beginning of the end. I didn't know it at the time, but now I look back, I'm sure.'

'What did he do?' In a whisper she added: 'Can't you say now?'

'We were drinking our morning coffee, sitting on our balcony. A couple were swimming in the sea. They left the water and it was apparent they were naked.'

'Nudist beach? I've never had the guts to go full tits and *minino*, have you?'

'Early morning. We couldn't see details, just there was no material where their swimming costumes would be. He was a little pot-bellied, and she more than a little rotund. There was no one else there. He was bald, and she had shoulder length grey hair. They stood by the beach and embraced. He had a towel around his waist, and she one tucked under her armpits. He held her close to himself, kissing her head, as she rested it against his bare chest. They stood still, then they kissed, a long slow kiss, holding hands and gazing into one another's eyes. It was so beautiful. I felt as if I were intruding, which was ridiculous since they were on a public beach.'

'Then what?'

Helen blushed slightly. 'They held hands and walked quickly to the apartment block, disappearing inside as fast as possible. It was obvious what they were rushing inside to do.'

'That's really sweet. Sounds like the sort of thing me and Arnie would have done – pre-kids. They obviously didn't know you were spying on them.'

'I most definitely was not spying, they were on the beach, unselfconsciously showing affection for one another until they could do this no more in public. I thought it was very sweet.' Helen swallowed, composing herself. 'I placed my hand in his, on the table, lacing our fingers together. Hoping he'd pull me in for a kiss, and we'd walk the few feet back to our bedroom and...'

'What did Bill think?'

'Not that. I told him and he said people ought to have more self-respect. Rutting on a beach was very unbecoming, especially at that age. He pulled away his hand, stood, shook his head and said he was going for a swim.'

'What had he been like before, about that sort of thing?'

Helen was disinclined to get into the details of her and Bill's sex life, even if she knew Gabriella would remain discrete. She'd found it difficult enough speaking to Bill about it, never mind a friend. 'A marriage, for forty years, is work. Lots of it. Making the effort to care. To humour, to spend time together. It was then that I realised he'd stopped seeing me.'

'Seeing you?' Gabriella frowned.

'It was as if I'd disappeared among the years of bringing up children, making house, being a wife, that he'd forgotten why he first fell in love with me. The real me, the young me, the original version of myself. I hadn't. Still remembered the twinkle in his blue eyes. The smile that made my heart thump in my chest. I'd have preferred him to have an affair. At least that's a logical explanation one can tell friends for why you've divorced. Rather than a wet fart of not seeing someone.' Helen shook her head.

Gabriella pulled her in for a hug. 'If I meet him, I'll tell him—'

'You won't. I couldn't, so you won't be able to.'

They drove back to Gabriella's house listening to the radio as the boys played in the back seat.

'I'm going to have a lie down,' Helen said at the bottom of the stairs.

A look of pity crossed Gabriella's face. 'I wish I could do something to help.'

'You are. Don't make the same mistake as I did.'

'I don't think I can because Arnie is—'

'Staying at home, cooking and cleaning and worrying about what someone thinks who's no longer with us, is no life for a beautiful woman like you. Take Simon up on his offer of a coffee.'

'Maybe.'

Helen narrowed her eyes, doing her best to share a look of imperious demand. 'Definitely.' She continued upstairs and lay on the bed as the fan turned slowly, circulating cool air. She was thinking about all the ways she could have lived her life differently, and whether, unlike Gabriella, it was too late for her now.

Chapter 24

Ian had been swimming at the lido – a wonderfully solitary hour of lengths, totally uninterrupted by children, their parents or people old enough to be grandparents. It set Ian up well for the rest of the day, regardless of him not having anything planned.

Gabriella, now that Thomas was at school too – or was it preschool, he wasn't sure – had been coming less often to the lido. She'd said that the house felt less empty and sad. Ian suspected it may have something to do with the handsome house-husband she'd met at the school gates. Gabriella had denied this very strongly and offered her house if Ian wanted to see her and Helen.

And of course, Helen was visiting less often since she was spending her days with Gabriella. Her husband still showed no signs of being able to come to the place where he understood what needed to change for him to win Helen back into his life.

Poor man, he reflected as he walked along the side of the outdoor pool to the changing booths. The sun warmed his skin and he stood facing it for a moment, with his eyes shut. If he imagined, very hard, he could pretend he was on holiday; somewhere on the Amalfi coast, or a small Greek island, having enjoyed the sea and now about to return to their villa for wine, reading and a conversation with Drew.

Drew, from whom he was still keeping the biggest, ugliest lie he'd ever created.

Sliding into the nearest booth, he then threw on his gym clothes and walked along the other side of the pool towards the gym and exercise machines.

Approximately half the sun loungers were filled with reclining people, some reading, some staring at their phones, others simply staring at the activity of people swimming in the pool. Ian nodded in friendly recognition at a few people he'd noticed before and exchanged pleasantries with.

At the far end of the pool, he looked through the glass wall into the gym, noting which machines were busy and which empty. He stopped still suddenly, then stood against the wall, doing his best to hide in the shadows along the wall.

Drew was on the running machine. He wore the white vest and black shorts Ian was used to washing, and a determined look on his face, staring straight ahead as he ran.

Drew. Here. My husband at my place, the lido.

Shit.

I need to work out what to do, before he sees me. Except all he could do was stare at Drew and hope he didn't look up and see Ian.

He turned, starting to make his way back to the changing booths at the opposite end of the pool. His brain had worked out that put him farther from Drew, and from there he'd work out more plan as it came to him.

'Ian, hello, how are you doing?' A woman he'd nodded at earlier, while swimming, asked him.

Ian tried his best to flatten himself against the shady wall, keeping his gaze fixed on Drew running inside the gym.

'What are you doing?' the woman asked, peering through the glass wall into the gym. 'Are you trying to avoid someone? Embarrassing isn't it, bumping into somebody you know from your real life, and seeing them in your swimming costume. I almost died when a colleague from work saw me here. We didn't talk about it at work afterwards. Suppose she must have been as mortified as me.'

Ian stood frozen, caught between Drew, who'd moved from the running machine and onto the bench-pressing machine, still, very unhelpfully he thought, facing towards the pool, and this woman, whose name he'd forgotten.

She peered at Ian and then into the gym. 'Who are you spying on?' She turned, and waved at someone inside the building.

Two people, no, three, left their exercise equipment and walked towards the glass wall, staring through at Ian and the woman.

This, in itself, wouldn't have been a problem, had the third person not been Drew. But it was. He leaned against the glass, shading his eyes with his hands. His eyes widened and he raised his eyebrows at seeing Ian.

Ian didn't need to know lip reading to understand that Drew was asking, 'What are you doing here?' and Ian would need to think of an excuse very swiftly.

Ian, even though it was too late, debated running away, gently skulking along the wall, through the reception and café, and into his car. Despite it being too late to make any difference, sheer desperation and terror were driving him, forcing him to make bad decisions. Later, he blamed the answer he gave on them, when Drew finally met him outside by the pool.

They hugged, the most awkward hug Ian had ever endured.

'What are you doing here?' Drew asked with a look of confusion. 'You should be at work.'

'What are you doing here?' Ian asked as his mind whirred and fizzed and tried to make sensible words come out of his mouth, and mostly failed.

'I asked you that. I'm trying this place for my days off, rather than going all the way into London.'

'Shall we get a coffee? The café is over here.' Ian nodded, gesturing they should walk in that direction.

Drew stood, his arms folded and worry clouding his face. 'Are you going to tell me what's going on?'

'I'll get you a coffee. Or decaf since you're in the gym, probably better for your stomach.'

Drew grabbed Ian's forearm, stopping him turning to walk away. 'I think we should have this conversation at home, don't you?'

Ian's body went limp. He was caught out and had run out of excuses. 'I'll follow your car.'

'No you won't, you'll come with me in mine.' He shook his head. 'For some reason I don't trust you to follow me home.'

Ah. Right. It was going to be like this.

Ian stooped forwards, feeling like a naughty schoolboy having been caught painting in large red letters on the side of the school – Mrs Miller Is A Cow.

They drove in silence, which was very unlike Drew, who normally liked to chit-chat with the radio playing in the background. His hands held tightly onto the steering wheel.

Ian's stomach rumbled with a deep sickness – perhaps he had food poisoning, or a stitch from breakfast and then swimming too soon or hard. Sweat accumulated around his waist and his trousers stuck to his legs. *Who has sweaty legs?*

No. This was guilt, plain and simple. Thick, ugly, unavoidable guilt, from the big deceptive lie he'd been telling every day for the last three months.

They sat in the living room, Drew in the chair and Ian on the sofa.

'Now,' Drew began, a tone of calm had descended over him, 'Are you going to tell me why you're at the lido when you should be working?'

'I booked a day's holiday. Thought I'd just have a day for me and enjoy what the lido had to offer.'

'I was off today. You knew this. It's on the calendar. You wanted to book a me day, when you knew I was at home too. What have I done for you not to want to hang out with me?' Pain appeared in his eyes.

Just tell him! He remembered Gabriella and Helen's advice. But the problem with a lie was how attached to it you became. It was almost as if it became part of who he was.

'Why here, why this lido and not somewhere nearer home?'

'I could ask you the same,' Ian said with as much confidence as he could muster, which wasn't much.

'I said. Local ones didn't have the gym equipment I wanted. Now your turn.'

Ian chewed the inside of his cheek in thought. He looked at the floor. 'I'm sorry. So sorry. I thought it would only be for a while, until I... But I've not been able to. So I've had to carry on.'

'Carry on with what? Say it.'

'The lie.'

'About what?'

'I'm not at work because I don't have to be there. They let me go.'

'When?'

'February.'

'That's five months ago.'

Ian shrugged.

'It is. You're telling me you've been getting up, dressed for work, every day, and instead you're spending it at the lido?'

The guilt was so much, it sat in his throat like a blockage, sickness filled his tense stomach. Ian nodded slowly.

'Why?'

Ian shrugged.

'Oh no,' Drew said, 'you don't get to shrug it away like that. This isn't something you decide to do on a whim, this has needed planning, consistency, it's a lie you've been telling me for over ninety days. Twenty weeks. Twenty weeks of lies, deception. Twenty. Weeks.'

'I thought I'd get a job before it became a problem.'

'Before *what* became a problem?'

'Not having a job.'

'Right. What about the lying?'

They sort of came with the not having a job. It had, at the time, seemed a very sensible solution to a temporary problem. 'You don't mind me being unemployed?'

'It's not ideal, but I'll live with it.'

'Right.'

'The bit I'm struggling with most is the betrayal. Why didn't you just tell me?'

'Like I said, I thought I'd have a job before I needed to tell you.'

'We talk about everything. Why not this? Am I that scary?'

Ian shook his head. 'It's not that. It's…' He struggled to explain. When rationalising it in his head it had seemed very logical. He'd lost his job, plus his other problem, therefore he was no use to Drew. Therefore Drew would break up with him. But now, all this time later, all those lies behind him, Ian wasn't so sure it had been the best decision.

'What happened at work? Let's start there.'

'Restructure. My job went. I had to apply for an events role and didn't get it. Me, events.' He rolled his eyes. 'So I'd had two times when I'd been shown I wasn't any good, all in the space of a month. I didn't want you knowing that.'

'In case I, what…? Divorced you? Don't be so ridiculous. You're still you, whatever job you're doing, or not doing.'

'Am I? Cos I don't feel it.'

'You are. Trust me.'

'And the other thing.' Ian looked at the floor.

Drew pulled him in for a hug. 'That's separate from the lying. I'm not angry, upset, or anything about that. That doesn't matter, understood?' He stared into Drew's eyes.

Ian realised how very wrong he'd got all of this. Shame, regret, guilt and sadness combined as he stared back at his husband. 'I've been very lonely.'

'Because you excluded me from this. Is it any wonder?'

'Suppose,' Ian said, and not really meaning it.

'There's no suppose about it.'

'You don't talk to me about work.'

'I would if I lost my job.' Drew looked exasperated. 'For fuck's sake, this isn't the same.'

Drew didn't bring work home with him in that way because he didn't want to bring the trauma, pain and hurt he'd seen from firefighting into their home. He'd explained that to Ian when they first met. 'It's not saving cats stuck up trees. Some of the things I've seen, I don't want to remember it myself, never mind telling you about it.' And, he'd gone on to say later, 'I have my buddies down the station. That's what we do when we're waiting for a shout.'

'Even when I'm trying to fix something I still buggered that up.' *God, I really am bloody useless.* Ian sighed as the weight of his mistake and misjudgement, and everything he'd ever got wrong, pressed down on his chest, so he almost couldn't breathe.

'Enough beating yourself up. If anyone's going to be angry with you, it's me. All right?'

Ian had always thought himself very lucky, a six or seven married to a solid nine or ten. He worried without a job he'd dip to a five and Drew would realise the error of his ways and that would be it.

'What are you thinking?' Drew lifted Ian's chin up, so they made eye contact.

'Nothing.' He shook his head.

'Did you think I'd throw you out like the recycling box?'

Ian said nothing because the long and the short of it was, that was precisely what he'd believed.

'You think I'm that shallow?' Drew asked. 'That I only love you for what you earn?'

'When you put it like that, I don't know. At the time, I wasn't thinking straight.' He'd been very depressed, struggling to motivate himself to rise every morning, so the routine of going to the lido had helped. But after his employer had told him he wasn't good enough and the job interviews failed to come flooding in, Ian had soon concluded he really was worthless. And then his health problem had made things worse.

'I'd love you if we lived in a tent under a bridge next to the Thames.'

'I wouldn't love me then.'

'Maybe that's your problem. You don't see why you're so amazing, why so many people do love you. You're far too hard on yourself.'

'Maybe.' Ian shrugged.

'Definitely.'

Ian began to cry. 'I'm so sorry. I thought this was the right thing to do. I never wanted to hurt you. I thought this would hide the mess from you, not make it worse.'

'I know. You must have been really lonely, with no one to speak to about it.'

The lie. Ian thought it was far too charitable of Drew not to refer to it as the lie, since that was exactly what he'd done. Lied. Again and again, over many days, weeks and months. To the person who he'd promised to share his life with.

'If you'd told me we could have worked out what to do,' Drew said.

But it was too late now, the damage was done. The lies were told. 'I'm so so sorry. I genuinely thought I was doing it for the best.' There was no more he could do than apologise. The intent had been good, even if the execution was shitty.

'I know,' Drew said.

They sat in silence for a few long moments.

'How did you not go mad, keeping this all to yourself? A trip to buy a pint of milk can end up with a ten-minute anecdote from you. How did you not talk about this?'

'There's more.'

'More lies?'

'No.'

'Good. What then?'

'What you said about keeping it to myself.'

'Right,' Drew said with uncertainty.

'I did have people to talk to.'

'About this?'

Ian nodded.

'Who?' The tone also implied *and why not me?* but Ian did his best to press on in spite of that.

'TheLonely Hearts Lido Club.'

'At the lido, there's a group?'

'Our group.'

'Your group?' Drew shook his head. 'I don't understand. Start from the beginning. There's a group for people who are lonely? Like exercise groups if you want to get fit? Or walking groups if you want to walk...'

'We mainly drink tea and coffee. With some swimming.'

'We? Who's we?'

Ian told him, how they'd met, who the members were, and how they'd repeatedly implored him to come clean with Drew about the lie.

Drew sat back in the chair, shaking his head in obvious disbelief. 'Can I meet them?'

'You've already met Helen.'

'Who?'

'When I told you about my medical issue,' Ian said.

'I didn't think you'd worked together. She didn't even name the organisation, which seemed a bit... Anyway, hindsight is always crystal clear, right?'

Just like how Ian knew his handling of this had been beyond bad, terrible, stupid, unbelievable. But then again he'd not been thinking straight, had he? 'You'd like to meet the other members of the club?'

'How many are there?' Drew asked.

'Three, including me.'

'I'd like to meet them all.'

'Don't see why not,' Ian said.

'You've not got anything else you need to get off your chest, while we're here, have you?'

Ian shook his head.

'I feel like I've been married to a different person. I thought you were an open book to me.'

So did I. 'Sorry,' Ian said quietly. The fact he'd taken to sharing his darkest most unpleasant secrets with two near-strangers filled Ian with sorrow, not just for himself, but for his marriage, his relationship, for the sake of being open with one another, being able to talk about anything and everything.

'Enough of the sorrys – now we need to work out what to do next.'

'I don't know.'

'Which is why you've told me, so I can help. That's kinda how this whole marriage gig works.' Drew said it as a joke, but the implication of what it meant was like a knife to the heart for Ian, reminded him how monumentally wrong he'd got this.

They hugged, Ian resting his head on Drew's chest as they lay on the sofa. Ian wept quietly until he'd soaked

Drew's polo shirt as he kept repeating that he was really very very sorry.

'We're going to be all right,' Drew said. 'You are. I know.' He rested his hand on Ian's stomach, stroking the hairs and his navel gently.

And Ian, despite how he felt, what he believed he should have done, found that with relief, at both unburdening himself of the lie, his body was responding in a way he'd not experienced in a while, not with Drew anyway.

Drew kissed him, his fingers gently caressing, stroking, and feathering over Ian's body as it responded in ever more needing, hungry ways until there was no mistaking the release, the expression of love that Ian needed.

Mostly clothed and on the sofa wasn't how Ian would have planned their great reconnection, but in that moment, with joyful abandon and sweet relief, it was exactly what they needed.

Chapter 25

Gabriella stood at the café's counter, waiting to give her – no, their – order. Simon had told her what he wanted. She'd been repeating it in her head ever since, because it stopped her mind buzzing about why she shouldn't be doing this.

Even the setting was unfamiliar to her – she'd suggested a café in the town centre, rather than at the lido because she knew she'd be put off her stride watching Helen and Ian out of the corner of her eye.

She gave her order and their names to the barista, paid, then stood waiting for her order to be prepared.

Simon – in a dark blue suit and white shirt, matching dark blue tie – sat at their table frantically typing on his phone.

She'd decided to leave him to it, rather than waiting at the table for their order. He seemed to be very busy. Perhaps, she reflected, he would be too busy to stay for long and this awkward part of her day would be over quickly.

'Gabriella and Simon,' the barista called, holding the cups aloft.

She took them and walked towards the table outside on the pavement beneath a parasol.

Gabriella and Simon – it was almost as if the universe was announcing them as a couple before she did.

Gabriella and Simon, she didn't hate the sound of that. She wasn't sure of his surname, how would it sound after her first name. Although not having the same one as the boys was an issue. And the boys, of course, wouldn't want to change theirs would they? *Why am I getting so ahead of myself?*

She sat at the table, sliding Simon's drink towards him.

He looked up from his phone, slipping it into his pocket. 'You look miles away.'

She had been. Hundreds, thousands of miles away, worrying about surnames and step-dads and what his girls would think about her boys and the load of old cobblers she had no business even thinking about just yet.

Ever, probably.

She laughed nervously. 'Yeah, I was. You know what it's like. Start thinking about one thing and then you've hopped, skipped and jumped to a dozen others.'

'I was just trying to sort something out – work-wise. Done now.' He patted his phone in his pocket for emphasis.

He had told her what he did for a living – she thought anyway. But her memory wasn't what it had been. He'd said something about acting or writing, or speaking, or something like that. It was definitely something about… Something.

He blew onto his coffee, looking at her from the corner of his eye. 'Do you work?'

God, this is hard work. I don't remember it being such a palaver with Arnie. A sigh. And oh, God, I've just sat down and already my dead husband is here with us. Christ, this really was such a bad idea, what the bloody hell convinced me to do it?

'I must get back to doing something work-wise. But it's hard when you're alone.' She giggled nervously. 'Course, you know. Same for you. I don't think I could go back to modelling, I'm pretty much past it for that. It's a young woman's game, is that. Not that it's like being on the game. Although if people want to do that, then it's their choice...What I meant to say is I don't know how I'd feel about being in front of the camera again. I mean, people say, when I tell them I done modelling, was it mucky. I mean, some of it was, yeah. It was just a thing I did, not who I am. That's what Arnie always used to say... So yeah, I'm still thinking about career options. I mean job. Something to do with my brainbox.' She picked up the mug and took a long slurp, more to stop herself talking than anything else.

He nodded slowly, blowing on his drink again, looking at her with concern, or worry perhaps.

If I'd just listened to someone saying that load of old cobblers, I'd have run a mile by now.

'Why did you give it up?' he asked.

He hadn't mentioned Arnie, which she reckoned was good. If her dead husband hadn't been part of the date — no, it wasn't a date, it was a chat — before, then he definitely was now. She smoothed her dress's crumples over her stomach — still larger than it had been in her modelling days. Never managed to shift that last half a stone after the boys. 'I never wanted to give it up. Well, that's not true. I did. But not without anything else I enjoyed as much. It was my passion. As a girl I couldn't do much else but look pretty.' She laughed at her very bad joke.

'That's not true, I'm sure.' He smiled. His eyes seemed to change colour from blue-green to green-blue.

They talked about their children, his girls were called Olivia and Sophie, one looked like him and the other,

Olivia, Gabriella thought, reminded him of his wife – he'd shown her a photo from his wallet.

At the mention of his wife who was very much no longer alive, the chatty banter came crashing to an end.

Her hands were sweaty. Very sweaty. She stood. 'I'm just going to nip off. Use the facilities.' She scuttled inside to the ladies' loo and surveyed herself in the mirror.

What on earth are you doing here? He was just being friendly, there's no way he wanted anything more. Who would? Two kids, dead husband hanging around in whatever she said like a lingering fart. She was hardly a catch.

Gabriella brushed her long wavy hair, noting the dark roots had returned, something to ask Helen for help with later.

Helen.

And Ian.

They were the reason she was here now. On the worst not-date in the history of human beings speaking to each other.

Reapplying her lipstick, she said, firmly to herself: 'No need to be nervous. He's just a friend. This is a casual coffee with a friend.' A firm nod at her reflection and she opened the door to return outside to their table.

Simon was frantically typing on his phone. He looked up, flipped it over and left it on the table. 'Sorry. Addicted. Bad isn't it? How did we manage without them?'

She laughed far too much and sat, berating herself again very strongly. A coffee with this much adrenaline pumping through her veins was a mistake. Arnie used to say she talked too much and should let others fill the silence.

Fill. The. Silence.

'Would I have seen you in any campaigns?' Simon asked.

She stared at him – neatly trimmed dark blond beard, bluey green eyes, tanned skin. He had big hands too – they rested on the table. Neat nails, long fingers and hairless too. *I wonder if he's hairless elsewhere…*

'Recently?' he asked. 'Campaigns. Adverts, you were in.'

She shook her head and let out the breath she hadn't known she'd been holding. This was bad news. Very. Bad. News. She'd seen enough romcoms and read enough books to know she needed to hold on tight to her hat because… 'I used to be the face of Manière, the hair dye people. Ironic since I didn't need it then, and now I do. I—' She stopped herself. Let others fill the silence.

'I remember that. You talked about how easy it was to apply and how natural it looked. You were brown haired then.'

'Contractually I had to be. Sad times, eh?' She shrugged.

He laughed. A loud reverberating deep booming laugh and she wasn't quite sure what to do.

'You're funny,' he said.

She shook her head. She really wasn't. No one had ever said she was funny before. Not except her family and they didn't count. *He's only saying this because he wants to get me into bed.*

Oh God. I need to make him hate me. Rabbit on about myself, not let him get a word in edgeways and he'll soon go off me.

'What else?' he asked and his tone implied he was interested.

She talked about the car she'd nearly launched – the little sports car that was practical as well as stylish, except she'd missed out to another model and had ended up being the hands and lips of a high street chemist's makeup brand for ten years; the high street face cream she'd fronted for most of the early Noughties – how each advert felt like a film because the shoots were so over the top and made no sense; she added that she'd been considered for the face of a premium dog food but had turned it down.

'Why, you like dogs, don't you?'

She didn't like dogs but equally she didn't dislike them. 'I was throwing up all over the shop, couldn't have sat down long enough for them to take the pics.'

'Bet you could.'

She blushed. Arnie had told her she didn't need to do it, that she could rest and concentrate on growing their baby inside her. 'That was my last job. Then Jack came along.'

'I remember that dog food. Who did the adverts? Can't remember. They weren't as memorable as you.' He grinned.

Is he just trying to charm me into bed, or is he really interested in me and thinks I'm memorable, pretty and funny? Gabriella's bullshit radar was very out of practice. She'd been with Arnie for so long that she'd not needed it.

'Do they know at the school they have an international supermodel in their midst?' He smiled.

Her heart went faster – bad sign, definitely. *I'm in trouble here.* 'Hardly international. Definitely not a super-model. I was like a jobbing actor, isn't that the phrase?'

He nodded.

'Yeah, I was a jobbing model. Chugging away. It was years ago. I don't look the same.' Two babies and a decade had a habit of doing that to a woman, she'd found out.

'You do.'

Her bullshit radar buzzed inside her head. It was difficult to tell because he'd been asking about her, taking an interest and yet he was a man. A charming one at that. She felt sure he was a salesman. Gift of the gab and all that.

She shook her head.

His phone rang. He checked it, then turned it upside down.

'Get it, I was going to make a call anyway.'

'Sure?' he asked.

'Positive. I've got a message from the school.'

'I'll give you privacy.' He stepped away.

She checked her voicemail and it was the school secretary asking if she had authorised her parents-in-law to collect the boys in the middle of the day. *For fuck's sake, what have they been and gone and done now?*

Before the receptionist could ask who was calling, Gabriella said, 'I do not give consent. No consent. I'm not having *them* two picking up my boys.'

'Yes,' she said, 'we wondered if that was a little peculiar.'

'What did they do? Did they turn up and try to kidnap them?'

'Let's not get too hasty.'

'They're my kids, I'll tell you if it's too hasty.'

'I don't think it's appropriate to say they're being kidnapped since they're the boys' grandparents.'

'You don't know the half of it. The way they brought up their son, my Arnie, I don't want any of that rubbing off on my boys. I need to be with them to protect them.'

'From their grandparents?'

'Bloody right.' Boarding school, bullying, and regular beatings, if Gabriella remembered rightly.

'I see.' There was silence. 'I'll tell them *you're* collecting the boys, shall I?'

'Yes.'

The receptionist said something else, but Gabriella wasn't listening.

She ended the call and her hands were shaking. If she smoked, this was when she could really do with one.

Simon was pacing up and down the pavement, speaking on his phone. The way he moved his hands and leaned forward to emphasise his point, was pure Arnie. He even looked like Arnie too – similar build, dark blond or light brown hair, dark brown eyes too.

'Everything okay?' Simon asked, stepping back to their table.

She jumped. His good looks were pretty striking and she'd been observing his movements and forgotten he was actually with her, having a coffee. 'Parents-in-law. Long story.' She rolled her eyes.

'Do you need to leave?'

Does he want me to go? Is this a convenient escape route to this not-date? 'I don't think so. No, I don't. It's sorted for now.' *Until I have a firm word with the pair of them, bloody pushy buggers.*

'Do you want to call someone, your parents maybe, talk it through? I can get us more drinks. Or go. If you need to.'

She did want to call her parents. Had done every day since they'd died. But it was impossible. 'Can we just sit for a bit? I've had enough of my life for today. What about you?'

'What about me?'

'Everything.'

And not just because it would be a distraction from her own problems, but because she genuinely wanted to hear from him, she agreed to stay a bit longer.

Simon ordered more drinks, this time iced coffees to cool themselves as the heat rose into the low thirties.

I'm enjoying this. Him. Being with him. It's nice to have some additional adult company, to be in the company of a man who's so fit and well-spoken. He is, she allowed herself to admit, watching him inside the café as he paid for their drinks, leaving a tip in the change jar, pretty damned near to perfect.

He placed their cream-topped, iced coffees on the table. 'When you say widower it sort of sends the conversation to a shuddering halt.'

'I know.' With care, she asked, 'What happened, if you don't mind me asking?'

'Blood cancer, leukaemia. It was quick, which if there were any small mercies, that's one. Less than three months from diagnosis to...'

Gabriella stroked his arm as it rested on the table.

'Every day, I miss her. Every. Single. Day.'

She nodded, leaning back on the table. 'When?' Gabriella asked carefully.

He counted on his fingers. 'Eight months.'

It was the same time since Gabriella had lost Arnie. She didn't say. It felt stupid. Like it made it any better. It didn't of course. Like they were members of a secret misery-guts-grieving-their-other-halves club. 'Do you reckon it gets less?' she asked.

'What?'

'The pain of losing someone. Grief. When Arnie first died it felt like I couldn't stand cos it was weighing me down. Pressing on my chest when I woke and remembered he was gone.'

'I've been reading lots about grief and went to a group too. You should give it a go, if you like.'

Gabriella nodded. Maybe she would. Maybe she wouldn't. But she'd never even considered it before.

'The grief is always there, because you don't stop loving the lost person, but it shrinks and doesn't touch your outsides all the time. Imagine a box with a big balloon inside. At first the balloon touches all the sides of the box. But over time it gets smaller, bouncing around inside the box, from time to time. That's when the grief touches you still, years later.'

She liked that. Could imagine it in her head. 'My balloon's pretty big still. Not like before, but still touches the box quite a lot. You know?'

Simon nodded. 'For me I can cope. Have to. It's the girls that make it hardest.'

'Yep.'

'They used to ask when Mummy was coming home from the hospital. I didn't let them see her right at the end. Wanted them to remember her healthy and full of life. Perhaps it was a mistake.'

Gabriella's heart squeezed tightly for him. He really had been through the worst experience someone could go through. 'You did what felt right at the time. That's all you can do, I reckon. Your best. That's what my old mum used to say.'

There was a silence for a few moments. Gabriella felt almost consumed by her grief, having made Simon talk about his. Which felt selfish. Plumping for an easy subject, she asked, 'What do you do for work?'

'I do voice-overs. I'm a voice actor. Narrating books, adverts.'

'I thought I recognised your voice. Did you do the advert with the puppy and the cat playing together?'

'I was the daddy dog. Telling the puppy off.'

'Right.' She smiled. *See, there is still plenty of joy around, if you know where to look for it.* 'Done anything lately?'

'I've been looking after the girls. I'll get back to it soon.'

'Course you will. When the time's right.'

He grinned at her. Twinkly eyes, perfect white teeth and a prominent but attractive nose.

Gave him a distinctive profile when he looked sideways. *Roman nose, that's what they say isn't it?* Gabriella suppressed a grin.

'Indeed. This has been nice,' he said, looking into her eyes. 'I didn't think I could do it. Thanks.' He leaned forwards, and was about to kiss her cheek.

Her phone rang in her handbag. Gabriella froze, then pulled back, scrabbling to answer it.

He missed her cheek. Kissed her hair. Bit some. 'Sorry. I shouldn't have...' He spat out the hair as he pulled back. *Mortified.*

She stood, walked away from their table, stumbling as she navigated past the other tables and chairs, until she was a short distance away, staring at the building, not sure what to do next.

Simon joined her. 'Sorry,' he said breathlessly. 'I didn't mean to scare you off. Are you all right?'

She shook her head, walked backwards as if he were about to harm her. 'My fault. I think I've made a mistake.' She turned away, half waved half shrugged as a half-arsed apology. She answered the phone. It was the school, asking when she was going to collect the boys because their grandparents were still waiting outside the school and now the school day had ended, she really needed to collect them. She ran towards her car and drove there as quickly as possible.

Chapter 26

A week later, Gabriella had asked Helen to collect the boys from school. Even though it was the last day of term, before they broke up for summer holidays, Gabriella had said she couldn't face it.

Since having coffee with that man – Sam, or Simon he was called – she'd been much more withdrawn. She'd returned from having coffee with him and been very shaken up. Almost as if she'd endured some sort of trauma, which seemed ridiculous given what had happened.

Poor confused, grieving woman, Helen reflected now.

'Hello,' a voice said from behind her.

She turned and it was Bill.

He wore a baggy, creased blue shirt and trousers that looked as if he had tied them up with a piece of string. He didn't look unkempt, just not well put together.

Briefly, her heart squeezed for him, feeling sorry for him. 'What are you doing here?' Helen asked, as she felt as if the hot pavement had tilted sideways.

'Don't be stupid, come home, will you?'

'I'm busy,' she said, turning back to face the school gates, stepping into the shade away from the stifling heat.

'Doing what?'

'Collecting Gabriella's boys from school. She's unwell and she asked me. I like helping her. She appreciates it.' She narrowed her eyes, staring at him for a moment.

'You can drop them home and then come back to your real home. With me.' It wasn't a question, instead a statement. An order of sorts.

Helen rolled her eyes. 'Just like that, eh?'

'Don't you want to come home?'

There was plenty she missed about her home, the space, not having to trip over toys on the floor, but there was also a lot she hated. 'I do not.'

'Why not?' He looked at her briefly, his light blue eyes showing worry for the first time in as long as she remembered.

'I was unhappy there. I'm not unhappy now.' She shrugged as if it were the simplest decision in the world. In some ways it had been.

'I knew you were okay,' he said after the silence.

'I think you're misunderstanding me. I was not okay, before. Hence why I left.' Or was it, she wondered, more accurate to describe that he hadn't been okay, which was why she'd left?

'Your phone. I saw it moving.'

She was horrified. 'You've been tracking me?'

'I knew you were okay because your phone was moving.'

'Someone could have stolen it.'

'They didn't.'

'Is that why it's taken you all this time to visit me?'

He looked at the ground. 'I thought you were staying with a friend.'

'Correct.'

'When you didn't come back, I realised something was up.'

'What, precisely, is that then?' This ought to be good.

'That's as far as I've got. Which is why I'm here.'

233

A bell rang inside the school signalling the children would shortly be finished.

'Don't be so silly, come home with me, will you?' Desperation had tinged his tone.

At least now it was a question, rather than an order. She responded better to those. Shaking her head, she said, 'No.'

'What do you want me to do?'

Children were pouring out of the school, running across the playground towards the gate. A teacher stood, watching children greet their parents, or whoever was collecting them.

Helen waved at the two boys, who waved back. She walked closer, so she could speak to the teacher. 'I'm Helen, collecting Gabriella's boys, on her behalf. She rang this morning to say so.'

The teacher checked a piece of paper on her clipboard. 'Can I see some ID, please?'

Gabriella had said they may ask for this – can't be too careful nowadays – so she handed over her driving licence.

The teacher inspected it, glancing at the clipboard. She stepped aside, and let the two boys through the gate to meet Helen.

Helen pulled them in for hugs, kissing their cheeks in turn, inhaling the scent that was peculiar to them and only them. 'Ready?' She stood, taking their hands.

'What about me?' Bill asked behind her.

She turned, still holding the boys' hands. 'What *about* you?'

'I need you.'

'I'm afraid,' Helen said with as much self-control as she could muster, 'you're just going to have to get used to managing without me.'

'Come home, please.'

'If you'd taken me by the hand, and gently led me home, shown me how you felt, perhaps accompanying me to our bedroom, then I may consider it. But this, this pitiful performance, it's just not going to cut it I'm afraid.' She turned, striding towards her car.

Content she'd lost him, she strapped the boys into their car seats as Gabriella had shown her, checked the seatbelts were correctly fastened, then buckled herself up.

Once back at Gabriella's home, she was leaning into the back seats to remove the boys from their seats and walk them inside, when she felt a presence behind her. Must be Gabriella. 'Could you help me, I can't seem to—'

'Won't you reconsider?' Bill said.

'I have my hands full. Time and a place. This is neither. I can't believe you followed me!' Anger warred with feeling slightly impressed at his persistence.

Gabriella had appeared from her house and stood next to the car. 'Are you Bill?' she asked him.

'You're Gabriella, I assume.'

She nodded. To Helen she asked, 'Are you all right here?'

'Can you take the boys inside please?'

Gabriella grabbed them by the hands and stood watching Bill with care. 'I can wait, see you inside, if you want.'

'That won't be necessary,' Bill said.

'I'll wait.'

Helen turned to face him. 'There are laws against this sort of thing. You followed me home, and now you're harassing me. I could call the police.'

'Go on then.'

She shook her head. 'Or we can just go inside.'

'I want to talk to you.'

'That's a first.' She chuckled to herself. 'I've had a lot of time to think and have made some decisions.'

'Good.'

'Not good actually. Very bad. Well, for you, anyway. I shall be fine. You, on the other hand…'

'Can we not do this here, with an audience? Couldn't we go somewhere quiet, talk it through?' He looked at Gabriella and the boys. 'I'm sorry.'

Helen walked towards him, fixing him with a stare. 'If you can tell me what you're apologising for, then we can leave to discuss things.'

'It's obvious, isn't it?'

She raised her eyebrows. 'Is it?'

'Plainly.'

Helen shook her head almost imperceptibly as she caught Gabriella's eye. 'I'm waiting.'

'You're unhappy.'

'I'm listening.'

'Isn't that it?'

At its core, he wasn't wrong. But the part Helen wanted him to understand was why. Why she felt this way and why he hadn't noticed until she had left.

'Well?' he asked.

'Do you remember that holiday in Greece when we saw the couple on the beach?'

'When?'

'Three or four years ago.' She described the couple, their being semi-nude and standing entwined for a while before adjourning to somewhere more private.

'You didn't want to swim in the nude, did you?'

She shook her head. *Jesus Christ, give me strength!* 'No. They saw one another.' Even the memory now, of the

236

couple and their obvious love, made Helen sad when holding it in direct contrast to her relationship with Bill. She didn't expect to be like a couple of teenagers, but she was sick and tired of him not seeing her, barely noticing her. That was why she'd left, to find out if he missed her.

'I see you. Like now. I appreciate you.'

Helen scoffed. 'What I do for you, more like.'

'They're the same. You're splitting hairs.'

'If I can,' Gabriella said, 'they're not the same.'

'I'm very sorry,' Bill said, 'but I'm trying to have a conversation with my wife. I'd appreciate if you didn't interject.'

Helen stared at Bill. 'Don't be so bloody rude. And at Gabriella's home too.' She shook her head and stared at him with disapproval.

'I was just saying it's a private matter between husband and wife.'

'Gabriella can say what she bloody well likes. She's more than earned the privilege since I've lived with her and she's listened to me for hours and hours, when you didn't. Wouldn't. Decades of ignoring me. Putting off conversations indefinitely.'

Bill turned to Gabriella. 'Sorry.'

She nodded in acceptance. 'It's the easiest thing in the world to take someone for granted, cos they're always there, dependable, in the background, keeping things running smoothly. But loving someone is a habit you have to keep.'

Bill stared at her, chewing the inside of his cheek. Clearly the message hadn't hit home, as far as Helen could see.

'There's a first time for everything, I suppose,' Helen said, walking towards the house, following Gabriella and the boys.

They went in and Helen stood on the step. She turned to face him. 'I was looking forward to retirement. Together. To doing all the things we talked about but couldn't when you were working and we had children. This is meant to be our time now. I've been patient. But I'm sick and tired of waiting for my life to begin because you're busy doing something else. Something that never involves me, so I spend my whole time in an endless queue, waiting to get to the front, to my time. When I got there, I realised I'd been queueing for nothing. For no one.' She'd not quite expressed it like this before and the blinding realisation that she'd wasted so many years hit her like a punch. She felt winded, sick with the wasted years, time she could never have again.

'I'm sorry,' he said. 'Very sorry. I didn't know—'

'Because,' she said, 'you never saw me. I'm a silly old fool for not being more forceful, for not telling you. But I tried. You didn't listen. I've spent my life supporting you in your endeavours, because that's what wives used to do. But Gabriella's generation has got it right. No sticking with someone for the sake of the marriage. Now it's generation *me*, and I've been generation *don't worry about me*. Well, I've realised if I don't worry about me, then no one else will.' She slammed the door behind her.

Gabriella met her in the kitchen. 'Okay?'

'I think I've done it.'

'What?'

'Left him. Properly. Permanently.'

'Right. Well done you.'

'I've decided I'm going to divorce him.'

Gabriella hugged her. 'I know some amazing solicitors. News spreads fast around the school.'

'Yes,' Helen said, 'I think it's best all round.'

'Good. Decision made. You'll feel better now.'

Helen hoped that was true. Because at the moment she felt worse than when she'd packed a bag and walked out. She was now going to divorce him, leave him, walk away permanently and all that would entail. 'Right,' she made it sound decisive, even if she didn't feel it. 'Where are the boys?'

'In their rooms, playing. Why?'

'I want to see them.'

'Fill your boots.'

Helen smiled weakly, trying to put on a brave face as she walked upstairs to follow the boys' voices and sit with them, each in turn, watching them amuse themselves with toys.

She didn't eat that evening, had lost her appetite for some reason. As she sat at the table in the garden, sipping wine in the warm evening air, while the others ate, a blinding realisation struck her: not only did Bill not see her, but he didn't know her either. He was a man entirely devoid of emotion – not just for her, but for himself too. How could she have missed this for so long? Or was it something he'd grown into over the decades?

'What would it have taken for you not to divorce him?' Gabriella said later, as they tidied the kitchen, after the boys were asleep.

Another glass of wine, she decided. She seemed to have consumed most of a bottle tonight, silently sipping while the others had been eating. Gabriella had said she shouldn't do that, it was a sure way to get drunk very quickly and Helen had said she needed something to take the edge off.

'He just needed to make a start. Show me he cared enough to want to change.'

'That makes sense,' Gabriella said. 'Half the time when me and Arnie used to fight, I just wanted him to see things from my side. Not necessarily agree, but just see there was another way of seeing things than his own. You know?'

'Absolutely.' Helen noticed her lipstick marks on the wine glass – a series of sticky red crescents. 'Do you ever wish you could live your life again? Differently?'

Without a pause, Gabriella shook her head. 'Not at all. I wish Arnie was still here, but anything other than that, no. If I did that, I wouldn't have my two beautiful boys, this house, you…' She smiled.

It was sweet of her to include Helen in the grand sweep of her life, but Helen didn't think it necessary. She nodded slowly in thought.

'You?' Gabriella asked.

'I think it's difficult to view my life from now. Through a lens of how women live now.'

'Yes.'

'Peter doesn't need me. It's how it should be. He's a grown man, with his own life. But I thought there would be more for *me* at this point.'

'With Bill?'

'And without him. Perhaps he's not completely to blame. Perhaps I should have been more forceful. Easy to think now, but forty years ago was a different time. For men, women, children, families.' Helen had done what she'd needed to back then. No point wishing she'd been more of a twenty-first century woman in the eighties, it was as impossible as wishing she'd had the Internet, or flatscreen TVs, or smartphones.

'You can say that again,' Gabriella said.

Helen walked towards her, kissing her on the head. 'You're very lucky. I was lucky in comparison to my mother and my grandmother.' Perhaps it was impossible to expect Bill to behave like young men nowadays. Maybe she was asking the unachievable. But he had been a good husband, father, at the time. Otherwise, why had she stayed married to him for so long?

Chapter 27

As July almost became August, the summer's heat continued. Ian was in bed, half asleep and half awake, naked, with only the sheet to cover him.

Drew had left for work very early, a kiss and a 'see you tonight' as Ian rolled onto his front. Drew had left, but not before showing Ian how much he loved him, and Ian had reciprocated, with sweet relief at how he, once more, could do so.

Ian rolled over in bed and his body responded at the memory of half an hour before, he grinned in anticipation of Drew returning that evening, his kisses, his hugs and so much more...

Unburdening himself from the lie had been the first step to physically recovering. Not working itself wasn't as bad as not being truthful to Drew. It had sat in such strong relief against his normal behaviour that it had eaten away at him, making him question who he was, what he could do, crippling him with anxiety which manifested physically in his impotence.

'You were impotent, so you became impotent,' Drew had said not long after Ian had told him.

'I hadn't thought about it like that.'

Ian was a man used to being able to resolve problems, to read around subjects until he felt a comfortable mastery and became an expert. He'd had that taken away from him, and his ability to do so while job hunting had eluded him.

'I know I asked before, but I'd really like to meet the other members of your club,' Drew had said last night.

'Why?'

'Because they saved you.'

'Did they?'

'Definitely. And from what you've said, you saved them too.'

'I think that's a bit much. Helped is probably a better word.'

'I'll meet them at the lido.'

The lido was their place, and not Drew's. 'I'd rather not.' The guilt and memories of all the times he'd shared his hopelessness and sadness with Gabriella and Helen, rather than Drew, would haunt him forever. He didn't want Drew to return to the scene of the crime, so to speak.

'They're your friends, you decide.' And that had been the end of the discussion.

Now, he rolled out of bed and into the shower, ready to meet Gabriella and Helen at the lido, see how they were getting on, before inviting them to his place.

At the lido, in the warming morning heat as the temperature climbed above twenty before midday, Ian completed his lengths of the pool, and had a few snippets of conversation with Helen, who seemed more than usually withdrawn. She volunteered hardly anything in response to his questions – and didn't ask him any back. There was obviously something going on there.

Gabriella had decided she was less keen on swimming, without the impetus of the boys wanting to do so. Instead she saved their corner table in the café, waiting for them.

Ian waited by the changing booths for Helen to leave, walking with her along the edge of the pool, past the fountain and people sitting on sun loungers, to the far end, by the glass window into the café.

'You seem contemplative,' Ian asked carefully.

'Correct.'

'Anything you want to share?'

She shook her head. 'No point.'

'Sure?'

She stopped walking, looked directly at him. 'Did you ever think you could have lived a better life if only you'd made better decisions?'

He hadn't. He reckoned his life had turned out pretty well, all things considered. 'You can't.'

'If you could, I said.'

'But it's impossible, that's the point of life. You don't get another go at it. No dress rehearsal, isn't that what they say?'

'I think I may slip off home. Don't feel as if I shall be much use today.' She sounded morose.

As they arrived in the café, Ian caught Gabriella's eye, nodding towards Helen, then shaking his head – hoping she'd get the message that Helen was very much not okay today. And although Ian knew nowadays it was supposedly okay not to be okay, he felt sure Helen would not agree.

'Do you know,' Helen said, holding the back of the chair, 'I think I'll pass today, if it's all the same with you two.' She looked from Ian to Gabriella and back.

'Please don't go,' Gabriella said, 'I have a lot to tell you.' Turning to Ian she went on, 'And you.'

Helen shook her head, staring at the floor.

Ian stood, and carefully guided her towards a chair.

She sat and looked glum, defeated and exhausted.

'I was,' Ian said uncertainly, 'going to invite you to mine. But perhaps I should wait.'

'Do please do so,' Helen said, sitting upright and a smile briefly crossing her face, 'I should like that. What is the occasion?'

'Drew wants to meet you both. Wants to thank you.'

'What for?' Gabriella asked, looking about herself. 'Can't get used to not having at least one kid to look after.'

'That sticks,' Helen said quietly. 'Where are the boys?'

'Simon's. We've been having play dates and it's my turn to have his two girls next.'

Ian looked from one woman to the other. 'It's a thank you, from Drew. For being there when he wasn't. Couldn't be, because Drew didn't know the truth. When you did.'

'I'd love to come. When?' Helen said.

'Doesn't he mind that you told two strangers the truth and not your own husband?' Gabriella said. 'I would. I'd be physically livid.'

Ian smirked at her turn of phrase that he'd by now learned to embrace and love. He shrugged. 'He knows I wasn't myself. Losing my job hit me harder than it would him. Not being good at something isn't my comfort zone.'

'Does that include *not* being a good husband?' Helen asked absently.

'Harsh.' A pause, and then: 'It should do.'

'Can I bring someone?' Gabriella asked.

'You must bring the boys. Drew is getting broody I think.' Ian smiled.

'Tempted?'

'Not just yet.'

'No,' Gabriella said, 'I meant someone else. Helen, you could bring Bill. Wouldn't it be nice for them all to meet? Like we have been…'

'I wouldn't hold your breath for Bill to come.'

'Drew will be there, and if I can bring Simon, a sort of thanks for the playdates and the coffees… That just leaves your Bill.'

Helen shook her head slowly. 'He's not my Bill. He never really was.' She stood, left her herbal tea untouched on the table. 'Please don't call me.' She left, walking slowly and carefully towards the door.

'What's wrong with her?' Ian asked Gabriella.

'She's been different lately.'

'Since when?'

'She saw Bill.'

'Talking is better than not. Where did she meet him?'

'He turned up at the boys' school. Since then she's been talking about repeating her life, me being lucky, that sort of thing.'

'Should we worry?'

'I'll keep an eye on her. See that she comes to your do. Even if it's without Bill. Which is most likely. Maybe I shouldn't bring Simon – makes a big point about Bill not being there.'

'When do you think?'

'Daytime, weekend, then I can bring the boys and Simon. Few weeks' time?'

'I'll check what shifts Drew's working – it's all or nothing with him.' In life as in work, he reflected with a smile.

Gabriella put her hand on his on the table. 'Me and Helen had been comparing notes, if you like…' She looked out of the window. '…the other thing. Just briefly, no details. She didn't want to pry. Said Bill had the same thing a few times. Come to think of it, Arnie did a few times – mostly too much booze, but he took it to heart. Got really worried it was permanent.'

Ian did *not* want to have this conversation, but he knew it came from a place of genuine concern. 'Everything's fine in that department.'

'Spect it's easier, with being two men. Knowing how things work, what it's like to… Or not to…' Gabriella raised her perfectly plucked and shaped eyebrows.

There was an awkward silence.

'I'll check with Drew and we'll sort out a date. Talking of dates, how did yours go with Simon?'

'I tried to talk to Helen about it, but she… Anyway, she's not herself.' A pause, and then: 'Well. It went well. I think. Except for the end.'

'Why, what happened?'

'Ten years I've been with Arnie. Ten years I've not kissed another man like that. Ten years I've only looked and not touched. And now… Well, I can touch. What's worse, is he looks so much like Arnie.' She shrugged. 'Must have a type. Didn't think I did.'

'Where did you go?'

'Café. Daytime. No kids. Felt funny at first. He's very interesting – does these books where you talk them and don't read them. And lots of adverts – voice-overs. We talked about my adverts, when I was modelling.'

'Sounds lovely. I can understand why you want him to come to the lunch. What went wrong?'

'Not wrong-wrong, just awkward. I knew it was a date, but wasn't sure what he was expecting by the end.'

'Not to get you in bed, surely?'

'Course not. What sort of girl do you think I am. It's all the hellos and goodbyes I can't get the hang of.'

'I don't follow.'

'He shook my hand when he arrived. It's not like he's not met me before. Held out my chair for me too. That was nice. Gentlemanly. When I left he went in for a kiss and I moved my head – didn't fancy a smacker on the lips.'

'Right,' Ian sounded uncertain. 'And?'

'He only went and missed my cheek and kissed my hair, bit some and spat a bit of it out.'

'Awkward.'

'Just a bit.'

'So you want to see him again, to rectify that? See if he's interested?'

'We've met since then. I apologised for running off, said I needed to pick up the kids.'

'So why do you want to bring him to my do?' Ian asked.

'I think,' Gabriella said with a tone of sadness, 'I need to see if I can kiss him back without wanting to run away and feeling guilty.'

'About what?'

'Arnie.'

'But he's dead!' Ian said, very confused.

Gabriella shrugged. 'Didn't say it made sense, did I?'

'Death and grief aren't simple. Or the same for everyone. I reckon it's normal to feel that way.'

'Good… I think…' Gabriella raised an eyebrow.

Chapter 28

Gabriella was enjoying – well, that was going too far, more enduring – having dinner with her two boys at Pru and Edward's home.

They had asked how each boy was getting on at school, Thomas was getting used to not being at home all day with Mummy, as he settled into both the routine and short days at preschool; Jack was learning he didn't like reading but all the adults told him he should. He'd also scored top points at a maths test – this last part impressed Gabriella very much. She had no head for figures, always resorting to her phone's calculator for the simplest sums, but Arnie had been a great whizz with figures, so he'd obviously got it from his dad.

'And what,' Pru said, turning to Gabriella, 'have you been up to?'

She hadn't expected to be asked this – she thought her main role was bringing the boys there and taking them home afterwards. Mostly she just sat at the table, listened and ate. Which made a change for her usually chatty persona.

Gabriella finished her mouthful and debated with herself whether to tell them, or just spring it on them as a surprise. Arnie was always for the first option, but if she decided on the second, she always had him there to protect her from any fallout.

'I'm thinking about going back to work,' she said.

'Doing what?' Pru asked.

'Not parading around in your underwear so people can photograph you, surely?' Edward said with obvious disapproval.

'That's not really how it worked,' Gabriella said, 'And Arnie was a great photographer. Very good eye.' A memory of him saying she was a natural in front of the camera, that her enthusiasm for life and joyful personality came through in her pictures, shot through her like a knife.

'You'll work in a shop, presumably,' Pru said.

'Why would I do that?'

'How on earth would you go back to modelling, with the two boys?'

The kids had politely asked if they could leave the table and been granted the permission by Pru – who very much believed that manners maketh the man, or whatever it was. They were playing in the lounge with the many toys Pru and Edward had bought them for when they visited.

'I have a friend who'll look after them. He has kids too. We'll share it. It was hearing about how he juggles his career with his two girls that made my decision to go back.' Simon fitted in his voice-over work between school runs and ironing uniforms. Not without a lot of juggling and help, but he did it. He'd told her at length and she'd been so impressed, realised how much she missed having a creative outlet for herself.

'Besides,' she went on, 'most of the work is during the week, when they're at school. I always planned to go back to work once they were both at school. It's something me and Arnie talked about.'

At the mention of her son's name, Pru visibly bristled. 'I see.' A pause, and then: 'And where has this sudden impetus come from?'

'Like I said, I was waiting until Thomas went to school. I have a lot of free time during the day now.' And what Helen had said to her about filling her days.

'I see.' Pru clearly didn't.

'Is looking after the home and boys,' Edward said, 'not enough for you? I think you do it so well.' He tilted his head to one side in a look Gabriella recognised as pity, with a side order of patronising.

'Thanks,' Gabriella said, 'I think. It's not that it's not enough, it's that I have time and skills to do more.'

Pru looked over the top of her glasses. 'I see.' Her tone implied she did anything but. 'And what, may I ask, do the boys think of this?'

She hadn't told them, because it hadn't yet happened. Seemed a bit pointless until she had something to say. 'They don't know yet. But they will. When I have something to tell them.'

'I see,' Pru said. Again.

The irritation bubbled up inside Gabriella's stomach and she couldn't bite her tongue any longer. If Arnie had been here, he'd have gently knocked her leg under the table. But he wasn't. He hadn't been there for a while now and Gabriella was getting more and more used to living without him, making decisions without him.

Gabriella looked about her, from Pru to Edward. 'I'm good at it. Did he ever tell you that?'

'Being a mother? Of course you are,' Edward said.

'Modelling. I was one of the highest-paid British models at the time. Not cos I got the big contracts, but because I worked so hard. All those high street chains and catalogues soon added up over the year.'

'Are you sure?' Pru asked as if she'd not heard Gabriella. 'We're very happy to take the boys more, if you need some more time to yourself. But surely there must be other things you can amuse yourself with?'

'Not that'll pay me two grand for a day's work.' The money, as always, would come in handy. If she earned enough it may mean less reliance on Pru and Edward for the boys' school fees and then these dinners would return to being optional.

'I've told you, you don't need to worry about that side of things,' Edward said with sincerity.

'It's very kind of you, but I like my independence. Something for myself. Earning my own money.'

'I see,' Pru narrowed her eyes.

'You really don't. Or you wouldn't have said that half a dozen times since we've been talking about this. Bottom line is, cooking and cleaning isn't enough of a life for me. Not now the boys have gone to school. I know it's fine for lots of other women, but I'm not one of those women. I don't mean to insult you, or anyone else who decided different. This is my decision to make and I will make it.'

'But you've not actually secured any photography work, as yet?' Pru asked.

Gabriella shook her head. 'That's the next step. My friend has contacts. I'm going to reach out to my friends from those days. Take some to lunch. You know. Networking.' She wished she felt more like a modern businesswoman rather than a naughty teenager trying to justify her decisions to her parents.

Gabriella's parents would have been nothing but supportive. Cheering her on, offering to take the boys

– which she'd have been glad to oblige. Her mum used to keep the magazines with Gabriella's adverts – framing them for the walls, despite it embarrassing Gabriella.

'Thank you for telling us,' Edward said with kindness.

They moved on to discussions about when the boys could next visit, and whether they could stay the night – 'especially if you're wanting some more space for yourself' – and Gabriella said she'd let them know, but at the moment she had plenty of help with her friend Helen who was staying with them.

'Auntie Helen,' Pru said, 'I believe the boys are calling her.' It came out as if she'd said she had found a large dog shit on the lounge carpet.

They had finished eating and Gabriella had declined sitting in their 'drawing room' because she wanted to get home.

She rested her hands on the table. 'That's right. And?'

'Who is she? And why is she living with you?'

'A friend. Who I'm helping out by letting her live in my house. The boys love her. She doesn't have any grandkids. And with Mum gone, it's nice having her there.'

Pru peered at her as if she was inspecting a mark on the carpet. 'Interesting setup.'

Gabriella stood. 'She's texted, we should get back. See how she's doing. Loneliness is a terrible thing.' She looked from Pru to Edward to emphasise that they didn't have this problem.

'Must you leave so soon?' Edward asked.

Gabriella was in the study where the boys had been playing, telling them to tidy up the toys and get ready to go. They had been there over two hours, and that was more than enough of Arnie's parents for one week.

'Thank you for coming,' Pru said, standing by the door.

'Thanks for having us. And the, you know, school… Much appreciated.' Gabriella avoided eye contact. She knew Arnie would have wanted the boys to continue in private school, but he also wouldn't have wanted his parents to be so interfering in Gabriella's life either.

'Happy to help.'

Chapter 29

Helen had been very pleased to help Gabriella resurrect her modelling career. She'd wished she had done something similar when her children had started school.

'It was,' she'd said, with a tinge of sadness, 'a very different time then.'

'Can you help me?' Gabriella had asked. 'I've contacted some old friends, asking them to lunch, but they're all so busy.'

'My friend, Lana – she used to be a PA, we were in the typing pool together – is now the publisher. Worked her way up. Twenty-five years. Very impressive.'

'Wow. And she'll get me work?'

'No promises. But she's the publisher. Brings the whole magazine together. Like a film producer. Her daughter must be nearly your age now.'

'She has kids?'

'One. Returned from maternity leave after six weeks so she could fill the deputy publisher's shoes.'

'Six weeks? Wow. I don't think I could do that. Not judging, but I...'

'She didn't think she could either – leaving a tiny baby with a near stranger, pumping her breasts for milk so she could be fed. But if she hadn't, the job would have gone to someone else and she wouldn't have made publisher two years later.' Helen shrugged. 'We all must make choices in life.'

'Definitely.'

'Do you have a portfolio we can show her?'

'Course. But I don't look like that now. They're from over ten years ago. I've had two kids, and things have started to go south.'

Helen shook her head, narrowing her eyes. 'I have seen you in a swimming costume and believe me, nothing of yours has even remotely started to go south. Besides, there's a resurgence in curvy, everyday-shaped women as models. None of the stick insects with gaunt faces and lots of eyeliner from my days at the magazine.' She remembered those days wistfully, wondering what would have happened if she'd continued with her career. If she now would have an illustrious career as a publisher, a director of some kind, her name in what Lana taught her was called the flannel panel of magazines from the last four decades.

No matter. That ship had most definitely sailed. No point in wondering about what might have been. Daydreaming did no one any service. That's what Bill had always said anyway.

Gabriella blushed. 'Anything else to give you?'

'Me? Why would you give *me* your portfolio?'

'I thought you were meeting your friend and showing it to her.'

'*With* you. Of course *with* you. How else can I show her how wonderful you are? Pictures won't do you justice. She's got to meet you.'

'Are you sure?'

'I shan't do it any other way.'

Gabriella smiled.

Helen rang her old friend. 'Sorry, bit out of the blue, wondered if you could do me an enormous favour.'

'Depends.'

'I have a dear friend who's looking to get some modelling work. Tasteful. Advertising, magazines, up your street. I wondered if you'd take a look at her.'

Lana sighed. 'That is a big favour. I have a pile of university portfolios sitting on my desk. I usually ask my PA to sift through them. We're always looking for new talent, but it's become so cut throat now. Everyone's looking for the next big thing, and the turnover is savage. It's not like the nineties supermodel era. Sadly.'

'Great days eh?'

'Indeed.'

'She's not a graduate. She's done it before. Looking to dip her toes in, since having children. Two beautiful boys. The spit of her husband apparently. I'm sort of surrogate grandma.'

'Right. You really do have a lot to tell me.'

A long pause, while Helen debated telling her friend or not. It had been a while, Bill showed no sign of changing. Biting her lip, she said, 'I've sort of left, Bill too. Hence why I'm living with Gabriella. That's the person who's looking for the work. Modelling.'

'Let's have lunch and we can catch up. You can tell me all about this Gabriella woman.'

'Splendid.'

'I'm presuming you're mostly free at the moment?'

Sadly it was the case. 'Yes.'

'I'll get my PA to send you some dates and we'll do lunch. I've an expense account that's rather underutilised at the moment.'

'Don't go to any trouble on my account, will you?' Helen didn't like the sound of this. It set her and Gabriella up for a fall.

'We'll be very low-key. Afternoon tea any good? Or brunch maybe?'

'Brunch will work better.'

'Of course.' Lana chuckled.

'I wondered, if rather than us meeting, catching up on my news, and to discuss you seeing Gabriella, if you wouldn't mind awfully, if we did it all together.'

'Together?'

'Two birds, one stone. Gabriella knows about my news, she's lived with me through it, blow by blow. And I really do think you need to meet her to fully appreciate her model potential.'

There was a silence as Lana obviously considered this for a moment. 'Okay. But no promises. Two birds one stone is fine. I am obscenely busy at the moment. I have a magazine to publish every month. I love it. Do you miss it?'

Helen did. Every day now, she let herself look back at her life. She missed being terrifically busy, working with people on a shared goal. Camaraderie, the rush of seeing the magazine on the shelves and flicking through to see a picture of the models she'd watched being photographed, talked to, fetched them coffees, all looking radiant, thriving, staring out at the reader. Being needed, wanted, useful...

Finally she said, 'A little. How's Liam?'

'Doing the milk round. Desperately scrabbling for a grad job that meets his exacting standards. And your Peter?'

'Very well. Let's do all that when we meet, okay? Bring pictures too please.'

'My PA will be in touch. Same number, of course?'

'Not the house. I'm not there at the moment. My mobile is best. This number.'

'Got it.' Lana ended the call.

Helen smiled, looking forward to both reliving the good old days, and catching up with Lana who she'd known most of their lives. She was lucky to be able to pick up their friendship, despite somewhat neglecting it over previous years. Helen wondered sadly quite what she'd been doing to prevent her from seeing Lana and others who would give her such joy, such a sharp reminder of who she'd been, and show her who she could be in the future.

Perhaps, she wondered with more than a tinge of sadness, that was where she'd been going wrong all those years.

The boys were both at Simon's, playing with his two girls. Gabriella said he'd insisted he look after them, that they join for another playdate, and he'd wished her luck, said she'd dazzle them with her personality. To which Gabriella had scrunched up her small and perfect nose and said to Helen he was always like that, paying her compliments and saying nice stuff.

'Is there a problem with him doing things like that?' Helen asked.

Gabriella shrugged. 'Missed it. That's all.'

'Nothing wrong with that.'

'I feel guilty at being happy,' Gabriella had said.

'What happened?'

'He kissed me. After saying I had a personality that would dazzle, he pulled me in for a hug, and held me and then we were kissing. I didn't think about it until afterwards and…'

'Good news, I should have thought.'

Gabriella shrugged. 'He's different, kissing-wise to Arnie. I can't believe I'm even telling you this. Shameful.' She looked away.

'It's not shameful to be happy. Arnie would, surely to God, want you to be happy.'

Gabriella nodded. 'Feels funny though. You know?'

Helen, who had only kissed Bill for forty years couldn't begin to imagine what it would feel like to kiss another man. She smiled and nodded. 'Nothing more, only a kiss?'

'What do you take me for?' Gabriella crossed her legs. 'I'm not giving it all away the first time he says something nice.' She looked out of the corner of her eye.

Helen felt sure Gabriella had considered going further with Simon, and hoped one day she would. The way Gabriella's face lit up while talking about this man showed Helen he was only good for her.

Helen had insisted they get a taxi to Park Lane for the Riley restaurant – an old car showroom converted to an exclusive eatery, overlooking the green of Hyde Park, surrounded by the opulence of the mansion blocks and Victorian terraced houses of Belgravia.

'We must not,' Helen had said, 'be late. On pain of death, will we be late. It sets such a negative start to the meeting. And I want it to be a meeting of great minds. I want Lana to immediately and completely fall head over heels for your natural and irresistible charms. Much more important than your photos, I think.'

And Gabriella had nodded and returned to her bedroom to try on another three outfits, until finally

Helen had nodded in approval and they'd set off, with plenty of time to spare, for their brunch appointment.

The taxi stopped outside the Riley. Helen paid, letting Gabriella out first.

The sun shone, the temperature a comfortable low twenties in the dappled shade, and the scent of pollen, flowers and mown grass from nearby Hyde Park filled the air.

'Is that an old car or something?' Gabriella stepped onto the pavement in treacherously high heels, a figure-hugging white sleeveless shift dress with a blue, red, green and yellow macaw print on the back. It had looked dreadful on the hanger, but on Gabriella it simply sang her personality and Helen had insisted she wear it.

Gabriella pointed at the restaurant window containing a small sixties saloon car based on a Mini. It had a chrome grille, circular headlights and tiny fins at the back in an understated nod to the American cars at the time.

'It is,' Helen said, leading the way to the entrance. She wore a long three-quarter-sleeved flowing aquamarine blue linen dress, matching small hat and high, but not dangerously so, heels.

They took their seats, having been led there by the waiter who greeted them upon entering.

No sign of Lana. Helen wasn't going to worry, she wouldn't have stood them up, it wasn't Lana's style.

Gabriella held her photograph portfolio tightly, then opened it as they waited at the table.

'Probably best if you put it away,' Helen said, 'don't look too try-hard.'

Gabriella replaced it in her large handbag on the floor, placing her hands in her lap.

The waiter arrived. 'Would you like something to drink while you await your friend?'

Helen found herself in need of a drink. It wasn't as if this was, for her, much more than a catch up with an old friend. And yet, she was nervous. For Gabriella, for not making a fool of herself, for not disappointing both Lana and Gabriella. For not, in short, having totally misjudged the whole thing and made a complete pig's ear of it.

'Can we see the wine list please?' she asked.

The waiter handed it to her, then left.

'I don't think I should drink, do you? If I drink I'll get loose tongued and make a show of myself. I'll stick to water.'

'I'm having some wine,' Helen said with determination, 'Lana, will too. I suggest you do as well, but keep a check on your consumption. Don't get too carried away.'

Gabriella nodded. 'Whatever you're having.'

'Too carried away with what?' a voice said from behind them.

Helen turned and saw Lana.

She held her hands aloft, wore a mauve jacket, white blouse and matching mauve trousers. A chunky silver necklace sat around her neck. Her hair was bright red and cut into a very short side-parting with an impressively large quiff at the front.

Helen stood, and they hugged, kissing both cheeks.

'This must be, Gabriella,' Lana said, leaning forward to kiss both her cheeks.

Gabriella obliged.

Lana sat, looking about her for a moment. 'Who's getting carried away? I couldn't help but catch what you were saying.'

'I was worried,' Gabriella said, 'if I had wine I'd get really drunk and make a right show of myself. Carried away. So Helen was saying cos you're both going to drink, I should too, but watch myself.' She shrugged.

Helen raised an eyebrow in a 'really, you told her that, just as you've met' gesture.

'Sounds very sensible to me,' Lana said with a smile. 'What are you drinking?'

'Haven't chosen yet,' Helen said, 'we'd only reached me giving advice.'

Lana gestured for the waiter to join them. She took Helen's wine list, peered at it for a moment, holding reading glasses to herself, not putting them on, then said, 'One bottle of that,' she pointed, 'and some sparkling water.'

The waiter left.

Helen felt her shoulders tensing, seeming to rise higher and higher so they felt as if they were by her ears.

'Tell me about yourself,' Lana said to Gabriella.

She explained she'd been a model before, talked about the clients she'd worked with, emphasising she wasn't a big name, but that she'd done more than her fair share of modelling. After being asked, she handed her portfolio to Lana and talked through each shot, each advert she'd been in, then explained about having two boys in short succession. She blushed. 'Arnie, my husband. Ex, is it now?'

'Late,' Helen said.

'Late, that's the one.' Gabriella blushed, looked at the floor, 'My late husband couldn't get enough. He said he wanted us to have half a dozen. Said we'd carry on trying until we got a girl.' Gabriella looked out of the window briefly, blinking furiously, sipped the wine then went on,

'Didn't though. Anyway, two boys. Now they're at school, I thought I'd see if I could give it a go.' She coughed, drank more wine. 'If I still had it in me, you know?'

Lana had rested her elbows on the table while Gabriella was speaking. Turning her head to one side slightly, and listening intently as she spoke. 'Yes,' she said, 'I do know.'

Their starters arrived – Helen and Lana had watercress soup with bread. Gabriella had more sparkling water.

Lana described *Simply You*, the high fashion and life-style magazine she published every month. 'It's not like our flagship magazine, *A La Mode* – which is about high-end fashion. This is about the everywoman. The mum who's gone back to work after having children. The stay-at-home mum who's looking to make more sustainable choices with her life. The young graduate who's finding her way in the workplace, working out how to politely elbow men out of the way while they continue to think she's sweet and charming.'

'Sounds marvellous,' Helen said, turning to Gabriella, 'Don't you think?'

'Yeah. It does.' She sounded a little unsure.

'Tell me what you're thinking,' Lana said.

She shook her head. 'It's stupid. I shouldn't say. I'm two glasses deep and I mustn't. Need to mind my Ps and Qs.' She bit her lip.

'If we're to have a fruitful business relationship, I must insist on total honestly, from day one. I shall give it to you, and you must reciprocate.' Lana caught Helen's eye.

This had been one of Lana's principles right from the start. She'd learned how to give honest feedback in such a way that she retained her job, and work associates. Helen believed it was this, as well as her endless appetite for work and ability to make each work relationship count, really work for all parties, that had seen her succeed so fully.

She just hoped that Gabriella wouldn't bugger it all up by being too honest, too soon.

Gabriella shook her head. 'No. It is stupid. I'm being a twat.'

'If you are, as you say, being a twat, then I should like to know why, so we can avoid it in future,' Lana said carefully. 'Do, please, go on.'

'When I was in this game before, my nose was on billboards, had my hands on double page spreads of glossy magazines, filled catalogues with my face, went to launch parties where they poured champagne over a tower of glasses and it flowed into them gradually. And *Simply You* sounds amazing. It really does. But it's just...'

'Not how you saw yourself?' Lana offered.

'I don't read stuff like that. So I don't really know. But from what you said. I was hoping I'd be, I dunno, a bit glam still.'

'You are glam. Very glam in fact. You are what these women aspire to. Having it all, as they say. The career, the family, the partner, the craft hobbies on the side. All of it. And we're about showing her how to make that happen.'

Helen gently kicked Gabriella under the table. If she wasn't careful, Gabriella was going to mess this up before it had even started.

'You're right. Sorry. I don't know what I don't know. I think I stupidly thought I'd go back to how I was before.'

'There is, I'm afraid to say, not much of that "back" to return to. Even *A La Mode* isn't what it was. The super glam look is very passé, it's now about a more natural look. Which, if I might say, you have in bucketloads.'

Gabriella blushed, blinked furiously, and put a hand over her mouth. 'Really?'

Lana nodded. 'Your pictures, but more importantly you, the way you've styled yourself today, the way you are with me, are all pointing me very firmly towards *Simply You*. You're glam, but not unattainable.'

Sensing Gabriella had probably saved it enough by now, Helen said, 'How would it work? An in-house model for the magazine, or what?'

'No, we don't have those. But we do have advertisers who want to get in our magazines with adverts, advertorials and more, but need the right face to connect with our readers.'

'And you think Gabriella has this?'

'Without a doubt. I have a skincare manufacturer, a hair product company and a clothes line that would break their arm off for you.'

'All at once?' Gabriella asked, open-mouthed.

Lana shook her head. 'Of course not. They'd want you to be theirs for a while, but we can manage that. There's plenty of other uses we'll have for you. Besides, I'm assuming you have limited hours available to work?'

'School hours. But I can be flexible, with notice. I've got friends who can help. Like Helen.' Gabriella held Helen's hand, squeezed it. 'I can't believe this. Is it really happening?'

'It is,' Lana said, 'I'll be in touch about you coming to the office for a new portfolio shoot, then I'll be in touch with the advertisers, with our editorial department, et cetera. It will all come from there.'

'Thank you so much,' Helen said. 'I, we, really do appreciate it.'

'Don't mention it. You've both done me a favour. You, my dear, are going to make a lot of money, for *Simply You*, and for simply yourself!' She laughed.

Their main courses had arrived and been eaten while they were talking.

Lana turned to Helen. 'Now we've done that, I'd like to hear what you've been up to. Leaving Bill, is that true?'

'She's living with me,' Gabriella said.

'Are you divorcing him?' Lana asked Helen. 'There's something about retirement that makes people do somewhat odd things. Three girlfriends have all done the same.'

'Divorce?' Helen asked.

'Bit like Henry the Eighth: one was divorced, the other's husband died, mercifully there was no beheading involved, but she did tell her husband of fifty years that she wanted to travel the world for six months, and if he didn't want to join her she'd make alternative arrangements when she returned.'

'Wow!' Gabriella said. 'Wish I had the guts to do that.'

'From what you've said, you never had need. Arnie seems like something of a saint.'

She shrugged. 'Not always, he wasn't.'

Helen said, 'He doesn't see me. Doesn't want to. So I've left him.'

'Permanently?' Lana asked with a frown.

'Who knows. What's permanent nowadays anyway?'

'Good point.'

And for the rest of the meal, over desserts – one bit of baklava for Gabriella and great slices of chocolate and raspberry roulade for Helen and Lana ('It's on expenses, so I might as well push the boat out!') – Helen explained what had happened, what had been the final straw and why, and she was happier than ever before, living with

Gabriella and helping to look after her two wonderful boys.

'Not all the time, they're not,' Gabriella said, licking her fingers of the honey from the baklava.

Lana laughed. 'I've got four grandchildren. Spoil them rotten. But they can also be the most terrible little rotters.'

'That,' Gabriella said with a nod and a smile.

Helen shook her head solemnly. 'Not with me they're not.'

After post-meal drinks Lana kissed them both on the cheeks warmly and slipped back to her office to start the ball rolling for Gabriella.

'That went well,' Helen said in the taxi on the way home.

'I didn't bugger it up, did I?' Gabriella asked with concern.

'You were splendidly yourself, as only you can be. I think she understood why you were asking that. I think we often want to see ourselves as the most glam version, despite evidence to the contrary.'

'You're sure?' Gabriella stared out of the window as the buildings passed in a blur.

'What's up?'

'Do you think I can do it?'

'If Lana does, then it's unimportant what I think. And Lana loved you.'

'I've not done it in six years. Have you ever done something you've not done in six years? Cos it's scary. I'm shit scared.'

'What's the worst that can happen?'

'I can't do it. I look like crap in front of the camera. I can't juggle the boys and modelling. I've lost that woman,

268

she's gone. I'm just me and no one wants to see *me* trying to sell makeup, or shoes, or even a loo cleaner.'

'Nothing that's worth doing is easy. New jobs are always terrifying. That's the point. It's how we grow into better versions of ourselves.'

'Did you just say that? For real? That's some meme-tastic shit right there.' Gabriella laughed.

'I said it, because I believe it. Especially about you. Lana does too. So you just need to get on board with that as well.'

Gabriella smiled, smoothed her dress on her lap. Caught her reflection in the window and smiled.

'Who wouldn't want this face selling them anything?' Helen pulled her in for a hug.

Chapter 30

August

Ian was in the kitchen, preparing food for the dinner party to which Helen and Gabriella were invited. Thin filo pastry with feta cheese was on the work surface, ready to be grilled. Whole trout with herbs and lemon slices were wrapped in aluminium foil. He'd parboiled pieces of potato ready to sauté them, and broccoli, carrots and mange-tout were prepared and waiting in their own layers of the steamer.

They weren't due to arrive for another three hours, but Ian had given himself plenty of time so he could enjoy the preparation and cooking.

The sun shone golden and hot, with a cloudless sky. They would eat outside this evening, once the temperature returned to twenty Celsius. Ian and Drew had a newish patio area with chairs and a table.

Gabriella was bringing Simon and all four of their children – ingredients for a kids' supper sat in the freezer, waiting for Ian.

Helen hadn't asked Bill, despite Ian and Gabriella suggesting otherwise. 'I'm still very angry with him,' Helen had said, 'I don't want to include him in this – this is for me, not him.'

Drew was due home soon, Ian reflected, checking the time. In fact, he was due home half an hour ago.

Turning his attention to the herb butter he was cooking the trout in, he looked forward to Drew's return, so he could help. He'd help lay the table, make sure the patio heaters were doing their thing, a quick run through the house with the vacuum cleaner – Drew really was the perfect husband.

All is well.

Ian's phone rang from its position on the kitchen windowsill. His hands were covered in herb butter. What a pain.

Withheld number. Of course.

Ian wiped his hands clean and answered it.

'Ian, is that Ian Oakley?'

'Speaking,' he replied lightly.

A cough, and then: 'It's Bob, from Drew's station.' A pause, and then: 'There's been an accident.'

The ground tilted, and Ian's blood ran cold in his veins. Sickness filled his stomach as it turned into a ball of anxiety. 'What's happened?'

'He's on his way to hospital.'

'Is he okay?'

'There was a lot of smoke.'

This was one of Ian's worst nightmares. He knew it was a risk with Drew being a firefighter, but he and his colleagues used to point out they had the correct equipment and had been properly trained and they never took risks.

But Ian knew Drew, he'd put himself out to help someone. He'd always put his own needs second, third, or last.

'Where is he?'

Bob named the hospital. 'We're following the ambulance.'

'He's in an ambulance?' Drew asked, desperation in his voice at what this could mean.

'He is.' A pause and then Bob said: 'See you at the hospital.'

Ian drove as fast as possible. He couldn't think about anything, not a single thought, until he'd seen Drew and knew how he was.

In A&E he gave his name. 'I'm here to see Mr Oakley, I'm his husband.' Their surname was a portmanteau of their own. Felt more *them* than double-barrelled.

The receptionist looked at her computer terminal, tapped the keyboard. 'If you could wait, I'll ask someone to speak to you.'

'I want to see him. I need to see him. Now.' Ian's hands shook with impotent rage. *Why can't they just let me see him now?*

'Would you like a seat?'

'I'd like to see my husband.'

She nodded.

Ian stood, pacing up and down by the reception desk. He couldn't sit. Couldn't read. Couldn't stare at his phone. He could hardly breathe until he'd seen Drew, knew how he was, only then could he exhale. The air was stifling, stale and smelling of bleach and... Too hot, didn't they have air conditioning in hospitals nowadays? Sweat ran down his back and under his arms, soaking his shirt. He untucked it – nothing mattered, least of all his appearance. Nothing was of any importance except Drew.

It felt like an hour later, but checking the time somehow it had only been five minutes, and a woman in blue scrubs arrived, called his name.

She led him into a room, closed the door. 'Your husband has been in a fire. He was wearing his firefighter equipment. I'm afraid he's inhaled a lot of smoke.'

'Is her burned?'

She shook her head.

'Is that good?' Ian asked, trying to cling onto the key words that she'd said, make sense of them, arrange them in a way so he could understand what had happened.

'It could be worse.'

'What happened?'

'Drew's name meant manliness, they'd found that out when agreeing on their married surname. He wanted to tell the nurse now, as if it would make Drew less likely to be...

'All we know is he went into a burning building and remained there for some time.'

'What about the people he was saving?' Ian knew that Drew would be as concerned about them, if not more, than himself. So he thought he should find out, for if – when – they spoke.

'Stable. They're in recovery at the moment.'

'They? How many of them?'

'Four. Two adults, two children.'

A whole family. *He's rescued a whole family, putting them before himself and now this. Oh Christ.* Ian bunched his fists so they went white. He was so angry that Drew would do this, to himself, risk his own life when he knew as a firefighter he shouldn't. But he would have bloody well ignored that.

Ian swallowed the ball in his throat. 'When can I see him?'

'Soon.'

Ian tried to read her expression – was it soon when he's dead, or soon when he can speak to you. Was it, *This guy's got no chance and I need to let his husband down slowly*? 'I can't see him now?' Ian asked.

She shook her head. 'We're treating him now. When he's stable.'

'Five minutes, fifteen, an hour, what are we talking?' *For fuck's sake!*

'I can't say. We prefer not to say because then it prevents disappointment. As soon as you can see him someone will get you from reception.'

Ian blinked away tears that had formed. He raked his hand through his hair.

Impotence, that really was the only word for how he felt. Completely unable to do anything to help, powerless. Much worse than his problem before, this really was life and death stuff.

The woman in scrubs showed him back to reception.

He sat, his legs jiggling up and down, stared at his phone, but nothing made sense, he couldn't focus on anything. Without Drew, nothing would make sense. It hadn't before and it wouldn't afterwards. He unfastened another button on his shirt, it hung on him, clinging to his skin in uncomfortable places. If he––.

His phone rang – it was Helen – he went outside to take the call.

'I'm at your house and it's locked,' she said calmly. 'In fact, I'm here with Gabriella and the boys too.'

'Shit. Sorry. Should have told you.'

'Is it cancelled? Simon is on his way too. It's taken quite a lot of coordination for them. Four children, I don't envy them.'

'It's cancelled.'

'Right.'

'I'm in hospital.' Ian swallowed. 'Drew is here. Smoke inhalation.'

'Oh shit. My dear Ian. I'm so sorry.' Muffled sounds on the phone, when she was probably telling Gabriella. 'Where are you?'

He named the hospital. 'I'm so sorry. Can you tell Gabriella and Simon too. The fish is on the side in the kitchen. I...'

'Don't worry about the fish. Just concentrate on Drew.' A pause, and then: 'We love you. We're all thinking of you. Is there anything we can do? Anything at all?'

'Not at the moment. Thanks.' Ian's voice came out as a strangled half moan half cry. It was as if he let out a tiny bit of the fear he had about what may happen. He bit his mouth closed firmly. He ended the call, staring at the phone in his hands as he turned it over and over.

He screamed, low and guttural, like an animal in pain. All thought of anyone seeing him completely gone.

Leaning against the wall outside the hospital, he took a breath, then stepped back inside.

The noise of the hospital seemed to wrap around him. Quiet beeping of machines, low chatter of people, the smell of lino and disinfectant, the sound of shoes squeaking slightly as people walked quickly across the hard floor.

He sat in the emergency department waiting room, leaned his head forwards and, despite his best efforts, sobbed.

Sometime later, he opened his eyes, saw two shoes as he stared at the floor. He looked up.

The woman from earlier. She was smiling.

This has to be good, right? 'Sorry. I had to make a call. Were you waiting for me?'

She shook her head. 'You can see him now. Drew.'

Ian stood, wiped his eyes and followed her to a cubicle surrounded by a curtain.

Drew lay in the bed, sitting up, with wires and tubes attached to his body. A machine beeped next to him. He had on a mask over his mouth and nose.

'It's to help him breathe,' the woman said. 'Tell him to keep it on. Even if he's talking.'

Ian nodded. Standing next to the bed, so he could stroke Drew's hair.

'Can you hear me?' Ian asked. He kissed Drew's forehead, it tasted salty.

Drew nodded, reached out a hand and held Ian's.

'Can you talk?' Ian asked.

'I... can... but... it's... hard.' He tried to remove the oxygen mask.

Ian gently replaced it, standing there, holding Drew's hand and hoping, praying – even though he didn't believe in God – that Drew would be well. Making bargains with a god he'd not acknowledged for years that if Drew came through this, he'd believe in him, he'd even go to church, just as long as Drew was all right.

'Look at the state of you, another mess you've got yourself in,' Ian said, attempting humour.

Drew blinked slowly and tears rolled down his cheeks. 'I... am... sorry.' He coughed, removing the mask then replacing it, gasping for breath a few times.

They remained like this until the woman entered the cubicle. 'Can I talk to you please?' she asked Ian, nodding to one side.

276

He followed her through the curtain and they stood in the middle of the room, surrounded by other curtained off areas, each with patients and relatives going through their own personal hells.

'Is he going to be okay?' Ian asked.

'He has *severe* smoke inhalation. His lungs are *very* damaged. But he hasn't sustained any burns, and he is breathing with the mask. His vitals are nearly normal – slightly elevated temp and pulse, but considering what he's been through, he's doing okay.'

'Will he live?'

She blinked slowly, staring into his eyes. 'We can't give guarantees. Anything can change very quickly. His body is in shock, and it's recovering now.'

'Right,' Ian said, trying to take in how she'd gently managed his expectations, that Drew could, still, very much die.

'Your husband is a strong, young, fit man. We are doing all we can.' She held his arm.

Yes, he bloody well is. He's my strong, young and fit man. My Drew. 'Can I go back to him now?'

She gestured towards the curtain.

Ian found a chair and sat next to Drew's bed, holding his hand, talking about how he'd been in the middle of cooking, and the fish was still out on the side, and he was glad that he hadn't put the feta and pastry wraps under the grill because they'd be burned by now. He burbled on, filling the air with chatter, because it felt better than listening to Drew's strained breathing.

A while later, Ian wasn't sure how long, he heard a familiar voice on the other side of the curtains.

'I'm family. Of sorts,' Helen was saying. 'I'd like to see my friend.'

Ian stuck his head through the curtains. 'What are you doing here?'

'Plans were cancelled. Thought you could do with some company.' She raised her eyebrows. 'Unless you'd prefer me to go.'

'Stay,' Ian said, gesturing into the cubicle where Drew sat.

Helen joined him in silence. She stared at Drew then took Ian's hand. 'Coffee, chocolate, whatever you want.'

Ian squeezed her hand. 'Stay.'

'I'm not going anywhere.' Helen placed her handbag on her lap and held it tightly.

They sat in silence next to Drew as he lay in bed, the machines beeping, sucking, and the quiet hissing of the mask over his face.

After some time, Helen said, 'I'll leave you to it. Sit in the waiting room.'

'Don't go.' Ian felt as if he were just about keeping a lid on his emotions. If Helen asked him to explain anything he knew he'd dissolve into a heap of tears and snot and wobbly nerves.

Helen held him tight, into a hug. 'It's fine. He'll be fine. I know it.'

'Will he?'

'Positive. He's very robust from what you've told me.' She looked at Ian from head to toe. 'And you are too.'

Despite the official visiting policy, they somehow managed to sit in the curtained area with Drew all night, until Ian fell asleep, with Helen holding him tightly.

Chapter 31

September

Gabriella picked up her phone. It would only take a quick text and she could cancel on Simon. Her proper evening date with Simon. The date she'd been looking forward to for three months since their first coffee together, which had become regular, alongside their playdates with the kids, video calls most evenings while they got on with their routines, bringing each other along for the ride while feeding their children or supervising their home-work, then sometimes they would watch TV together, remaining on the phone. She had really enjoyed getting to know him better. Until he'd finally asked if she wanted to have dinner.

'I'll get a babysitter.'

'Right,' she'd said, understanding the implication of this — it was a proper adult date, time away from the children where they could be themselves, away from being Mummy and Daddy.

Except now, the bloody babysitter had called to say she was sick. 'Vomiting every five minutes,' she'd said.

Gabriella had known the right answer was to say, 'Of course, take care, thanks.' But as soon as she'd put the phone down, she'd wanted to shout and rage and scream at the sky – at whoever it was that looked after luck and chance and really mouth off at them.

Simon's number was a swipe and a click away and she'd tell him what had happened and then she'd stay in with the boys. Have a nice night at home. Except, that's all she ever seemed to do at the moment, theLonely Hearts Lido Club hadn't met much over the last few weeks. All too busy with their own adventures, having supported each other with taking the first steps.

She'll cancel on Simon and have a cosy night in. Alone. Except she didn't want to.

'Mummy,' Thomas said, walking into the kitchen, 'When are you going?'

Good question. 'Where is your brother?'

'I want a bath.' He stuck his bottom lip out in a gesture that reminded her as strongly as possible of Arnie.

Gabriella took a deep breath. She could always call Pru and Edward. The babysitters of last resort. The two people who were absolutely guaranteed to make her feel inadequate and that she wasn't able to cope.

'Mummy will be with you in a minute.' She tried to keep the tension out of her voice.

Phone a friend, fifty-fifty, ask the audience. She felt as if she were on a game show, with a difficult question and fifty grand riding on it.

Phone a friend.

She rang Helen.

'I thought you were going out tonight,' Helen said.

'How's Ian?'

'I won't be back at yours any time soon.'

'That bad, eh?'

A pause, as Helen moved, then, quietly, 'After a few days, I had to forcibly remove him, bodily, from the hospital or he'd never have left. The staff were very under-standing, bending all sorts of rules, but in the end, it was doing Ian no good.'

Gabriella let that sink in for a moment. Her stupid problem shrivelled in comparison, while Helen and Ian had spent the last month making sure Drew was okay. She swallowed. 'How are you?'

'Fine. Rather enjoying feeling useful to be honest. Not that I wanted this to happen to Drew, of course.'

'Course.'

'How are you?' Helen asked.

'Fine. Good. Well, actually. It's stupid. Feel silly asking.'

'You're seeing Simon, tonight, aren't you?'

'Meant to be.'

'Aha.'

'Thing is, the babysitter's throwing up and, well, I could cancel. He'd be okay. I wouldn't die. No one would. It's just…'

'You'd rather like to go out with him?'

'That.' Gabriella nodded, she loved how Helen always cut to the chase so quickly. She bit her lip carefully. 'Doesn't feel right though, does it? Me gallivanting around while Drew's—'

'As much as we don't want it to, life does go on. Want me to look after the boys? You'll have to bring them to Ian's. I can't leave him. He's exhausted from driving to the hospital and back twice a day every day for weeks.'

Deep into the countryside. Nowhere near her place. She'd still be late to meet Simon. 'Let me call him, explain. Are you sure you're okay to take them?'

'I love your boys. Besides,' she said in a whisper, 'a bit of life around here wouldn't go amiss. He's very maudlin of late. Keeps talking about arrangements. Mentioned the crem a few times. I told him Drew's past the worst, if anything bad was to happen, it would have, well, happened. I tell him not to be so silly, but he will worry. He's a worrier, is Ian. He won't believe Drew's okay until he's home.'

'Let me call Simon. Thanks.' Gabriella ended the call.

They were meant to be eating at a West End restaurant Simon had said was very good, but not too formal. Although, Gabriella was looking forward to dressing up – her sparkly red cocktail dress was hanging on her bedroom door. Matching red satin heels sat by her dressing table.

She videocalled Simon – he preferred that to a phone, said it was more personal, liked to see what she was doing. He felt as if they saw each other more often that way.

'You look very casual,' he said, taking in her clothes.

Worry crossed her face. 'I'm not dressed yet.'

'What's up?' he said. 'Is it Ian's husband?'

She'd been keeping him updated about the situation, since he appreciated how important Ian was to her. Gabriella shook her head.

'What's happened? Is it your boys?'

'They're okay.'

'Thank Christ for that.'

'The babysitter, not so much.'

'Ah.'

'Sick. Like, being sick. All the time.'

'That bad, eh?'

'Helen said she can take the boys, but she's half an hour away. She's still staying at Ian's.'

'Because his husband is in hospital?'

Gabriella nodded. 'I don't want to cancel. Feels wrong, while Drew is in hospital. Helen said life goes on.'

'Indeed it does. Even if you don't want it to.' A faraway expression crossed his face.

'So I'm coming, but I'll be late.'

'Or…' he said.

'What?'

'Your friend's got enough with looking after Ian.'

He wasn't wrong. 'What shall we do?'

'I'll cancel. You come round to mine, with the boys, and I'll cook. Give them a chance to play together while we're both there.'

They'd been talking about a play date including her *and* Simon. Their kids knew each other from school, and had spent time at hers and Simon's places, helping each other out while they worked, but Gabriella hadn't been able to find out if they all got on with both her and Simon too. It would make it easier if they all got on.

'What about the restaurant?'

'What about it? I'll move it to another time.'

'Sure?'

'Wouldn't have said it otherwise.'

'Thanks,' she said then ended the call.

It felt much more them than a child-free dinner up west. As much as Gabriella didn't like to admit it, she was much more comfortable slipping on smart jeans and a long jumper cinched in at the waist with a belt, with comfortable trainers, than dressing up for the West End. She'd have plenty of time for dressing up with her modelling career relaunched.

Gabriella called Helen and told her.

'Thanks anyway.'

'Relieved to be quite honest.'

'Why did you offer then?'

'Because I know how much you were looking forward to this date, no children, big deal. I'd have muddled through. Always do.'

'Ta. I'll tell you all about it next time we're at the lido.'

'I want all the gory details.'

'Course.' Gabriella ended the call.

As she gathered the boys together, packed anything she thought they may or may not need while away from home and placed it in the car, she reflected that they were seeing each other less often at the lido. It was as if they needed to remind each other where they'd met, even though that was less important to their friendship now than at the start.

Simon held the front door open, his two girls standing either side of him. 'Come in.'

The air was cooler, a few leaves had fallen from the trees as autumn announced its arrival, slipping away from the long hot nights of summer. The heatwave had become boring after a few months. Gabriella had taken long cool baths and found herself able to sit with the silence after the boys were asleep, and didn't find herself overwhelmed with sadness as before.

Gabriella's heart thumped in her chest as she stared at Simon. Why was she more nervous than if they'd been eating at a swanky restaurant up west?

Because this somehow felt easier, without any airs and graces, as if they'd somehow slipped into being this natural with each other.

Gabriella ushered her two boys into the hallway. 'Take your shoes off!' she shouted.

Simon shrugged. 'Doesn't matter.' He pulled her in for a hug, and a kiss on the cheek, pausing for a moment to kiss her lips.

She inhaled his woody aftershave scent and closed her eyes, imagining what his hard body would feel like next to her own.

It was something she'd allowed herself to see in her mind, late at night, and now he was standing next to her, she found her thoughts running riot, joyfully skipping through the fields of her imagination, a quick skip and a jump into the bedroom.

For the first time, since allowing herself this skip into her imagination, she didn't immediately feel jolted back to terror, the gripping fear at thinking about herself, naked with a man who wasn't Arnie.

'You look beautiful,' Simon said, placing his hand in the small of her back as he guided her through the hallway into the kitchen.

Gabriella giggled a little. 'Whatever.' She never quite believed it when he said stuff like that. It always seemed a bit cheesy. But with Simon she found she was starting to enjoy cheesy. After time with nothing – no love, no romance, nothing – she reckoned she deserved a bit of cheesy.

'You'd look radiant in a brown paper bag.'

Gabriella shook her head. 'Now I know you're taking the piss.'

Simon's eyes widened. 'I mean it. Most sincerely.' He pulled out a chair at the kitchen table, indicating for her to sit.

She did. 'What are we eating tonight? I've brought something for the boys, so you don't need to worry about them.'

'I've done fish fingers, chips and peas for the kids. Won't yours want that?'

They would. Much prefer it to the cheese sandwiches she'd thrown together before leaving. 'Spect they'll force it down.'

The noise of children playing came from the lounge.

'They seem to be getting along fine.'

'It's not like they don't know each other, is it?'

A shout, she thought it was Thomas, came from the lounge.

Gabriella ran to see what had happened.

Thomas was sitting next to Simon's girls on the sofa, playing with My Little Pony dolls. 'Can I have one of these, Mummy?' He looked at her with Arnie's facial expression.

Jack screwed his face up. 'It's for girls.' He shook his head.

'Dinner will be ready soon,' Simon said.

They fell silent.

'Does anyone want a drink?'

Gabriella's boys held their hands in the air like the well-behaved children they sometimes were.

Gabriella knelt on the floor. 'Are you going to be good for Mummy?'

They all nodded.

'Can I have one?' Thomas held the pink toy horse in the air. 'Please?'

She kissed his forehead. 'Let's see.'

Simon left for the kitchen and Gabriella followed.

'You'd think they'd never seen girls before,' he said, opening the oven, pulling out an oblong dish topped with brown mashed potatoes.

The room filled with a rich fish smell, cream and spices mixed to make Gabriella's mouth water.

'Maybe it's their toys?' Gabriella shrugged. 'That smells nice. What is it?'

'Fisherman's pie.' He closed the oven.

'You made it?' He'd had just under an hour since she'd phoned.

'You're joking, aren't you?'

He seemed so perfect that it would be just the sort of thing he'd do.

'I'm good, but I'm not superhuman. It's out the freezer.'

Relief washed through her. At least he wasn't perfect in every way. 'So is now a good time to show you the pudding I brought?'

'Whatever it is, I'm sure it's delicious.'

She removed a trifle from her bag. It had been at the back of her fridge, hidden by strawberries that went mouldy, and in a mad panic before leaving she'd grabbed it.

He held it, inspecting it carefully. 'And it's only three days out of date.' He placed it on the table.

She checked the date and he was right. 'It's not been a good day.' She put her head in her hands, resting elbows on the table. Taking a long sigh, she wished the day would just bloody well end.

Simon stood behind her, hugging her, kissed her neck, said quietly, 'Doesn't matter. Most things don't matter much. When it comes down to it. After you've had really important stuff happen, it shows you what matters and what doesn't.'

A shiver of desire ran down her spine. Gabriella couldn't disagree and yet she still found herself worrying about the small things. Possibly because she wanted to come across as perfect in Simon's eyes.

'You're right,' she said finally. 'You're always right. Basically whenever I need to know what to do about something I'm going to ask you. Cos you've always got the right answer. You and Helen. Maybe you should get together, make a life coaching company or something.'

'I'd really like to meet your friends,' Simon said. 'You talk about them like they're family. How's Ian's husband?'

'Still in hospital.'

Simon's girls walked in, followed by Gabriella's boys.

Olivia sat at the table. 'Daddy, when are we eating?'

'I'm starving,' Sophie said, yawning.

'Wash your hands, then sit at the table. Show the boys how it's done.' Simon nodded at Gabriella's boys.

The girls walked to the sink, standing on a step, washed their hands, then watched as the boys did too. They sat at the table, once Olivia had laid the table.

Gabriella looked at Simon, widening her eyes, mouthing 'How?' at him. How had he ended up with two perfectly behaved girls, while she had two of the naughtiest boys ever.

As they ate the fish fingers, chips and peas Simon served, Simon poured them a glass of wine.

Gabriella said, 'When.'

He continued pouring.

'Enough,' she said. 'Driving.'

He stopped, pouring himself a full glass. 'When?'

'Say when, that's what people say, isn't it? So I said when. Isn't that right?' It was what her mum had always said and she'd not thought anything about it until now.

'It is,' Simon said, nodding. 'You can stay. Plenty of room for all four of you.' He looked at her over the top of his glass, narrowing his eyes. 'Spare room. Of course.'

She looked away, wondering if he was thinking what she was. Possibly. But it was hardly the most romantic evening, with four kids playing in the background.

She had brought overnight things for the boys. She could stay. It would be much nicer, having a drink and relaxing after what had been a stressful evening beforehand.

'Unless…' he said. 'No. Obviously not. Forget I even suggested it. Presumptive of me. Rude in fact.' He held the wine bottle in the air.

'Spare room sounds great, thanks,' she said trying to keep the uncertainty out of her voice.

'I'll make it up now, before I get too pissed.' He stood, walked out of the kitchen.

He had, she noted with pleasure and a small smile, a very attractive bum. Encased in dark denim. Two round half moons. And, she reflected, as he stood, his height was pleasantly enough that she needed to look up when they kissed.

A little flutter of excitement bubbled up in her chest. Good and wide shoulders too – he somehow managed to make a white T-shirt look as if it had been designed by one of the luxury diffusion brands she used to model for. When, she suspected, it had probably come from a department store.

As she thought about where he may have bought the T-shirt, and how dashing he'd look in a suit, she felt something tugging her sleeve.

Jack stood at her elbow, with a sad look on his face that spelled trouble.

'What's wrong?' Gabriella asked, ruffling his hair in the hope it would stop him crying.

Simon appeared at the door with a concerned look. 'I think you should join me in the drawing room.'

She followed him.

A box of makeup sat on the floor and Thomas's face was covered with lipstick, blusher and mascara. He looked like a clown and on the verge of tears.

'What have you lot been up to here?' Gabriella said, putting her hands on her hips.

Simon stood next to her, staring at his girls. 'You know Mummy's makeup case isn't a toy, don't you?'

The two girls looked at the floor, obviously clear they'd done wrong.

He turned to the two boys. 'What happened? Daddy's friend,' he nodded towards Gabriella, 'and me need to know.'

For a brief moment, Gabriella had a glimpse of Simon and her parenting their children, together. And she didn't hate it.

After the children had been put to bed, Gabriella and Simon sat on the sofa, with another bottle of wine and talked. He was very interested in her modelling.

'I told you Lana wouldn't be able to resist you,' he said.

'I'm up west most days. They've got me doing a clothing range for a high street shop. Next month it's washing up liquid and a new fabric softener from the same people. Or is it the same ad agency, I can't remember.'

He looked deeply into her eyes. 'What's it like, being in front of the camera again?'

It was amazing. Everything she remembered and more. Because now, she had her two boys to love very hard at the end of a long day. Sometimes she missed Arnie, because he'd got her into this game in the first place, but she didn't tell Simon that now.

'I arrive first thing, leave the boys with Helen to take to school, and they do my hair and makeup – God I forgot how much I loved that. They send a car to collect me sometimes. Lana says I'm worth it. All day it takes, early, and then I wear the whole wardrobe of clothes from the shop. This is for next summer, so it's swimwear, shorts, floaty dresses, all that.' She told him about her first shoot, a few weeks ago.

They'd had her standing in front of a painted wall of flowers, peering from behind trees, sitting on a park bench, reading in a deckchair, then used a large fan to blow her hair about, giving her a windswept look. They threw leaves and then rose petals in the background as she caught a beachball, laughing, then licked an ice cream, letting the red sauce drip down her arm. She loved wearing the yellow suit – had bought herself the skirt and jacket from the shoot at a massive discount. The photographer was friendly, helped bring her out of her shell; she'd arrived really nervous, convinced she couldn't do it. He'd handed her a coffee and chatted to her, asking about her life, her journey. Soon she'd been rabbiting on about the taxi and how she couldn't believe they'd sent one just for her.

'You've seen yourself, right?' he'd said and began taking photos.

She put her hands in front of her face, saying she wasn't ready, but he'd continued and showed her and she was shocked at how natural, happy, glowing, she'd looked.

'When will I see the photos?' Simon asked now.

'Magazine's not out for two or three months.'

'You're more than worth the wait.' He kissed her.

She leaned into it, opening her mouth, tasting him, letting herself be lost to the moment, the joy, the desire, of this man, the love she felt for him, and he for her. He really cared for her, was interested in her, just like when she'd been married. And she reckoned there wasn't anything else she could ask for from Simon, and so she didn't.

Chapter 32

Helen had finished clearing up Ian's kitchen and had seen him off to the hospital. They'd fallen into a routine very swiftly after she had moved in. She'd not brooked any argument or debate from Ian.

'You're not,' she'd said, after that first night in the hospital, 'of sound mind. You shall concentrate on being there for Drew, while he heals. And I shall focus on looking after you.'

'I don't need anyone looking after me,' Ian had said the morning after that first night, looking like he'd been dragged through a hedge backwards, red-rimmed eyes, stubble and hair going in six directions.

She'd followed him home and put him to bed, then made him some food, giving him strength, so when he returned to the hospital that afternoon, he looked like something approximating himself once again.

The crumbs on the table now, at least signified Ian was eating before his first daily hospital visit.

He'd be back at lunchtime, when they'd eat together; sometimes Helen would supervise him, mouthful by mouthful, until satisfied he'd eaten enough. Now, at least Ian understood if he was to make two return journeys to the hospital daily, he had to look after himself.

Drew starting to talk had definitely been the turning point for Ian caring enough about himself to eat at least once a day, under Helen's watchful eye.

The doorbell rang. Ian wasn't expecting anyone, or at least he'd not told her that morning. He usually left her with a list of things he'd find helpful for her to do. At first he'd felt like it was an imposition, but Helen had quickly explained that was the precise reason for her staying there.

Helen looked through the window. The lawn was greener than its faded yellow during the summer heatwave. She recognised the car – a blue Ford of some type. Reminded her of… No, it couldn't be… Why would he be here?

She opened the door.

Her son, Peter stood with a look of contrition. 'Will you let me in, please?'

'What are you doing here?'

'Peace offering.'

She frowned. 'What for?'

'Not from me, from Dad.'

Helen shook her head, started to close the door.

Peter put his foot in the way, stopped it. 'Can't I come in, please?'

'I'm not interested in a peace offering from your father, especially if he can't even be bothered to deliver it himself.'

'Please, Mum,' Peter said with feeling.

Helen's heartstrings were pulled. But not because the message came from Bill, but since it was delivered by her son. Their son. She leant her forehead on the door and closed her eyes. With great reluctance she stepped backwards and let him walk in.

They stood in the hallway.

She folded her arms. 'If you must, you must.'

'He's a bit lost.' Peter coughed. 'Dad.'

'I got that. Go on.'

'Can't we sit? Five minutes and then I'll go.'

Helen knew when she was beaten. In silence she turned and led the way towards the kitchen.

'Thanks,' Peter said as he sat at the table, removing a light jacket and hanging it over the chair back.

Helen busied herself making them coffee. She felt she at least deserved something stronger than her usual fruit tea. 'What I fail to understand,' she said, 'is why he's sent you. Why, of all things, he can't come here himself to speak to me. His wife. Of over forty years.'

'He's lost without you.'

Helen laughed, shaking her head. 'So if he's so lost, why isn't he telling me?'

'Because he's so lost, Mum.'

She turned to continue with the coffee in silence. Finally she joined Peter at the table with their drinks.

'I don't disagree with him,' Peter said.

'Do go on.' Helen rested her elbows on the table and stared at him.

'Why are you here with…' Peter waved in an attempt to remember Ian's name. 'Your friend? And not Dad?'

'Ian,' she began with emphasis, 'needs me.'

'Dad needs you.'

'Very different. Ian needs me because his husband is in hospital. I'm his oxygen mask while Drew wears his own.'

Peter shook his head. 'I don't follow.'

'On a plane you're told to put on your own oxygen mask before helping others. Because without looking after yourself you can't care for others. Drew has his mask, after the smoke inhalation. I'm making Ian look after himself.' Tears filled her eyes at the memory. 'You should have seen him that first night in hospital. He was beside himself with grief.'

'Grief? Isn't Drew okay?'

'He is. As well as can be expected. But we didn't know he'd live at the time. Ian believed he was about to lose Drew. The love of his life. The husband he never thought would fall for him, who he still, in some small ways, believes is out of his league.' A pause, and then: 'He's not. Ian is splendid. As is Drew. They deserve one another. Unlike some couples I could mention.'

'He misses you,' Peter said, trying to make eye contact with her.

Helen looked away. 'Odd way to show it.'

'He's lost without you.'

'You said.'

'I've been taking food for him. Showed him how to use the washing machine and dishwasher. He was wearing very odd clothing combinations when I visited. Asked him why and he said he'd run out of clean clothes.'

Helen rolled her eyes. She had no intention of returning to Bill if they were the only reasons he missed her. 'He's not a child, he's a grown man.'

'One who's let you do everything for him his whole life.'

'It's what women did. It's what was expected of me. He went to work, I made house and brought up you and your sister. It's all very well and good for you to lecture me on making your father helpless, but he let me. He enabled it. It was not a one-way street.'

'Come home and talk to him, will you?'

'Absolutely not! I have nothing to say to him. I'm needed here. Just like I was at Gabriella's.'

'He said he'll get a cleaner.'

Helen laughed. As if that would solve the problem.

'What's so funny?' Peter asked.

'If he thinks that's going to fix things then he's sorely mistaken.'

'What else? Tell me and I'll tell him.'

When did he become an emotionless, joyless closed book? When did he slip from being committed to his work, into being *obsessed* with it, at the expense of everything and everyone else? It wasn't worth the effort, she'd tried many times to no effect.

'The only difference,' she said, 'with this time and before, is that I've walked away.'

'Do you want a divorce?'

'Yes. No. Haven't decided. I needed to do something to change the cycle we'd found ourselves in.' A divorce, she admitted, felt very final. Perhaps a tad too forceful. Yet, she hadn't considered the alternative: go back to Bill and their old, unhelpful behaviours.

'Well you've definitely done that. I think he's struggling with why you'd prefer to look after strangers than family.'

'Then I'm afraid he's very much mistaken. Ian and Gabriella aren't strangers. They're...' She struggled for the right word. 'They're...'

'What are they, Mum? Because I'd like to know too.' He leaned forwards, elbows on the table.

'They see me. That's what they are. People who see me. Understand me. Appreciate me. And until your father can do that, I see no point in speaking to him.'

'You've got to come home at some point.'

'Do I?' She shrugged. 'I think – in fact I know – Ian's very grateful for me being here. As was Gabriella.'

'Why did you leave her place?'

'Because Ian's husband nearly died in a fire. I told you.'
She shook her head. 'It's very simple really.'

'What about when his husband comes out of hospital?'

'What about it?'

'Surely,' Peter said, 'you won't continue living here with them.'

Helen hadn't quite thought that far ahead. Much like Ian, she was living from one day to the next. 'How are you? Work? House? Anyone on the horizon, romantically perhaps?' Why was Peter such an enigma when it came to matters of the heart?

Peter sighed. 'Nothing to report. Is that the subject closed?'

'For now,' Helen said with great care. *I hope he's more emotionally open with his friends.*

'We need you too.'

Helen was unconvinced. 'Did you secure that promotion you were angling for?' He'd mentioned it a while ago and then she'd heard nothing. She liked to see him succeeding in his endeavours, as any good parent should, of course.

'Dad and I. We both need you.'

But you don't see me. 'Needing and appreciating aren't the same thing.'

Peter shook his head and sighed. 'Dad will be very disappointed.'

'Of what?'

'That I've not managed to get through to you.'

'If he wants to get through to me, then I suggest he tries to do so himself.' *In person, preferably.*

Peter left shortly afterwards, after revealing he'd not secured the promotion but wasn't bothered about it, that his house was as she'd seen it the last time she had visited.

And that he was very happy, thank you very much, without a significant other, as some people termed it.

Helen stared at the two mugs on the table where they'd been sitting and wondered if Bill would ever describe her as his significant other. And with a sadness she'd not felt before, she decided that no, in fact, he probably wouldn't, that she'd be relegated to being the woman who stood behind the successful man, and no more.

When Ian returned at lunchtime, she was still staring at the mugs on the kitchen table. She'd spent the time appreciating Ian's garden as some flowers went over, returning to just their foliage as the lawn recovered and became green after weeks of brown from the hosepipe-banning heatwave. A light drizzle had fallen for a brief spell, the first rain since… Well, in as far as she could remember. Certainly since moving in with Ian.

'Did someone come round?' he asked, staring at the mugs on the table.

'In a way, yes. In another way, no.'

Ian frowned. 'What do you mean?'

She didn't want to burden Ian with her concerns. If Bill was so much in need of her, he should tell her himself. She refused to not be seen any longer. Having experienced being seen, appreciated by others, she had no desire to return to her family and the status quo. 'Don't worry. No one for you to worry about. How is Drew?'

'Much better. We're having proper conversations now. He still gets a bit breathless though. No burns, which is good. On his skin anyway. They say his lungs are burned. Which—' He swallowed, blinked quickly.

Helen gave him a hug. 'On the mend though?'

Ian nodded. 'Yes,' he said tightly. 'It could have—'

'But it didn't. He didn't, did he?'

'No. Quite right,' Ian said. 'How's Gabriella and Simon?'

'Her date went awry.'

'Did it?' he asked.

'Nothing too bad. She slept at his place, by all accounts. So…'

Ian's eyes shone. 'Shall I call her?'

'Or we could ask when we're next at the lido.'

'Better,' Ian said with a knowing nod.

It had been a while since they'd all been there. Ian had almost completely stopped going, as had Helen, except for the occasional swim alone. She bumped into Gabriella from time to time, but not as much as before. Gabriella said she was busy with the modelling work. That reminded Helen, *must ask her about that too*.

Chapter 33

Ian had spent the afternoon with Drew by his bedside in the side room he'd been moved to, since Ian visited so long and frequently. It was very considerate of the staff. Ian felt optimistic that he'd be home very soon. The nurse in charge had mentioned something about him being ready for discharge in the next fortnight, and said that she'd seen that the next of kin had been told.

Ian hadn't heard this before, so he reckoned there must have been crossed wires somewhere at their end, but didn't want to cause a fuss since they were giving Drew such great care and it felt churlish.

'I'll go,' Ian said, kissing Drew's cheek. 'Is that okay?'

Drew smiled. 'At least Helen is looking after you.'

The door opened and there stood a brown-haired woman in a fake fur coat, holding a boy's hand.

'Sorry, this is a private side room,' Ian said.

She looked about the room. 'Drew Oakley?'

'Yes,' Ian said with confusion.

'This is the right place,' she said, walking in.

'Who are you?'

'I'm Carol. The hospital rang. Said he was here. Don't know why I hadn't been told before. It's been a while, so... Suppose it makes sense.' She shrugged.

'What makes sense?' Ian asked.

Drew's smile had been replaced by a look of horror.

'Drew?' Ian asked.

Drew's face had gone ashen grey.

'Who are you?' she asked.

'I'm his husband,' Ian said carefully. 'Who are you?'

'His girlfriend. Well, ex.'

Ian knew Drew had dated women, he'd always been open about being bisexual. 'Why are you here now?'

'He told you he swings both ways, then?'

Drew shook his head. 'I think you'll find we say bisexual now.'

'Right. Bi. Yeah.'

'He did,' Ian said. 'If you don't mind, this is a private conversation, in a one-person side room. There's no point talking about exes when Drew's got more than enough on his plate.'

The little boy looked at his mum. 'Is this Daddy?'

She stroked his hair and nodded. 'Yes, love.'

'What did he just say?' Ian frowned.

'Daddy,' she said.

'Daddy?' Ian asked with incredulity. 'Drew has a son?' *Drew. Has. A. Son.*

'He does, yeah, as it goes.'

Ian felt the ground whooshing up to meet him as blood rushed in his ears and his heart beat like he'd been running a marathon. An icy cold terror grabbed his gut, squeezing it tightly. 'What?' he managed to say, but only just. Turning to Drew, he said, 'You've got a son?'

'Apparently,' Drew said.

'And you didn't think to tell me?'

'When we split up I didn't know Carol was pregnant.'

Ian turned to Carol. 'Didn't you tell him?'

She shook her head. 'I didn't know myself. I'm always all over the shop. Didn't know until I went to the doctors feeling sick and needing a wee all the time.'

'You didn't know you were pregnant?'

She shrugged. 'It happens. He was my first.'

'You didn't know you were carrying a whole actual human inside your body, for nine months?'

She shook her head.

'You didn't know you were carrying a baby?'

'Like I said, no.'

He didn't think Drew would have cheated on him, but given this, anything was possible. Carefully, he asked, 'This just gets better and better. I'm not sure I want to know the answer to this, but I feel duty bound to ask anyway. How old is he?'

'Four.'

'Right.' Ian nodded. 'That's one question answered.'

'I wouldn't have, not while I've been with you.'

The emotion of it all was too much and Ian shouted, then began to cry. Tears fell down his cheeks. He'd had enough of this, worrying about Drew, but now this woman and little boy had come crashing into their lives. The relief at discovering Drew hadn't cheated on him ran through his veins like cool ice. But the anger at this, the sheer bloody terrible timing, had him bunching his hands into fists and banging them against the wall.

'Look, I know it's lousy timing, but I thought he was at death's door, see,' Carol said, with a shrug.

'Right. Yes.' He blinked away the tears, tried to compose himself. It wasn't really her fault – or was it? The anger warred with confusion and then sparks of joy mixed in as he considered them having a little boy in their lives. 'Course.'

'I would say sorry,' Drew said, 'but...'

'He didn't know.' Carol nodded at Drew. 'Blame it on me, if it helps.'

It might have helped, but then again Ian wasn't sure. He'd gone from shock to confusion, to worry and anger, and then briefly joy, and now he was just flabbergasted. 'He's four?'

'He is,' Carol said.

'And we met three years ago, which is fewer years, so that means it's after. Right.' He almost felt as if he needed to draw a timeline to reassure himself. But the maths wasn't that complicated, even though his brain was struggling to process it.

'I was with Carol well before I met you.' Drew squeezed Ian's hand.

Ian wasn't sure how he felt about Drew, so carefully removed his hand. 'Well, that's at least something. We can cross off infidelity from the list.' Louder now, he went on, 'Splendid. Wonderful. Marvellous. Bloody fantastic!' His face heated and a prickly sensation trickled through his arms and hands.

'Calm down, will you?' Carol asked.

'Calm down? You're telling me to *calm down*? When my husband is in hospital, fighting for his life and you turn up out of the blue with a child neither of us even knew existed until five minutes ago?' He took a deep breath. 'I think, of all times, of all the things I've been through in my relatively uneventful life, up until this point, *this*, what's happening now, is an occasion when I'm well within my rights not to remain calm, don't you?' He pursed his lips, looking at Drew, then Carol, then the little boy.

'Please yourself.' She shrugged.

'Does he have a name?' Ian asked.

'Lennox,' she said, rubbing his hair affectionately.

Ian raised his eyebrows.

'He didn't stop kicking and punching me when I was pregnant. Once I realised I was, er, pregnant. First scan and then he didn't stop. Before that I just needed a wee all the time and then I knew it was cos he was punching my bladder.'

It was a lot for Ian to take in. The lack of cheating, the addition of a son, the arrival of an ex, all within five minutes. He felt as if he was on a TV show set up for maximum conflict and confusion.

Drew being in hospital was one thing. Drew being in hospital with an ex-girlfriend, and a son who'd sprung fully formed from this Carol woman, without her knowing, and who had been living perfectly well, in wherever it was Carol lived, for four years, was too much to process.

And so, as the anger, frustration, confusion and surprise combined, the sickness took over the feeling of serenity and optimism he'd had before the door had opened. And then there was nothing except blackness.

He woke in the relatives' room with a nurse sitting next to him. He was laying on the sofa.

'What happened?' he asked.

'You sort of passed out,' the nurse said. 'It's my fault,' she went on with concern in her voice.

'It's not your fault. It's… That woman's. My husband has a child I didn't know about. Neither did he, to be fair. But it was…'

'A lot?'

Ian nodded. 'Right.'

'I'm really sorry.'

'No need to be sorry. It's not your fault.'

305

'It really is my fault. Which is why I'm really sorry.'

'Why?'

'N-O-K, I rang them.'

'But I'm his next of kin.'

'And Carol.'

'How can you have two next of kin contacts?' Ian asked, as confusion continued to rein supreme in his world.

'I looked at an older record.'

'Right.'

'She was his N-O-K. Before. Didn't check the date. I was in the middle of talking to a relative on the phone and I'd left the drugs trolley in the ward to answer the phone. Locked of course.'

'Of course,' Ian said, as if he knew the significance of this.

'I'm sorry. I was just going to ask if you could, maybe, not complain about this?' She looked at the floor.

'Sounds like you had a lot on your plate.'

'Right. Yeah. I did. So will you not complain?'

'I won't. But I'm going to have some very stern words with Drew.'

'The little boy? No, your husband. Course. Yes. Well, I would if I was you.' She stood. 'Can I leave you, it's just I think I'm wanted in the ward?' She nodded at a male nurse who stood at the door, peering through the small window.

'Thanks.'

The nurse left, shaking her head as she met her colleague.

The door shut.

Later, in the side room, where Drew lay, with Carol to one side and Lennox the other, Ian entered.

Carol stood. 'I'll leave you to it.'

'You can stay if you want,' Ian said.

'Best I don't.' She grabbed Lennox's hand and they left.

'I swear I didn't know,' Drew said with contrition in his voice.

'She seems nice,' Ian said, doing his best to be magnanimous about the whole thing.

'She was. I mean, she is. But we split up, so...'

'Obviously.' Ian coughed. 'Why? Just out of interest, did you split up?' Drew had mentioned an ex-girlfriend when they'd started dating, but just said they weren't right for each other.

'She's a bit, er, mad. Mood swings, anger, flying off the handle. Then—' Drew stopped himself.

'What?'

He shook his head. 'Doesn't matter.'

'Your actual son has just turned up. I think you owe me at least some details.'

Drew shifted uncomfortably in the bed. 'Make-up sex.'

If ever Ian had heard a two-word horror story, that was definitely one.

An awkward silence settled in the room.

Ian coughed. He had enjoyed more than his fair share of fun with "gentlemen friends for the night" at uni and it didn't bother him that Drew had been in relationships with women. He knew it didn't make Drew any more or less likely to cheat on him – *if he's going to cheat on me, he'll do so* he'd reasoned to his friends. But a child, he begrudgingly admitted, did change things. Very significantly.

'Not all details need sharing,' Drew said staring at the bedsheets.

They nodded.

'Why didn't she tell you about Lennox?' Ian asked.

'We didn't split up on the best of terms.'

'Who does?' Ian shrugged.

'I mean, like shouting and screaming, throwing my stuff into a pile and burning it in the front garden.'

'Ah.' *Hence the mood swings comment.* 'Is she still the same?'

'She says not. She's got a boyfriend, who she's very happy with. Apparently.'

Apparently. Apparently Drew and Carol had been catching up while Ian was passed out. He did all he could not to feel uncomfortable about that. 'What about him raising your son?'

'What about it? I've only just found out he exists, never mind thought about how he should be brought up.'

'But you must have some thoughts.'

'I do. But I wanted to talk to you first.' Drew made eye contact. 'Cos we're a team, right?'

Right. Ian's heart, despite the anger and surprise of earlier, felt as if it would burst with love. Ian nodded.

'I know you've never wanted kids.'

'Haven't I?' Ian asked.

'You've never mentioned them before.'

'I spent the last eighteen years knowing I liked men and that made it harder to have children. I don't *not* want them, I'm probably ambivalent about children. I don't know if I want them or not. Which probably tells me I'm leaning more towards not. Anyway, it was just easier to focus on my career and friends over trying to have a family when I've never had a relationship with someone who I could make a baby with. And then I met you.' And he didn't need anything to change their relationship.

They'd always worked on the basis that each other would be enough for them. As long as they were a team, working in the same direction, in unity, they didn't need any other additions to their family.

Finally, Ian said, 'A theoretical child is very different from one that very much exists. Sitting by your bed in hospital, finding out his dad could have—'

Drew squeezed his hand. 'I'll be home soon. That's what they said, isn't it?'

Ian nodded. He wasn't going to let Carol and Lennox reduce him to tears. 'Lennox, I mean, what a name!'

'I know, right? If I'd had anything to do with that, well… Anyway.' After a silence, Drew said, 'I want to be part of his life. I know you might not. But I need to. I can't let him be brought up by some other man. Not know I know he exists.'

Ian had once told Drew that he could deal with anything – debt, exs, health conditions, even being into country dancing, but that if Drew wanted children Ian would be out. That conversation haunted him now. At the time Drew had said he didn't want children, not if he had Ian. As long as they had each other, he'd be happy.

'Thinking?' Drew asked.

Ian nodded.

'What about?'

'What I said when we first met.'

'I can't choose between you and him,' Drew said. 'You can't make me.'

'I wouldn't.' Not least, Ian reckoned, because he may well lose. A husband he'd become used to and who was far from perfect versus a handsome boy he'd just met, a shiny new piece of his own DNA to whom he could pass on his knowledge and skills. Ian knew who'd win that competition. Easily.

'Means we'll, or I'll have Carol back in my life.' Drew grimaced. 'But she is his mum.'

'And you're his dad.'

'And you, if you want to be,' Drew said.

'A team dad.'

'Right. I know it's the last thing any of us needed, but I'd rather know about Lennox than not. Even if the way it happened wasn't... Great.'

Ian enjoyed Drew's familiar understatement. It meant they had, and could, face anything life threw at them together. 'Shall I ask them to come back?'

'If you want.'

Ian left the room, met Carol and Lennox sitting in the relatives' room where he'd woken.

'We'll get off,' she said. 'I've said once he's home, we'll sort out seeing Lennox. If you want to? No pressure.' She shrugged.

Ian wanted to ask her why she could have excluded Drew from Lennox's life when she knew he could have enriched it. But he knew it was pointless. Carol had made the decisions she had, for her own reasons. Perhaps her boyfriend was more than enough dad in Lennox's life. Perhaps the way she and Drew had ended meant she never wanted anything to do with him again.

After an awkward silence, Ian said, 'That would be great.'

'I'm doing okay now.' She pointed to her head. 'Not like before.' A pause, and then, 'I meant to tell Drew. You know what it's like.' She shrugged. 'Still, it's all out in the open now.'

Ian smiled. 'Absolutely.'

They walked to the ward entrance, waiting by the buzzer to be let out.

Carol waited for Lennox to walk into the corridor. She told him to stay there, as she looked at him. 'I'm much better now I'm with my man. Me and Drew sort of rubbed up the wrong way. You know?'

Ian had no idea how anyone could become rubbed up the wrong way by Drew, who was the most unargument-ative person he knew. To be kind, he nodded.

'Lennox's gonna be lucky, with three dads. Like I said, no pressure. As much or as little time as you want with the lad is okay with me.' She narrowed her eyes at him, looked back to her son, who remained in the corridor.

'We'll be in touch,' Ian said.

'Thanks.' She slipped through the door she'd been holding ajar and into the corridor, holding Lennox's hand and walked quickly away.

Chapter 34

October

Gabriella hadn't been swimming at the lido for weeks. Since the first meeting with Lana, she'd returned and done jobs for a footwear brand, clothing and sunglasses. The staff at *Simply You* had become her new family. And she remembered so well why she enjoyed working. The pain at not being able to share this with Arnie had reduced somewhat, as she could talk endlessly to Simon about it.

Today, she had completed thirty lengths of the lido's outdoor pool, grateful it was heated, as a light steam rose from it in contrast to the cold autumnal air. The trees had golden yellow, orange and red leaves, the ground covered in them, the car park slippery as she'd walked towards the lido. Too cold to sit on the sun lounges and no sun to sunbathe in, no one hung around the pool's edges any longer, everyone chose the indoor pool or ran back to the warmth of the wellness centre after their swim. She had changed and sat in the café, her hair damp, and waited for the other members of theLonely Hearts Lido Club to arrive.

Helen had said she'd swim, but obviously hadn't. Ian had said he'd do whatever Helen told him since she was bringing him.

Gabriella saw them arrive out of the corner of her eye.

312

Ian waved, then Helen strode to order their drinks.

Excitement bubbled in anticipation in her stomach. It had been ages since they'd done this. Something which, some weeks ago, had been the core of their friendship, had somehow fallen away.

'Sorry we're late,' Helen said, sitting at the table.

Ian followed and he looked about a decade older than before. Gabriella didn't say anything. What he'd been through with Drew would age anyone. It was a miracle that he wasn't much worse, especially since the ex and son had appeared from nowhere.

'You look well,' Gabriella said to Ian.

'Some days I feel dead. Some days worse,' Ian said smiling awkwardly as he sat.

'You're doing very well,' Helen said, patting him on the back. 'So, what caused you to call this meeting?'

'I wanted us to return here, to where we met. Since so much has changed with our lives.' She hadn't thought too deeply about it, except that she missed them and their time together.

'Did you swim?' Helen asked.

Gabriella nodded.

'I must get back to that.' Helen rolled her eyes. 'I've not had time, with one thing and another.'

'What like?' Ian asked.

'Neglecting my family. Apparently.'

'Says who?' Gabriella asked.

'My son, among others. And my husband. I'm waiting for my nieces and nephews to make an appearance and tell me too.' Helen sighed loudly.

'I've got unknown family coming out of the wood-work.'

'I heard,' Gabriella said. 'Is Drew home now?'

313

Ian nodded. 'Could be much worse. He can't wait to see Lennox.'

'Who?'

'Drew's son.'

'Wait a minute, this is a lot to take on board. What happened?'

Ian told her. About the ex-girlfriend and the little boy and about how Drew hadn't known about Lennox until then.

'When he was in hospital?' Gabriella asked.

Ian nodded.

'I can think of better timing.'

'Indeed.' It was Helen, who'd been listening in silence.

'Why are you neglecting your family?' Gabriella asked.

'I left them. Dereliction of duty. Left my assigned post. That sort of rot.'

'Is that what Bill said?' Gabriella asked. Helen had rarely mentioned her husband since leaving, which Gabriella had taken as a sign she didn't want to discuss him. But now the issue of her neglecting her family had been mentioned, Gabriella felt she could ask.

'If he had, I wouldn't mind so much. But instead, he sent Peter as a messenger. Apparently he didn't understand why I had left. He needs me, or so he says.'

'Right,' Gabriella said.

'Needs me and can't manage without me are, I pointed out to Peter, two entirely different things. And, until Bill deigns to deliver the message himself, I shan't be entertaining any notion of a reconciliation.'

That, Gabriella felt, was very final. Helen was a woman who always seemed to know her mind and had no problem telling everyone whether they wanted to listen or not. An enviable quality, Gabriella felt.

'No chance of going back?' Helen had what Gabriella felt was an enviable advantage to herself. Arnie was, and always would be dead, whereas Bill could change. Being dead was a permanent state, that Gabriella had no hope of changing no matter what she did.

Helen shook her head. 'I know what you're thinking. I'm lucky he's not dead. Well, I'm going to say it: I'm unconvinced of that. If he'd died, at least I could move on without all this terrible guilt hanging around me like a noose.'

'Don't wish him dead,' Gabriella said, trying to keep control of her anger. 'It's not something I'd wish on anyone, not even my worst enemy.'

Helen gathered herself together, sitting straight on the chair. 'Sorry.'

'Don't be sorry, just think about talking to him.'

'I can't. Not until he speaks to me. Until he sees me.'

'What would it take for you to know that Bill wanted to make an effort? To see you, I mean?' Ian asked with great care.

Helen shook her head. 'Enough of me. I'll think about it.' She turned to Ian. 'Tell us about this Lennox child.'

Ian said, 'I didn't think I'd want children. I didn't. But now there's this person who exists, who's part Drew, of course I love him. Both of them.'

'What's the ex like?'

'Carol is, I believe the phrase is, as mad as a box of frogs. Although, by all accounts, she's calmed down since Drew was with her. I think she's grateful to have two people to offload Lennox on every now and then.'

'Why didn't she tell Drew he was a dad before?' Helen asked.

'They left on less than perfect terms.'

'How bad?' Gabriella asked, intrigued.

'She burned his belongings and threw him out of the house.'

'Aha. That'll do it.' Gabriella took time to appreciate this. 'Didn't he call the police?'

'Domestic – they wouldn't have done anything. Besides, he just wanted out of the relationship. He jumped in his car and never went back.'

'Wow.'

'Indeed,' Ian said. 'That's more than enough about me. Even I feel embarrassed talking about my stepson. They're working out shared custody at the moment. It's a good job we're married or it could have become very convoluted apparently. Or so said our solicitor.' Ian smiled. 'Our solicitor. Get us. How glam. Not as glam as you, though.' He turned to Gabriella.

She blushed. 'I'm so grateful.' She looked to Helen.

Helen shook her head. 'I didn't do anything. Lana loved you. That's all you.'

'You must know what I've been doing from her?' Gabriella asked.

Helen shook her head. 'Nada. Zilch. Rien.'

'Oh,' Gabriella blushed. 'Since we're all talking about family – of sorts – I feel like I've found a new one.' She rested her hand on theirs, on the table. 'Except you two, of course.'

'Of course,' Ian said with a smile.

'Everyone at *Simply You* has been so welcoming. I didn't think I'd be able to do it. Go back to work. Thought I'd be shy. But as soon as the photographer looked through the lens, I was…' How would she describe it? It reminded her of the first time she'd done a photo shoot, when she'd met Arnie. Except now she had the confidence and experience of an older woman.

'Happy?' Helen offered.

'Back?' Ian asked.

'Home,' Gabriella said carefully. 'Like I'd never left. I took direction from the photographer and came alive. Mum said I always loved the camera. Since I was a little girl, I'd dance about and pose when Dad took pictures. I've never felt prettier. More confident.' She stopped, feeling she was verging into big-headed territory.

'Show us the pictures, then,' Ian said.

'I've not got them with me.'

Ian narrowed his eyes. 'Pull the other one, it's got bells on. You can't tell me you don't have access to an online folder where they're stored? Printouts? What do you think this is?'

'My brief Nineties magazine career,' Helen said with a smirk.

They laughed.

Gabriella hadn't touched her drink, the time had passed so quickly and she felt as if she were slightly tipsy from only drinking coffee. She'd told Arnie this after her first photo shoot and he'd said it was dopamine, which gives you a natural high.

'When will we see the adverts you're in?' Helen asked.

'A few months. One is on those boards you get outside. By the side of roads. Another is in *Simply You* magazine, with an interview about my life, makes me seem more like their readers. Having kids is doing me a favour. Lana is even talking about something in *A La Mode* magazine, but I don't think it'll happen. Me, in *A La Mode* magazine?'

'Don't do yourself down,' Helen said.

Keen to change the subject, Gabriella said, 'Who wants to swim?'

'You've just had one,' Helen said, unconvinced.

'So?'

'You're far too modest for your own good. Lana said you're beautiful and natural in front of the camera and completely professional.'

'You said she'd not told you anything.'

'Not details. Not about, you know, the photos. Which reminds me. Can you log onto the whatever it's called, so we can, you know, see them?'

Gabriella did, as Ian had suspected, have access to a folder where all her photos could be viewed. She'd first viewed them and hadn't wanted anyone to see them because she didn't want to seem too full of herself, as her mum used to say.

'Budge up.' Ian moved his chair next to Gabriella's.

Helen copied.

'We're waiting,' he said.

With reluctance Gabriella logged into the folder and laid her phone on the table, as the photos appeared. 'Fill your boots.'

'We intend to. If you're not going to blow your own trumpet, we shall for you,' Helen said.

Gabriella sat back as Ian and Helen swiped through her photos, asking questions about what they were intended to be used for, what it had been like, was it cold, did she feel self-conscious wearing that. And Gabriella felt grateful her friends cared so much about her passion, her work, her life, in a way she'd not experienced since her parents and Arnie had been alive.

Chapter 35

November

Helen was at Gabriella's place, holiday brochures splayed out on the dining room table. The nights were drawing in, grey, cold and rainy most days. The heat of the summer and sunbathing by the lido felt like a lifetime ago. The lure of a winter sun holiday had proved too irresistible, so she'd stopped resisting. She'd considered holidays for single travellers but, since she was still married, that hadn't felt right. Then a company specialising in holidays for retired people, and after some research she'd concluded maybe she was just not yet old enough to holiday like a scene from *Cocoon*.

There was a loud knock on the door. It would be Peter, keen once again to persuade her to return to the family home and to Bill's side.

Helen stood, resolute with the decision she was not doing either, ever again. But it felt motherly to allow Peter to try and persuade her otherwise.

She opened the door and assembled her features into something resembling a smile. Whatever happened, it would be nice to see Peter.

They hugged, he kissed her cheeks.

'Home alone?' he asked as they walked to the dining room. 'What's this?'

'Gabriella's working. Boys are at school. I'm having a bit of me time.'

'You hate me time. You've always hated sitting around doing nothing. Even on holiday you hate it.' Peter picked up a brochure, flicking through it slowly. 'Aren't you going to offer me a drink?'

'Not if you're that cheeky.'

'I would help myself if you were at home. But since I don't know Gabriella, nor her house, it feels a touch presumptive.'

He wasn't wrong. 'She has a very impressive coffee machine. It's like something from a science fiction film.'

'Good–oh.' He put the brochure on the table. 'When are you going to end this nonsense and come home?'

Helen narrowed her eyes and clenched her jaw. 'If your father is so lost without me, he should tell me himself. It's neither right nor proper for you to behave like some marriage counsellor for your parents. In fact, it's rather distasteful.'

'Why? I just want things back to how they were before.'

Helen stood, walked to the kitchen. 'That's where you and I differ, very considerably. I don't want anything to return to how it was before. In fact, I think it's a physical impossibility.'

'You're so dramatic, Mother. It doesn't suit you.'

'What would you know about what does or does not suit me? You know nothing about me. Me as me. Not a mother or wife. But me.' She shook her head. 'I think you ought to leave, if you're going to speak to me like that.'

'Sorry,' he said quietly. 'Only trying to help.'

'I'd prefer if you didn't.' She busied herself with the coffee machine.

It whirred and lights flashed, beeping in a sequence Helen recognised to mean it was doing as she'd asked. If only people were as compliant.

There was silence.

She handed him a coffee, then took her own.

'Are you planning to live here forever?' Peter asked in a tone she recognised as very sarcastic.

'Very unbecoming is that.'

'What?' He tried his best to look innocent.

'Sarcasm. I'm evaluating my options. Ian doesn't require me any longer, now that Drew is home. They're working out how to accommodate a son neither of them knew existed.'

Peter frowned.

'It's complicated. Suffice it to say it's better I leave them in peace. Ian knows where I am if he needs me.' Wistfully, she reflected how they saw each other much less frequently than the early days of swimming in the lido, of her trying the gym equipment and meeting in the café. But life had moved on for them all, so it was to be expected.

'So you're finding somewhere to live and planning a holiday alone?' Peter summed up.

'Correct. Gabriella would never say anything, but now she has Simon, it's quite crowded here sometimes. I feel like something of a gooseberry on occasions. She has him to babysit, and she for him. It seems to be an arrangement that works for them both.' Gabriella had kept very tight-lipped about her relationship with Simon, probably not wanting to jinx it, but Helen could see how happy Gabriella was; the combination of working and having someone to love her in a way she'd missed since being widowed was doing her the world of good.

A pang of loss crept across Helen's heart at her own situation. Bracing up, she said, 'I don't suppose you'd be interested in holidaying with me?'

'Not on some cruise that'll remind me of *Cocoon*.'

'How rude.'

'Come on, Mum, you can imagine what it'll be like.'

She had. And he wasn't wrong. She held a brochure and flicked it open to the page she'd been considering that described a European cruise for a fortnight. 'Tell me you don't want to do this.' She showed him.

He read it with interest. 'Sharing a cabin, I don't think so.'

'I'll pay.'

'You can pay me for my time as well, but the answer is still no. It's my precious annual leave from work. I can afford that if I wanted.'

'Ah.' Helen put the brochure down, with a great deal of disappointment lodging itself in her heart. 'Of course.'

'Sorry, Mum. But I think it's a recipe for disaster, don't you?'

She hadn't before. But now he mentioned it, she could see his point of view.

'Couldn't you ask one of these new friends to go with you?' he suggested, not unhelpfully.

'Good idea,' she said, not believing it for an instant. Gabriella wouldn't take a holiday without the boys, nor should she. Besides, she'd want time with Simon anyway. And Ian, although she could imagine enjoying a holiday with him, wouldn't want to, at the expense of one with his family.

'Gabriella must be grateful,' he said, obviously sensing she wanted to change the subject to something entirely less depressing.

'For what?'

'Introducing her to your magazine friend.'

'She is,' Helen said. Although, now, if she considered it, would she do it again? Possibly not. It had taken Gabriella further away from her, to a place where she didn't need Helen nearly as much as before. Into a confidence with Simon that had pushed Helen even further into second or third place in Gabriella's life.

'Maybe move out, before you outstay your welcome?' Peter said.

Helen stared out of the window. She'd done it again, been so helpful she'd done herself out of the job. And yet, with Bill it was the opposite; he was so reliant on her that he'd developed some sort of learned helplessness.

'Thank you,' Helen said finally. 'I shall bear that in mind.'

'You seem... Not yourself. What's wrong?'

'I should return to my volunteering. That's all. I've found myself in the position of having too much time and not nearly enough to do with it. Once again.'

'Come home. He's sorry.'

'I don't need him to be sorry. I've had enough of sorry to last me a lifetime. I want him to change. I want him to—'

'See you, appreciate you, yes, I know. But how's he supposed to do that if he can't see you.'

'You're seeing me. He can see me. He knows where I live.' All she was asking for was one step. In the right direction, to acknowledge how wrong Bill had been for all those years. How she'd let him get away with it. But now she'd realised her errors, he needed to build a future together with her. Rather than in spite of her.

'He—'

Helen bunched her fists up tightly. 'If you're going to say he's a proud man, please don't. It's not an excuse for anything. I'm all done with him using that as an excuse for all sorts of unacceptable behaviour. As much as he dislikes it, we're not in the eighties. He might be, but I'm not.'

'What can he do to show you he sees you?'

'Not be such an emotionally stunted fuckwit! Not complain about everything, despite it not making the slightest bit of difference. Not choose to search for the bad in everything when there's so much joy to see and experience. And not to see straight through me. To see me, to listen to me, to want to be with me.' *Like the Greek couple on the beach all those years ago.*

Peter looked at her wide-eyed. 'That's… a lot.'

The front door opened, and the boys shouted they were home.

Gabriella shouted, 'Chaos is back, silence is gone.'

'I've put up with a lot,' Helen said, with barely disguised rage.

Gabriella arrived in the dining room. 'Still thinking about holidays?'

Helen stood. 'I'll be out of your hair soon. Don't worry.' She left the room for the hallway, standing at the bottom of the stairs. She took a deep breath then walked up slowly.

'I didn't mean—' Gabriella said.

Peter followed her, calling up the stairs.

Helen turned halfway up, held onto the bannisters. It had all been too much for her. She never failed to underestimate how fragile she still was about this. About Bill's complete failure to see her. To understand her point of view. To even speak to her properly.

'I didn't mean to upset you, Mum,' Peter said.

Helen slowly sat on the stairs, feeling like a crumpled heap of washing. 'I know. Ask him if he remembers the Greek couple on that beach when we were on holiday.'

Peter frowned. 'What on *earth* are you talking about?'

'He'll know. And if not, then I don't know what to say or do.' She turned and walked up the stairs slowly.

From behind her she heard Peter say, 'The Greek couple and the Greek holiday?'

'Correct,' Helen said as she reached her bedroom.

Chapter 36

December

Ian wanted to take Drew and Lennox to a place that had been very special to him over the last few months. Saved his life in some ways.

While in hospital, Carol brought Lennox to visit his dad a few times a week. Ian timed his visits so he got to know them better. Having children wasn't something he would have planned for, but now Lennox was in his life, he enjoyed it much more than he'd anticipated.

Once Drew was home, a few weeks ago, signed off from work, they had made the most of this spare time to get to know Lennox and Carol, visiting their home twice a week. Ian found a part time job, similar to what he'd done before, but more junior. It took a little more juggling of timetables, but they made it work. With Lennox to look after, he didn't mind the step down. He was grateful for the routine, the intellectual distraction that work provided, but he no longer felt his job dictated who he was. He was many things: husband, stepfather, colleague.

His new colleagues asked about the little boy whose photo he kept on his desk.

'He's my husband's son.'

There had followed comments about how of course gay men could have children nowadays, it was marvellous what they could do with surrogacy and adoption.

'Drew did it the old-fashioned way,' Ian said with a smile. 'With an ex-girlfriend. It's all very amicable now of course.' He left out the fact that both the son and the ex-girlfriend had come from nowhere, but he went large on how he enjoyed his guncle duties. So he resumed his commute from the end of the Piccadilly line into London's West End, three days a week, but he looked forward to the time off, in ways he'd never found before. Appreciating Drew after his accident, getting to know Lennox and his other family, were delightfully complicated and interesting in equal measure. And completely different from summarising a ninety-six-page policy document about care systems into a two-page briefing.

At first he and Drew would hang out with Lennox while Carol was in the house, then she would pop out for a short while.

'Mummy's going out, but you're okay with Daddy and Uncle Ian, aren't you?' she would ask, with a laid-back tone she'd told them was the best approach for anything new in Lennox's life.

Lennox would look up from his drawing, grabbing a coloured crayon. 'Okay.'

The first afternoon with Lennox, a few months ago, while Carol went shopping and met a friend, had felt like a big deal. Ian sensed the terror creeping up his arms as pins and needles, making his chest tight.

'I've got my phone. You know what he likes to do and eat, just play with him. Take him for a walk if you like. He's into football at the moment.' She picked up a ball from the corner. 'The park we went to earlier this week.' She kissed Lennox's head, then left.

Football with a four-year-old wasn't half as bad as Ian had thought. Nowhere near as terrible as playing sport at school. They kicked the ball for ages, bought Lennox an ice cream from the van and ate them sitting on the park bench, as other children played on the swings.

'Can I go on the swing?' Lennox asked, licking his hands of ice cream.

Ian reached into the bag of tricks Carol had given them, pulled out a wipe and cleaned the little boy's hands.

'Look at you, Guncle Ian.' Drew winked and elbowed him playfully.

'Hygienic.'

'Can I?' Lennox asked with those wide eyes and the cheeky grin that reminded Ian of Drew.

'You go.' Ian nodded at Drew. 'What if he falls off the swing?'

'He won't.' Drew stood, taking his son's hand and leading him to the swings. 'Watch!'

Lennox sat on the swing.

Drew pushed his son on the swing and Lennox held on tight, with his freshly cleaned hands.

Ian smiled. He'd not checked his watch all afternoon for when Carol was due home. *I could get used to this. Part time, anyway...*

One day they discovered that Lennox hadn't been in a pool, nor to the beach, when telling Carol their plans to take him to the lido.

'With all that seaweed?' she'd asked, with a look of disgust.

'Doesn't do anyone any harm,' Drew had said. 'We're thinking of taking him to swim.'

'He can't. So you can't.'

Drew had shown his frustration, and started to respond.

Ian, knowing he could diffuse the situation had said to Carol, slowly and calmly: 'It's a lovely place. It sort of saved me, these last few months.'

'I don't like swimming pools, all those plasters floating about in the water.' She shook her head.

'It's not like that now.'

Carol narrowed her eyes and pursed her lips, her arms folded.

'Swimming is a great life skill.'

'Is it?' Carol shrugged. 'Hasn't done me any harm not being able to swim.'

'We'll teach him. If he hates it, we'll stop.' Ian knew Lennox wouldn't hate it because he loved exercise and Drew had said he enjoyed bath time when Carol had asked him to put his son to bed. 'There are children's swimming classes.'

'How deep is the water?' Carol asked with uncertainty.

'Deep enough.' Ian looked at her. 'Trust us.'

Lennox had been sitting on the floor playing with his toys, completely oblivious to the discussion going on over his head.

Carol put her hands on her hips. 'You're not gonna take no for an answer, are you?' She looked at Ian then Drew.

'Let us, will you? You've had all the other firsts – word, step, solid food. This can be our thing.'

There was a silence as Carol stared at the floor. 'Fine.'

Now, they arrived at the lido – Ian's lido – for the parent and child swimming class. Drew and Ian were going to take turns looking after Lennox in the water. Apparently there wasn't space for two parents with each child, which had frustrated Ian slightly, but not as much as the looks they'd received arriving in the pool, pushing Lennox in a buggy.

Carol said he should really be walking by now, but sometimes it made it easier if he was going to new places, to make him less anxious. So Ian and Drew had taken her advice.

Two men with a child somehow screamed something that a man and a woman with a child did not.

There was a crowd of parents and children in the shallow end of the indoor pool. Much too cold for children to swim outside apparently, even though the water was heated.

'Is this the parent and child swimming class?' Drew asked.

'It is,' said a lithe red-haired woman in a one-piece blue and white swimming costume. 'I'm Amy, the teacher.'

'Drew,' he replied. 'Lennox.' He nodded at his son.

'We're not starting for a bit, so you've time to change.' She smiled.

Ian noticed the eyes of all the mums raking over Drew from head to toe. *Wait until you see him in his swimming shorts.*

Ian stayed with Lennox, who stared at the water, while Drew changed in a blue changing booth. Then Drew returned, took Lennox back into a booth, then reappeared shortly. Lennox wore long red swimming shorts – it reminded them of lifeguards. Drew, as usual, looked magnificent in his well-fitted aquamarine swimming shorts. His broad muscular chest had short, slightly stubbly hair from when he'd shaved.

Twelve pairs of eyes – the mums and the few dads – followed Drew as he walked from the changing booth, holding Lennox's hand, and into the shallow end of the pool.

Lennox cried loudly, asking for his mummy, screaming as the water touched his feet.

'First time,' Drew said to everyone.

After more crying, Drew sat Lennox on his lap as they took their places in the shallow end. The water came up to Drew's navel.

Ian had taken a seat by the edge of the pool.

Drew and Lennox's head shape was the same. As was their hairline, and eyes, Ian noticed now.

Amy clapped, stood by the edge of the pool and the class began.

They held the children on their fronts as they thrashed arms and legs about in the water. Taking them further into the water, the parents held their children as they became used to having the water up to their stomachs, while bobbing them up and down upright in the water.

Lennox soon stopped crying and was transfixed by the other children, all splashing and enjoying themselves in the water.

They flipped the children so they lay in the water on their backs, supporting them so they were only just getting wet. Lennox didn't like this and screamed and cried loudly until Drew returned him to his front. He shrugged at Amy.

She said, 'Well done, Daddy.'

The parents stood in a circle, each holding their child's hand.

Amy stood in the centre and began to sing 'Ring a Ring O' Roses'.

The parents walked clockwise, singing, allowing their children's legs to flow through the water. They walked anti-clockwise. At the chorus, the adults knelt on the bottom of the pool, submerging themselves and the children with them, up to their necks.

Then they started 'The Hokey Cokey' and as Amy led the singing, about putting your left arm in, the parents held the chubby limbs of their children and put them in the water, taking them out in time with the song.

This was repeated with their right arms, and then the children's left legs, as they went in the water, and then out, finally ending with their right legs.

This was accompanied by lots of shouting and laughter from the adults and children.

It was delightful, and Ian found himself becoming a little emotional watching on. He'd believed he didn't have a paternal bone in his body, but that was before he'd been presented with the living embodiment of Drew in miniature form. And how on earth could he resist having a child like that in his life? And indeed, why should he?

The class finished sooner than Ian expected. He'd thought there would be a natural gap, so he and Drew could swap.

'Everyone clap for yourselves,' Amy said. 'You've done so well.'

The adults clapped and some children shouted their gurgling happiness.

Drew carried Lennox out of the water and sat next to Ian on a plastic chair. 'I should have swapped. Sorry.'

'Doesn't matter,' Ian said, meaning it. 'Next time.'

It was a ten-week class and since he and Drew had Lennox every Sunday, they'd be able to complete it together.

'Shame you couldn't take any pictures or video,' Drew said.

'We can tell Carol when she picks him up.'

Drew said to Lennox, 'Are you gonna tell Mummy how much you enjoyed this?'

Lennox smiled and gurgled and laughed and nodded.

The way they stood, the angle of their heads, their smile, mirrored one another perfectly. Ian had never seen Drew look more like his son than at that moment.

'Is Gabriella meeting us here?' Drew asked, looking about.

It would have been a nice idea, especially if her boys were doing the swimming class too. But they could all swim and didn't need the teaching. Apparently Arnie had taken them almost before they could walk, according to Gabriella.

'At hers,' Ian said. He gestured for him to take Lennox. 'You change.'

Drew winked. 'Thanks.'

Ian shrugged. 'Whatever, it's nothing. You did the class with him.'

'Not that. Everything.' He stared at Ian for a moment.

Ian raised an eyebrow.

Drew strode towards the changing rooms.

Ian took Lennox to a cubicle and changed him into dry clothes. It had been quite a journey from ex-girlfriend and unknown son turning up to here now, putting Lennox's T-shirt over his small head. But Carol understood how Drew wanted Lennox in his life and she admitted she should have told him sooner. But she lived a busy and often disorganised life, and Drew was out of sight and out of mind. Except when he wasn't.

Ian smiled at the simplicity of that. Much more likely than Carol being a controlling mother and not allowing Drew to see his son. But just like Drew, Carol was remarkably uncomplicated. She conceded to liking the freedom that time without Lennox gave her and her boyfriend Ty.

Ian left the booth with Lennox dry and dressed. Holding his hand, they walked towards the café.

Drew, with damp hair and dressed, met Ian in the café. 'All right?'

'Yeah. Really all right.'

'You seem too zen for someone who was looking forward to the class and who missed out.'

'It doesn't matter. We'll have him next week.'

'We will,' Drew said.

They put on their coats, Drew helped Lennox with his, then they walked to the car and after securing Lennox in his car seat, they climbed into theirs and drove to Gabriella's home. The windscreen misted up as the rain fell and Ian turned up the car's heater. The weather forecast said it would snow later, but Ian would believe it when he saw it.

Gabriella showed them inside and into the kitchen. As she made coffee she said, 'I think you're both saints.'

'Why?' Ian asked.

'If I'd missed the first few years of my boys I'd... Well, I'd be really pissed off.'

Drew shrugged. 'Doesn't change anything though, does it?'

'She did apologise. Carol,' Ian said.

'I know,' Gabriella went on. 'But I'd still be physically livid. How can she forget about the father of her kid?'

'Because,' Drew said, 'I don't think she did. I think she was okay because she had her boyfriend.'

Gabriella handed their coffees over. She shook her head. 'He's the spit of you.' She gestured at their chins, eyes, noses. 'It's always the way. I read that a baby resembles its dad more so it's easier to tell who is the father. It's obvious who's the mother, right?'

'Anyway, who would it have helped to fall out with Carol?' Ian asked.

'I'd already done that.' Drew grimaced. 'If *I'd* been left pregnant, I don't think I'd have got in touch with Carol. Not after how it ended.'

Ian wondered if Carol had experienced addiction issues as well as mental health problems back then, but he kept it to himself. From what Drew had described, the relationship was passionate at best and stormy and volatile at worst. Was it any wonder Drew never thought of her again and Carol wanted nothing to do with Drew either?

'She met Ty a fortnight after we split,' Drew said.

'Do you think she was seeing him before?' Gabriella asked, sipping her coffee and staring at him over the top of the mug.

Drew shrugged. 'Maybe. Doesn't matter, does it?'

'Would to me.'

'Carol was seeing someone when she met me. I think she's a serial monogamist.'

'Unless she was cheating,' Gabriella said raising her eyebrows.

Sensing this conversation wasn't particularly helpful, Ian said, 'Where's this play centre?'

'One of the school mums told me. Offered to have a play date there with her kids too.' She shook her head tutting loudly.

'What?'

'Never shared the time of day with me before. Probably wouldn't have pissed on me if I was on fire. But since I'm in *Simply You* magazine, I'm her best friend.' A pause and then: 'Not exactly original is it?'

'At least they're friends with you now,' Ian said.

'If you can call people like that friends.' Gabriella shrugged.

'How's it all going? Helen said you're the face of everything and anything.'

Gabriella blushed. 'Not quite. Three products so far. Cover for the December issue. They interviewed me and some other mums about going back to work. Told 'em, me modelling was hardly down to earth, like their readers. Lana reckoned it was inspirational. Probably cos I'm not posh.'

'You're delightfully you.'

'Common as muck, more like.'

'Individualistic.'

'Nice one,' she said, looking at Lennox. 'How was he with swimming? Jack loved it. But Thomas, Christ, he screamed blue murder the first time we brought him to a pool. Arnie took him to the deep end and let go. He went under, and then up he came. Bobbing up and down like those things they use in boats. What are they called?'

'Buoys?'

'Is that what they're called? Like my two boys?' Gabriella asked.

'Different spelling,' Ian said.

Gabriella stood. 'Shall we go?'

'Do you have copies of the magazine you're in?'

'Later. It's in tomorrow's recycling bag. It's nothing too great. Not like you two, giving Lennox three dads. That's amazing I reckon.'

'Talking of dads, how's Simon?' Ian asked.

'Can we get going?' Gabriella said, urgency in her tone.

At the play centre, they left the older boys climbing ladders, slipping down slides and throwing balls at one another. Gabriella, Drew and Ian took Thomas and Lennox into the soft play ball pit.

The children were partly submerged in the coloured plastic balls while their parents made themselves comfortable, then handed the children balls to play with.

After a while, Gabriella left Thomas to crawl through the balls alone.

Since Thomas was nearly the same age as Lennox, Drew followed, while keeping a close eye on the two children.

Gabriella pulled her hair away from her shoulders, tying it up in a band. 'He's too perfect. I keep thinking he's going to grow another head and bite my head off when he's pissed off. Or something.'

'Simon, I presume?' Ian said.

'Course. I was told so many horror stories about dating. I didn't have that before Arnie – just boys and men I didn't want to date. They weren't terrible.'

'Tell, please. Cos I've got dozens of dreadful dating stories.' Ian chuckled.

Drew had joined them, still keeping an eye on the two boys as they played.

Gabriella laughed. 'Okay, keep them clean, little ears always hear the wrong things,' she said to Ian.

'I spent my twenties experimenting and wondering why none of the men I slept with wanted to see me afterwards.'

'Because they had no reason,' Gabriella said wisely. 'Once you've given it away, there's no need to come back. That's what Mum used to say.'

'You're telling me you were a virgin for your wedding night with Arnie?'

337

'Christ no! Neither was he. Although his mother believed otherwise. Probably why she disapproved of me. Still does.'

'Harder now you're the mother of their grandchildren,' Ian offered.

'They're not as bad as before. Although they're pulling the strings with the boys and I don't like it. Didn't have any choice but, well, now things are different.'

'How?'

'They might be. Not sure. I just wish I had my parents to even things up a bit. You know?'

'You've got us. And Helen.'

'And Simon.'

'Who's perfect. Like I said, I can't believe it. I keep thinking I'll wake up and he'll be a dream. I've just gone from boyfriend to boyfriend without any gaps. Much. I think it's cos I can't be single. People are gonna think I got with Simon too soon, aren't they?' She looked at Ian with those big brown Disney princess eyes and tears formed at the corners.

He pulled her in for a hug. 'None of their business. He wouldn't want you to sit around mourning him forever. He'll always be the boys' dad. Nothing anyone does can change that.'

'Some of the mums at school, they say little things about how lucky I am to have found someone so soon. Soon, they always sort of hang on that word.'

Drew checked no children were in earshot. 'Fuck 'em. It's jealousy. You've got it all. You've gone from the poor widowed housewife to this fantastic creature we see before us.'

'He can come more often,' she said to Ian with a wink.

'I aim to please,' Drew said with a smile.

'You should have seen everyone staring at him at the lido earlier.'

Drew looked from Gabriella to Ian. 'What's the point going to the gym if you're not gonna show off the hard work?'

'And you do mean hard, right?' Gabriella grinned. 'Simon used to go to the gym. Reckons he doesn't now. I reckon that's a lie.'

'Based on what?' Drew asked with obvious deep interest.

'Never you mind.' She blushed.

The children played until they'd had enough and arrived where the adults were with the two youngest, complaining they were hungry.

That evening after putting Lennox to bed, Ian was exhausted but with a generous side order of satisfaction. He wanted to tell Drew this and reflect on how it felt to have the best of both worlds, being able to give Lennox back to his mum on Tuesday. But he didn't want Drew to think he wasn't grateful for their time with Lennox.

'Knackered?' Drew asked as they sat on the sofa. He lay flat.

'Yep.'

'Maybe next time we do something less...'

'Knackering?'

'That's right,' Drew said with a chuckle. 'Looking forward to going to work for a break.'

'How about reading club around Gabriella's, with Thomas?'

'That. Yeah. I never know what to read him. We need to get some more kids' books.'

'And toys.'

Drew fell silent, making a quiet low snoring noise as he fell asleep.

Ian felt his eyelids becoming heavier, and lay next to Drew on the sofa, so they were like spoons in a drawer.

Sometime later, Drew said over Ian's shoulder, 'How do people do this full time? And with two of them. Gabriella is a superwoman.'

'I keep telling her this. But she thinks she's remarkably unremarkable.'

'She's a fucking warrior princess.' Drew sighed, his breath against Ian's neck. 'They all are. I'm looking forward to it being just us two for a bit. Is that me being a bad dad?'

Relief washed through Ian at this familiar sentiment. 'It means you're a normal person. It's hard work having children. Or so it seems based on our extensive few months' experience. We've got two other adults to share it with.' He kissed Drew's hand and placed it on his chest.

'Right.' Drew's hand went limp as he fell asleep.

Ian decided he'd do the same as he thought about all the women like Gabriella bringing up their children without complaints, without help, and those who juggled family and jobs and other commitments.

Fucking warrior princesses, the lot of them.

He wasn't sure what that made him and Drew after two days with Lennox, asleep at seven o'clock, too tired to make themselves dinner after doing so for Lennox, then bathing him and reading a night-time story to him, now asleep on the sofa. Warm, contented, exhausted and wondering how they'd make this work when Drew went back to fighting fires…

Chapter 37

Gabriella had done her sums, checked them and spoken to Lana and felt confident she could make it work.

They stood at Pru and Edward's front door, the doorbell echoing around their large hallway.

Another week, another Friday night.

She stamped her feet on the ground and sheltered under the porch against the rain as an icy wind blew. She knew it wouldn't snow, which the boys would have loved, but instead, as always, it would be bloody freezing and rain day in, day out.

The door opened. Edward stood in a smart jacket and chinos. 'How lovely to see you.' He sounded as if it was a surprise, although it was anything but.

She'd been there every Friday night since the conversation about them continuing to pay the boys' school fees.

Her boys ran up to their granddad and hugged his legs.

He knelt and brought them in for hugs and kisses.

In the hallway, the door closed behind them, Gabriella stood silently, watching as her boys showed how much they adored their grandpa. She'd brought them here not for Edward and Pru, but for the boys themselves.

It didn't seem possible that this gentle elderly man and woman could have parented Arnie so strictly. Boarding school, telling him to man up as a teenager when he was still being bullied by boys in his year.

'I'm so pleased you're here,' Pru said from the corner of the hallway, her arms folded.

'Wouldn't miss it.'

Pru walked forwards. 'Really? That's wonderful to hear. Only... No, doesn't matter.' She pulled Gabriella in for a hug.

'You've both taken to nanny and grandpa duties very well,' Gabriella said.

'We're their grandparents. What did you expect?' Pru smiled.

To ask me to send them away to some draughty boarding school and tell them to just get on with it whenever they had any problems. Gabriella bit her top lip.

'You're thinking. I can tell because you're quiet.' Pru sighed. 'Bringing up Arnie was very different. *We* were different. Times have changed.'

Gabriella nodded. 'I'm just made up they have you in their lives, even if they don't have their dad no more.'

'Well, there's nothing to be done about that, so no sense in dwelling on it.' Pru coughed, knelt on the ground and said to the boys: 'What have you been up to?'

Thomas put his arms around her for a hug and Jack stood swaying gently before joining his brother when Pru gestured with a waving hand.

Gabriella's heart nearly burst with love, and squeezed with pain that her parents had missed this.

They walked into the lounge and the boys told Edward and Pru about the play centre.

'Aren't they,' Pru said, 'somewhat unhygienic? All those children putting the plastic balls in their mouths.'

'These lot aren't afraid of a few germs.'

'That's as maybe, but I am concerned. As their grand-mother. I'm sure Arnie would be the same.'

Gabriella bit her tongue, sure that Arnie would *not* feel the same.

'You seem to have gone all red. Is there something wrong?'

She had planned to save this until after they'd eaten, but now was as good a time as any. She'd rehearsed what she was going to say and double-checked the figures and she was sure it added up.

'I need to say something,' Gabriella said with care. 'And I don't want us to fall out over it.'

Pru and Edward withdrew, their faces appearing very pinched all of a sudden.

'I'm afraid that,' Pru said, 'very much depends on you.'

'Thank you for paying for the boys' schools. It's very generous. Arnie definitely wanted them to stay going private. He told me—'

'And me.'

'He obviously never expected… What happened… To happen.'

'Who does?'

'Nobody. The boys love coming here. But now I can, I want to pay for their schools myself.'

'How?'

'The modelling work.'

'That's making money?'

Gabriella nodded. 'From next term I'll pay their school fees.'

'It's an awful lot.'

'I know.'

'Wouldn't you be better spending it elsewhere?'

On the tip of her tongue was *who do you think you are to tell me how to spend my money?* but she bit it back. Falling out over this wouldn't help anyone. 'I want to spend it like this.'

'What about your other living expenses?'

Gabriella's life insurance policy and pension from Arnie paid for modest everyday living expenses, now she was better at managing her money. She told Pru.

'I see.' Pru folded her hands in her lap, staring at the floor for a moment, in obvious discomfort. 'And you don't think this will disturb the boys' routine?'

'What will?'

'Stopping them coming here. They've become very used to it. I understand they look forward to it. We've never seen so much of them. It's a shame we couldn't when Arnie was alive. But I'm sure you had your reasons.' Pru looked very sad, lost, out of control. As a woman used to being in charge, this was obviously uncomfortable for her.

'I never said that,' Gabriella said.

Edward frowned. 'I don't follow.'

'We'll carry on coming here. I'll cover the school fees. Quite simple.'

'Why?'

'Because you're their grandparents. Because they love coming here. Because you won't be around forever. Because you're the only grandparents they've got. Do I need to go on?'

Pru shook her head. 'What else?'

'That's it.'

'Well, that's very kind of you.' Pru looked away awkwardly, clearly uncomfortable with not having to fight Gabriella over this.

'I have a lovely home, why don't you come to mine sometimes?'

'We could,' Edward said, looking at Pru with uncertainty.

She shrugged.

'And,' Gabriella went on, 'you could meet Simon. And his kids.'

'He is,' Pru said, 'I presume, the gentleman you're seeing?'

'He has his own kids. He's spending time with the boys. He loves me.'

A look of horror crossed Pru's face. She bit a hanky she'd taken from her pocket.

'Arnie will always be their dad. Please, just meet him.' Gabriella stopped. She could have said so much more, but decided silence would be better. More powerful, Simon had said. Let them sit with the awkward silence, he'd advised.

'He loves you?' Pru asked finally.

'He does,' she said plainly and with confidence. 'Definitely.'

Gabriella had been surprised Simon had said the 'L' word first, worrying she'd let her joy and happiness bubble through her and one day she'd say it casually. But it had been Simon.

He'd said it on a bright Sunday morning at his place, after eating breakfast in his kitchen, she had slept in the spare room, no pressure to do anything else.

Reappearing at the bathroom door wearing blue pyjamas, with rumpled hair and stubbly face, looking every bit as lip-bitingly sexy as always, he said: 'Thank you.'

'What for?' She looked away, carefully buttered a piece of toast.

'For being you. For not feeling sorry for me. For just loving me as a man, and not a poor widower.'

She shrugged. 'You're a man first, widower's like, fourth, or fifth down.'

He smiled, resting a hand on the doorframe.

'Man, dad, son, voiceover thingummy, boyfriend, friend, colleague, then widower.' She counted them on her fingers. 'Widower's right at the bottom.'

'You're Gabriella, fantastic, fearless, caring, strong, sexy.' His eyes shone as he grinned.

She blushed. 'You're just saying that.'

He shook his head. 'I love you.'

What did he just say? She frowned. *I. Love. You.* 'Your words for me don't work. They're different.'

'Mine are nouns and the ones for you are adjectives.' He folded his arms. 'You're a woman of emotions, on your sleeve, up front, *describing* words.'

She felt herself both in awe and on the edge of confusion. She'd never spoken about love in this way, not since… She bit her lip at that. *Will I ever love without thinking about Arnie?* Taking a deep breath to compose herself, she went on, 'You're all those things – man, dad, son – and you do them all at the same time and they're separate. I can't describe it.' He was clever and complicated, and yet also as comfortingly simple and straightforward as herself. She stared at him. 'I love you.'

He strode over to the table and kissed her with passion, with love and with all the other describing words Gabriella might sometimes forget, but felt, deeply within her. She knew Simon would love her and although Arnie had said he'd love her forever, he hadn't managed to. And she couldn't live in a world without love, as much as she'd tried. She felt sure the tinges of guilt at gently moving

346

on from her husband, who was no longer in this world, would subside, replaced by joy for her love of Simon, who was very much with her, here and now, in this world.

Now, after a long silence, Pru asked, 'And the boys, does he love them?'

'Like they were his own. Same as his daughters. He's just so nice. But not boring nice. Interesting nice, prince on a horse rescuing you nice.'

'I see,' Pru said narrowing her eyes.

'In that case,' Edward said, 'I think we shall have to meet him.' He looked to Pru.

She nodded slowly. 'What does he not eat?' She looked at Edward. 'Unless you want us to yours next week? I don't think we've got anything in especially for next week. I can always bring something. If that's okay with you.'

'Yes,' Gabriella said, 'that's great. He'll eat anything. Including offal, but I don't hold that against him.' She laughed nervously.

'I'll strike stuffed sweetmeats off the menu.'

Gabriella frowned.

'Offal,' Edward said.

'Right.'

'Are we ready to eat now?' Pru asked.

Later, after they'd eaten and neither Pru nor Edward had mentioned their earlier conversation again, Gabriella had to check that she'd told them. In the car on the way home, she recalled what they'd said and how it had all felt like a dream. A surreal, unexpected dream.

Once home, she told the boys to get ready for bed. 'I'll be up in a minute to read your stories.'

They climbed the stairs. Thomas yawned. 'Will you help me with my pyjamas?'

'Ask your brother,' she said.

347

Jack held his brother's hand. 'Come on.' They walked upstairs together.

Simon was watching TV in the lounge. 'World War Three?' He took his feet off the foot stall, stood to greet her with a kiss and hug.

'Where are the girls?' Gabriella asked.

'In bed. Probably not asleep though. I read them a story but they wanted to see the boys before going to sleep. I said they'd see them tomorrow.'

'They're coming round next week.' Gabriella sat, allowing it to sink in.

'Who? Pru and Edward?' Simon asked.

'Yep.'

'No tempers and tantrums?'

'I don't think they believed me at first.'

'Money-wise?'

Gabriella nodded. 'I'll bring them a copy of *Simply You*. See if they can ignore that. Stick that in their bloody pipe and smoke it.'

'You seem very undecided about your feelings for your in-laws. I think you should be much clearer about them.' He smirked.

'I am a terrible person. They are the boys' only grand-parents.'

'True.'

'I just told them. What I was doing and gave them no option to disagree.'

'Quietly and calmly, leaving the awkward silence?'

'Like you said,' Gabriella added. She thought for a moment. This hadn't occurred to her before, she'd been so focused on what they might or might not say to her.

'No disagreements?'

'I did what Arnie used to do. He used to tell them. Make it clear they're our kids. They're just the grand-parents. Second-in-command he always used to say. Tell them.'

'Just like they told you at the start?'

'They had the money. They knew I wasn't going to take the boys out of their school. Not after me and Arnie had agreed. They had all the cards. This time I had them.'

'Well done.' He stared into her eyes. 'Love you.' Simon hugged her, kissing her on both cheeks, then her lips.

His hard lips pressed against hers and she inhaled his woody, citrus scent as she pressed against his hard, muscular body. It took her by surprise, not for the first time he'd told her he loved her, but for the first time she'd said Arnie and hadn't felt a stab of guilt or pain. He was up there, looking down on her, helping her look after their children. While Simon was here down with her, on the sofa, doing his bit too.

'Thanks,' she said, putting her arms around his neck. 'Love you.'

Later, when she told Helen and Ian in the lido café, grateful for the warmth as sheet rain fell and a biting cold wind blew, she explained it didn't feel like such a big deal because she'd known how she felt for a while before that. Their lives were interwoven: he stayed at her place with the girls, or she at his with her two boys; they worked around each other's work commitments for childcare, and that evening, when she'd arrived home to Simon relaxing in her lounge, she'd finally been able to let go of any remaining guilt. Guilt for her happiness. Guilt for making a new life after Arnie. Guilt for not living her life in continuous mourning. Guilt for not keeping the house as some sort of museum to Arnie.

'Don't go chasing misery,' Helen said to her. 'Grab any joy you can. You're a long time dead. Sadness is every-where. But so is joy — don't run from it. Would Arnie want you to be alone?'

Gabriella blinked away a tear as it rolled down her cheek. 'He was a brilliant husband and dad. But he's dead. So I'm going to run towards Simon.' She looked to the sky. 'I hope that's okay, Arnie?'

The chatter of the café, the clanking of crockery and whoosh of steamed milk were the background when Gabriella realised she knew exactly what she wanted.

'I'm going to ask him to marry me,' she said, wiping her cheek with her sleeve.

'You don't muck around do you?' Ian said.

She shrugged. 'When you know, you know.' She looked at Helen. 'Right?'

'Indeed.'

Gabriella held their hands. Looking to Ian, she said, 'Right?'

'If you know, you know.' Ian leaned forwards. 'Can I just say one tiny thing?'

'When has it stopped you if I said no?'

Ian grinned. 'Live with him first. Get engaged. Plan the wedding together. There's no rush.'

'Right. But I'm gonna tell everyone now. I don't see why not. Once I've asked him. Assuming he says yes.'

'He'll say yes,' Helen said calmly.

Chapter 38

January

Early one morning a few weeks later, Helen was swimming in the lido's outdoor pool. Steam rose from the warm water as it met the cold air. Only a few others were there too, most others had retreated to the indoor pool. *Wimps*.

She'd left Gabriella's at sunrise. Gabriella had plenty to keep her busy now, didn't need Helen in the same way, now that Simon had practically moved in.

She really must find herself somewhere to live, alone. Six months, with a spell at Ian's and she'd definitely outstayed her welcome at Gabriella's. She knew Gabriella would never tell her to move out.

She reached the end of the swimming pool, caught her breath, then turned around for another length. Where would she want to live, if she could choose anywhere?

Helen tried very hard not to feel slightly cynical about Gabriella's decision. She was sure it was the right one. But Helen couldn't help but remember back to Bill proposing to her, all those years ago and now look where they were. *It's easy to keep things interesting at the start, you try doing it after forty years.*

She reached the far end of the pool as she contemplated this; the colourful changing booths were empty.

Two shoes and trousers she recognised fell into her field of vision. She held onto the rail on the pool's edge.

Must be water in my eyes. Clearing them, she looked upwards.

Bill stood, in a winter coat, scarf and hat, looking down at her. He held flowers in one hand and a pile of papers in the others. He was saying something.

Helen removed her swimming cap and ear plugs. 'What are you doing here?'

'I'm an idiot.'

'What's new?' She peered and squinted to make sure her eyes weren't deceiving her.

Next to him stood a suitcase.

'What's that?' she pointed.

'What does it look like?'

'Suitcase. Where are you going?'

'Wherever you want.'

Helen laughed.

He held the papers aloft. 'I've got brochures. Let's pick somewhere.'

Helen swam to the shallow end so she could get out of the water. Away from this nonsensical demonstration of nothing of any real substance. She walked out at the shallow end, took her towel from the sun lounger, wrapped it around herself, shivering at the cold air against her skin.

Bill met her. 'I mean it.'

'I wish I believed you.' She walked to the far end, grabbed her clothes from a sun lounger then slid into a changing booth where she began to dry herself and dress. Her teeth were chattering, perhaps the wimps swimming indoors had the right idea.

Bill had followed her and stood outside the booth. 'I've stopped work. I want to go on a cruise with you. There's one for four weeks, all around the world. Northern Europe, then southern Europe, around Africa, South America, and then back. Leaves from Southampton. The food options are amazing. We can eat twenty-two hours a day.'

This piqued her interest. Never before had he shown anywhere near this much interest in a holiday. 'You've retired?'

'Yes.'

'Prove it,' Helen said, shaking her head and rolling her eyes, with more than a smidgen of cynicism. Dressed and much warmer, she left the booth.

He handed her a letter, headed with the hospital's logo. It thanked Bill for thirty-seven years' loyal service and wished him well for his retirement with his wife and family.

She handed it back. 'You did this before.' And he'd returned part time on the following Monday. Plus the other project he'd been doing that seemed to involve reviews and some sort of regression to the mean, whatever that meant.

'This time I mean it.'

'Why?'

'Because I'm lost without you. Still am. There's no point whatever I'm doing if you're not with me.'

'And now, you realise this?'

'I do.' He shrugged. 'Better late than never.' He removed his shirt, kicked off his shoes, sat on a sun lounger and took his trousers off. He stood, wrapping his arms around himself against the cold, in a pair of swimming

353

shorts she'd bought him for a holiday they'd not gone on due to a work emergency. 'I'm not too late, am I?'

He wasn't wrong. But Helen remained to be convinced. 'Why didn't you speak to me before?'

He handed her a bunch of flowers. 'It's in there.'

They were roses and carnations, reds and pinks, her favourite flowers in her signature colours. They were mixed with baby's breath and in the centre was a card. She opened the envelope and read the note inside: *I'm sorry. I love you. I'm lost without you. Looking forward to retirement together, Bill Liphook xxx*

He put a toe in the water.

'What on earth are you doing?' she asked. 'It's very cold. Even for me. You're not going to swim, are you?' He'd never been a fan, especially in the winter, never mind outside in a lido.

'You'll see, I want to understand why you love it so much, why you've been coming here all the time. It'll be something we can do together,' he said, then obviously debating diving in, then thinking better of it, he walked to the shallow end, walked into the water, swam to the deep end, where Helen remained.

He looked up at her. 'It's freezing!'

'Told you.' But he'd done it. He'd actually dived in and stuck to his word, which was more than she'd expected.

He smiled up at her. 'Will you do me the great honour of renewing your vows with me?'

Helen laughed, put her hands over her face in shock and confusion. 'What?'

'I can't ask you to marry me again. I want to show you and everyone else how much you mean to me.' He stared at her. Really keeping eye contact. 'All the things you've done for me, for the children, for the house, everything over the years. I took so much for granted.'

'You can say that again,' Helen scoffed.

'It's a cliché but I didn't know how much I needed you until you left.'

Helen shook her head. She'd heard enough of this cheesy rubbish.

He beckoned to her.

She knelt by the edge of the pool.

'I want to stand on a beach with you, watching the sunset. Meanwhile, why don't you come in?'

She shook her head. 'I've just dried off. I'm cold. I want a fennel tea to warm myself up.'

He waggled his eyebrows suggestively. 'I can think of something else to warm you up.' He held his hand out.

She grabbed it.

'Come on.'

She shook her head. 'I'm dressed. Why don't you get out, you're going blue.'

His teeth were chattering and his lips purply blue. He swam to a ladder, climbed out of the pool and wrapped her towel around his torso.

'Dry yourself off, before you catch your death.'

Bill scurried to a changing booth, shortly reappearing dressed and with damp hair. Next to her now, he said, 'You didn't believe I'd do it, did you?'

She shook her head. 'Swim?'

He nodded. 'Told you I meant it. It's exhilarating.'

Seeing Bill like this was exhilarating.

He pulled her to his torso, putting his arms around her, pulling her close, so their bodies touched.

She couldn't remember the last time he'd done that. The last time she'd felt his hard chest against hers, his

355

thighs pressing next to hers. *His... Is that what I think it is?*

Helen's eyes widened at the unmistakable recognition of what she felt poking into her hip.

He pulled her close, in for a kiss.

She was confused, unsure if it was appropriate for a swimming pool, or if it was some kind of elaborate joke. But she trusted in Bill's arms as they encircled her, as he pulled her close, as he kissed her cheeks, then her eyes, and then oh so joyfully, her lips.

She felt herself melting into him, onto him, towards him. Wanting desperately for this to be true, not to be a dream, not to be some sort of ruse.

His eyes shone and he smiled.

The man she'd married was back. She recognised him, after so long when he'd been absent.

'Shall we go home?' he asked.

'Just like that?' she asked, feeling somewhat swept away with this. Whatever this might happen to be.

'If you like.' The desire in his eyes was unmistakable, as was the firmness against her hip.

They walked to the café holding hands, and stood by the door, bracing themselves against the weather, as coffee smells, clattering crockery and talking filled the air.

He pulled her close, kissing the top of her head, putting his arms around her, pulling her against his firm body.

They stood still for what might have been moments, but felt to Helen like hours.

'I'm sorry I've been missing,' he said quietly, staring into her eyes and holding her hand.

She nodded.

'And thank you for waiting for me to return. I'm back. I want to show you how much I love you. How much I've always loved you. Will you let me do that?' he asked in a whisper just next to her ear.

Butterflies spread from her stomach, up through her chest and she felt light. Anticipation, excitement, desire uncoiled from deep within her. 'Yes,' was all she managed to say as a lump formed in her throat.

He took her hand and led her out of the café, and into his car, and went home as quickly as Bill could drive.

They fell inside, and he pressed her against the wall, leaving her in no uncertainty how much he wanted this. She too felt warm, felt liquid desire course through her veins. It had been so long since they'd... But it was, as Gabriella had said a long time ago, just like riding a bike.

They rushed upstairs into their bedroom, and to Helen's blessed relief, it was precisely like riding a bike. Neither of them had forgotten anything. It all came back to them very naturally, joyfully, lustfully, and all at once.

Afterwards as they cuddled in bed, Helen pulled the duvet around herself and Bill said he wasn't sure why they'd stopped doing that, when it was such fun. Helen blushed, imagining telling Gabriella how much of a fool Bill had made of himself, kissing her like a love-sick teen-ager in the corner of the café.

'I laughed at that Greek couple on the beach,' Bill said, after bringing tea and biscuits back to bed for them.

'I remember.'

'I've been so wrong about so many things for so long. It's a wonder you're still here.'

'I wasn't. Remember.'

'Yes.' He paused, stroking her hand. 'But you're here now.'

'Evidently,' she said.

357

'Where do you want to go first? I was looking into buying a camper van. We can drive it all around Europe. Stop wherever we want. Go wherever the mood takes us.'

'What about Peter?' she asked.

'What about him?'

'You're happy to walk away from the hospital and do that?'

'A few weeks ago we had a man in with a heart attack. Thirty-five. Dead. His poor wife was beside herself. Left two small children. Like your friend Gabriella. I got home that evening – empty house, shattered – and I thought, why am I doing this? There are doctors thirty years younger than me who can do it. I've done my time. I could drop dead tomorrow. They'll manage without me. They'll have to. But I couldn't manage without you.'

'I said this to you.'

'I know. But, in case you didn't know, I can be quite stubborn.' He coughed. 'Can't see what's at the end of my nose. What's right in front of me. You. I stopped seeing you. Don't know when. But I did and I'm sorry.'

'Did Peter speak to you?'

Out of the corner of his eye, he glanced at her. 'Yes. Why?'

She wanted to be sure it wasn't just Peter putting him up to this, that it was Bill wanting this himself. 'Nothing.'

'So where do you want to go first?' he asked.

'Where would *you* like?'

'I'm not falling into that trap. That's how the rot set in. My fault entirely.'

'Trap?' she asked.

'Being too busy to talk to you properly. This is our retirement, not yours with me as a passenger.'

'You've got the brochures, where do you think is nice at this time of year?'

'I hear Greece is very nice at this time of year. Blue seas, long sandy beaches, red and golden sunsets.'

After the last time they'd been, when Bill had missed the significance of the couple on the beach, she'd wanted to go back on her own to experience the magic. But now he understood the magic, she wanted to go with him.

'It is,' she said.

'Greece it is then,' Bill said.

'Greece it is.'

He kissed her again, moving from her lips to her cheeks, to her neck, and then under the duvet...

Chapter 39

February

'Are you sure you've got everything?' Ian asked.

Drew shook his head. 'If we've forgot something we can buy it. We're not going to a desert island.'

Ian checked the packing list, ticked everything off, but couldn't help but wonder if he'd forgotten to add something onto the list, and therefore hadn't remembered it.

They were on their way to a holiday park on the Kent coast. Normally it was their turn to have Lennox from Saturday night to Tuesday, but since it was half term... Apparently, up until very recently, Ian had no concept of half term, summer holidays or anything related to children and school.

Drew started the car and they set off towards the coast. They hadn't gone on this sort of holiday before, preferring instead to fly and flop somewhere sandy, sun-drenched and surrounded by sand. But Carol wasn't keen on eating food she didn't recognise, so she and Ty had visited a holiday park every half term since Lennox was born.

'I'm sure it'll be fine,' Ian said resolutely, determined to convince himself and overcome the significant nerves that had been plaguing him.

'I don't know why you're so worried,' Drew said as they pulled onto the motorway, the windscreen wipers doing their best against the driving rain.

'I want it to be perfect,' Ian said.

'You'll be very disappointed then. There's nothing about Carol that's perfect. And who knows what her boyfriend's going to be like for more than a chat at their doorstep.'

'Least it's only two days. Well, two and a half,' Ian said.

They had agreed to join the others for the weekend, which had proved hard enough between Ian and Drew's part time hours, meant to make looking after Lennox much easier, but often doing nothing of the sort.

Drew nodded wisely. 'You're telling me you've never been on this sort of holiday before?'

'I have not.'

When Drew had suggested a holiday together with Carol and family, Ian had – naively he now knew – assumed it would be a city break somewhere in Europe.

'A holiday park?' Ian had asked, in bemusement at its mention.

'Static caravans, lodges, swimming pool, entertainments, club house.' Drew had said.

'In the UK?'

'Yes. Didn't you have UK holidays as a child?'

Ian shook his head.

And Drew had laughed very long and very hard, until finally saying, 'Did you go to Brittany as a boy?'

'We did. But I don't know what's so amusing.' Ian frowned.

Ian's parents had taken them to various rented villas in France, Germany, Italy, Spain and Portugal as children. Since his mother and father were teachers, they always took the opportunity to tour Europe for six weeks in their estate car.

He'd told Drew and asked, 'Didn't your parents?'

More laughter from Drew. 'Nope.'

Ian had felt embarrassed.

Now, Drew said, 'You never thought your European tours were a bit… Posh?'

'I went to a grammar school. Parents came from all backgrounds.'

Drew nodded in a way that Ian knew meant he wasn't convinced but wasn't about to say so. He put the radio on and they drove in silence as rain fell.

Much to his surprise, the static caravan was larger and better fitted out than Ian had expected. Each room had a radiator, with an electric fire in the sitting room.

Carol stood with her hands on her hips as they parked next to their car, on one side of the 'van' as Ian soon found everyone referred to it.

'You made it then!' she said, pulling Drew, then Ian in for a hug. 'We've got so much to show you. Shame you couldn't come yesterday too. We've been getting right stuck in since we arrived. The entertainments are wicked. Been reading the programme. Lennox's already had a swim with Ty. I stayed in the van having a bit of me time, you know?'

'Where's Lennox?' Drew asked.

'Ty's taken him to the crazy golf course with some friends.'

'He's like me, making friends just like that.' Drew snapped his fingers.

'School friends. They always come here half term.'

Drew nodded. 'So what's the plan now?'

'Fancy a look around the site?'

'I've read the map,' Ian said, waving it aloft. 'I think we're—'

Drew jabbed him in the ribs. 'Sounds great, we'll follow you.'

Carol showed them the swimming pool, the entertainment complex with slot machines and fruit machines like in a seaside arcade, the pub, and all along the beach with golden sand covered in bits of seaweed and shells.

'Fancy a vino?' she asked, as they stood outside the entertainment complex.

Ian checked the time: it was ten o'clock. 'Maybe a coffee?' He shared a look with Drew.

Drew shrugged. 'When in Rome.'

Ian stuck to coffee until midday, when he was convinced to 'go on treat yourself, let your bloody hair down,' by Carol, and had a small glass of wine.

Unsurprisingly, as he had more alcohol, he found himself relaxing and enjoying the afternoon as it unfolded in front of them.

He didn't usually do well in places like this. He tended to be easily spotted as what he was, and used to attract unwanted comments and attention. But he felt safe with Drew there, and Carol worked very hard to make him feel comfortable.

'You okay?' she asked. 'Looks like you just got some really shit news. You're on holiday.' She squeezed his thigh. 'Another one?'

Ian was feeling more than a little tipsy, two glasses of wine with no lunch had, unsurprisingly, gone straight to his head. 'Can we eat?'

'I've done my holiday special.'

'Sounds great,' Drew said with enthusiasm. 'What is it?'

'What it is, is I fry some sausages, onions, add baked beans, and top it all with slices of potato. It looks like the tiles on the wooden cabins. The roof does. You'll love it.' She left for the bar.

Ian turned to Drew. 'I'd have cooked. If she'd asked me. I'd have gladly cooked. I enjoy cooking. It would give me something to do.'

'I think she wants to show us how *they* do this. Maybe next time you can cook, eh?' Drew said.

They had Carol's round of drinks and she said, 'Best get back for lunch.' She led them back to their van.

Carol's boyfriend was called Tyson, shortened to Ty.

He was a large, beefy man, bald, thick–set with tattoos on both his forearms and on his chest since he'd been in the navy as a young man. He arrived with Lennox in a pushchair and shook their hands firmly, staring into their eyes, smiling, saying it was wicked they'd made it.

They unpacked and settled in to the bedroom, listening to Carol and Ty arguing in the kitchen.

'What's wrong with them?' Ian asked, sitting nervously on the bed.

Drew shrugged. 'I think it's just how they talk.' Drew unpacked his suitcase then sat next to Ian on the bed. 'Ready to go out and face them?'

Ian felt sure he wasn't ready, but instead smiled weakly and said, 'I suppose so.'

'Lennox's been asking about you,' Drew said.

'He has not.'

Drew nodded. 'Carol said. She and him were looking forward to spending more time with you.'

'They did not.'

Drew crossed his heart. 'Cross my heart and hope to die.'

Ian smiled. 'What did they say?'

'What I just said. And Ty is okay. You're just being prejudiced.'

'I am not.'

'I know you are. If he's happy to take you as he finds you, you should do the same.'

'Even if,' Ian said, standing, 'in school he'd have beaten me up and flushed my head down the loo?'

'This *isn't* school,' Drew said, opening the door.

They walked into the small galley kitchen.

Carol said loudly, 'What's this about school?'

'Nothing,' Drew said.

Ian stood, getting in the way. 'Can I do anything to help?'

'Sit at the table and enjoy my food,' Carol said. 'And start enjoying yourself.'

Ian did as asked, as best he could.

Ty helped Lennox into a chair, then sat next to him, holding his knife and fork upright and gently banging them on the table. He winked at Ian.

Ian wasn't sure what to do, so he copied.

'Why are we waiting?' Ty sang, 'We are suffocating. Why oh why are we waiting…' He looked at Ian out of the corner of his eye.

When in Rome, Ian decided and quietly started to sing along with Ty.

Carol completely ignored them, continuing to prepare the food in the kitchen.

Drew joined them at the table, sitting next to Lennox. 'Can I take him swimming later?'

'Be my guest,' Carol said as she carried two plates with her holiday special onto the table. 'Hot.'

The sliced potatoes did resemble the roofs of the log cabins Carol had shown them earlier. The sausages were full of flavour and melded well with the baked beans and onions that had some sort of kick to them Ian couldn't recognise.

'You must give me the recipe,' Ian said, as he finished.

Carol laughed. 'Recipe. I wouldn't call it that. It's all up here.' She tapped her head. 'But I can tell you if you like.'

Drew helped Lennox with his food, and what didn't get thrown on the floor, the little boy seemed to enjoy. Drew wiped his son's mouth with some kitchen towel.

'Was that okay?' Carol asked everyone.

Ian, contrary to his expectations, which he now admitted to himself had been those of a snob, had enjoyed the food. 'Definitely making that myself,' he said, standing and stacking the plates, taking them over to the sink.

Drew collected the sauces and remaining plates.

'I'm not used to this,' Carol said. 'Men helping.' She laughed. 'I think I'm gonna sit and watch, while I let my lunch go down. Make some space for pudding.'

Lennox shouted very loudly, 'Want pudding! Want pudding!'

Drew and Ian did the washing up and dried everything, stacking it neatly on the work surfaces.

'You two can come again,' Carol said, reaching into the fridge. She pulled out a box. 'Jam roly poly okay for everyone?'

Ian thought of his waistline and knew that Drew would disapprove of something so calorific, but when he saw the way Drew looked at his son, Ian knew the dessert's calorie count didn't matter.

Carol opened the box and put the dessert into the oven. 'Little top up anyone?'

Ty stood, retrieved wine from the fridge. 'Beer anyone?'

'I will,' Drew said.

They drank and chatted while the van filled with the mouth-watering smell of the suet jam-filled dessert.

Carol kept offering them more to drink. She asked when they wanted to go swimming later. 'It's lovely and warm. I'll show you where the steam room is if you want.'

Ian smiled. 'Sounds great.'

Carol sat back on the seat, putting her wine on the window ledge. 'Lennox likes swimming now. Can't get enough of it. Thanks to you two.'

Ian's heart burst with pride. They had done that.

'I can't swim,' she added. 'He said I'd make Lennox scared, like me. So I never took him. Kids learn fear, isn't that what you read?'

Ty nodded slowly, rubbing his belly in satisfaction. 'That's it.'

Ian wasn't sure if it was the wine, or the way Drew couldn't stop looking at and playing with his son, or how Carol and Ty seemed to do everything possible to make them feel comfortable, but Ian soon relaxed and leaned into it all. Ian decided he was going to enjoy this weekend, for his and everyone's sake.

That evening they went to the pub.

Carol said, 'I'm glad you two come here. It means a lot to Lennox. And me and Ty. Wish I got in touch with Drew before. But I genuinely thought Lennox was Ty's.' She paused, staring at the optics for a moment. 'It's like nachos.'

Ian wanted to ask if she'd been seeing Ty at the end of the relationship she'd had with Drew, but didn't feel it was any of his business. He knew Drew wouldn't care – the past was the past, Lennox was his son and that was all that mattered.

They sat in silence, waiting for the barman to make their drinks. 'What's like nachos?' Ian asked.

Once their drinks arrived, Carol proposed a toast: 'To mixed up families.' She smiled. 'Like nachos.'

'Mixed up families, like nachos.'

'You're back at work now?' Ty asked.

Ian nodded. 'Part time.'

'He did say what you did, but I can't remember.'

'I work for a think-tank.'

Ty nodded.

She looked at him, smiling. 'I'm glad you came. I really hope you enjoy it. We do.'

'I will,' Ian said. 'I am.'

'Good. Cos when you got here you looked really scared. Upset.'

'I wanted it to be a good weekend. For everyone. First one together as a nachos family, right?'

'Right. We don't have holidays like you and Drew do. It's not our thing. But this is our thing. I hope it's okay.'

'It's more than okay,' Ian said. 'I'm on holiday, so I'm gonna treat myself.'

She raised her glass and they toasted to that.

The next day they went to the beach, a short walk on the other side of the park. Lennox built a sandcastle with Drew and Ty. The little boy wasn't bothered about the cold, he just enjoyed playing in the sand. Carol and Ian sat in thick coats watching the people. Carol said in summer she didn't even paddle because she was so scared of the water.

Ty said, 'I tried mate. No good.'

Lunch was a picnic in the van, sitting around the table, picking from a buffet Carol had made, then an afternoon in the amusement arcade playing the slot machines.

Lennox was transfixed by the lights and coins falling as Drew held him close so he could see properly.

They enjoyed ice creams and coffees in the café next to the pub.

Drew and Ty went to the gym for a while and Ian and Carol made a cake with Lennox in the caravan. Ian had brought ingredients just in case and Carol had said of course they could, but normally she didn't bother with all that, but if she thought Lennox would enjoy it, then of course.

They ate the cake sitting in the lounge, once Ty and Drew had returned from the gym.

'Shouldn't,' Drew said as he grabbed a slice.

Ty shrugged and did the same, sitting at the table.

Sunday afternoon was quiet, with Carol making a full roast dinner, serving it that evening. Ian helped her in the kitchen, doing whatever she needed.

Drew and Ty promised to clear up afterwards, and as they finished eating, Ian feeling stuffed to the gills, he watched as they did so.

'Haven't got 'em too badly trained, eh?' Carol said to Ian with a wink.

Lennox fell asleep across Carol's lap.

Drew, leaving a tidy and clean kitchen, joined them in the lounge area. 'I don't want to leave,' he said sitting.

'Stay then?' Ty said. 'We're here 'til Friday. Plenty of room.' He gestured inside the caravan.

Ian would have gone along with whatever Drew suggested; he had no work until Wednesday, and if Drew could get the time off at short notice, they'd spend more time together, as this slightly odd and messy, blended family.

Drew looked at Ian with a tired gaze.

'If you want,' Ian said simply.

'Let me check with work.' He went to their bedroom, reappearing with his work phone. He shook his head. 'Couple of the other guys are on holiday, there's no way. Next time.'

Getting the whole weekend off had been almost an impossible ask for Drew.

Carol nodded. 'Next time, eh?'

'Next time.'

Ty smiled at them. 'Any time.' He stroked the sleeping Lennox's cheek as he lay on Carol's lap.

They left late that evening to miss the Monday morning rush. They hugged Carol, who kissed Drew and Ian's cheeks, holding them in tightly. She looked a bit teary as they stood outside the caravan.

They went in for shaken hands with Ty, but he pulled them in for a big bear hug, wrapping his large arms around them. 'Cheers,' he said looking them both in the eye.

In their car as they drove out of the holiday park, Drew said, 'Carol's quite upset. Wished she'd told me sooner. I didn't see Lennox as a baby.'

'And how do you feel?' Ian asked.

Drew shrugged. 'It is what it is. Can't go back and see him as a baby. Can't not split up with Carol cos I wouldn't have met you.' He looked straight ahead through the windscreen at the headlight beams piercing the darkness. 'She said she's got thousands of videos and photos of him as a baby. Next time, she said she'll show them to me.'

Ian nodded. Next time. It seemed like a good way to end the weekend. He knew there would be a next time, because now they were part of Lennox's life, just as Carol and Ty were. The thought of being a part time dad to Lennox had seemed scary at first, but when Ian realised he had three other adults to help, it didn't feel so daunting.

'Next time,' Ian said.

Drew turned the radio on. 'Who knew a kid would be so knackering?'

'Gabriella. Carol. Ty. Everyone who's got them, I reckon.'

Drew nodded. 'All right?' He squeezed Ian's knee.

Feeling needed, having Lennox in their life, adjusting to a new way of living, all filled him with anticipation and joy and excitement. Because, after all, life's for living and although it had felt like he wasn't for so long, simply circling in the same holding pattern, his life had resumed. Only different, better, messier, more blended.

With Lennox.

He'd found a new openness to he and Drew's marriage. They talked about everything, shared worries, issues, joys, challenges, wins. Ian knew he'd always share his worries with Drew, rather than keeping them to himself.

Chapter 40

Twelve Months Later

Gabriella walked into the large airy dining room. French windows on one wall filled it with light. She placed the magazine on the table. A picture of herself smiling on the front, in jeans and a loose-fitting T-shirt. No make-up — it had been her idea, to lay herself bare like that, to show the readers what she, Gabriella, the face of four household brands, looked like when she woke every morning.

It had been the deciding factor in her landing the *Uniquely You* brand skincare range advertising campaign.

Simon entered. 'Is everything ready?' He looked at the magazine. 'I still think we should frame it.'

Gabriella blushed. 'Put it where? I don't wanna be one of those people who has massive blown-up prints of themselves on their walls. It's a bit… I'm not full of myself.'

Her mum's most frequent criticism of others was them being full of themselves. Despite having her face on the front of magazines, she was keen to avoid that.

'Not in the sitting room. The study. My study,' Simon said.

Gabriella shook her head. 'If you want, but don't tell me.'

'Am I allowed to put up a picture in the study?'

'You,' she stepped towards him, putting her arms around his waist, looking up at him, into his eyes, 'can do whatever you want. Your study.'

He kissed her, leaning her backwards slightly.

She closed her eyes, allowing herself to lean into the moment, the wonderful feeling of him holding her, his lips pressed on hers, his arm steadying her, keeping her safe. God, she'd missed this. Needed this. And she knew Arnie would want her to be happy.

Simon pulled back from the kiss. 'What?'

She shook her head. 'Nothing. Usual. Fine.' She looked up at him. She didn't even need to tell him now, he sensed when she was having a memory or a thought of Arnie and he'd let her experience it and come out the other side. They happened less often now. Arnie was still here, even though it wasn't their house. It was Gabriella and Simon's home. But every time one of the boys walked in the room, they had Arnie's smile. When she washed their hair, lathering it with shampoo, it was Arnie's hair. Each time they asked Mummy for something, their eyes were his.

But leaving behind the home they'd made had been an important step for Gabriella into creating and accepting her new life with Simon and his girls.

'I was thinking,' Simon said, 'One metre squared and in the kitchen. On the wall opposite the windows.' He mimed the size with his hands. 'Your very own poster campaign in our home.'

'When is everyone coming?' she asked.

'Soon. Is Helen bringing Bill?'

'He insisted apparently.' She smiled. 'Won't let her do anything on her own now. Almost.'

'Is Ian and Drew's little boy coming? Can't remember his name.'

'Don't know. I lose track of when they do and don't have him. It's all pretty messy now. But I think they like that.'

Simon nodded, smiling. 'Same.' A pause and then: 'Is the food done?'

She'd laid sandwiches, sausage rolls and crisps on the dining room table. 'Just the drinks. Can you be in charge of them?'

'My pleasure,' Simon said, taking her hand.

And yet it was so much Gabriella's pleasure. The first time they made love was in the afternoon, in a hotel, because it felt wrong in her old house, and Simon had agreed.

The kids had been with various friends and relatives, being looked after. They really must try to combine that at some point.

They had a drink in the hotel bar, relaxing, or trying to, and not succeeding very well.

Simon had said after two glasses of fizz, 'I'm really nervous. Feel like I'm sixteen and doing it for the first time.'

'Yep.' Gabriella looked up from her champagne glass.

'We don't have to do it if you don't want.'

She really did want. Had for months. The warmth of desire uncoiled in her belly as she stroked his hand as it rested on the bar. She finished the fizz in one gulp. 'Come on, let's get it over with.' She grabbed his hand.

He stuttered, nearly fell off the bar stool, finished his fizz and followed her.

Gabriella had wanted to be wanton and like a woman possessed, but instead she knocked her head on the wardrobe door as she jumped onto the bed. Simon appeared naked from the bathroom, looking like he'd just had some very bad news.

He ran to the bed and scrabbled beneath the covers and with the curtains closed and lights off, they fumbled and laughed until they finally consummated their relationship.

The next time, later that afternoon, was what Gabriella remembered. Making her blush and smile and glow with the love and pleasure Simon had shown her, making her want to show him even more how much he meant to her, all those weeks, months together.

My pleasure.

Now, they walked into the dining room and Simon opened the wooden drinks cabinet. 'Cocktails?'

'Who doesn't like cocktails?' Being with Simon made her feel both more sophisticated, but also more confident in her lack of it.

The school mums were speaking to her now, possibly something to do with seeing her face in magazines they thought beneath them at the newsagents. She didn't let it make her bitter, just rose above it, passing the time of day.

'Cocktails it is.' Simon turned. 'Did you invite anyone from school?'

'They'd only want to check out the house. Have a nose around.'

'You didn't invite any of them?'

She shook her head. 'Probably a bit petty of me. But they're not friends. Never were, never will be. It's too late for that. After how they treated me. I wanted to share this with people who mean something to me. That lot are just filler.'

'Presumably I'm not filler, am I?'

'You are,' she said without thinking.

'Right.' He sounded uncertain.

'But in a good way,' Gabriella said.

'Back-pedalling?'

'Are you sorting the drinks, or what?'

'Depends.'

'On what?'

'How I can be good filler.'

The doorbell rang.

Saved by the bell! 'It'll be Helen, she'd be early to the first day on Earth.'

Simon busied himself with the drinks, arranging glasses and a bucket of ice next to the various coloured bottles of alcoholic drinks.

She greeted Helen at the door.

Bill stood next to her, holding Helen's hand.

Simon shook Bill's hand, taking his jacket and hanging it in the hallway. 'Drink?'

Bill looked uncertain. 'Do you know what, I think that sounds like a perfect idea.'

Simon led him into the dining room where he began talking Bill through the cocktail options.

'He's really nervous,' Helen said to Gabriella as they walked to the kitchen. 'Don't know why, he used to talk in front of hundreds of medical students. Presented research papers at medical conferences. But this.' She shook her head. 'Sorry, I shouldn't bother you with this. I'm very happy he's here. I can't expect him to be a new man, even though he's retired. He's still Bill.'

Gabriella leaned against the work surface, indicated for Helen to sit at the table. 'Simon's the barman, but in case you don't want a cocktail, fancy a cuppa?'

Helen's face lit up. 'Don't suppose you've got any fennel tea have you?'

'For you, I have.' Gabriella searched in the cupboard, turning round and placing the box on the side with a flourish. 'Shall I have a coffee, like old times?'

'Have a cocktail if you want.'

Helen shook her head. 'Is Ian coming? Haven't seen him in ages. He's never at the lido now.'

'Not even at weekends?'

'I don't go then. We're away most weekends. Mini breaks here there and everywhere. Did I tell you I've, well, we've booked a cruise for later this month?'

'You didn't. Where are you going?'

'Bill has always wanted to discover the Canaries, away from the tourists and the hotels. This boat sails from Southampton, all the way down there. Then goes between all the islands. It's a month I think.'

'A month?'

'Four weeks. Yes. Why?'

She'd been thinking about asking Helen to take the boys for a few days so she and Simon could have a child-free weekend in a hotel, like that first time but without the awkwardness. 'Nothing.' She shook her head. 'Don't matter.'

'If it's babysitting you're after, I'm afraid I'm very much out of action for the foreseeable. Sorry. Surely Arnie's parents would have the boys.'

'They would. It's complicated.'

'Is it all right?'

'It will be. If we give it long enough.' She shook her head. 'Nothing. Just finding it tough with Simon on the scene. I don't know what they expected me to do for the rest of my life. Join a nunnery? None today, none the next day and none the day after, as Mum used to say. I thought I could do it alone. And I could. But with Simon it's much easier. More complicated. But better. Good complicated, you know?'

Helen smiled. 'Your life seems very full now.'

'Right.' Gabriella sipped her coffee. 'Reminds me, I was telling Simon about the school yard bitches.'

'Now they're giving you the time of day?'

Gabriella nodded. 'More than that. It's bloody play dates here and play dates there, and it's getting embarrassing to keep saying no. Feels fake, you know?'

'I do. Maybe give them a chance.'

'Having additional adults is never a bad thing. Unless they're, you know, twats.'

'Any twats coming today?'

'No fear.' Gabriella shook her head. 'They're filler. But not in a good way.'

'Quite. Bill's realising a lot of his work friends were just that.'

'Filler?'

'Work friends, filler. Casual acquaintances. You know.'

'Do you want the grand tour?'

'How long have you been here now?'

'A month. Just under.'

'It's looking wonderful. Very polished and finished.' Helen looked about her.

'We just moved in.' Gabriella led her to the dining room, where Bill and Simon were talking and enjoying cocktails. They walked through the lounge, with bi-folding doors along one wall, looking out to the large garden. A sofa sat in the middle of the room with a coffee table in front. A TV was wall-mounted above the fireplace flickering with flames and filling the room with warmth. Gabriella walked behind the sofa. 'I've made it.' She walked from one end of the sofa to the other.

'I don't follow,' Helen said with a puzzled expression.

'Mum always said if you can walk behind your sofa you'd made it. First time this, for me.'

Helen looked around the spacious room. 'She wasn't wrong.'

There was a silence as Gabriella remembered her mum and dad and wished with all her heart they could see her now, happy.

'Wish I'd met your mum,' Helen said gently.

'You'd have had nothing in common. But I reckon you'd have got on all right.'

'So do I.' Helen nodded and smiled.

They walked past Simon's study; a small square room with desk computer, office chair and shelves on two walls. 'There,' Gabriella put a hand on the wall opposite the computer screen. 'He wants to put my magazine pictures.'

'And?'

'Cringe! No!'

Helen shook her head. 'Not cringe. Absolutely not! Be proud. Take the praise.'

'Maybe.' Gabriella closed the door, led them up the wide stairs, turned a corner, and they were soon on the landing.

'Five-bedroom houses don't come up too often.' Gabriella rolled her eyes. 'Who knew?'

She showed Helen their master bedroom with a large double bed, mirrored wardrobe along one wall, a pink and mirrored curved leg dressing table in one corner. White sheepskin rug on the floor either side of the bed. 'He let me do what I liked in here.'

Helen's eyes widened. 'It's very... You.'

'Right.' They walked past two small bedrooms, each for one of the children. 'The other two are downstairs – or will be once the garage is converted.'

'You've really moved-in moved in, haven't you?'

Gabriella raised an eyebrow. 'Right.'

'Wedding bells?'

'We will. Just not yet. He's asked me and I've said it feels too soon. Arnie wouldn't give a shit. As long as I was happy. But I just need to get used to it for a bit, you know?'

'Very sensible. I'm so pleased for you.'

They stood at the top of the stairs on the wide landing, looking down at the hallway. Bill and Drew's voices floated up, the odd word was clear, but mostly it was just a series of deep noises, mixed with laughter.

'It had been done up by the previous owners, then they got divorced. I told Simon it was a bad omen and he said if we couldn't stand up to some superstition, we'd have no chance. He's had similar to me, about moving in together.'

'What like?' Helen asked.

'Too fast, his wife's only just buried. That sort of thing.'

'How long's it been?'

Gabriella counted on her fingers. 'First date about a year and a half ago.'

'When did he lose his wife?'

'Just over two years. Same for me.' Gabriella made an awkward facial expression.

'Fuck 'em!' Helen said with feeling.

'Don't mince your words. Tell it like it is, will you?' Gabriella chuckled. 'Some weeks I don't know how we do it. We look at our schedules, the kids' and yet somehow it works. We make it work. Being busy is the best cure for grief, you know.'

'I heard it too.' Helen stroked Gabriella's shoulder.

Gabriella looked at Helen as tears filled her eyes. 'Sometimes I feel guilty...'

'For being happy?' Helen shook her head, pulled Gabriella into a warm hug. 'Don't ever run from happiness. Grab it with both hands and run after it if you need to.'

'Sometimes, when I have a minute, which isn't often, when I sit and think about everything that's happened, it sort of pushes down on me. Like I can't breathe. But then Simon walks in and asks if I want something, if I've washed the girls' PE kit, or if I've chased the builder for the quote to do the garage. And I'm fine again. I know I can do this, because he's with me. I would never have met him if Arnie hadn't died. That sort of haunts me. Shouldn't. But it does.'

'That's because you're a heart on your sleeve person. Right from when I first met you I knew that. It shines out of you. Don't change that. It's a wonderful quality.'

Gabriella brushed away the tears, pulled a stray blonde hair from her eye, blushing and shaking her head. 'I need to get a grip. Ian's going to be here soon and he doesn't want to see me like this. Not after what nearly happened to Drew.'

Gabriella swallowed. She'd been almost beside herself with worry when Drew was in hospital. But she'd kept it to herself since Drew wasn't her husband. But she'd felt Ian's worry and pain like Drew was her husband. She'd always experienced all her emotions, deeply and on the outside.

The doorbell rang.

'Speak of the devil,' Gabriella said reflexively.

Simon strode across the hall and opened the door. He greeted Ian and Drew with firmly shaken hands.

'Hi,' Gabriella said, waving down at them. 'No Lennox?'

'He's just gone back,' Ian said.

'We've come here for a rest,' Drew added with a smile.

'And to have a nose around,' Ian said.

Gabriella walked down the stairs, hugged both men, kissing their cheeks. 'Bill's been drinking with Simon.' She narrowed her eyes at Simon. 'You're not getting him too pissed are you?'

Simon held his hands up in surrender. 'As if I would.' He turned to Drew and Ian. 'Drink?'

Drew shook his head. 'I'm working later. But I could murder a sausage roll. I heard a rumour they're home-made.'

'They are!' Gabriella said with triumph.

'Don't think I've forgotten you calling me filler,' Simon said to Gabriella. 'Me and Bill have been discussing it.'

'I said, it's different.'

'Good different, or bad different?'

'Good, of course.'

Drew walked towards the dining room. 'Tell me all about it over a plate of sausage rolls!'

'What's that about?' Ian asked.

'That's what I wondered,' Helen said.

Gabriella told him. 'Want a tour?'

'Of course,' Ian said.

Gabriella started upstairs, room by room, accompanied by many oohs and aahs, and *I like what you've done here*'s from Ian, and once they'd reached the family bathroom, she perched on the edge of the bath.

'I should be friends with the school mums, because they're in the same boat as me. But I'm not. Cos when I needed 'em they didn't let me into their boat.' She shook her head. 'I'm talking rubbish. Ignore me. Simon's probably winding me up. He'll forget it by the time we eat.'

'You two helped me even when I didn't want it,' Helen said slowly, avoiding eye contact. 'That's proper friendship.'

'Or being interfering.'

'Absolutely,' Helen said. 'Thanks. For interfering in my life.'

Gabriella nodded. 'Yep. You too.' She looked from Ian to Helen.

There was a loud laugh from the dining room. 'It's taking me a while to get used to the new gregarious Bill. The more I see of him, the more I realise it's just normal Bill, but with a drink in his hand. He forgot how to have fun. He enjoyed work so much he didn't realise there are millions of other ways to enjoy yourself. He's like the man I married. And I mean in all ways.' She smiled and colour rose on her cheeks. 'I suspect if we leave them any longer, they'll be incoherent.'

'But friends,' Gabriella said.

'Indeed,' Helen said. 'Filler, do go on?'

'I should have said another word. There's filler and there's filler, you know?' Gabriella struggled to explain what she meant.

'Filler is something you stuff in to fill a gap,' Helen said. 'That's what those horrid school mums are.'

'So what's Simon?'

Gabriella thought for a moment. 'They tried to fix the tower block where Mum and Dad lived. Concrete cancer apparently. Put stuff in the cracks. They've pulled it down now. Not long after they died.' She paused, took a breath. 'But the lido, after they nearly pulled it down cos it was falling apart, when they fixed the lido building, cos it was so old, they filled in the cracks in the concrete and now look at it. So not all cement's the same. Not all concrete's fixable. But now the lido's as good as new.'

'That's how I feel,' Helen said. 'And Bill.'

'Simon filled my heart with love, when I thought I'd never find it again. I thought it would always hurt, that I'd always be broken down, like an old tower block, only in my heart.'

'So really, Simon's cement, not filler?' Ian asked.

Gabriella nodded. 'Can you tell him? I'll get it wrong.'

'Glad to.'

They walked downstairs. At the bottom they inter-linked arms, then walked into the dining room together.

Bill was in the middle of a very in-depth conversation with the other two. He was indicating parts of his body with one hand, while holding a glass in the other.

Drew sat, transfixed by whatever Bill was saying.

Simon held a cocktail shaker aloft. 'We've been awaiting your arrival!' He asked for their drink orders, then made them, handing the glasses out as they talked about their journeys, the food and how great it was to all be together.

In a lull in the conversation, Ian coughed, looked at Simon. 'You're cement,' Ian said. 'Not filler.'

'Fills in the cracks?' Simon asked with a smile.

Gabriella walked up to him, putting her hands around his waist, looking up at his face. 'Keeps things together. Repairs them. Makes them better. Fixes things.'

Simon nodded in understanding, kissing her lips. 'I think that calls for a toast.' He turned to Gabriella, raising his eyebrows.

Gabriella missed their time at the lido where they'd met, found it harder to visit, but the reasons were because their lives were stuffed full. They had no need of the lido to kill time, fill their empty days, maintain lies, avoid grief, separate from emotionless responses.

She knew the best part of the lido hadn't been the building, the swimming, the sun loungers or the endless coffees and teas they'd consumed, but the people she'd found there. People who, in ordinary circumstances, she wouldn't have spoken to or even met. But who had all felt drawn to that place and had helped each other put themselves back together, repair themselves, their lives, their relationships, their professional selves.

Gabriella bit her bottom lip in thought. She was going to toast to theLonely Hearts Lido Club, but they'd moved on from that to here, now, with her new fiancé in her new home she shared with his and her kids. To Ian and his husband, working and raising their son. To Helen, on her second honeymoon that seemed to last forever.

'To being cement and fixing each other, when we couldn't fix ourselves,' Ian said loudly.

Simon nodded. 'To fixing each other when we couldn't fix ourselves!'

They raised their classes and together repeated the phrase.

Gabriella knew she'd probably never go back to the lido, but she didn't need it. She'd found these people and they had, even if they hadn't wanted to at the time, slowly but surely fixed each other, in ways at the time they hadn't even noticed, or thought possible. And if that wasn't some sort of magic, Gabriella didn't know what was.

She looked to the ceiling in the sure knowledge that everyone who'd loved her when they were alive had been making sure she and her two boys were all right down here on Earth. Maybe everything did happen for a reason, and although losing Arnie hadn't made sense at the time and still caused her pain at missing him, now that she looked at it from afar with the benefit of hindsight, it seemed, albeit in some painful way, to make sense. She had lost someone dear, but gained two of the best friends she could ever have wished for.

Acknowledgement

As with all books, this is the culmination of efforts from a whole host of people – it really does take a village!

Tim, as always is supportive of my writing and understands when I'm absent due to a deadline or an idea striking me. I can't imagine having a partner who wasn't supportive of my writing, and for that I'm very grateful.

Thanks to my caravan club writing buddies, who were with me on a windy wet October 2021 weekend on the Kentish coast as I wrote about 16,000 words of this story. Thanks for the wine, the chat, the food, the space to unwind and the friendship. Clare London, Sue Brown and a particular thanks to Ali Ryecart who helped with the parent and child swimming class scene.

Thanks to Tim, Gregor and Colin who were with me in sunny Rhodes during autumn 2021, as I wrote the middle 30,000 words of this story. Every morning, as they read, drank or swam, I quietly slipped away and made myself comfortable to write on the first-floor balcony overlooking the sea. I can write in most places (planes, trains, airports, libraries, hotel rooms) but I've found I write best in the sun, overlooking the sea.

Thanks to Emma, my friend and neighbour for talking about 'additional adults' as, one afternoon, she watched her daughter playing in our garden with a friend, at a barbecue. It sparked something in my brain and very shortly afterwards Gabriella sprang, almost fully formed onto the page.

Thanks to Nick and Lorna for telling me the story of Penny and her 'absolutely not!' retort when someone suggested she watch a long home movie about metallurgy that she'd missed, having arrived late for a lunch. Her phrase sparked inspiration and soon Helen and her story were flowing out of my head onto the page.

Thanks to Carol who has followed my writing career with much-appreciated levels of interest. I know talking about writing isn't for many non-writing friends, and that's absolutely fine, but you've been there for all the ups and downs, changes of genre, publisher, pen name, everything really. I hope you can grab a few well-earned moments to read this story.

To the Romantic Novelists' Association (RNA); as an organisation it's been wonderful for introducing me to other authors and publishers. The committee has been particularly supportive while I've been writing this story.

Thanks to BBC Radio 4 who broadcast a feature discussing a swimming pool suspended between two luxury apartment blocks in London. They described how exclusive that pool was, only available for the residents of the two buildings. As a contrast, they interviewed people who enjoyed their local lido, because it's a much more accessible place for everyone and anyone to swim, to escape life's worries. That gave me an idea for this story's setting.

Thanks to the Hera Books team including Danielle, Gareth, Keshini and Rose Cooper (who designed the cover) I'm so grateful to everyone for helping me bring this story to life.

Love and light,
Charlie Lyndhurst xx

Author's Letter

Thanks for picking up a copy of *The Lonely Hearts Lido Club*. I hope you've enjoyed meeting the characters and sharing their journey.

With this story, I wanted to show how even when your troubles seem too much, even when you feel unable to take the next step, talking to friends, no matter how different their lives are from your own, is a good starting point. Helen, Gabriella and Ian are deliberately very different, but at their core, they all just want to have meaning and love in their lives.

If you're struggling, talking to someone is usually the best thing you can do. Even if it's a stranger you turn to. Men, in particular tend not to be good at opening up about their problems. Women tend to use their friendships like a coffee shop and men use theirs like an A&E department. Maybe ring that friend you lost touch with, call someone even if you're feeling a bit low, people are naturally sociable creatures, it really is great to chat.

Reviews help others find their next story to enjoy. It would be wonderful if you could add a review of *The Lonely Hearts Lido Club* on your favourite review platform. Even a few words and a star rating make all the difference.

If you're interested in meeting my alter ego, who writes sweet to steamy gay romance and gay fiction, check out liamlivings.com I love to hear from readers who've read my stories. You can also check out charlielyndhurst.co.uk where you can find information about my other Charlie Lyndhurst books, my latest news and social media links.

Love and light,

Charlie Lyndhurst xx